THE SWAN

Also by Tania Park

Mistaken
Blind Justice
Retribution
Road Trip

THE SWAN

Tania Park

A catalogue record for this book is available from the National Library of Australia

ISBN: 9780994284785 (Paperback)
ISBN: 9780994284792 (Ebook)
Book Cover Design: Pickawoowoo, Laila Savolainen
Interior Design: Pickawoowoo Publishing Group

Printed & Channel Distribution
Lightning Source | Ingram (USA/UK/EUROPE/AUS)

Dedication

Writing a book is a lengthy and challenging process. Ideas stream but often don't coalesce without numerous deletions, additions and structural changes. When you think you've got it all together you seek the opinion of others, who somehow always find anomalies or have fantastic suggestions.

My heartfelt thanks go to Dennis Talbot who gave his expert thumbs up to the psychological aspect of my protagonist but didn't like the secondary character one bit, causing a major change of direction.

Thank you to the members of my writers group who read the manuscript and covered it in read marks. Each suggestion is important and mulled over whilst re-writing.

The final hurrah is when you think your manuscript is perfect and is put in the hands of the person you have chosen as editor. Ted Witham, even though you caused another major re-write, you did a sterling job. I can't thank you enough.

To the children whom I knew were going through the same kinds of trauma, way back then when I was teaching – I'm sorry. I did what I could but my hands were tied. Getting authorities involved to ease your suffering was beyond difficult. Despite your bruises and flinches, I could not prove how you received your injuries. Like the main character in this book, you kept your dark secrets because you were too darn scared to tell the truth.

Chapter One

Breathe, you fool.

In… out… long… slow.

Breathe.

Even though Melanie Jones focused on breathing the way her singing maestro had taught her, this time it didn't work. Blood still pounded through her veins, the adrenaline surge hyping every cell in her body. If her nerves were violin strings they would have snapped by now. In accompaniment, frantic thoughts galloped through her mind making it impossible to concentrate on the pieces she was about to perform. A more sinister picture kept interfering, the black crotchets and quavers all having the same grotesque facial features.

What if he was here?

Lurking outside.

Waiting.

A dense fog of fear swirled then engulfed her. Feeling faint, she staggered, grabbed the table edge then found her balance. Heavens but she shouldn't even be here: shouldn't be doing this. Had she lost her mind? She tossed the mascara onto the table, jolting at the clunk, the tiny noise tensioning tight nerves even more.

She was an idiot. It was too dangerous. But she had to - for her mother's sake. Besides it was one thing she was good at: the only thing and she couldn't let the other girls down. Not now.

To rid her mind of seesawing thoughts she peered into the mirror, forcing her concentration on checking her appearance yet again. Tweaking a long black ringlet into place over her shoulder, she lowered her eyes to inspect the satin of her black gown for wrinkles. As she lifted her eyes she caught sight of a reflected print on the opposite wall and wondered if the smiling woman depicted in the glossy photograph had used this room. She couldn't have been all that famous for Melanie didn't recognise the image, but then having been overseas for so long she wasn't up with famous locals any longer.

The soft green paint on the walls caught her attention. Wasn't it supposed to be the calming colour often used in doctor's surgeries? Well it wasn't working here. But compared to other dressing rooms she'd been in, this one was modern, if not plain. She snorted when she pictured the dump she was living in. She'd prefer this room any day.

A hushed whisper of sound echoed from the hall. She stilled on a sucked in breath then glanced around for something she could use to defend herself. And her mother didn't know where she was. What if something happened to her here? Nobody knew to check on Mum. Her hand automatically lifted and rubbed at her throat. She dragged her hand away and reached for the chair, hefting it high.

'Five minutes, Miss Jones.'

Held breath whooshed out. Shaken, she dropped the chair then flopped into the seat with her eyes shut. Oh, my! This was too hard. Willing her racing pulse to slow, she sucked in three long calming breaths and slowly hissed each out. Then she stood, brushed down her gown, picked up her instrument and whisked the door open in an act of false bravado. She wouldn't be scared.

Yeah, right, she thought as she sped along the underground passages searching the dark shadows for any sign of movement. Tense nerves didn't ease until she was standing behind the central gap of the backstage curtain where she waited by the side of the stage manager, his presence easing but not quite dismissing her fear.

***

Taller than any other person in the crowded concert hall foyer, it was easy for Guy Harris to search for his friends. There, on the far side of the room. He wove through the noisy melee, doing his best to avoid jutting elbows and held drinks. The sensation of eyes following his passage sent his feeling of dread about being there even deeper. Unbidden, his left hand brushed the scar that slashed down the side of his face. Normally it didn't bother him but he felt people stared despite the plastic surgeon's expert repair job. He forced a smile as he reached Neil and Louise Cummings then stooped low to greet the diminutive woman with a brief kiss on her cheek.

'Told you there was no blind date,' said Neil.

A growl rumbled from Guy's chest. 'How many times have I heard that promise? I'm still recovering from the last woman you set me up with. She chattered about nothing all night and wouldn't shut up.'

'Yes, well, I hadn't met her. She was a friend of a friend.' Neil paused then a wry grin spread across his face. 'She was awful, wasn't she?'

'Probably the worst night of my life – and I had to drive her home. So you understand my mistrust?' Guy straightened as he scowled at his best friend.

'I take it she didn't get a goodnight kiss.' There was dead silence then a stifled giggle gurgled from Louise, which was followed by a shout of laughter as her husband spied the look of disgust on Guy's face. Neil was still chortling when the warning bells began dinging. Louise dug him in the ribs to indicate they needed to find their seats. Thank goodness for bells, Guy thought as the three mounted the marble steps.

Settling back in his seat, Guy suspected he was going to be bored. Much as he enjoyed listening to background music at home, instrumental concerts were not his idea of a pleasant night out. Even though Neil had assured him she was internationally acclaimed, Guy had never heard of Melanie Jones. Opera, he would have appreciated – or even a musical where there was singing and acting. A folk or blues group would be even better. But a single instrument for an entire evening? Not his scene. Still, he thought as he peered at Louise's programme, a disastrous night would give him an excellent excuse to refuse Neil's next invitation, of which there had been a constant stream to various functions so he could meet people – in particular, women. For some reason his friends thought his single status meant he was lonely. Who had time to be lonely?

His eyes came to a sudden standstill on Lou's programme when he spied a photo of a woman playing panpipes. For heaven's sake! Sighing in disgust he sank back into the seat as the lights softened. Closing his eyes he prepared for the worst.

***

The lights in the auditorium gradually dimmed until darkness settled in an unspoken message to silence the audience. The moment the stage was immersed in shadow Melanie straightened then waited until her support musicians moved to their places. When the rush of fabric from long gowns ceased she lifted her pipes into position, filled her lungs and waited for her cue.

'One, two, now,' the stage manager whispered at the same time relaying the message through his headset to the light controller. She breathed out in a controlled gentle *whish* through pursed lips. The first long haunting note quivered as blue lights shimmered, giving the stage the appearance of gently lapping water. Over and over, Melanie had practised and knew exactly how slow she would tread, how long each step would be and her position at each bar of music. The piece was one of her favourite and her signature tune. But most important – on stage she was safe.

***

The first note to reverberate against his eardrum demanded Guy's immediate attention. The long soulful sound caused the hairs on the back of his neck and arms to stand to attention. His eyelids shot apart to see the blue shivering hue on the plain backdrop and stage. Then his eyes were drawn to the sole spotlighted figure standing at the back of the stage. Wearing a long black dress that seemed to float from her shoulders, the tall slender woman drifted forwards with such fluid grace she appeared to be gliding. It was the hair that grabbed his attention. Long, black shiny ringlets flowed down her shoulders and back almost reaching her waist. Melanie Jones was an extraordinarily beautiful woman and was playing extraordinarily beautiful music.

Peering through the blue tinged gloom, Guy dragged his eyes from the stage back towards the programme still open on Lou's lap to find the name of the piece he recognized but couldn't put a name to. It was difficult to make out the words so he leant closer, squinting hard.

'*The Swan* - Saint Saens,' Lou whispered in his ear.

'Thanks,' he whispered back as he straightened. The setting suited the music, he thought as he studied the vision floating across the stage. It felt weird to hear the melody played on such an unusual wind instrument when it was so well known as a cello solo but there was some special essence in the sound that kept him spellbound. Around him there was an eerie silence. When the piece drew to an end there was an uncanny stillness. Then applause exploded.

After the first solo piece a small group of instrumentalists joined in one-by-one in accompaniment while Melanie Jones played the pieces for the first half of the performance. Guy counted ten young women seated on chairs in a semi-circle around the edge of the stage. When spotlights highlighted each as she was featured as a soloist, he studied each lady in detail but his eyes kept swinging back to the woman in black as she moved amongst the group in a tapestry of mimed storytelling and play-acting, in humour or pathos, depending on the mood of the piece and drawing sighs and laughter from the enthralled crowd. Clever stage lights created a different but magical atmosphere for each piece.

While they stood sipping drinks during interval, the conversation around him confirmed that he wasn't the only one who had been touched by the poignant sounds. It would be impossible to better what he'd already heard, but the second half soared to exceptional heights. He lounged back in his seat, much of the time with his eyes closed to allow the seductive tones envelop him.

After the final piece the ovation was thunderous with the entire audience rising. As he stood, Guy cast his eyes downwards and felt shocked when he noticed Melanie Jones appeared shaken by the reception. There was a stunned expression on her face as she stood under the spotlight giving only a nod of her head in acknowledgement. In that brief moment before her face broke out in a smile, she appeared to be so timid - ready to take flight like a startled animal caught in the headlights of a car. There was an almost imperceptible shiver along her shoulders before she indicated to her fellow players with a slight turn of her head before lifting her instrument to her mouth. There was an instant hush before the audience regained their seats.

As an encore, the opening piece was repeated but this time with the accompaniment of the stringed instruments, each joining in one after the other. Instead of moving forwards, Melanie Jones floated backwards, disappearing behind a side curtain with the final few lingering notes being played from the wings. Despite the continuous applause, she didn't reappear. Disappointment flooded. He wanted more – a lot more.

***

Despite the incessant applause, Melanie refused to return to the stage for another encore. There were to be no other pieces. A pre-booked taxi was waiting behind the hall to take her home. It was too risky to stay. After collecting her things, she snuck through the rear exit with her eyes darting around seeking the slightest sign of an unwelcome presence in the darkness.

The moment she crept into her apartment she poked her head around the door to the main bedroom. A huffed sigh of relief escaped at the sight of her mother asleep on the single bed. Her body looked tiny under the covers, the graceful line marred by the thick heavy cast on her leg. Melanie tiptoed across the worn but scrubbed linoleum, stood by the bedside and peered at the peaceful face. 'I'm sorry, Mum,' she whispered. 'You should never have sent me away and I should never have come home but I promise we'll escape soon. That's what tonight was about.'

Reaching out, she was drawn to caress her mother's gaunt cheek but yanked her fingers back before touching the soft skin. They would talk in the morning. Instead, she turned and crept to her room where she changed, scrubbed the make-up from her face, hid her dress away in the back of the scarred wardrobe then crawled into bed.

Even though she kept her stretched-out body still, willing it to relax, deep thoughts about the evening hurtled through her mind in an unceasing eddy. Even after splitting the profits with her friends she would earn enough from this one concert so she and her mother could stay in this dump for another two months. Maybe then, she could go back to work, save enough to escape. By then, the compound fractures would have healed, the pins could be removed and her own lung would have healed enough to allow her to fly with her mother back to Greece, to a new life – a safe life.

***

The late night café where he had taken his friends for supper was small and intimate. Guy leaned back in his chair with his fingers outspread tip-to-tip, feeling devastated that the magic had ended. Emerging from his introspection he leant forwards. 'Neil, I owe you an apology. That was the most enthralling performance I have ever experienced. Thank your sister-in-law for not being well, although I sincerely hope she is soon much better. And thank you for insisting I join you. What I would give to see and hear that incredible woman play again?'

'Unfortunately, tonight was the only performance.' Lou settled her cup in its saucer. 'It's a pity for I would have come again. The way Miss Jones interacted with each of the girls was amazing. Such acting ability. I loved it when she pinched that violin bow and she bowed while the violinist did the fingering.'

'I was amazed when she swapped instruments with the cellist. She played the cello as well as she does the panpipes,' said Neil with a laugh.

'And the cellist could only get a screech from the pipes,' Lou added. 'With two and half hours of playing and constant movement, that poor girl must be exhausted. I wonder if she has ever recorded her work.'

Chapter Two

Sleep was elusive. Flopping over again to seek comfort, Melanie wondered whether her insomnia was a result of feeling pure pleasure in performing again. She shivered as she relived the exhilaration of standing on a stage being immersed in her music, the one haven where she could completely forget about the harsh reality of her life. She smiled into the darkness heightened by the close drawn curtains, folded over each other to ensure spying eyes couldn't see in.

A shudder wove up her body. Maybe her inability to relax was from the adrenaline rush caused by the fear of being found. Had he seen the advertisements? Was he there? Did he follow her home? Frown lines settled between her eyes as a solitary tear slid down her cheek. After brushing it away with a clenched aching fist, she forced pictures of her new and only friends in this country to the forefront of her mind.

Had it only been four months ago when she'd met them? So much had happened since the evening she'd been hurrying past the hall after making a few emergency purchases at a nearby delicatessen. So entranced by the music she'd edged the door open then slunk inside to listen to the two cellists, four violinists, three viola players and one harpist who had great talent and she hadn't been shy in heaping praises on the young women. After introducing herself and spending an hour chatting while the girls continued their rehearsal, she asked if she could join them during their practice sessions. This chance meeting had resulted in tonight's single concert. It had been a hectic four months in organisation, planning and rehearsal. But the audience reaction told her that it had paid off.

Her fingers danced around on top of the thin blanket in rhythm to one of the pieces they'd played, her soft voice humming the melody. At a dull creak she stilled. Terror replaced joy as she swung her legs over the side then shivered when bare feet met cold linoleum. Creeping to the door, she un-wedged the chair from under the handle then settled her ear against the flaking wood. Was someone else in the flat? Unsure whether or not to take the risk of venturing out, she waited, attuning for ears for the slightest sound.

Utter silence pressed against the edge of her consciousness making her oblivious to the cold penetrating her cotton nightgown until her body trembled in response. What to do? Her need to check on her mother won the war of uncertainty in her mind. With practised slow precision she turned the key in the lock then twisted the knob around until she heard the slight snick as the barrel released. As she opened the door a fraction her muscles tensed, ready to slam it shut again. She set her eyes to the crack and peered into the gloom of the lounge area.

The moon streaming through the gauze covered kitchen window was her only light. She swung her gaze at the heavily curtained front windows. With no light being able to penetrate it was impossible to discern any unwanted shape but there was no crack of light indicating an open door. But that lack of light meant nothing. Continuing her zigzagging sweep of the room, she searched the gloom until her eyes were back at the kitchen then peered beyond the glass. With a sheer drop to the ground from the second storey kitchen there was no need for the same heavy drapes at that particular window but she still searched the night sky for some sinister shadow.

She neither heard nor saw anything unusual so ventured out on tiptoes, twisting her head in all directions – ever alert. With her mother's door still ajar Melanie could see the sleeping form. Held breath whooshed out in relief then she returned to her room, ensuring the key was turned and jamming the wooden kitchen chair in its nightly position under the knob.

All pleasant thoughts had vanished as she stood behind the vaulted door. All she could envisage was the horror of finding her mother's comatose body on the kitchen floor in a pool of dried blood. After a spasm of trembling Melanie skittered across the floor to her bed and sat in the middle with knees drawn up and her arms hugging them tight. Relentless thoughts recalled details she was desperate to forget but never could.

Shivering, she yanked the blanket from the folded restraints and wrapped it around her body, holding the ends tucked in against her chest as her mind remembered. After the ambulance had driven them to hospital, Melanie hadn't dared return to the rented house to live. Even though the bastard often disappeared for weeks at a time to evade possible questions from authorities after causing such shocking injury, she hadn't been able to find the gumption to even go within cooee of the neighbourhood.

While her mother recovered in hospital, Melanie was sent to a safe house organised by a social worker attached to the hospital. Deep shame accompanied her. Washing her only outfit each evening and sleeping naked so her clothes had a chance to dry overnight became an impossible chore: she had to collect their belongings. The humiliation of her life prevented her from asking anyone to assist or for charitable handouts. She and her mother didn't possess much. Having very little money and mounting medical bills meant they weren't able to afford the purchase of new clothes. In the end she knew she had to return to the house.

How many times had she maintained vigilance, waiting in dark shadows until the bastard left the premises? Even though she'd watched him vanish down the street it had been impossible to pick up the courage to go inside. What if he returned and found her while she was still there? She had no doubt she would end up in the same pitiful state as her mother if she were caught.

A cold sweat broke out as she visualised the night she took a chance out of sheer desperation. Waiting until she had the shield of darkness, she had hovered under the darker shadows of overhanging trees, darting across lighter areas then hiding behind whatever cover she could find until she reached the corner pillar of the neighbour's tall fence. There she paused then stuck her head around the corner to see if any lights were burning inside. The darkness should have given her courage but it felt so evil. Even having seen him leave, the dread of uncertainty preyed on her mind.

Instead of entering through the gate, Melanie perched her backside on the corner of the cracked brick fence, swung her legs over then crept down the shadowed fence-line until she was level with the front veranda. Keeping to the fence in order to blend with the shapes of the darkness, she circled the house twice to check for any movement before plucking up the courage to move closer. After peering in all the windows in another closer circuit, even without the benefit of lights, she felt certain the place was empty.

She snuck through the back door then allowed the powerful surge of darkness and silence to envelop her until her senses became attuned with her surroundings. Even though she moved quietly, each scrape or hiss of noise appeared to magnify a hundred-fold and then echo. She grabbed as many belongings as she could carry, stuffing them into two large, striped, plastic luggage bags she'd purchased for only a couple of dollars at a disposal store.

When filled, the bags were bulky and heavy but after locking the rear door and pocketing the key she'd brought with her, she hoisted the short handles onto her shoulders, snuck to the corner of the house, peered around through the gloom then shot full pelt to the fence as though a torpedo from its cocooning chamber. As she sidled along the fence, she hoisted the heavy bags back up each time the slippery handles slid down. Once she reached the front corner, Melanie searched both ways up and down the street, slithered over the fence then tore down the pavement in the opposite direction from which she'd seen him leaving. Bags slapped against hips in a rhythmical rustle of cheap plastic against nylon. With her fingers gripping the handles on her shoulders she didn't cease running until she was several blocks away. Her constant peering in all directions continued until she was relatively safe on a train heading towards her one-bedroom unit.

She didn't give a damn about what happened to him with her paying no more rent on the place. The cheap one-room hovel the authorities had found for her until she was allowed to take her mother home from hospital was reasonably secure. Then they moved to this new apartment. She snorted derisively. Apartment was too grandiose a name for the dump they now lived in but it was cheap and more important - furnished.

Dragging the blanket tighter, Melanie wondered whether she could find another job. Maybe she could apply under an assumed name. But then there was the problem of ID and taxes. She wriggled to get more comfortable. He would only find her again. Somehow he always managed to find where she worked. But this time she knew he would carry out his threat to kill her. He'd almost succeeded last time. Her hand slid to her throat and rubbed. She yanked it away. She couldn't, just couldn't take a chance on working full time. But she knew he would be looking for money, searching for her – his only source of ready cash apart from illegal methods and she had no doubt a lot of his income was obtained by nefarious means.

No, better to stick to the plan she had in place. Mum needed to regain mobility and independence before Melanie could find another job. No way could she leave her mother alone when she couldn't move far or fast. Apart from the money she had in an overseas account: money they would need when she managed to secrete her mother onto a plane, all her meagre savings had been used up. It was the only reason she had taken the chance to play in a concert. Terrified he would have seen the publicity, she had taken great pains to keep her whereabouts unknown. Even if he did turn up at the concert, which was highly unlikely since he couldn't abide either her or her music, he didn't know where she lived and the concert hall had been given strict instructions to never reveal any details about her.

She stretched out on her side, pulling the blanket snug then shuddered. If he did find them, both their lives would be over.

Chapter Three

Guy slouched back in his office chair and stared out of the window, thinking about the evocative music and the beautiful woman. For almost four weeks he'd found it impossible to erase her from his thoughts. The opening scene, especially, was a vivid picture imprinted in his memory and he felt a desperate need to meet the woman in person, thank her and hear her play again.

A phone rang in another office, startling him. He spun from his unseeing reverie and sighed as he recalled how many times he searched the crowds for the incredible hair. Estimating her height to be slightly above average for a woman, he dismissed any one much shorter or taller but he never spotted anyone having the same mass of long ebony curls. He'd searched through the phone book only to discover how many Joneses were listed.

A search of the electoral rolls had been in vain. There was no Melanie Jones registered as being an eligible voter and she was definitely older than eighteen. The programme had said she was locally born. So maybe she no longer lived here but was revisiting. During his search he rang then visited in person the concert hall to make inquiries as to her whereabouts. Surely they must be able to contact her, he had insisted to the manager after a lengthy stonewalling conversation. How had they paid her? He was told in no uncertain terms, 'Privacy laws prevent us from disclosing any information about any individual.' Such a well-worn cliché he had thought at the time. Even when he insisted he only wanted to send her flowers of appreciation, he came up against a solid brick wall.

By searching the Internet and music stores, Guy discovered there weren't any panpipe recordings by Melanie Jones or Melanie anything. He found several recordings of pan music and bought most, along with several recordings of *The Swan*. He listened to them all, but none had the magical soul of Melanie's playing.

To ease his unceasing thoughts Guy began pacing, forcing his mind to think of the new venture he was planning. With business going so well, he intended to open a new factory to manufacture air-conditioning units. The expansion had come at an opportune time but they had hit a major snag. After spending an inordinate amount of time searching for vacant land or empty premises while co-ordinating all the aspects required, they'd come up empty handed.

The photo sitting on top of a bookcase caught his eye. He paused and studied the features of his parents and brother. Seeing the love in his parents' eyes brought his thoughts to the woman he'd recently begun dating as a means to forget Melanie Jones.

Linley Miller. He thought of the three times they'd gone out. He'd enjoyed the evenings as a change from his normal solo existence but he felt no emotional spark and couldn't ever imagine having a long-term or physical relationship with the woman. Despite his less than enamoured feelings he'd tried to convince himself that maybe things would improve given time, so there was another dinner date coming up. His thoughts wavered between *make a go of it* to *why did he bother?* Deep down he knew that Linley, like any of the women he'd dated before, didn't interest him enough to seek a permanent romantic liaison. Maybe there was something wrong with him and he was expecting too much.

Another phone rang, this time much closer. He reached out to lift the receiver at the same moment his second in command and best friend, Neil Cummings swung into the open door. Raising his hand as indication to wait a moment, he watched Neil step back outside as he took the call.

The call dealt with, Guy replaced the receiver. 'Yes, Neil?'

'I think I've found empty premises which might be suitable for the new factory,' Neil said as he crossed the carpet.

'At last,' Guy sighed as he indicated for Neil to sit.

They sat opposite each other while discussing Neil's findings. Ever efficient, Neil had several sheets of paper with all the details for Guy's perusal. A single phone call gave him an appointment with the selling agent for the following afternoon to inspect the premises.

'I might drive by the factory site this evening and fit in a swim on the way,' said Guy as he shoved the papers into a file.

'You seem to be throwing yourself into the fitness mania a lot these days,' remarked Neil as he rose to leave.

'Gives me something to do and I enjoy the feeling of being fit. I always have.'

'You need a new woman in your life, my friend.' Neil grinned from the doorway.

'Don't go getting any more of your brilliant ideas. And just to make sure you don't, I've been dating,' Guy called after him.

Neil stopped in his tracks and spun around. 'You have?' He took two steps back into the room. 'Details, mate? Who is she? How serious is it?'

'None of your damned business! Now scoot and let me get back to work.' He grinned while listening to Neil's diminishing laughter as he returned to his office next door.

Chapter Four

After completing a hard swim in his favourite bay that was protected by a reef, keeping it relatively shark free, Guy gave his body a vigorous rubdown then sat on the warm sand to enjoy the beauty and serenity of the sun easing its way behind the undulating waves. The rhythmical sound of the crashing water lulled him as he savoured the crisp scent of salt from the fresh evening breeze. It was amazing how every sunset was different, with cloud formations diffusing the sun's rays from deep indigo through a wide range of reds and oranges to the softest of salmons with purple tinges. He sat, elbows resting on bent knees, appreciating the tranquillity until the velvety mantle of darkness fell and caressed him. Returning to his car, he pulled a tracksuit over his bathing costume, brushed sand from bare feet then settled them into worn but comfy leather loafers. Feeling totally relaxed, he drove to the proposed factory site.

There was enough street lighting to gain an idea of the layout of the buildings and grounds as he circled the well-fenced block twice. It looked to be suitable with large, well-constructed buildings in top condition and plenty of space for machinery and truck movements. Things were looking positive. To assess the surrounding area by walking, he parked in a side street. The place seemed almost deserted except for one rough looking character trawling the other side of the road. The man looked unkempt and shifty, lurking in the shadows as he shuffled close to the fence. Guy kept to the opposite footpath. He wasn't afraid of the man, being a good deal taller and a lot fitter but he wasn't about to look for trouble and since he spied glimpses of a length of wood every time the man swung his left hand forwards, Guy thought it wiser to keep a healthy distance. Dismissing the stranger from his thoughts, he made his way down a side street edging the factory site then veered off at right angles to see what other buildings, facilities and amenities were around and whether the area was suitable. Easy access for large trucks was vital. Maybe a deli or café would be useful for his employees. Add somewhere pleasant to sit during the lunch break. A park would be good: with shelter for stormy days. He grinned. The list of wants was getting longer.

The church hall he neared had lights blaring and appeared in good order so some sort of community-based events occurred. Another tick for the position. At an unmistakable sound he stopped mid-stride then backtracked a few paces. Someone was playing the panpipes. He closed the distance then heard the harmonies of stringed instruments in the background. Hope soared so he stayed, leant up against a railing until the music ended. Could two people play the same instrument with such pathos? Then he heard the solo rendition of *The Swan* and knew for sure he had found the musician he had tried so hard to track down. A wave of pure pleasure swept upwards, even the hair on the nape of his neck bristled to attention.

He strode across the road to the closed hall door then waited to one side in the shadows. It wasn't long before a small group of women carrying instruments came out amidst happy chatter, calling goodbye to each other as they loaded belongings into cars or set off in various directions on foot. The moment he saw her, Guy recognised the hair on one of the last group of three. It had to be Melanie Jones. A few tendrils of tight curls fanned around her face. As she turned to farewell a friend he spotted her hair tied back in a long braid before she pulled a hood over her head the moment she stepped from the portico onto the pathway. The other two women waited until she had tucked her instrument underneath her long flowing jacket then the three turned away, hurried to the corner, crossed the road then paused while they had a few quiet words. After farewell hugs, Melanie swung back around while the other two turned the corner.

Without moving, Guy watched, intrigued until a niggle of concern shimmied up his spine at the way the woman moved. Imitating mercury, she flowed against the brick wall, keeping to the darker areas. She walked briskly, pausing a brief moment when he suspected she spied him from the corner of her eye. She hesitated as she shot a quick glance in his direction, the panic in her eyes impossible to miss even in the half-light. For a moment he thought she would stop to address him but she spun back and quickened her steps. He wondered if he should call out to assure her that he was no threat but she turned the corner and vanished. Guy followed, keeping well back so as to not alarm her. He felt uncomfortable about trailing and had no idea what he was going to do now he had found her, but maybe she would lead him to her home. Then he'd know where she lived.

He was about to cross the road when a high-pitched scream echoed through the silence. He began jogging. As he rounded the corner he saw, half-way down the long road, the rough character he'd noticed before, drag Melanie along by her hair. The back of her heels scraped along the rough pavement then her backside dropped to the ground. He wondered what had happened to the jacket then spied it in a heap in the middle of the road. Lying next to it was the length of wood. He shuddered at the thought of what the man had intended by carrying such a weapon. Thank goodness he'd dropped it or had he already used it to subdue Melanie? Oh, God!

A hard twist and yank to her braid forced Melanie to coil over and land roughly on her knees. Loud sobs were interspersed with panicked shrieks of, 'No, no.' Guy ran full pelt, shuddering each time Melanie squealed in agony with her arms tucked over her head for protection. All the while, the man yelled abuse while lashing out with a fist. Guy winced when he heard the sickening sound of knuckles connecting with bone. Dread settled in his gut at the sudden cessation of the woman's screams. Again the man lifted his fist and was about to strike again when Guy reached them, grabbed the thug's wrist then yanked the arm behind the man's back, ignoring the grunt of pain.

'What the devil do you think you're doing?' Guy gasped. 'Leave her alone.'

The older man swung around to face Guy then lashed out with one leg in wild panic. There was a loud scream from Melanie as her hands flew to the elastic band where her braid sprung from her head. The man released his hold and she dropped to the ground with a thud and *oomph*.

'She's my daughter, I'll do what I want to teach her a lesson,' came the belligerent, drunken reply.

His daughter? Oh, whew. Guy recoiled at the overwhelming smell of stale alcohol and filth. He felt a sudden need to retch from the stench but swallowed down the rising bile. 'That doesn't give you the right to hit her. Only a coward hits a woman.'

Yanking hard on the wrist he still had in a firm hold, he wrenched the man away from Melanie and flung him across the pavement. A sharp crack cut the air like a whip as the man's skull connected with concrete and he dropped to the ground like a full sack of grain. Guy grabbed Melanie, drew her upright and held her in a protective embrace while surveying the result of the altercation. As he twisted around he tensed, ready to strike again to protect the woman, but the man lay sprawled and unmoving on the pavement. He looked to be unconscious but Guy was more concerned about the daughter – if she was really the man's daughter and that seemed unbelievable.

With utmost gentleness he turned the badly shaking woman around so he could see her face, sucking in his breath with a loud hiss when he spied a trickle of blood dripping from a ragged vertical cut on her cheek. Though it was difficult to see in the dim beam of an overhead streetlight ten metres down the road, there appeared to be a dark bruise already crawling out from the gash and mingling with the rapid swelling.

'Are you all right?' he asked while he searched for further wounds. 'Do you know this man?' He ran a fingertip down the gash to ascertain how deep it was. Not as deep as he first thought but it was nasty and surely must hurt.

Melanie shuddered then sagged against him. 'That bastard is my father. I hate him,' she grated. 'How did he find me?' she managed to splutter against his shoulder before dissolving into tears as she huddled so close it felt as though she was attempting to melt into his skin for safekeeping.

Not caring about the condition of the bully who treated his daughter with such cruel contempt, Guy turned to lead Melanie away. 'Come with me and I'll see you home.'

'My pipes! Where are they? He grabbed them and threw them away. I can't leave them here.'

Guy glanced around the surrounding pavement and roadway while keeping Melanie tucked close but she broke free and tore over to the other side of the bitumen then bent to retrieve three broken pieces from the gutter, her face distraught. His heart hitched at the pathetic sight as she knelt in the road holding the fractured pieces against her chest. Striding over to her, Guy paused to snag the strewn jacket then dropped down on his haunches and gathered her into his arms, lifting her slender body with ease. She felt unnaturally light for a woman of her height and the thought worried him. Why was she so thin? Unsure as to what to do about the father, Guy slid Melanie's feet to the ground to check that the man was still alive. There was going to be hell to pay if he wasn't. The man moaned. Guy sent a prayer of thanks skywards then waited while watching the drunkard struggle to sit. At first he wobbled but then straightened. If he was well enough to sit then he was okay. He might end up with a severe headache but right then, Guy didn't care.

Confident the man had no serious injury, Guy turned away then assisted Melanie the few blocks to his car where he opened the passenger door and settled her into the seat. He crouched down on the kerbing to her level. Chucking his fingers under her chin, he lifted her face to look at him under the glare of the car's interior light then dragged in a deep breath when he noticed the extent and nastiness of the gash and bruises on her face. She'd been on the receiving end of more than one punch. 'You need your face attended to. Can I take you to an emergency night surgery?'

'No, please? Will you take me home? It's not far. I need to get home to Mum. I can't leave her alone any longer.' With a look of determination she brushed the remnants of moisture from her eyes with clenched knuckles. When she drew back in obvious pain Guy grabbed the damp beach towel from the rear seat, shook out the worst of the sand then gently dabbed tears and blood from her face, pausing when she flinched and hunched back as he reached out to brush stray tendrils of loosened hair from her eyes.

'It's okay, I'm not going to harm you,' he said quietly but it concerned him the way she reacted.

Moving lower, he wiped the dirt of the gutter from her hands and lower legs, pausing to carefully remove traces of blood from grazed knees before tossing the towel into the rear seat. He eased her legs into the front cavity then closed the door and strode around to the driver's seat.

Shock hit when he saw where she lived. A rundown apartment at the top of a flight of stark grey concrete steps looked as though the only thing it was good for was a bulldozer. It was squalid with only remnants of flaking paint left on the outside. A single un-shaded light globe was the only light on the lower floor while the upstairs was in relative darkness. He offered to walk her to her door but she pulled away, insisting her mother wouldn't approve as she limped up the steps. Feeling uneasy, he waited by his car until Melanie mounted the steps. He figured now was not the best of times to pursue his quest of getting to know this lady better. Besides, he now knew where she lived.

He slid into his seat when she opened the door and turned on the light. The instant he shut the car door, there was a blood curdling, high-pitched scream.

Guy shot out of the car and lunged up the steps three at a time. Surely the man couldn't have arrived here before them. He shoved the still open door with an outstretched hand, prepared to defend himself as he stepped into the doorway.

Oh, merciful heaven! He reeled at the sight of Melanie hunched on the floor cradling what could only be her mother's badly beaten body in her arms. A low mournful keening echoed around the trashed sparsely furnished room. The sound curdled his innards as he took three steps inside and dropped onto one knee next to the injured woman. A rush of dread surged as he reached down with two fingers to feel for a pulse under her jaw. Somehow, the battered woman was still alive but her pulse was thready. Nausea churned as he stared down at the remains of the face, which was a pulpy mess of raw meat, blood and torn skin. Her closed eyes were so swollen he doubted she would be able to see through them even if she were awake. As he scanned the woman's body he could tell there was more than one broken bone. He swore under his breath when he noticed one leg was already in plaster from the ankle all the way up her thigh and by its tattered condition, had been for some time. By her laboured shallow breathing he guessed Mrs Jones was barely alive.

'Phone, where's your phone?' His eyes flicked around the room in search of the instrument as he stood.

'We don't have one.' Melanie sounded strangled, barely able to get the words out.

'I've got a mobile in my car.'

Melanie shot a fearful look at him as he backed towards the door. He didn't have to ask the reason for her terrified glance. 'Its okay, the car's at the bottom of the stairs. I won't let him in. I'll come right back.' He flew down the stairs, removed his mobile phone from the console then dialled the emergency number while he climbed back up the dingy steps.

'Your address - street name and number?' he asked as he reached the open door.

After giving the details to the emergency services, he rang his detective brother to ask advice. He then did his best to tend to Mrs Jones while they waited for the ambulance and police to arrive, but there was not a lot he could do. Moving her was out of the question. Finding a couple of towels hanging in the bathroom, he lifted them to his face and sniffed to ascertain the cleanliness. A sweet floral aroma and soft dry feel told him they were freshly laundered so he used them as pressure packs in an attempt to staunch the flow of blood from numerous gashes. Thank goodness the woman was unconscious for her injuries must be agonising.

Melanie appeared too distraught to do anything other than stroke her mother with quivering fingers, silent tears coursing down her cheeks as she whispered quiet words even though they would be unheard by the recipient.

It seemed like an eternity before they heard sirens wailing in the distance then nearing, but once there the paramedics moved rapidly and had the injured woman ready for transport. One made a quick assessment of the abrasions on Melanie's face.

'I'll attend to Melanie. You just get her mother to hospital.'

'Thanks, mate. This lady is critical. I believe the police are on their way so can you give them the details?' asked one man as they manoeuvred Mrs Jones through the doorway.

'Go, I'll see to things here.'

Within seconds the ambulance left with siren blaring. While waiting, Guy urged Melanie to not touch anything but she kept fidgeting, so he reached out and eased her against his body to prevent her interfering with any possible evidence. After an initial jerk she cowered when he reached for her. But then she went limp and pressed her face against his chest. Her arms wrapped around his waist and gripped tight.

'Guy, what the devil have you been up to… strewth, mate, what a mess!' Looking shocked, Iain paused before stepping across the threshold. After Guy gave the meagre details he knew about, Iain tried to elicit more information from Melanie.

'It must have been my father, he must have found us,' she repeated over and over but trying to get anything else from her was useless. Guy mentioned where they had last seen Mr Jones and Iain sent two officers to search.

The entire time the police sieved for evidence Melanie perched unmoving on a tattered lounge chair, her eyes staring into space. Every time someone went near her she flinched. He watched her wince again as Iain approached. It didn't take high intelligence to figure out why. The poor woman was terrified. The forensics team began packing up their gear and he was told he could leave.

Iain stood to one side of Melanie. 'You can't stay here. Your father may return. Have you anywhere else you can go?'

There was a shy shaking of her head. 'There's no one else,' she murmured.

Well, damn it. What was he supposed to do? If she stayed here alone the father would probably return to finish off what he'd started. He'd already had one attempt. It was too late to settle her into a hotel, even if he could find a suitable one at this hour of the morning and then how safe would she be, alone and unprotected? Squatting in front of her, he stared into vacant eyes until they focussed on him. 'Melanie, this officer is my brother, Detective Iain Harris. I'm Guy Harris. He can vouch for me.'

'Good idea, little brother,' Iain interrupted as he pressed a hand into her shoulder, frowning when she shrank away. He caught Guy's eye as he lifted his hand and slowly dragged it away. Then he took his time to move where she could see him. 'Miss Jones, you'll be safe with Guy. I promise you. Go with him tonight and I'll call around to see you some time in the morning to get a few more details. Knowing where you are will make it much easier. '

'I can't,' Melanie stuttered. Her eyes blinked rapidly as she squished further into the corner of the chair – as far from Iain as she could get.

Her actions concerned Guy. Was she really terrified of every man, even a police officer? Very slow, so as to not alarm her, he reached for her chin so they were eye-to-eye. 'You said you have nowhere else to go.' He waited for a response. All she did was lower her eyes. 'Gather together a few clothes and you can stay at my home tonight then we can sort something else out in the morning. You need to get cleaned up, treatment for your face, a shower and some sleep. We'll call at the hospital on the way to see how your mother is. Come on, it's impossible for you to stay here, especially with your father still roaming around. I'm assuming from what I've seen tonight, that you don't want him finding you.'

A shudder and moan gave him the only answer he needed. 'I didn't think so. Now how about packing a few clothes and toiletries? Yell if you need any assistance.' After helping her to her feet, Melanie swayed then finding her balance she stumbled into a room he'd not been in. She had only been gone a few seconds when a distressing cry echoed through the unit. Guy wove his way through the maze of broken furniture to her door. She was holding up the black dress she'd worn for the concert. It had been ripped to shreds, the long skirt looking like the unwoven ribbons on a maypole.

'Oh, sweet mercy!' he muttered. His gut wrenched as he strode across the room and gathered her close. What type of animal would do this to his wife and daughter? Glancing around, he noted the room was in much the same condition as the rest of the flat – pretty well destroyed. It looked as though someone had been searching for a particular item and not finding it, wrecking the place in retribution. Maybe the man's anger had been because Melanie hadn't been home. A breath huffed out. Thank goodness she wasn't.

He settled Melanie on her bed then picked up strewn clothes and shoved them into a striped plastic bag he found hurled in one corner. He didn't have to search through drawers and cupboards – everything had been tossed over the floor. Moving into the bathroom he swept all the brushes and toiletries from the top of the vanity into another small bag he retrieved from the floor then handed both to Iain so he could assist Melanie to his car.

On the way home, Guy pulled into a lay-by to ring the hospital, grimacing when told Mrs Jones was clinging to life by the slimmest of threads. Still undergoing emergency surgery she would be there for several hours. Guy passed on the information then added, 'We'll go home first to get cleaned up since we won't be able to see your mother until she comes out of the operating theatre.' He couldn't tell whether or not Melanie heard or absorbed his words as there was no acknowledgement.

While driving back along the coast, he mused about how quick things could change: from the pleasurable drive and swim he'd had only a few hours earlier, his joy at hearing the music and finding Melanie, to this ghastly outcome. Life sure threw you strange curve balls when you least expected them.

Once home he led Melanie to his guest suite where he settled her on the edge of the double bed, carried in her bags, turned the shower on then suggested she undress and shower. When she appeared to ignore him, he threatened to throw her under the water, clothes and all. This seemed to bring her out of her daze. With reddening cheeks she moved like an automaton towards the bathroom.

In his own room, Guy had a quick shower to rid himself of the salt from his swim and splashes of blood, changed into jeans and a fine knitted navy sweater then since he'd missed his evening meal, began to rustle up some food. The finger food snack ready, he went in search of his guest. At her mumbled answer to his knock he opened the door feeling apprehensive. Dressed in a similar outfit, Melanie was sitting on the side of the bed attempting to towel her hair dry but it was obvious the movement was causing considerable pain. Why she had washed her hair at this ungodly hour of the night, he couldn't fathom.

He strode across the carpet, drew the towel from her hands and frowned as she flinched even before he'd reached her. That simple jerk said so much and it worried him. But right now there was not a lot he could do about it apart from let her know when he was going to touch her. 'If you sit on the stool in the kitchen, I can do that for you.'

There was another disturbing flinch as he took her hand. He grimaced then loosened his hold as he led her through the house then settled her on a high stool at the granite topped kitchen bench. A gentle spin on the swivel stool had her back facing him. He proceeded to towel through the lovely long locks. Her hair was so thick it took almost thirty minutes to lift each black, silky strand and rub the water from it. When he'd finished, he returned to her room to find the brush he'd packed and swept it in a gentle rhythmic motion through her hair until it laid knot free, flowing down her back.

Next he removed his medical kit from an overhead cupboard and tended to the cuts and bruises on Melanie's knees and face, apologising every time she winced or sucked in her breath as a silent acknowledgement of her suffering, but not once did she turn away or complain. With one cheek swollen already, she was going to sport a black eye for quite a while.

Neither said a word until Guy's ministrations were complete and they tucked into the meal. He attempted to coerce Melanie into an amiable, light-hearted conversation. She appeared to be very reserved, only answering in monosyllables or very short sentences while she picked at her food. He kept to general topics of conversation to keep her mind away from the trauma of the previous few hours.

'Can I clean up for you?'

At the unexpected request Guy could only stare at the woman.

'Please,' she begged, 'I need to keep busy so I don't think about… you know.'

Maybe keeping busy was a good idea and her way to deal with the horror. Even though he felt guilty to see her carrying out his chores, he acceded to her wishes then poured coffee from an already brewing pot, all the time keeping a watchful eye on his guest as she rinsed off plates and cutlery and settled them in the dish-rack.

He made a late call to Neil to cancel the next day's factory inspection due to him taking a day off. This was such a rarity he smiled when Neil yelled, *'Alleluia,'* down the phone. Neil would suspect something was up especially since he had been woken from his sleep. Guy would never ring at such an hour unless it was urgent.

After coffee, Guy bundled Melanie back into his car for the short drive to the hospital. Her mother had just come out of surgery and the amount of machinery and tubes surrounding the poor woman looked scary, even to him. Her face was an unrecognisable mass of swollen blood blackened flesh interspersed with taped gauze patches under which, he assumed were hundreds of tiny sutures.

Melanie sank into a chair by her mother's side, her hand shaking as she grasped the fingers of one hand poking out from the edge of new plaster. 'Oh, Mum, I'm so sorry I wasn't there for you.' The whispered words sounded tortured as silent tears slid down Melanie's cheeks.

Guy slipped out the door to have a quiet word with the attending physician to give Melanie time alone with her mother.

'Mrs Jones is alive – but only just and it will be a miracle if she survives. All four limbs have fractures along with several ribs and some facial bones as well as internal injuries. The poor woman has literally been bashed within an inch of her life.'

Bile churned in his gut at the brutal honesty. He shuddered. Melanie probably would have received the same treatment if fate hadn't stepped in.

'I have to report this. Are you able to give me any details?'

'The police know. They know who did this and are already searching for him. How can any man do this to his own wife?'

'Believe me, it happens a lot more than either of us would ever want and much of it goes unreported.' The buzzing of the doctor's pager meant he had to go, leaving Guy standing alone in the middle of the passage feeling bewildered.

It took a while to persuade Melanie to leave so they could grab a few hours' sleep. 'Come on, Melanie. There's absolutely nothing we can do at the moment. Your Mum is to be kept in an induced coma for as long as required. It could take several days.' He held back the brutal truth figuring Melanie had had enough traumas to deal with for one day.

The silence during the trip home was unnerving.

'How did you know my name?' Melanie asked as she settled onto the stool at the kitchen bench soon after arriving home.

'I was at your concert last month and recognised your playing as I passed the hall last night. I was waiting outside for you to come out to make sure it was you. Your music spun me out - I've never heard anything so exquisite. Tell me, can your instrument be repaired?'

'Not here, no. I had it specially made for me. It needs to go back to Greece where I learned to play.'

'Would you allow me to get it repaired for you? I can have it flown over and back in a short space of time.'

'You don't have to do that.' Melanie sounded a tad too defensive for his liking.

'I know I don't have to, but I would like to. Think of it as a thank you gift for the wonderful night of pleasure you gave me at your concert. I could have them on the courier tomorrow. Please?'

'You've done more than I deserve already. I'll never be able to repay you.' There was a hint of desperation in her voice as she dropped her eyes.

Pulling out a stool, Guy sat opposite then grasped her hands. 'Are you trying to tell me you think you and your mother deserved the abuse you both received tonight?'

The way she shrunk and turned her face away gave him every indication that she in fact did feel that way. Why?

'Melanie, look at me.' She slowly turned her head but even though she lifted her face, her eyes remained shuttered behind dark lashes. 'Nobody deserves to be treated that way. All I have given you is a little care and offered you a temporary safe haven from that bully. I don't expect any kind of repayment.'

'You punched the bastard. I'm glad!' The sudden outburst of vehemence from this quiet, insecure young woman surprised him.

'I didn't punch him, just pulled him away from you. That's the first time in my life I've ever used physical force on anyone. I can't abide violence and it's not something I am particularly proud of but I had to stop him somehow.'

He wanted to ask about the abuse, whether or not it was as frequent as he suspected from the way Melanie flinched unconsciously whenever he got within cooee of her, but not tonight. She'd been through too much. 'It's almost morning and we both need some sleep so why don't you go and lie down. You're safe here. Nobody except my brother knows where you are and the house is secure with a top-notch alarm system.' He led Melanie to her bedroom, pausing in the doorway where he bade her good night before retreating to his own bed.

He was in that half-aware state just before falling into a deep sleep when he was roused by an unusual sound. Afraid Mr Jones had followed and broken in Guy threw his covers back then slid out of bed to investigate. He almost tripped over the huddled form curled up in a ball on the floor by his bed, a doona wrapped around her.

'What the devil?' Squatting down, he discovered Melanie was moaning but appeared to be asleep. Indecision hit. What was he supposed to do? It was obvious she had sought him out for security. She needed sleep; he needed sleep. He figured if he put her back into her own bed, she would probably return to his room with neither of them getting much sleep. He could settle her in the lounge-room, but there was only one sofa and she'd probably still come his way. Scooping her up, doona and all, he laid her in his bed then spooned his body around hers, one arm around her waist as he pulled the covers over them both. She'll probably be mad as hell when she wakes but he'd deal with that later.

Chapter Five

Yawning, Melanie prised her lids apart, wriggled upright then wondered where the heck she was. The room was strange and the bed far more comfortable than she'd been used to. Heat rose when still fuzzy brain cells processed grey and white décor indicating a truly male domain. Visions of the night before stabbed her to awareness. Last night. When the dark had pressed in and thrust her fear into overdrive she'd crept into Guy's room just because she felt safer having him nearby. She certainly didn't recall climbing into his bed. Oh, my, what had she done? How stupid and so unlike her.

With cheeks searing she wrapped the doona tight around her body and went in search of her saviour. After reading the note she spied on the kitchen bench, she searched for *downstairs*.

Opening every door she came to, she peered inside each room and cupboard. The house was large with comfortable furniture indicating quality. The lack of feminine knickknacks confirmed her earlier thoughts that Guy Harris was a single man, which was a relief considering she had slept in his bed but it didn't in any way assuage her embarrassment. Where had he slept? So far she hadn't found any rumpled bedclothes but then maybe he'd already put them away. Please let him have put them away!

At last, a door with a staircase leading down. She crept halfway down polished wooden steps then settled on a step to watch. The vast carpeted room below appeared to take up half the floor-space of the area above. Long, high windows along one side with the trunks of trees visible indicated the room was dug into the ground at the rear of the building. A series of gym machines and equipment was spread out across the floor but there was still plenty of space. The room could be made into three and each would still be larger than average.

When roving eyes settled on Guy her blood warmed at the sight of a magnificent, artistically perfect body. He had stripped down to only a pair of shorts exposing a mass of smooth skin glistening with sweat. His legs were long and muscular, his stomach flat and taut and she marvelled at the way his perfectly sculpted chest and arm muscles rippled while he pumped a pair of large dumb-bells. She had never seen a male body like it and the only time she had ever seen a man wear so little was at the beach. She had certainly never slept in a man's bed before. Another hot flush crept up her face. The unbidden thought of why such a caring man wasn't married centred in her brain. His face wasn't model perfect with a slight dent from a scar that had obviously seen the touch of a plastic surgeon's skills. Ruggedly handsome was the term she would use but maybe the scar put women off. She should know since she had enough of her own to put any man off.

'Good morning, sleeping beauty.' Melanie shot upright at the sound of his voice so nearby. She grappled with the doona as it began to slide away. With her mind in places it shouldn't be she hadn't noticed him replace the dumb-bells on the rack and now he was standing right in front of her swiping sweat from his body with a towel. A body that close up was even more magnificent. Oh, my gosh! She forced her lids to drop, embarrassed at being caught staring. What must he think?

When he laughed she peeked only to catch him pulling a plain black T-shirt over his head. She couldn't figure why he bothered since the shirt hugged him like a second skin, the black enhancing the outline of his muscles even more and contrasting so well with his blond hair. He appeared to be unconcerned about her watching him. Well, she felt more than concerned: guilty and embarrassed came to mind.

'Give me five minutes to shower then we can have breakfast,' said Guy as he indicated for her to precede him up the steps.

Still mystified as to where he'd slept, she raced to her room to freshen up and make herself a little more decent after suddenly realising how little she had on. She dragged on a pair of jeans and a long-sleeved top. They were crumpled from being jammed into a bag but wrinkles were far better than a thin cotton night-gown that probably outlined far more than she wanted to think about. And the scars – please don't let him have seen the scars. They were so ugly.

When she returned to the kitchen Guy was dicing fresh fruit with a small sharp knife, had cereal and milk on the bench and a heating coffee percolator was emanating a rich aroma that made her mouth water.

'Can I help?' she asked feeling hesitant as she neared the bench where two places had been set out. Good grief, but she felt so unsure of how she was supposed to act.

'Sure, sit down and help me eat. How does the face feel?' She felt her cheeks redden yet again as he peered at her. 'It looks like agony to me. Let me know if you need any painkillers.' He handed her a bowl of fruit salad accompanied by a spoon and a cheeky grin.

Melanie tried to smile back but instead winced at the sharp pain from her face wound. Without asking, Guy searched the same overhead cupboard that contained his medical kit for painkillers, removed two from the foil and handed them to her with a glass of cold tap water.

'These will help.'

She hesitated, preferring not to take medication but she wasn't up to giving explanations as to why so placed them on her tongue and washed them down with a few sips of water before tucking into the fruit. She wouldn't become addicted taking only two. Swallowing the first mouthful made her realize she was hungry so she ate, feeling guilty about the amount of food sitting in front of her. She hadn't had this much food in one sitting since she'd removed her mother from the hospital. With money short, she'd given most of their meagre supplies to her mother in an attempt to strengthen her health.

When he slid a steaming mug of coffee across the bench, Guy settled opposite. 'We need to talk. Do you feel up to it?'

Oh, oh, this sounded serious. She gave a brief nod but kept her eyes averted, feeling nervous. Life had taught her to never trust a man and this one was so overwhelming. Could she put her faith in him?

'You know you can't go back to your apartment until the police have caught your father. It wouldn't be safe, especially after seeing what he did to your mother. You're welcome to stay here for as long as necessary.'

He smiled when she dared to shoot him a glance. Stay here? She couldn't but before she had a chance to say anything his mouth opened.

'Nobody apart from Iain knows where you are. We could go by your place today to pick up whatever else we can salvage. Which reminds me, let me have your instrument and tell me where it needs to go. I'll send it off today. Let's do that first.'

With a gentle nudge from Guy, and too scared to say anything, Melanie hurried to her room, brought back the three pieces and laid them on the bench. She couldn't find the gumption to look at him so kept her eyes downcast. A pencil and writing pad appeared before her face.

'Write down the name and address of where they are to go.'

When she had finished she slid the pad back, peeking under lowered lashes. He read the address then smiled as he looked up.

'Nice place, I've been there. I hiked right to the top of Lykavittos Hill. The view was magnificent and worth the hot walk. Would you like to enclose a note?'

Stunned, Melanie could do no more than once again nod her head. He'd been to Greece?

Chapter Six

Wispy clouds feathered an azure sky, promising a perfect day as Guy headed towards his office. It worried him how skittish Melanie had been when she alighted from the car at the hospital entrance. She had begged to sit with her mother while he packed the panpipes. He wasn't so sure it was the best of ideas so lingered until she was safe inside, ignoring the wrath of other drivers waiting to pull into the set down only bay.

He grinned to himself when Neil followed him into his office.

'Okay, what's going on? You said you had private business to attend to and yet here you are. And what is this?' Neil pointed to the three pieces.

'I saved a woman whose mother was brutally bashed and is in hospital. These belong to the woman. I said I'd send them off for repairs. Now leave me be. Aren't you supposed to be running this place today?' As Neil held up his hands in submission and left, Guy wondered what Neil would say if he knew the particular lady was staying in his house and had shared his bed last night. While he wrapped the pieces in bubble wrap he kept expecting Neil's curiosity to get the better of him and start asking more questions, but he didn't.

Before leaving Guy stepped into Neil's office. 'Anything I should know?'

'You have three interviews booked in tomorrow morning for the assistant's position and I've re-scheduled the estate agent for two in the afternoon. Will you be here or do you want me to postpone them?'

'No, I'll be here.' The decision was immediate. What to do with his guest while he was at work would be solved later but he felt sure his brother would supply protection if needed. More important was to get back to the hospital to ensure Melanie was safe.

After collecting a morose Melanie they returned to her apartment to gather her belongings. On the outside the building looked worse in the day than at night, but the inside smelt clean and fresh underneath the odious stench of spilt blood. It was obvious Melanie and her mother had worked hard to improve their living conditions but he had to ask why she was living in such a decrepit building.

'It was all I could afford. Mum's leg was broken six weeks ago. When she was discharged from hospital I brought her here. We couldn't go back home – ever. I had to give up my job to care for her. That's why I played the concert, to earn enough for us to live on while Mum is recuperating.'

Her head dropped. 'The concert was a mistake. He must have seen the advertisements and tracked me down,' she mumbled to her chest.

'How long has this abuse been going on?' He felt cautious about probing especially when he noticed her shoulders stiffen at his question, but he had to know.

'With Mum, for as long as I can remember,' she murmured before lifting her head and staring at the far wall. 'Or almost as long. When I was very little things were different, happier. Just before I started school the bastard lost his job. I don't know why but later when I asked, Mum said something about some goods had gone missing and he had been blamed. I don't know the full story. Then he started drinking – a lot. When he drinks too much he loses his temper at the smallest provocation. Mum said it hadn't been so bad while I was away, but it became a lot worse after I returned from Greece.'

'And with you?' Guy asked, not really expecting an answer and knowing he was treading on dangerous ground. There was a long pause after a hiss of sucked in breath.

'Mum always protected me.'

It scared him the way an involuntary shudder wove down her body.

'He started on me when I returned.'

Guy wasn't sure how much truth was in her statement. Somehow, he got the impression she was being very sparing with the true facts. 'How long have you been back?'

'Eighteen months.' Melanie shuddered again as she slid her eyes shut for a few moments then they skittered open.

Watching the fear return to the brown depths, he gritted his teeth to refrain from saying what he thought. 'How long were you away?'

'When I turned eighteen, Mum sent me to live with my grandparents in Greece. She had scrimped and saved, hiding money. She wanted me to learn about my roots. Mum is Greek. My… that bastard isn't. I trained in office work and lived and worked in Greece for over four years as the personal assistant to my boss. I saved as much as I could for Mum, but I couldn't send it home because I knew the bastard would steal it to buy alcohol. When he's drunk, he's not a nice person.' She paused. 'In fact he's worse than a vicious wild animal.'

That's an understatement, thought Guy. He was mighty curious about the results of the viciousness but figured from how she'd reacted so far, those types of questions would have her clamming up. Better to keep to general topics. 'You said you learned to play the panpipes there.'

'Yes. I heard a man playing one day when I hiked through the National Park in the hills soon after arriving. The music was so beautiful. I asked him if he would teach me and he agreed after we discussed my musical knowledge. I spent all my spare time with him, learning and practising. Stephan made me those panpipes as a gift before we played our first concert together. I loved my time with him so much.' She sighed. 'I miss Stephan. He's a special man.' A wistful smile played at the corners of her mouth.

'Is that the person you have sent them back to? He did a fantastic job of teaching you.'

'Yes.'

It worried him that Melanie reverted back to silence after the simple reply. He kept close as they meandered through the apartment, finding very little that hadn't been wrecked apart from the linen, which they folded and piled near the front door. The furniture, according to Melanie, came with the unit. Staring at the two tiny piles while

Melanie sorted her personal belongings in the bedroom, Guy wondered why there was so little. They must have fled their home with the barest of essentials.

He was setting furniture to rights when he heard a stifled moan. Dropping the chair he was attempting to force back into shape, he tore into the room to find Melanie kneeling on the floor with an empty cardboard box she had pulled out from under a loose floorboard.

'He must have come back. My money has gone. It was here last night.' The anguished whisper caused the hairs on his arms to rise.

'Why didn't you tell me? I would have taken it with us.' Kneeling next to her, he drew Melanie against his chest, the empty box crushed between them.

'I thought it would be safe. I can't keep this place. That money was all I had,' she wailed as she pulled away then flung herself onto the bed. 'I feel so angry with myself and at that bastard,' she cried out.

Guy settled on the edge of the single, plain bed that had been stripped of its linen, rubbing his hand in a gentle circular motion across her shoulders. There was not a lot he could do except comfort her but he felt so helpless. 'Melanie, have you thought that your father came back here last night looking for you?' Her entire body tensed under his hand.

'You can stay with me until we sort things. Allow me to deal with the owners of this place. Their insurance should cover any damage. Come on, there's nothing else here that's worth taking, except this.' Muttering the last two words under his breath, Guy picked up the black dress he had been so enamoured with, tucking it under his arm as he ushered Melanie to his car. He settled her into the front seat then retrieved the measly piles of belongings, locked the apartment door and then drove home. He didn't know why it was important but he planned to have a replica of the dress made. Lou would know how to go about it.

Chapter Seven

As the last of the three applicants left, the temporary receptionist handed Guy several sheets of paper. He scanned the pages then glanced up in surprise. 'Melanie has applied?'

'Yes, she saw the position advertised on the desk. Would you like me to show her in?'

'No, give us a couple of minutes to read this through.' Guy passed two sheets to Neil while he read the other. 'It seems she held a similar position in Greece. Personal assistant to the owner,' Guy murmured as he read. 'Manufacturing company. Well, that's good. She'd know the ropes somewhat more than the others.'

'Can't be any worse than the three we just interviewed. I had no idea it was so hard to find experienced staff.' Neil flipped to the next page as he held out the one he'd read to Guy. 'Let's give her a go. Her credentials are very good. Much better than the others.'

Guy strode across the room and stuck his head through the door. 'Melanie, you applied for the job?'

'Yes, why not? I need the work and I can sure use the money. It's what I'm trained to do and the company in Greece was much the same as this one, only larger. Is it too late too apply?'

'No, of course not. Come in. We'll give you the same interview we gave the others.'

The interview left Guy impressed with Melanie's capabilities. She had included the name and number of her Greek employer, who he was anxious to speak to. What surprised him was the way Melanie spoke with a confidence he'd not seen in her before, and her intimate knowledge of the industry was even more surprising. Taking into consideration time differences, this one call would have to wait until the evening while the other three referees he could phone straight away.

***

During his lunch break, Guy drove Melanie to the hospital. He watched her bowed head as they listened to the doctor.

'I'm sorry, but your mother's condition has deteriorated to such an extent she has been put on life support. There was some internal bleeding causing her brain to swell. We've operated again to relieve the pressure but the prognosis at the moment is not good. The next twenty-four hours are critical.'

Melanie glanced up. Tears clung to her lashes. Reaching up he used his thumb to wipe away the few that fell.

'Please, can I stay with Mum?'

'Of course! How about I pick you up after work?' Slinging one arm around her shoulders, he wasn't shocked when she jerked as he touched her but he didn't pull away, instead giving her a gentle squeeze. 'But take care. Your father may guess your mother was brought here. Please don't go outside. Here…' he removed a business card from his wallet and held it out. 'Do you have a mobile phone?'

'Umm, I… no. It's not connected.'

Which means she can't afford it, he thought then said aloud, 'I'm sure the nurse will let you use a phone here if needed. Ring me on my mobile if you want me. Neil and I will be inspecting a property this afternoon.' To ensure her safety, he walked her to the door of her mother's room then scanned the area for any sign of her father as he left. The unease in his gut disturbed him but what could he do? If Melanie stayed put she'd be relatively safe. He doubted her cowardly father would take the chance of attacking inside the hospital. He prayed not.

While ambling next to Neil through buildings that were more than promising, his phone rang. Melanie, he thought, as he flipped it open.

'Do you think Melanie is up to a few questions regarding her father?' asked Iain.

'I can ask but her mother's not doing so well. Melanie is with her. How about coming for dinner tonight? I can leave you alone for a while. How about six-thirty?'

'I'll be there.'

Thoughts of Melanie gnawed for the rest of the afternoon. When he picked her up a grey haggard face greeted him. Maybe she won't be able to handle Iain's intended interview. 'Iain is joining us for dinner tonight. He wants a few details about your father. Are you up to it?'

She trembled, paused then sighed. 'I guess. If it means catching the bastard then I'm fine.'

She didn't look fine. She looked downright ghastly. Apart from the vivid bruise and cut, she looked as though she needed a solid night's sleep. He turned into his local shopping centre and parked. 'I just need a few supplies for dinner,' he murmured as he eased out of the car.

'Can I cook a Greek dish for you?'

The unexpected request was accompanied by such a pleading gaze Guy wondered if she needed to keep busy. 'Sure, why not? Choose whatever ingredients you need.'

He enjoyed the time wandering the aisles with her. Suddenly she seemed more alive. His only concern was the furtive glances they received from other customers. 'I sincerely hope these people don't think I had anything to do with your black eye,' he murmured as they approached the checkout.

Melanie winced as she swept one hand to her cheek. 'I was wondering why we were being stared at. I'd forgotten about it.'

'Surely it must be sore?'

'I know it's there but I try not to think about it.' She fell silent again as Guy paid for the groceries. It really concerned him that she remained introspective and gnawed at the corner of her bottom lip all the way home. The troubling silence continued while she prepared the meal of tomatoes and green peppers stuffed with minced meat and rice. Thinking back to when she fell into this contemplative silence he realised it was when he'd mentioned the injury. But was it significant? His own scar centred in his mind and he had to force his hand from rising to brush the side of his cheek.

Iain arrived bearing a bottle of red wine, which Guy opened immediately. Melanie refused the wine with a vehement shake of her head, accepting fruit juice instead. Mentally kicking himself for not thinking, he assumed she never touched alcohol because of her father. He swore to be sparing with his own alcohol intake when she was with him.

After a delicious meal of what Melanie called *Yemista*, Guy wanted to keep her in a good frame of mind so heaped praise on her then insisted he and Iain would do the dishes while she relaxed. He kept up a joking banter and was pleased when Melanie laughed at some of his weak jokes. But hell, he wasn't good with jokes and by the time the last dish was put away he was pretty well scraping the wood from an empty barrel.

While Iain questioned Melanie, Guy retreated downstairs for a workout to give the pair privacy. Continual thoughts about this incredible woman consumed him while he worked up a sweat. He enjoyed her company and didn't find her presence intrusive. He'd had his share of girlfriends, including a couple of long-term relationships but nowhere near as many as Iain, who always seemed to have plenty of female friends he could call on for a date. After experiencing the loving partnership their parents had enjoyed, both wanted the same in their marriages but neither had found the one person they wanted to share their life with.

'You make me feel exhausted just watching you. I wish I had your energy.'

Guy spun around then grinned at his brother. 'I enjoy the exercise; it makes me feel alive. You should try it some time, both of you. The fitter you are, the more energy you have,' he teased as he picked up a towel and wiped the sweat from his face and arms.

'You're almost obsessive with your workouts, little brother.'

'Obsessive?' Guy was taken aback by how serious Iain sounded.

'Yes, you never miss a session.'

Guy laughed. 'I miss plenty. It doesn't bother me if I don't workout for a day or a week. I've always kept fit so it's not hard maintaining the level. It's no different from somebody playing regular football or squash. I'm just fortunate I have the room here to play my sport at home. And I don't work out every night, big brother.'

'I'm off,' Iain said as he lifted a hand in farewell. 'I'll let you know if we find your father. Stay safe until we do.' He waved as he turned at the top of the stairs.

Melanie followed and retired to bed whilst he showered and then made his phone call to Greece, more than impressed with what he heard.

***

Darkness still pressed between the Venetian slats when the strident ring of the phone call roused him. One hand fumbled for the receiver as he yawned. Still half-asleep he clamped it to one ear. The news from the hospital shocked him to full awareness. How on earth was he going to tell Melanie? After replacing the receiver, his hand swept through his hair then down his face. Damn, damn, damn.

Bare feet slapped against tiles down the passage. He called at the closed door. When there was no response he paused then pushed the door ajar. Padding across the carpet, he gazed down at the woman curled on her side with her loose hair tumbled across the pillow. Reluctant to disturb her but knowing he had no choice he turned on the bedside light and placed a gentle hand on her shoulder. 'Melanie, the hospital rang, we need to go. Get dressed.'

His heart turned over as he watched her jolt upright then alarm spread over her face. He didn't have the heart to impart the bad news, so left her to dress when she shot out of bed and grabbed the clothes she'd worn earlier. Back in his room he yanked on jeans, shoes and a sweater and was waiting by the door when Melanie rushed out still braiding her hair.

Once inside the hospital, Melanie sped along eerily quiet corridors to her mother's room, while Guy spoke with the duty doctor. Pausing in the open doorway, his innards hitched when he saw Melanie gently caressing her mother's hand while whispering private words into her ear. Hell, why did he say he'd break the bad news? Sucking in a long breath he stepped further into the room. 'Melanie?'

Her glance held such hope it twisted his insides. He moved over and placed a comforting hand on her arm. 'Melanie, your mother had a massive heart attack.' Coward, she's dead, you fool.

'But she's alive! She's breathing. Look, you can see her chest moving.'

Hell, this was going to be harder than he'd thought. 'The machine is breathing for her.' He paused but Melanie didn't appear to have understood. 'She's gone, Melanie. She passed away. They kept the respirator going so you could say goodbye.' How he hated telling her, and he felt sure he wasn't doing a very good job. Was there an easy or right way to tell a person that her much loved mother was dead? Remembering the day of his father's accidental death, Guy felt positively ill.

A loud wail erupted. His words must have finally registered. He gently wrapped his arm around her shoulders but she shrugged him away and leant over her mother then began shaking her. Guy swore under his breath then pressed the button to summon the doctor who'd said he'd be waiting outside. Thank goodness the man entered immediately and began explaining the details of the tests they had carried out but Guy doubted Melanie heard a word.

'Can you give her a few minutes please?' Guy asked when he noticed Melanie's distressed face.

After the doctor left Guy held Melanie close while repeating the doctor's words. He didn't have a clue how much she absorbed for she was like a solid statue. She was still clinging to him when the doctor returned fifteen minutes later. He stood in front of the life support system.

'Miss Jones, we need to turn the machine off.'

'I can't!' The distraught wail echoed around the room as Melanie twisted around and settled her eyes on her mother.

'Would you like me to do it?' The doctor waited patiently until he received a shy nod of assent then reached up and flicked a switch.

Apart from the slowing beeps of the machine, the silence pressed in while they watched the chest rises and falls slow and finally cease. A mournful sound rumbled from Melanie. Guy turned her around, tucking her head against his chest. Tears soaked his shirt as she released her agony. There was nothing he could say or do to ease her distress so he just held her close to give what little comfort he could.

It felt like forever before her tension eased. Keeping his hands on her shoulders he stepped back. 'Would you like a few minutes alone to say your farewells?'

When Melanie nodded weakly he moved into the corridor where he stood leant up against the wall, giving her as much time as she needed. When she emerged, her tears had dried but her face wore a haggard vacant look. Ignoring the telltale jerk when his arm neared her, he slid his arm around her shoulders and steadied her as they walked to the car in silence. Having experienced the sudden loss of a parent, he understood her pain. Right now she'd be in a vacuum of disbelief. Denial would follow, then anger, all accompanied by an agonising pain.

Once home he led the morosely silent Melanie to her bedroom where he laid her fully clothed on the bed, removed her sneakers then covered her with the doona. He crept to the door.

'Guy, please don't leave me alone?'

The whispered plea was so plaintive. What the devil was he supposed to do now? They both needed sleep but that mournful cry for help came from her soul. He recalled the first night when she had been too afraid to sleep alone. He eyed Melanie's bed. It was way too small for the both of them with his big frame. Without any further thought of rights and wrongs, he lifted her still wrapped in the Doona and carried her to his room, where he slept with her in his arms until strident jangling woke him from a restless sleep. Reaching over to his bedside table, he grabbed the receiver, hoping it didn't wake the still sleeping woman by his side.

'Guy, where are you? It's nine o'clock. Are you coming in?' Neil's worried voice penetrated Guy's foggy brain.

'Sorry, Neil, I was up most of the night and you just woke me.' He dropped his voice. 'Melanie's mother passed away early this morning, so no, I won't be in. We haven't had much sleep and I figure Melanie is going to need someone around. I'll ring you later in the day but phone me if anything urgent crops up.' Replacing the receiver, Guy stared down at the curled up woman, wondering what was the best thing to do. Let her sleep. He lay back down and dozed off again.

Melanie's stirring woke him. He leant up on one shoulder, gazing down at her. 'How are you feeling?'

Her eyes widened then a scarlet blush rushed up her face as she realised where she was. Even her bruises seemed to redden. He smiled. 'You seem to be making a habit of sleeping in my bed, but I'm not complaining,' he teased.

With her blush of embarrassment deepening even further Melanie tried to get up but was entangled in her doona. She struggled to free herself and then fled.

He slithered out of bed and pulled the covers straight, wondering what the day held for him. It wasn't going to be easy. A swim was high on his priorities to clear away the cobwebs and maybe it would give Melanie something to do instead of being submerged in grief.

It took a while to coerce Melanie from her room. Figuring she felt embarrassed at sleeping in his bed, he was amused when she kept her eyes averted for most of the drive along the coast to his favourite bay. One of his incentives to tempt her from her room was to promise brunch by the seaside as long as he could swim first. After parking the car he suggested Melanie could either stay in the car or sit on the sand. When she opted for the first he left her the key with the remote locking device attached so she could lock herself in if she felt the need. Stripping down to bathers, he jogged to the water's edge.

***

Melanie watched Guy's every move, mystified at the strange fuzzy feelings at the sight of his massive frame covered only in a brief skin-tight bathing costume. She compared him to his brother. Apart from also being a tall, well-built man, Iain had little resemblance to Guy. With mousy brown hair, blue eyes and about two inches shorter, Iain was not in the same physical condition and was beginning to show a small paunch. But Guy? Oh, boy! That he was fitter than most, she had already sussed out and he was muscular but not the bulky over-developed muscles of some gym fanatics she'd seen.

Her thoughts centred on him as she watched Guy swim out to what seemed to be a long way. Then he turned and swam parallel to the shore. Becoming worried when he moved out of sight, Melanie walked down the beach then sat on his towel, keeping an eye on the spot from which he had disappeared. Relief surged when she spied his strong arms cutting a neat swathe through the water on his return. Her innards lurched when he rose out of the ocean, the sun glistening on his wet skin. To her, he looked like a golden Adonis rising out of the water, the sun turning the glistening water on his body to a rich gold sheen. She couldn't suppress the gasp that escaped at the awe-inspiring sight.

When Guy reached the sand, Melanie was standing holding his towel in her outstretched hands. As he took it from her their fingers touched for the briefest of moments. Never had a mere touch generated such charged sensations that travelled through her body. Knowing she needed to break the tension Melanie blurted the first thing that came to her mind. 'I just want a simple cremation service so that, one day, I can take Mum's ashes back to Greece.'

There was a long pause, during which Guy's hands stilled from rubbing the water from his musty blond hair. 'I thought the Greek Orthodox didn't believe in cremation.'

'Mum had no faith in religion. She denounced her Greek roots years ago. Although Mum taught me the language from an early age, I didn't even know I had Greek grandparents until Mum sent me to live with them.'

'So why then do you want to take her ashes back?'

'I promised her we would escape. I promised I would take her back to Greece to live. I intend to keep that promise.' Unbidden tears slid down her cheeks as she thought of the two tickets she'd purchased before she had come home. Circumstances had prevented her from making use of them and now they were out of date. An all-consuming pain of emptiness swept over her. Mum was gone – for ever.

Chapter Eight

Guy swallowed a mouthful of cereal, settled the spoon in the bowl then glanced at Melanie. She looked as though she'd not slept well with indications of tears having flowed for much of the night. Who could blame her?

'How about coming into work this morning so you can have your second interview?' He grinned at Melanie's dropped jaw then picked up a paper napkin and wiped the dribble of milk from her lips before jabbing her jaw closed to prevent any more spillage. 'By the way, Iain rang while you were in the shower. Because your mother's death is now a murder investigation, there will be a formal autopsy, which means we can't organise a funeral until her body is released.'

The instant change in her demeanour alarmed him but he said nothing. Knowing the news would give her grief he had wondered how to tell her. After his last attempt at breaking bad news slowly, he figured straight out was better, but it still didn't sit well. Either way it was going to hurt.

A few tears escaped from the corners of already puffy eyes, but then she shrugged her shoulders with a deep sigh and shook her head in several shivery quick movements as though shaking away bad thoughts. 'I'm sorry it has to be this way, but it's the law,' he added as he placed one hand on the long sleeve of her lower arm and gently squeezed.

An unladylike sniff escaped then Melanie sighed. 'I know, but it doesn't make it any easier.' She paused. 'The thought of Mum being sliced open…' She shuddered. 'But then Mum will never feel any pain again and I have to keep that in mind.'

He gave her arm another squeeze. 'She suffered a lot, didn't she?'

Melanie's eyes shuttered closed. The pause was palpable. 'Yes,' she whispered.

'I'm really sorry. Nobody deserves that kind of life. What I don't understand is why she didn't leave him.'

Her shoulders rose, tensed then fell. 'We tried.'

By the quietness of her words, he knew she was struggling. 'And?'

Her chest heaved. 'He always found us.' Another lengthy pause. 'The reprisals weren't worth it.'

While ghastly images jostled through his head, Guy stared at Melanie's bowed head. What the hell was he supposed to say to that?

'You need money to move any distance. He drank every spare cent we had – and then some. People who have never been in the situation just don't understand.' She turned away. 'I don't know why I'm telling you this. I've never told anyone before. Can we change the subject?'

The heartrending appeal twisted his innards. After seeing the butchery carried out on her mother, he didn't have the gumption to probe any further. He wasn't sure he really wanted to know if Melanie had been on the receiving end of the same brutality but after seeing how she cowered in fear or flinched at sudden movements, he was afraid she had.

'I'm sorry I brought up bad memories, now how about today? Are you coming with me?'

'Thank you, yes, but how come I get a second interview?'

'Because your experience is just what we want.'

'Truly?' She looked amazed. Then just as suddenly her face altered leaving her eyes bleak. 'I don't relish the thought of staying in the house alone all day.'

***

As they entered the foyer of his office Melanie halted then glanced around. He followed her line of sight, trying to absorb the scene from an outsider's point of view. For a reception area of an industrial manufacturing factory it wasn't too bad. He'd seen a lot worse. Two potted palms at either end of an L-shaped arrangement of seats softened the starkness of black fabric. A glass-topped coffee table held another small leafy plant and a pile of magazines. The only other colour was a multicoloured mat underneath the arrangement

'Give me something to do, Guy. I need to keep my mind occupied,' Melanie said.

He swung back to her. 'Let me find Neil so we can give you your interview first. Then I'm sure we can find a few files that need sorting. We've been busy planning a new factory and have been short-staffed with my last assistant leaving two weeks ago. We've been using temps, who have been fine, but the routine has gone out the door and it takes me hours to sort the mail each day. Wait here a minute.'

He left Melanie seated in one of the four faux suede chairs. She looked so forlorn. After gathering the paperwork on the applicants, he collected Neil for a short private conversation.

He was surprised at Melanie's confident poise when Neil ushered her in and settled her in the seat opposite the two men. It was as though in the few minutes she'd been alone, she had completely changed her personality from sad and timid to an unfazed businesswoman. 'I spoke with your Mr Panegyres last night. Would you like to know what he said?'

'I can imagine,' she replied with a wistful smile. 'He was a hard taskmaster with his men, but to me he was a gentle pussycat. I liked him a great deal.'

'Then you won't be surprised that he said, "Oh, my sweet little angel, how is Melanie? If you don't employ her then send her back to me. The place has gone to ruin since she left me. I had to employ three girls to take her place".' Trying his best to imitate the Greek accent Guy kept an eye on Melanie's face, absorbing her reaction. She smiled, but blushed at the same time then looked highly embarrassed. George Panegyres had also said he had never had anyone as efficient as Melanie and to trust her judgements and decisions, adding that she had run his empire better than he could. It had been very high praise indeed. After relating the call to Neil, both had agreed Melanie was by far the best candidate for the job.

'I wonder if you will have such a sweet smile and glowing praise when you remember your new boss. The job is yours. Welcome aboard, Melanie.'

For a few seconds Melanie sat dumbfounded, a look of sheer amazement on her face. 'Are you sure? It's not just because of what happened?' she asked when she finally found the ability to speak.

'If we didn't think you were the best person for this position, you wouldn't have won it. Your Greek admirer had nothing but high praise for your abilities. What helped was your experience and knowledge of our industry. Now, I'm afraid you are going to have to fill out the appropriate forms and I guess process them yourself, but I want them to cross my desk before they are filed. I believe we have a file for new employees somewhere.'

When Melanie stifled a giggle, Guy raised his eyebrows. 'You find something amusing?'

'The thought of Mr Panegyres being my admirer - he's over sixty! Can I start straight away?'

As an answer he handed her a large, untidy pile of papers relating to the new factory. 'See if you can put these in some form of order. It will probably take the rest of the day.'

Before starting work, Melanie was shown around the offices and introduced to a number of people. Then she was shown her work area, an office of her own.

'We'll leave you to find your way around the filing system. Feel free to re-arrange things to suit how you like to work,' said Guy before leaving her standing in the doorway.

***

She was elated being back at work but couldn't believe she had beaten the other applicants. No way was she good enough to be Guy's personal assistant, which meant she was given the job because of her predicament. This thought made her determined to earn the position – if she didn't get sacked after the first day. Needing to really apply herself to shove depressing thoughts of her mother away, she opened drawers and cupboards to see what each contained then engrossed her head in the pile of papers. Two hours later and afraid she'd taken way too long, she knocked on Guy's door and presented him with a number of newly created files, each clearly labelled.

'Would you like me to deal with the mail?' she asked while he studied the files.

'Sure, this is yesterday's mail here. I haven't had a chance to open it yet. Go for it.' He handed her a pile of unopened letters.

Since he hadn't given her any feedback with her first task, she felt sure he hadn't been pleased so she worked like a slave opening, reading and sorting then was back standing in his doorway in less than thirty minutes with a tray containing two items for him to read. The rest she had dealt with herself and delegated to people she thought were right for each item. To her, this was not a job for the boss. 'That's today's mail as well,' she murmured under her breath.

Guy looked stunned. 'Where's the rest of it?'

Oh, no! She'd made a bungle. Unsure how to handle her mistake she figured she should show him what she'd done. 'Come and I will show you, if you have the time.'

Guy followed. 'With the mail sorted I have plenty of time.'

Was that a compliment? Unsure, she handed him a neat stack. 'Have I done this right? These are receipts and invoices. I've matched up each with appropriate order forms and paperwork. I figured they should go to your accountant, Mr Smythe – have I got his name right?'

'Yes.'

She lifted a separate paper from her desk. 'This one, I believe is a bogus account. The order number is different to the system you use and I couldn't find any paperwork to match so I will investigate.' She handed it to Guy for perusal and picked up the next. 'This one has charged you more than the quote, so also needs checking.' There was a deathly silent pause while Guy studied the document.

Things were not going so well so to cover her humiliation she pointed to another small pile. 'This is junk mail and over here,' she stepped over to a low bank of cupboards, 'are some advertising brochures that could relate to your business, so I'll create a box file, in alphabetical order so that if you need to find them they will be on hand.' While she spoke, Melanie dared a peek at Guy to see his reaction for he had said nothing. He looked bemused as he followed then stood next to her, moving out of her line of sight unless she actually turned her head to look him square in the eye and she sure wasn't going to be so forward.

She picked up three more letters. 'These three, I believe you would pass on to Neil.'

Guy scanned the three letters. 'I can't believe this. You've sorted them exactly as I would have done, but in a quarter of the time. You've saved me at least three hours work. I can see why your Greek God called you his angel and why he wants you back. This is amazing.'

All she could do was stare at him with her mouth agape.

'But now you need a break. With your permission, Neil and I are taking you to lunch to welcome you to the company.' He placed his fingers on her elbow and steered her, via Neil's office. She had little choice in the matter so followed with her mouth firmly shut, not that she could think of anything to say.

Chapter Nine

At what sounded like shattering glass, Guy jerked awake in an instant. Had he been dreaming? Ears alert he swung his legs over the side of the bed. Hearing an almost imperceptible whimper he shot across the carpet. A sudden thought of Mr Jones breaking in had him pausing at the half open door. He needed a weapon. With the majority of his sporting gear and extraneous belongings stored in the gym below, the only thing he could think of that would do any kind of damage was a hiking boot.

He sped across the room and eased the wardrobe door open then felt around in the darkness until he made out the correct shape. Grasping the boot, he flew back to the door and eased it open. A quick peak both ways along the passage ensured there was no unusual shadow waiting to ambush him.

'No! No, don't!' The hysterical words broke the eerie silence.

Guy followed the sound and tore along the passage then shot into the kitchen. With this side of the house not having the benefit of moonlight, he stilled for a moment to allow his eyes to adjust to the darkness.

'No, Please don't!' The words were hushed but there was a definite hint of terror in her plea.

'Melanie?' Guy called into the darkness as he lifted the boot head-high, ready to wield. There was a snuffling sound followed by silence then another whimper. Following the sound, he moved further into the room, searching the darkness.

Another whimper like a mewling newborn kitten searching for its mother. Guy paused then glanced down. Melanie was on her knees huddled in a tight ball with both hands gripped behind her head in a protective pose.

'What the hell?' Guy muttered. 'Melanie?' He bent over her then reached down to pull her up. Just before he touched her she released a blood-curdling scream and even in the darkness he noticed how her body quivered then shrank into en even tighter ball.

Realisation hit. She must think he was her father about to belt her. His massive body hulking over her in the darkness was terrifying her. Well that reaction answered one question. There was no doubt she had been a victim of her father's brutality.

What has he done to you? Guy thought as he wracked his brain on what the heck he was supposed to do. He felt so damn helpless and inadequate. How do you convince a petrified woman who had been physically battered, that you meant her no harm?

'Melanie?' There was no response – not even an indication she had heard him. Was she so terrified that she didn't know where she was?

Confusion reigned. As he stepped away, glass shards crunched under his bare foot but he ignored the acute jab of the razor sharp edge penetrating his skin. When Melanie keened again he swore under his breath and backed away. Reaching out behind him, he felt around on the wall until he found the light switch. Flicking the tiny lever down, the room flooded with light.

Melanie whimpered again then huddled even tighter.

Dropping to the ground then lying prostrate on his stomach he slid both hands through the remnants of a smashed water tumbler, sweeping the pieces out of the way with the boot as his hands neared Melanie's face. At each sweep Melanie whimpered, causing his stomach to wrench. Flinging the boot across the room, he held both palms upwards. 'Melanie, it's me, Guy. I'm not going to harm you,' he said gently.

'Look at my hands, Melanie. They are right there in front of your eyes.' He paused, waiting for some kind of response: some indication she was aware of being in the here and now. Gut instinct told him she was so terrified she was almost catatonic.

'I'm *not* your father,' he said louder. 'It's Guy. Look at my hands.' He noticed a slight movement of her head then an uncanny stillness.

'Look at my hands. These hands will never, ever be used to hurt you in any way.'

The only indication of Melanie hearing him was the easing of the tense grip on the clenched fingers behind her head. Blood began flowing, turning the whiteness of her knuckles into pink.

'Melanie, I promise I won't hurt you. Put your hands into mine.' He waited, his breath held.

'Guy?' The single word whooshed out. Her fingers released their death-like grip and in an incredibly slow movement, quivering hands reached out until they slid into his palms. They were icy cold.

His held breath eased out as slow as his fingers curled around her frozen hands.

'Guy? I… thought… it was…' Tears began tumbling.

Keeping a gentle hold on her hands Guy eased into a sitting position. All of a sudden Melanie sprang up like a panther pouncing on its prey. One second she was crouched on her knees, the next she was curled up in his lap with her fingers gripped around his neck.

'I'm so sorry. I dropped a glass. It brought back…' She clamped her mouth shut then flopped against his chest.

Something told him not to ask any questions but he was mighty curious. What memory did a broken glass bring back? What was so ghastly that it made her react this way? She hadn't just been scared. She had been beyond terrified. He slid his arms around her and held her close, rocking her like a baby. 'It's only a glass. It doesn't matter.'

Nothing else was said. They remained cuddled up on the kitchen floor, shattered shards of glass surrounding them while Guy whispered calming words into her ear and his hands rubbed circles on various parts of her body where he could reach until her tension and tears ran their course. All the while, Guy couldn't help but wonder about Melanie's past. What had happened to cause this type of terror when all she did was drop a glass in the dark? And how the hell was he supposed to handle such severe insecurities? Despite being aware that familial abuse happened, he'd never experienced it before and really didn't have a clue as to how to treat an abused person.

It wasn't until Melanie began pulling away that Guy eased his hold. 'Do you want to tell me what that was all about?' Guy asked as he searched the depths of her tear-ravaged eyes.

She immediately dropped her eyelids. 'No. I never want to talk about it. Please don't make me?' The plea twanged his heart into suffocating tightness.

There was a long silence while he considered whether or not to push for an explanation. What was the right thing to do? He was no psychologist and had never encountered such deep-seated fear in a person. He figured his honesty to be the best course of action. 'Okay, I'll not push you, but it makes it hard for me to understand what's happening with you when you react like this. I have no idea how to handle things if I don't have a clue as to the reason.'

'Please, Guy, I can't talk about it. Ever.' As though to ensure he didn't pursue his questioning Melanie wriggled from his lap and stood. 'I'll clean this up. Go back to bed. And... I'm sorry, but thank you for being there.' Without waiting for a response, she scampered into the laundry in search of a broom and pan. She was already back by the time Guy had unfolded his cramped body from the floor.

He took one step and winced in pain. 'Damn.'

'What is it?' Melanie dropped the implements and rushed forwards.

'I think there's a piece of glass in my foot. Stay back in case the same happens to you.'

Picking up the broom, Melanie swept up the glass remnants then ordered Guy to sit on a stool. She grinned when he swore as she removed the offending slither from the pad of his foot. The sight of her smiling as though the past hour hadn't occurred caused his heart to flip-flop in his chest.

Chapter Ten

It stunned Guy how, over the ensuing week, Melanie began creating order in the office with phenomenal efficiency. Each item of mail had a typed letter in response, already attached before he read it. All he had to do was sign at the bottom. Every day, something new would amaze him about how she forethought every detail and organised things to function better. What disappointed him was the way she appeared to be humbled every time he gave her praise. It was as though she felt she wasn't worthy of compliments yet she was the most efficient assistant he'd ever had. Telling her that had caused her to redden then flee. Everything he'd learnt about her so far indicated she had an introverted but generous nature.

Mystified as to how Melanie exuded a different persona at work, he studied her without seeming to be blatantly obvious. Within days she had won the office staff over. One young man in particular looked at her with adoring puppy-dog eyes. It amused him to see the tactics the young man used to find ways to be near Melanie but he said nothing especially since Melanie appeared to be blossoming under the attention.

Friday evening Melanie hovered in the door after saying goodnight, looking as though she wanted to say something but didn't know how to broach it. 'Spill it out, Melanie.' Guy said without looking up.

'Huh? How did you know?'

'You look as though you are tiptoeing on red-hot coals. What's the problem?' When he raised his eyes he spied her rising blush before her chin dropped.

'Umm, I won't be home for dinner tomorrow night.'

The words were so soft he could barely make them out. 'Can I ask why not?'

'Umm, Rod Stevens asked me out on a date.'

Guy did a double take as his innards clenched. 'He's only a kid and has to be a couple of years younger than you.' At her flinch he realised his words were a bit harsh. 'I'm sorry, that came out wrong.' It shocked him to feel such a deep thrust of jealousy at the thought of this young man taking Melanie anywhere. 'Do you know where you're going?' he added. His curtness managed to raise her eyes, which spat shards of ice at him. Oh, wow!

'We're going out for a meal. Does it matter? Surely I can make up my own mind if I want to go out with someone. I am a single adult. I'm delighted he asked me.'

Phew, that was putting him in his place. 'I'm just worried about your father. What if he sees you? Does Rod know anything about the danger you could be in?'

'I promise I'll be careful. You don't need to worry. He won't attack me when I'm with someone else. He never does it with an audience.'

Guy contemplated the scornful words as he watched her scuttle away. The last sentence had him thinking. She'd told him her mother protected her but the way she said those few words… it sounded as though she was speaking from experience, which only confirmed his suspicions. So why wouldn't she tell him?

***

Despite Melanie saying he had nothing to worry about, Guy worried. When Rodney knocked at the door early next evening, Guy swung the door open. The poor young man's jaw gaped. He couldn't hold back his grin. It was more than obvious Melanie hadn't told Rod with whom she was staying.

'Uh, ah, I'm looking for Melanie.'

Guy didn't think any person could blush more than the man standing in front of him. He smiled as he ushered Rod inside. 'Melanie is staying with me until she can find a new place of her own.' Over my dead body will she be moving out. 'I'll see if she's ready.' I hope she's changed her mind.

Stepping into the passage, he called, 'Melanie?' His heart went to his mouth when she emerged from her room. With her hair down loose and wearing a flowing floral dress, she looked downright gorgeous. He bit back his feelings as he bade them good-bye, wishing them a pleasant evening while silently hoping it was ghastly and Melanie hated the company. To purge his body of unkind thoughts about this young kid who dared take Melanie on a date, he spent the next hour in the gym working his body until it hurt. Thoughts of Melanie refused to give his mind any peace.

He recognised the jealousy for what it was and it stunned him. There was nothing between them for such feelings to even arise. They'd never dated, never kissed, never anything romantic. Yet he felt insanely jealous and it didn't sit well.

Settled in the sofa with paperwork he couldn't concentrate on and listening to music he wasn't really hearing, Guy waited for her return. When he heard the front door opening he made a concerted effort to focus on the papers, but his thoughts were on how the young upstart hadn't better be thinking of even attempting to kiss her.

Melanie closed the door before turning around, looking surprised to see Guy still up.

'I trust you enjoyed your meal?' He tried to give the impression he didn't care but his pulse was racing and his heart pounding. Had she been kissed? He studied her mouth to see if her lips were moist or swollen.

'Yes, thank you, it was very pleasant. Goodnight, Guy.' She walked straight past him.

His eyes bored into her back as she headed to her room. He fought down the impulse to chase after her and wipe the feel of Rod's lips from her mouth and replace it with his own. Disgusted with himself, he tossed the papers to one side and stalked to his room where sleep eluded him.

***

The following day, Iain visited to ask Melanie necessary details to aid in the investigation. Guy left them alone while he went for a swim and was most surprised they were still talking when he returned. 'How about staying for a bite to eat?' Guy asked when he noted the tense lines on Melanie's face. Despite her trying to hide her distress, it was obvious she was upset about something so he figured a casual meal with company might ease her tension.

'Sounds great, thank you,' said Iain as the two brothers exchanged a silent look of understanding over Melanie's downcast face. Guy tried the teasing banter again in an attempt to ease the atmosphere during the light meal. It worked on Iain but Melanie remained morose.

On his way out Iain turned to his brother. 'I've already mentioned to Melanie that the coroner is releasing her mother's body on Tuesday. You can organise a burial service. Melanie said she may need some assistance.'

Iain turned to Melanie and grinned. 'I'll pick you up at seven.'

Staring in stunned surprise, Guy waited until the door was closed before making any comment. 'What was that all about? Picking you up at seven?'

She half turned and spoke to the wall. 'Iain asked me out. We're going to the cinema tomorrow night.'

'You're going out with my brother?'

She spun around and planted hands on hips. 'Why not? He's a nice man and he invited me out. So I said yes.' Turning her back on him, she fled to her room leaving him scowling after her. He didn't like it one bit the way things were evolving. He was going to have to do something about these intense feelings of jealousy. Soon.

***

When the next morning's mail included a parcel couriered in from Greece, Guy asked Melanie to stay. 'This is probably for you.'

'I was hoping. It looks about the right size.'

'You could have opened it, after all you are my assistant.' He took his time in opening the packet then handed Melanie a letter addressed to her along with the repaired instrument, which was wrapped in layer upon layer of fine tissue paper and bubble wrap. There was also a letter for Guy.

After tearing the wrapping off, Melanie studied the instrument with a critical eye before breaking out in a beaming smile. 'I can hardly see where they were damaged.' She ran her fingers over each pipe in an almost reverent touch. Picking up her letter, she retreated to her office.

Guy's letter contained the money Guy had included to pay for the repairs.

It is an honour to help my precious Melanie.
The talent she has and the fun we shared is
the only payment I need. Take good care of
my precious girl.

Slumping back in his chair with the letter clutched in one hand, Guy mulled over the words. It seemed the whole world loved this woman as much as he did. He jerked upright. Was he in love with her? Impossible. They'd only met a few days ago. He'd never been in love with any woman so how was he supposed to know how it felt. Then he realised that Melanie had entranced him from the very second he had first seen her on that stage. Sitting at his desk, he contemplated for a long time trying to sort out his feelings.

That night he hated seeing Iain place his arm around her waist. Even though his brother always treated his female companions with utmost respect, Guy was well aware of the number of conquests Iain had made in the past. His stomach churned at the thought his brother would add Melanie to his list. What if Melanie fell for his brother? He shuddered at the thought.

Minutes before Iain was due to arrive, Guy hid in the gym where he worked out half-heartedly until he heard Melanie leave. Ceasing his bench work, he sat on the weight lifting bench with elbows on his knees, his head in outstretched hands. He had no idea how Melanie felt about him but he sure knew how he was feeling about Melanie. The searing jealousy towards his much-loved brother stabbed him deep.

While he waited for Melanie's return, Guy mulled over the situation. At work, it was as though Melanie was a different person. She spoke with ease to everyone, worked hard, was super efficient and was always smiling and happy, but when they were together at home she was so different. It was difficult to get a word out of her. She appeared shy and reserved and rarely smiled. It was as though she pulled herself into her shell like a startled, shy little tortoise. He wondered if she didn't like living in his house or if she just didn't like him. He sure liked having her around.

When the pair returned, Guy was once again attempting to read. His book was open but the blurred words he stared at didn't register. When she opened the door, Iain waved in acknowledgement then turned to Melanie, bent and gave her a quick kiss on her lips before he left. A surge of sheer envy and resentment tore through Guy.

Melanie almost skipped past him then called goodnight before closing her bedroom door, leaving Guy staring after her. He was going to have to do something drastic, very soon. The very thought of his brother beginning any type of a relationship with his Melanie was just too much.

Chapter Eleven

Even though they were only in the reception area of the funeral parlour, the place still gave Guy the creeps. The young lady assisting them with plans for a cremation service was exactly as a funeral assistant should be: smart sober outfit, pleasant and quietly spoken. Her name went against the grain – Missy Barnes. He couldn't figure out if it was the real name, a diminutive or maybe a nickname. For the life of him he couldn't think of any name it could be a diminutive of. But she was certainly good at her job, showing a depth of understanding and compassion. At first, Melanie had looked scared but now was wringing her hands together and looking stricken.

'What's the problem, Melanie?'

'Can we speak in private for a minute?' she muttered after a hesitant pause.

Without a word, the young lady left, leaving him even more impressed with her understanding. As soon as the door closed, Guy settled one hand on Melanie's writhing fingers.

'What's bothering you?'

'I feel so embarrassed.' She hesitated but her face told him she was really upset about something. Embarrassed wasn't a strong enough word to describe the anguish on her face.

'I can't afford this yet. I never thought it would cost so much to have Mum cremated and I don't have the money. I don't know what to do.'

Ah, now he understood. He gently squeezed her entwined hands. 'You don't need to worry about anything. Let me take care of things for you.'

She blushed as she gnawed the same corner of her bottom lip that she often did when feeling self-conscious, which was far more often than a normal person. Her insecurities were deep.

'You don't understand. I've worried about money all my life but I've never borrowed before. Everything we ever managed to save was stolen to feed an alcohol binge. That's why I didn't have a bank account here. He forges my signature and empties my account. I don't know how he finds out where I have my accounts because I am forever changing banks but he steals everything.' Her quick glance showed how uncomfortable she felt. 'I've never owed anyone money before and I don't like the feeling but it seems I don't have any choice. I have a small amount in a term deposit in Greece but it would take some time to have it sent here. I promise I'll pay you back every cent.'

Sensing her intense discomfort Guy leant over and gave her a gentle hug. 'I understand. How about we make a deal?

You organise whatever you want, allow me to initially foot the bill and we'll discuss repayment later. What's important right now is for your mother to have the service she deserves.' Silently he prayed that she would forget about repayments because he would never be able to accept them.

***

Two nights later they were on their way home from work and Guy was wondering why Melanie was fidgeting. It was obvious she wanted to say something. 'Spill it, Melanie.'

She jolted. 'Umm, I… I'm returning to the music group tonight.'

'Tonight? But it's the funeral tomorrow.'

'I know but playing music allows me to forget for a couple of hours.' She turned away to stare out of the side window. It was a habit he'd noticed. There was a distinct lack of eye contact when she felt uncomfortable about what was being said.

'I think I understand,' said Guy as he glanced at the back of her head, 'but your father knows about the hall. There's a chance he'll be waiting for you so how about I come with you. If you don't want me inside, I'll wait in the car or stand in the shadows.'

'He's no man! He's a bastard!' she spat as she swung her head back to face him. Her eyes held menace, her unusual vehemence causing Guy to take his eyes from the road for a second. As soon as they had eye contact her eyelids dropped. 'Sorry, but I would really like to go. We were working to put together enough pieces to cut a CD and I feel like I'm letting the others down. I don't mind if you come in with us, in fact I would feel safer. I'd really appreciate it if you could spare the time but I'd hate to impose.' The head had turned away again. Damn, but she was so humble and apologetic for even the tiniest gesture as though she was asking for the world, yet he felt overjoyed. He'd hear her play again.

'Let's do it then. We'll have a quick snack before we go and then have a meal afterwards.' He paused. 'It's a good excuse for *me* to take you out.' Risking another glance, he couldn't help but smile as her face shot back towards him. A stunned look turned into a sly smile before she turned away again. Yes!

The sun had just dropped behind the horizon but daylight was still lingering when he parked right outside the hall door. He shielded Melanie as he guided her inside while searching the surroundings for any sign of her father. After acknowledging each woman when introduced, he edged around the group to find somewhere to park his backside. As they began setting up he dragged a chair to the back of the hall then eased his tall frame down and sat where he had sight of both the door and the group. He glanced around the bare brick walls that were a drab salmon colour. A row of high windows graced both sides. During the day they would let in sufficient light while providing privacy for inside activities. A human would fit through each but they'd have to be Spiderman to climb the outside walls to reach them. He rose then checked each to ensure they were secure. Continuing on, he searched the tiny spaces behind the kitchen area at the rear for further doors, jiggling locks and sliding bolts backwards and forwards before yanking on the handles to ensure each door couldn't be forced open. A dank smell of mouldy mops and antiseptic made his nose twitch but he held back a niggling sneeze. It was only after a second examination he felt satisfied the hall was secure and he settled back into the chair.

As the girls perched on chairs that looked uncomfortable and readied music sheets and instruments they chatted amongst themselves discussing the intricacies of what they were doing. Most of it was incomprehensible to him. There were a series of long notes played as instruments were tuned to the panpipes. After a short introduction by one violin, another joined in harmony then the other instruments entered the musical conversation until finally Melanie played.

The rich haunting sound carried Guy back to the magic of the concert. To him, the music was perfect so he couldn't understand why there were continual stops to repeat small sections again and again. The entire two hours was spent on the one piece and then the girls began packing up. He wanted more. Standing, he strode across the room to Melanie.

'Please play *The Swan* for me?'

She stilled, staring back at him. As though sensing the atmosphere the other women egged her on until she agreed. Moving to the middle of the room, she lifted the instrument to her mouth, closed her eyes and began. Guy stood mesmerised as the sound surrounded him. He was entranced at the passion flitting across her face as though she was in a world of her own. Then he recalled her saying that when she played, she could forget about unpleasant things. Now he understood. She was in a different world: one of peace and harmony instead of horror, pain and constant fear.

Chapter Twelve

Iain, Neil and Louise were hunched together in a single pew when Guy ushered Melanie into the crematorium. The office to this complex had given him the creeps but this room had an entirely different atmosphere: one he couldn't find the right word to describe. It wasn't spooky but more chilling and other-worldly, more so with so few people. The slightest sound seemed to echo. Melanie must have felt the same eerie sensation for she stalled then stiffened in the open doorway. He moved his hand from her elbow and slid it around her shoulders, giving her a gentle nudge before steering her to the front pew on the other side of the aisle. The moment she sat she shivered then stilled, remaining tense until the end of the brief but very touching ceremony. Silent tears slid down her cheeks and plopped onto her blouse but she didn't move to mop them up.

It surprised him when she stood by the side of the casket with one hand resting on the lid and spoke quietly while looking anywhere but at those inside. Nothing about the history of Maria Jones' life was revealed. It was more about happy times and how she felt about her mother. That they had such closeness was not a surprise but the fact that it was the first time Melanie expressed such positive emotion, was. While she spoke, tears hovered in the corners of her eyes but she held them back. Then she played *The Swan* as the casket slowly dropped into the mysterious void under the floor. His skin prickled at the echoed haunting tones.

Afterwards he drove a subdued Melanie home where she went straight to her room without having uttered a single word. When he looked in on her she was lying on her bed, seemingly asleep but a closer examination revealed moisture clinging to shuttered lashes. Kneeling by her side he brushed the fingers of one hand across both eyes to scoop up the moisture. At his touch she stiffened then immediately relaxed. He hated that she was so skittish at any close encounter. 'Dinner will be in about twenty minutes,' he murmured as he left.

When he called her to eat, Melanie's face appeared less tense. He suspected she'd flooded her face with cold water in an attempt to wipe away any evidence of tears but he could tell she'd been crying. Who wouldn't after such an emotional ordeal? They carried their meals into the lounge to enjoy a more relaxed atmosphere. Melanie turned on a CD of tranquil background music then perched on the leather sofa with her legs curled under her and the plate nestled in the hollow of her lap. She had let her hair loose and changed into well worn but comfy looking jeans and a simple long-sleeved cotton top. They ate in companionable silence.

After scraping the last remnants of food from his plate Guy placed the empty dish on the carpet by the side of his chair, noticing that Melanie had barely touched her food but under the circumstances food wasn't a high priority so he said nothing.

A sudden loud banging at the door felt like a violation of the atmosphere. He wanted to ignore the unwelcome intrusion but a second round of thumping had him stride across the room to find out what the ruckus was about.

Yanking the door open he reeled back when he saw the woman standing there with a raised clenched fist. 'Linley! Dinner. Damn. I forgot.'

'Forgot?' the tall skinny woman screeched as she stormed into the room, shoving Guy aside. She stopped short, anger suffusing her face even further when she spied Melanie.

'You bastard, Guy Harris! Who is this bitch? You leave me sitting in a restaurant waiting for you and all the time you're making out with a gypsy whore,' Linley spat, her hands wildly gesticulating in Melanie's direction then poking Guy in the ribs.

'I'm sorry, Linley. Things have been a bit…'

'How dare you stand me up for this piece of trash?'

Appalled at the uncalled for words, Guy twisted around when he heard a thud. With one hand pressed against her mouth and a fresh wave of tears tumbling, Melanie was standing looking distraught, her dinner plate upside down on the floor. With a mewling sound of distress, she fled.

'So, not only do you stand me up but you also have this bitch staying with you.' Linley squawked. 'How dare you date me while you're having an affair with someone else?'

Steaming with anger, Guy stepped towards Linley who had reached the middle of the room. 'I'm really sorry,

Linley. Forgetting our date was unforgivable but there were extenuating circumstances and if you had rung or given me a chance to explain you would understand. Your accusations about Melanie are inexcusable. You don't even know her, or why she is here. I'm not having an affair with anyone – especially you. I'm not too keen on people who jump to such hasty conclusions and are so vindictive in their wild assumptions. Now if you would be so kind as to leave?'

When Linley remained exactly where she was, clenched fists planted firmly on her hips and with a tense screwed up face showing her obvious fury, Guy reached out and placed his hands on her shoulders. It took some effort to turn the woman around. She wriggled and squirmed to free herself but furious for her unthinking insults, he finally managed to get her to the door where he shoved her out. 'I'll ring you to explain,' he forced out through a tight throat before slamming the door.

With his chest heaving, Guy stood contemplating Melanie's closed door, knowing full well she would be beside herself. Tamping down his temper, he strode down the passage and knocked. Hearing her sobbing, he tried to push the door open but it had been locked from the inside. Attempts to talk to her through the barrier were met with silence. Swearing profusely, he sank into a chair with his head in his hands. With all that had happened over the past week he'd completely forgotten about the date with Linley. In fact he hadn't even thought about the woman at all since the time he had met up with Melanie. His ire calming, he knew Linley had a right to be angry and he would call to apologise. Hopefully she would give him a chance to explain but he'd never date her again.

He sat mumbling self-recriminations under his breath then picked up the remains of Melanie's meal and cleaned the carpet and kitchen. Mad at himself for being so downright stupid he retreated to the gym where he worked at a furious pace for an hour. His muscles hurt, his head hurt and his heart hurt. After showering he lay on his bed unable to sleep; the scene with Linley galloping through his head time and time again. He was amazed at how nasty she turned out to be although he couldn't blame her after being stood up – something he had never done before. No wonder he had no romantic feelings towards her. What hurt the most was the look of utter devastation on Melanie's face. He was still lying awake when he heard a noise from the vicinity of the lounge. He rose then crept to his partially open door. In the dim moonlight he spied Melanie sitting huddled in his favourite chair, her chin resting on her knees and the doona wrapped around her like a little papoose.

'Melanie?' he queried softly as he approached.

She stared up at him.

'I'm so sorry about Linley. I completely forgot I had asked her out to dinner. That was weeks ago, before you and I even met.'

'You are not the one who should be apologising. You did nothing wrong.' Melanie's voice sounded vacant and raspy.

Moving closer, he crouched next to her, afraid of her reaction if he touched her. 'I forgot a date which is unforgivable but you did nothing wrong to be on the receiving end of such vitriol. She had a right to be angry with me, but not with you.'

Melanie managed a weak smile. 'I liked what you told her when you threw her out.'

'You heard, eh?'

'I think the whole neighbourhood heard. I heard you swearing too. That's not like you.' She paused while holding his gaze. 'Guy, right now I feel so darn empty and sad. I can't stop thinking about Mum. I'll never see her again and it hurts so much inside me. Everything aches and feels like lead. Would you hold me for a while?'

Surprised at her request but understanding her feelings, he eased Melanie up then sank down with her settled into his lap, setting the seat back into the reclining position with the footrest up. Grasping the edge of her doona, he pulled it up around them both, rested his chin on top of her hair and tightened his hold.

'I understand how you feel. When Dad died it hit us all very hard. Iain and I were still living at home but after Dad passed away neither of us could bear to be in the house. I kept walking into a room, expecting Dad to be in his usual places. I could feel his presence all the time. I even found myself beginning a conversation with him. It began to feel creepy. I think Mum and Iain had the same experiences because Iain moved out first. Then Mum began making noises about going back to Norway. As soon as I bought this place, Mum put the family home on the market. I wasn't sorry. Much as we all loved the house where we'd grown up, it just wasn't the same without Dad.'

He twisted his head to see her face when he felt her relax. Her lashes were wet but her tears held back. 'It takes a while for the pain to ease but gradually it does. I still think about Dad and miss him every day but the pain isn't quite so acute.'

He settled his chin back on her head. 'It's okay to hurt, okay to grieve. Just like we are now, if you need me, I'm here.'

Chapter Thirteen

A kaleidoscope of mixed dreams jolted Melanie awake time and time again. Each time she stared into the darkness with a heavy weight of emptiness pressing her insides. When salmon-tinged rays began edging through her window she was lying in tangled bed linen, thinking of the mixed day she'd just experienced.

Deep sadness swamped her as images of her mother swept through her brain. She would never see her again. Then a tremendous sense of peace brushed against her soul. Mum would never again feel the physical and emotional torture that had been inflicted on her for almost as long as Melanie could remember. Never again would Mum have to endure unwarranted drunken beatings. Never again would she have to work long dreary hours at low-paying jobs just to keep a roof over their heads. Never again would she have to hide away measly coins to have on hand to buy a loaf of bread when there was nothing else because all her hard-earned money had been sopped away after being beaten out of her.

A physical ache centred in her chest. 'I'm going to miss you, Mum. You were the only person in this world I could ever talk to.' Then a sinister image of her hated father leapt into her mind. She had loved him once, a long time ago. She recalled as a young child, the happy times when there was laughter around the dinner table and they'd gone on picnics. There was a time when he pushed on the swing as high as she begged, her mother sitting on a blanket, yelling out to be careful but looking happy and smiling. She could feel the whiz of wind against her skin as she'd been tossed in the air, then laughing hysterically as she was caught against the slight rasp of his chin.

Then things changed just after her fifth birthday. How often did he sit in the lounge chair looking solemn as he drank bottle after bottle of beer? She'd never understood why he would burst out with angry words when she made some noise or tried to run up to him with a picture she'd drawn. She recalled forgiving him over and over again for his drunken outbursts. After sobering up, he had always been contrite, promising it would never happen again. But he broke his promise every single time, instilling in her that a man's word meant nothing. It might have been weeks or even months in between bouts of drunken outbursts, times when everything was wonderful again but it gradually drew to only days before he lashed out at her laughter because she was too loud or he'd slap her face because she'd run full pelt inside eager to tell him about some treasure she'd found.

She couldn't recall how long it had been before she was too scared to speak or do anything when he was around.

Gradually, as the need for alcohol became more deeply entrenched, the beatings became more frequent and more vicious, especially with her mother. She had no idea how things had been for Mum while Melanie was away, but when she returned from Greece, life had been beyond terrible for both of them. He began taking his revenge out on her, making her believe he never forgave her for returning or maybe it was because she had dared to leave in the first place. Yes, that sounded more likely. Even though Mum always tried to intervene, Melanie rarely escaped unscathed, although she'd never received a beating like the one that had killed her mother.

Oh, Mum, why? Darling Mum. She had been the one who had earned the bulk of the money to keep food in the fridge. Melanie tried counting on her fingers the number of homes they had been thrown of out for unpaid rent then the number of times she had gone hungry because her father had drunk away what little money they could scrape together. She snorted a very unladylike sound. He'd never held down a job for more than a few weeks and he always drank what he earned.

After returning home, Melanie had become the breadwinner and somehow he always found her little stash of savings and turned it into liquid amber. A second scornful scoff escaped. If he had used his cunning and wiles in some paid job, they would have been millionaires.

Over the years she began to understand the meaning of hate, and lost faith. She knew it and even though it was illogical to not trust all males because of the actions of one, it didn't make it any easier to put her entire faith in a man. It had become entrenched to never trust a man's word. It had also been drummed into her to hide pain and never reveal inner emotions. For to show either meant harsh retribution. The only person she ever trusted was now a pile of ashes she could pick up in a week's time. A pile she was determined to take back to Greece. One day.

Her thoughts turned to the dreadful skinny scarecrow that had invaded their peace the previous evening. The hair had been bleached to something resembling straw and the bony hollows of her collar bones indicated extreme dieting to the extent she looked anorexic. How could anyone be so nasty and vindictive about someone they didn't know? She figured the woman couldn't be a regular girlfriend since Melanie hadn't seen her before nor heard Guy talk about any romantic interest. Even though Guy had spent his time making sure she was safe, he'd had plenty of opportunity to go out and leave her hidden in the house. She'd been out on a couple of dates. If he could forget to go on a date with the ghastly woman, she couldn't have been important to him. Melanie smiled in the half-light of dawn. Guy had been as shocked as she. She recalled the words used when he threw the woman out. They were much worse than the words she'd been on the receiving end of and she doubted Linley would ever be back.

Her grin widened. Gypsy didn't bother her. She'd heard that particular descriptive word before, and often wondered herself if she didn't have Romany blood flowing through her veins. What had thrown her were the words *whore* and *bitch*: they had cut deep. But then she probably deserved them because she was flawed. Look at how many ugly scars she had. She'd never have a decent relationship or get married. She wasn't worthy of any decent man's love.

Just as her restless dreams had changed during the night from one thing to another, her thoughts now changed with Guy coming to the forefront. She couldn't figure him out, but she liked him. No, more than liked him. He was kind and gentle-natured. She knew he went out of his way to make sure she was okay and he'd put his life on hold to make sure she was safe from her father but his every action and the way he spoke to and treated others showed what kind of a man he was. Did she trust him? Could she trust him or would he turn out to be just like her father if she let her guard down? She couldn't ever afford to make a mistake to find out.

An unbidden heat suffused her cheeks as she visualised the sight of Guy in the gym. How could any man look so hunky and not know it? The good-looking men she'd seen strutting around on the beaches in Greece had a different attitude. They enjoyed women staring at them while they flexed their muscles to show off, often wearing nothing more than barely-there bathers or skimpy shorts and sleeveless shirts – muscle shirts, she thought they called them. Arrogant twerps! They thought they were wonderful but were so full of themselves. Maybe that was the only way they could get attention.

Guy was different. It didn't seem to concern him if you watched him or not. He never showed off and she felt certain he never looked for adulation. He simply enjoyed the exercise and not what his body looked like. She wondered if he even knew how attractive he was to women. Somehow she doubted it.

She recalled the time he had risen out of the water at the beach. Her breath hitched at the vision of Guy glowing gold in the sunlight. It was awe-inspiring. Her body felt warm and tingly at the memory.

Guy was so self-assured and confident, whereas she hardly ever felt confident. Playing music and working as a secretary were the only times she wasn't afraid of what she was doing. She certainly didn't feel confident with men.

A wry grin spread across her face as she visualised her date with Rod. Poor boy had been devastated when he found out she was staying with his boss and after his discovery he'd been too afraid to even hold her hand. Dinner had been pleasant but all he had been able to talk about was what Guy would think.

The date with Iain had been better. They'd had a fun time but she didn't feel anything for him the same way she felt for Guy. She was stunned when she suddenly realised she felt comfortable with Guy. She loved living with him but knew it couldn't last. As soon as her father was found there would be no reason for her to stay and she would have to move out. A sigh of regret escaped.

Melanie climbed out of bed, showered and dressed. Expecting Guy to be up, she went in search of him. Finding his bedroom door open she crept over to knock. When she peeked in, she saw him spread-eagled diagonally across his bed, lying on his stomach and still asleep. She tiptoed across the soft wool carpet and gazed down. Oh, wow. He looked so awesome. She had an urge to reach out and run her fingers over his bare skin but didn't dare. Instead she pulled the doona up over him as she recalled the two times she had woken in his bed. She'd been mortified at the time but had enjoyed the feeling of security when he'd held her close. It was the safest she'd ever felt, even counting her time in Greece. But he was a man. She could never trust a man.

Deciding to practice her music as something to do, she collected her instrument then crept down the stairs to the gym.

***

In his semi-comatose state Guy thought he was still dreaming. He shook his head to clear away the cobwebs.

Man alive, he felt exhausted. It took him a few moments to clear his foggy brain and realise he wasn't dreaming. Music was being played somewhere in the house. Melanie had never played at home before so he threw back the covers and pulled on a pair of track pants over his shorts; shorts he had only taken to wearing since Melanie had arrived. He'd always slept in the raw. Grinning, he recalled how he'd almost been caught out the first night. He had a strong suspicion that, if she knew she'd slept in his bed with him buff naked, Melanie would die of shame.

In the bathroom he splashed cold water over his face to try to bring some sanity back. With only a couple of hours of sleep after a restless night filled with many deep thoughts, he felt completely drained. His muscles hurt from the vicious workout he'd undertaken, causing him to walk gingerly following the melodic sounds. He stepped through the gym door. Melanie stood at the far end of the room with her back to him. All he could see were long lean legs, white cotton shorts and black waves flowing down her back. He lowered his aching body onto the top step to listen. The pieces she played were different, from lively to low and melancholy - pretty much echoing his confused feelings. She played four pieces before turning around and spotting him and ceased playing in an instant.

'Guy?'

'Good morning.' Wincing in pain as he rose, he continued down the steps.

'I woke you.'

Damn but she looked so scared at the thought of having woken him. It shouldn't be like that. She should be vibrant and laughing, not so submissive and conscience-stricken. 'And it sure was pleasant waking to such wonderful sounds. I'm just glad we don't have to go to work today since my brain isn't functioning so well. I spent most of the night thinking and haven't had much sleep. Melanie, I want to show you something and then I want to put a proposal to you. I have a new business venture I'm thinking about and I want your opinion.'

Melanie looked mystified as he neared. Gently grasping her hand he led her back upstairs. 'Coffee first, I think. I need to chase away the fug in my head.'

While waiting for the coffee to brew, he strode into the lounge where he pulled a pile of CD's from a cupboard. 'Let me tell you about the concert I heard you play. I was prepared to be bored because I knew nothing about you or your instrument but your very first notes had me entranced. I'm not exaggerating when I say it was the most enthralling concert I've ever been to. At the interval, every single person was saying the same thing; how well you played. I spent weeks trying to track you down. I wanted to thank you in person, shower you with flowers and beg you to play for me again - if only once. In my search I bought these.' He spread the pile of CD's on the glass-topped coffee table. 'I've played every single one of them and not one, and I repeat, not one is a patch on you. Some are good, but none of them turn my nerves and emotions into jelly like you do.'

'Jelly? Truly?' She looked so surprised.

'Yes, truly. You have great talent.'

When she blushed and dropped her eyes, he felt distressed that she couldn't accept a simple compliment for what it was. Did she feel so unworthy of praise?

'I tried the concert hall, pestered them to pass a message on to you. Boy, did they give me the royal run-a-round. I now understand why. It could have been your father trying to find you. I'd given up. Then, by pure accident, I found you.' He dared to cup her face with his hands. 'You have an amazing natural gift. You have done your best to share it but circumstances have been against you. You mentioned that you and your friends want to produce a CD. I want to put a proposition to you - a properly constructed, legally drawn up proposition. Allow my company to fund the production for you. Make your CD and put on a few more promotional concerts. From what I heard those people in the audience saying, you can't lose. You could have sold a thousand CD's that one night I was there and I think I may be rather conservative in my estimation.'

He grinned at the bewildered look on her face as Melanie tugged free and plopped into the chair behind her. She looked stunned. He turned away to finish making the coffee to give her time to absorb his words.

Looking so contrite, Melanie removed the hot mug from his hand and sipped the aromatic brew but said nothing. He waited. He'd said his piece. It was up to Melanie now. He'd thought long and hard about his idea in the early hours of the morning and part of it was selfish. It was a way to keep her tied to him while he figured out how to convince her they should stay together on a permanent basis. He'd thought long and hard about that as well. He wanted marriage but gut instinct told him that if he imparted that little piece of information, she would run and disappear from his life.

It took so long for Melanie to answer that he was beginning to worry.

'I'm overwhelmed…' she began then paused as though not knowing what to say. 'Look, we have a rehearsal Monday night. Could you come and explain your idea to the others and let them make the decision? Thank you, Guy. I'm absolutely certain they will say yes.'

Humble as always and putting the accolade towards her friends and not herself. 'I'll be at your rehearsal in any case because there is no way I'd allow you to go alone. I'll see if I can come up with more detail by then, but right now I need to go for a swim to clear all this cotton wool out of my head. I spent most of the night thinking about you and haven't had much sleep. Would you like to come for a drive? We'll have breakfast out if you like.'

Chapter Fourteen

Leaning on the backrest of the chair he had straddled backwards, Guy couldn't stop grinning. Excitement was in the air. After outlining his proposal the ensemble was playing through their repertoire giving him a repeat performance of the entire concert he'd attended. After each piece they discussed the merits on whether or not to include it on the CD, asking Guy's opinion. All he could offer was his *tingle* rating - which tunes made his body tingle the most but he insisted *The Swan* be number one track, suffering the raised eyebrows and cynical groans from all eleven women. And now Melanie was playing it, much to his delight.

A sound of smashing glass came from outside. The girls ceased playing almost on the same note. Glancing at Melanie, Guy saw a look of sheer terror sweep over her face. Then she whimpered as one hand swept over her head for protection. Damn, he hated that she was so skittish when a simple unexpected sound had her react like this.

He shot from the chair, grabbing it when it threatened to crash to the floor, then sped down the room then slowly lifted his hands upwards to grasp her tense fingers, pausing when her entire body shuddered. Will she ever feel secure enough to not think he was going to belt her whenever he touched her?

'It's okay. I won't let him near you. It may not even be him.' He prayed it wasn't but instinct was shouting otherwise. 'It could just be some idiots skylarking around.'

'I know he's here,' she gasped. In the background, mumbles of, 'What's going on?' and 'What's happening?' were echoing.

'Look at me, Melanie.' With his hands resting on her upper arms he waited until she raised her eyes. 'I promise to keep you safe. Stay with the girls. Do they know about your Dad?'

She shook her head.

He wasn't surprised. 'Now might be a good time to tell them while I check outside.'

He strode to the door, gripped the handle and turned the knob. Feeling the lock free itself he eased the door open a fraction, taking care to stand back in case the perpetrator was waiting on the other side. Hearing nothing out of the ordinary, he peeked around the edge of the door, his eyes taking a few seconds to adjust to the sudden gloom. He didn't spot anybody lurking in the shadows but felt and smelt the presence; the same odious smell that had assaulted his nostrils the night Melanie had been attacked. Damn, it was Jones. He'd probably been dropping by every night waiting for Melanie to make an appearance.

Turning back, he searched around for some form of weapon. His eyes rested on a few cleaning implements stacked in one corner. None of them afforded much protection but he selected an industrial sized broom. With it held in both hands and the brush ready to swipe, he took a few tentative steps onto the small concrete portico. He searched the dark before daring to venture down the three steps to the pavement.

Some inner instinct told him Jones hadn't waited around. The sudden cessation of music would have warned the man that he had been heard. But then why make such a racket if he didn't want his presence known? After searching the area he noticed the windscreen and driver's window of his car had been smashed, leaving pellets of shattered glass scattered over the bitumen and pathway. One door was hanging open. A surge of anger rose then he sighed in resignation. It was pointless to allow feelings of wrath to cloud his management of the situation. There was absolutely nothing he could do – the damage had been done. He reached into his pocket for his mobile phone, punched in his brother's number then waited for a response with his back leant up against the side of his car.

'Iain, I need your help. We're at Melanie's rehearsal and have had a visit from Jones. There are a few young ladies who are going to need to be escorted home. I don't trust the man. If he can't get to Melanie he may attack one of her friends instead.' Pacing around, he continued searching the shadows as he listened to Iain's questions.

'Melanie and I are fine but my car has looked a lot better. Jones obviously needed money to feed his habit and broke into my car. Stupid fool wouldn't have got much.' After giving Iain details of his whereabouts he returned inside to see the girls huddled together. Rounded eyes stared his way.

They were scared. 'I believe it may have been your father, Melanie. Iain is on his way. He asked us to all remain inside until he arrives.'

There were a few gasps as the girls huddled even closer. They chattered quietly amongst themselves. 'I don't think it would be a good idea to continue your rehearsals here until this man is caught so how about rehearsing at my place until the police arrest him?' He smiled at the collective gasp. 'My gym is sound-proof with plenty of room. It won't be a problem to re-arrange my gear down one end. You'll find the acoustics excellent but I want none of you walking. Give Melanie your addresses and I'll have taxis sent to pick you up and return you home if you don't have your own transport.'

He caught Melanie's surprised frown then watched those who didn't have transport silently scribbling details on a scrap of paper.

Sirens sounded. He heard Iain issuing orders for officers to scour the surrounding area seconds before he stepped through the doorway.

'Guy, ladies,' he acknowledged with a nod of his head and a smile that was flashed to all before he turned towards Guy. 'Your car looks pretty, little brother. We'll need to take fingerprints. I'll have the boys tow it away and deliver it to the panel beaters for you. Is there anything missing from inside?'

Melanie gasped. Guy eased his arm around her shoulders, ignoring the slight tensing of her muscles when he touched her. 'It's okay, Melanie, the car is insured and can be fixed. It doesn't concern me. Your safety is the important thing.' He swept his arm around to indicate he was talking to them all then stepped outside with Iain.

'Melanie's jacket is missing and I had a half dozen CD's in the console. I don't keep much in my car,' Guy said as he searched around. 'A bit of small change in the ashtray has gone but no more than a few dollars. That's all, I'm fairly certain.'

Back inside Guy introduced Iain to each woman while they waited for the officers to complete their search of the surrounding area. The tow truck arrived at the same time as empty-handed officers. After the car had been towed away, the three girls without transport, along with hastily packed instruments and sheet music, were crammed into the rear seat of a police car to be driven home. Melanie sat in the back of Iain's vehicle while the two brothers chatted in the front.

Being still on duty, Iain didn't stay any longer than ensuring the pair was safe. As he left, Guy locked the front door behind him.

'I'm so sorry, Guy.'

He twisted around, 'I remember a young lady a few nights ago who was very unfairly verbally attacked and who wouldn't accept my apology for it but laid the blame on the perpetrator of the crime. Melanie, you did nothing wrong and don't need to apologise. You are in no way responsible for your father's actions.'

'He knows where I am.'

'Without a doubt! On the plus side, we now know he is still close by which narrows down the search area somewhat. Now, how about hopping into bed and try to get some sleep while I ring Neil to pick us up in the morning?'

After making his phone call and preparing for bed, Guy lay on his bed, waiting, gut instinct telling him what would happen. Every time Melanie felt this vulnerable, she sought security. He was beginning to understand her behaviour. She'd lost her only protection and he was only too thankful she trusted him enough to seek him out, but then again he was all she had. He was also under the impression she didn't trust men in general. He snorted. Any wonder why when she'd had no guidance by a trustworthy man whilst growing up. How much would it take for her to trust him on an emotional level? He felt gutted that such a beautiful, wonderful woman didn't know how, or was simply too scared to let go all her tightly held insecurities and love a man.

The wait was shorter than he anticipated. Melanie must have only lingered long enough to assume he would be asleep. Either that or she was too damn scared to stay by herself a moment longer. As soon as he heard her stealth-like footsteps brushing against the carpet he watched while she crept into his room and curled up on the carpet beside his bed. Without a word, he climbed out of bed, scooped her up and lay her down on his sheet. She stiffened, ready for flight as he tucked her shaking body into his.

'Melanie,' he whispered in her ear, 'you trust me enough to keep you safe. Please have enough faith in me to know I would never, ever take advantage of you. I promise you that. You are a guest in my home. I will not harm you in any way. You have my word. Now go to sleep.'

Tugging her closer, he settled his arm over her waist and waited for her tension to ease. He could tell when she finally slept but at least she had stayed, which, he figured, was quite a leap for her.

Chapter Fifteen

'Dessert?' Guy asked as the waiter neared.

'Not for me but you go ahead.' Melanie settled the knife and fork across her plate and delicately wiped her mouth with a serviette.

'How about coffee?'

'That would be nice, thank you.'

Guy turned to the hovering waiter and ordered then waited until the waiter had cleared away the remains of the meal before reaching across the table and taking a hold of Melanie's hand. He ignored the tiny wince as they touched. 'Are you happy with the pieces you've selected for the CD?'

'I guess we should be since we'll be recording soon. I still can't believe this is all happening. The girls are thrilled.'

'And you? Are you thrilled?' He wasn't really interested in her answer. He was more interested in the fact that Melanie hadn't tugged her hand from his. After several weeks of self-procrastination he'd finally asked her out on a formal date. His heart started beating faster at the memory of her shy but immediate acceptance. And she looked gorgeous with her hair flowing loose over a bright multi-coloured dress. She'd caught the front strands of her hair, twisted them into a dozen rope-like threads and pulled them back to the top of her head, pinning them in place with a sparkling hairgrip.

As if she'd just become aware of her hand being held, she yanked it back. 'More than thrilled, I can never thank you enough for organising all this.'

Feeling a sense of loss he began spinning his water glass around. Over the past few weeks he'd come to recognise how Melanie would speak and act freely about anything that didn't involve her emotions. As a consequence he'd kept the evening's conversation to general matters. 'Believe me I'm enjoying this new venture as much as you. We need to finalise the details for your concert tour.'

'I'm happy with the concert hall here but I'd like to visit the others to make sure they are suitable.' He noted how she kept her hands hidden in her lap.

'Surely if it is a theatre, it will be fine. That's what they are built for.' Guy sat back to allow the coffee to be placed on the table.

'You'd be surprised. Some auditoriums have terrible sound problems.' She began stirring the thin layer of froth on her coffee.

'You sound as though you're speaking from a lot of experience.' Guy became intrigued at her sudden stillness. Then her face became a mask for a brief moment before she pushed her chair back.

'Excuse me a moment, but I need the rest room.'

As she skittered between the tables, Guy watched after her wondering what in hell's name had just happened. Sipping on the coffee, he replayed the conversation until a feminine squeal echoed through the restaurant. It took a moment before he registered the voice as Melanie's. He dropped the cup into the saucer as he rose and shoved back his chair. A surge of adrenaline accompanied him as he wove through the tables, muttering apologies as he ran.

Planting an outstretched hand on the door leading to the rest rooms, he shoved so hard the door bounced off the wall. Then he came to a grinding halt at the sight of Melanie cowering against the wall with a man frantically trying to calm her with his hands grappling at her shoulders.

'Sir, please, I don't know your name but you need to drop your hands by your side very slowly.' Guy took a couple of tentative steps into the narrow passage; his heart pounding at the frightened mewls gurgling from Melanie's throat.

'Is she crazy or something?' asked the man as he dropped his hands. Poor man looked as though he was jammed in a crushing plant.

'No, just frightened,' Guy answered. 'Now, slowly back away.'

The man crept backwards until he reached Guy. 'What happened? Did you try to come on to her?' Guy whispered.

'No way! She bumped into me as I came out that door.' He pointed to the door with a brass moulding of a man. 'What's with her?'

'It's a long story but basically you frightened her. How about keeping anyone else away until I can calm her?'

The two men sidled past each other then Guy approached Melanie slowly. With her hands held over her head and her fingers gripped tight, she was whimpering like an injured puppy in rhythmical accompaniment with the shudders weaving down her body.

'Melanie, its Guy, I'm not going to hurt you.' As he spoke, Guy slid his spine down the wall then crab-walked until he was under her arched body. Turning his palms upwards, he slowly raised them until he felt sure Melanie could see them. It had worked last time but all he needed was for her to open her screwed-shut eyes.

'Melanie, open your eyes and look at my hands. I'm not going to harm you. It's me, Guy. Your father isn't here.'

'Father? Her father caused this?'

He turned his head towards the stranger who had taken a couple of steps towards them. 'Please, sir, keep back and keep quiet. Right now she sees all men as a threat.'

Turning his eyes upwards, he noticed Melanie was peering at him but he wasn't sure if she was yet aware of exactly who he was. 'Melanie?'

She blinked. Then a single tremor snaked down her body. 'Guy?' She slumped against the wall.

He caught her as he rose from his haunches. Her hands gripped tight around his waist. 'I'm sorry,' she mumbled against his shirt.

'It's okay, you were frightened.' With one hand cradling her head against his chest and the other running up and down her back, he turned to the man whose faced looked stunned.

'I'm sorry about this, but she's fine now.'

'He beat her?' the man asked, sounding incredulous.

'And her mother. He beat her mother to death.' Guy felt Melanie jolt at the same time the man swore profusely then left.

'I'm sorry, Melanie, I shouldn't have told him that. Are you ready for your coffee?

'Can we just go home? I feel so stupid but he came out the door as I passed and… and…'

'He scared you witless,' interrupted Guy. 'I need to collect my jacket and pay on the way out.' Holding her hand he led her back into the restaurant then slung an arm around her waist as he collected his leather jacket from the back of the chair. Pausing only long enough to pay at the counter, he kept one hand touching Melanie until she was settled in the hire car.

There was thirty minutes of silence before he pulled into the drive. 'Now what?' he muttered as Iain strode towards them from the front step then followed the car into the garage. His brother wouldn't be here at this time of the night if something hadn't happened.

Melanie alighted from the passenger side looking shaken. Iain moved towards her. Feeling a stab of jealousy, Guy stepped between his brother and the car then strode around to Melanie and placed one arm around her waist and possessively drew her close as they entered the house. His unspoken message was received when Iain raised his eyebrows and stepped backwards. 'What's the problem?'

'Your silent alarms went off at the security firm. I'd like to check your house to make sure there hasn't been an entry. Keep Melanie with you while I check.'

The gasp of shock and sudden trembling of her body caused Guy to tighten his hold. He settled her on a bar stool at the kitchen bench then began preparing for the coffee they'd missed. The hot drinks were ready before Iain returned.

'Will you join us for coffee?' Guy asked.

'Just a sip. I'm on duty and had better get back. I'm sure no one's been in but I'll send a patrol car for regular checks of the area during the night. It's my last night of night duty for a while. I'll call you tomorrow afternoon after I've caught up on some sleep. Take care.'

As Guy ushered his brother out, he thought of Melanie. Her usual practice if she felt threatened was to seek him out in the dark. Two incidents in one night would probably spin her out. Returning to the lounge he found the room empty and Melanie's bedroom door shut. Did she skedaggle because she was uptight or because she was embarrassed about earlier? Was she okay? Knowing he was too stirred up to sleep, he figured a hard workout might ease his frustration so changed into gym shorts.

After showering away the sweat of a harder than normal routine, he lay across his bed still unable to relax. Churning thoughts tumbled around his brain. He felt sure Melanie wouldn't be asleep, she'd be too afraid to close her eyes. Was it at night when her father beat them? Was that the reason she was so afraid of the dark? He tried to imagine what type of injuries she had sustained, wincing at the thought of the pain she must have endured and unable to comprehend why a man would ever lay into a woman like that. Still restless, he clambered out of bed then wandered into the kitchen for a drink of water. He came to a standstill when he heard muffled sobbing. Creeping over to her door, which now stood open, he took a step into Melanie's room but her bed was empty.

'Melanie?'

A strangled sound came from behind. Spinning around, he spied Melanie huddled on the floor against the wall hidden behind the door. Even in the shadows and with only moonlight to see by, it was obvious she was trembling.

'Guy, please hold me?' she whimpered.

'Hell, Melanie!' He sank onto his haunches and gathered her up.

Her arms gripped his neck like a vice. Rising up with her in his arms he carried her to the lounge where moonlight streamed through the large uncurtained window which faced the backyard.

'Why didn't you come to me?' He held her close, one hand caressing her back through the thin layer of her cotton nightgown.

'You weren't there.' Her voice hitched on a swallowed sob.

'I went down to the gym for a while. I wouldn't leave you alone without telling you first, especially at night. You're safe in here. He can't get you. You're freezing cold,' he added as he felt the cold of her body penetrate his skin.

Carrying her into his room, he wrapped her up in the spare wool blanket he kept on the top shelf of his wardrobe then lay down with her on his bed, pulling his Doona over them both.

She snuggled into him with her head on his shoulder while he held her tight with one arm and caressed her back in long gentle sweeps until her trembling ceased. It took a lot longer for her to calm this time but he waited for her to fall asleep before relaxing his hold. Then he turned her over and gently spooned her back against his body, draping his arm over her waist.

Chapter Sixteen

The sun's first rays were barely tinting the darkness when Guy roused. Feeling strange warmth against one side, he glanced towards the sensation. Melanie had turned over and was lying on her side watching him. He gazed into her wide-open eyes noting the smile tugging at the corners of her mouth. There were no apparent signs of her fear from the previous night. She opened her mouth to say something.

'Don't you dare start apologising to me, Melanie Jones,' he murmured with a smile.

Her grin widened. 'Okay, I'll say the second thing I was going to tell you. Thank you for dinner last night. I really enjoyed it, more than you could ever know.'

'So did I, a great deal.' He thought it wiser not to mention the interlude in the passageway. If Melanie wanted to forget about it, that was fine by him. 'Would you like to go for an early morning drive to watch the sun come up? We can sit on the beach with our backs to the water while we watch the city wake. Then you can join me for a swim followed by breakfast somewhere. We don't have to come home for the rest of the day if you like. Tell me where you would like to go and we'll go, or we can drive and stop where it takes our fancy.'

'Sounds wonderful - I'll beat you to be ready.' Melanie was up and running before she'd finished speaking, leaving him stunned but delighted at the change in her demeanour as he took up the challenge. He wondered if she would join him in the water. She never had before and he doubted things were about to change. To save time, he shaved under the shower, threw casual clothes on over a pair of bathers, grabbed extra clothes to change into because he didn't know what he was in for and finally raced to the kitchen. Melanie had beaten him and was standing by the bench waiting with an over-acted nonchalance.

'You cheated, you didn't tie your hair back,' he teased as he grasped a willing hand and strode to the garage. For once she hadn't shied away. Progress.

Melanie braided her hair while they drove, a cheeky grin spread across her face for outsmarting him but he didn't mind in the least. At last he was making some headway in breaking down her ironclad defences. What delighted him even more was the knowledge that she was emanating unbridled happiness.

A molten gold ball hovered over the horizon when they reached the beach, so they settled on towels and watched the shifting shadows awakening the city in the distance. Being so early and a Sunday, there was no one else around. Even the breakfast kiosk had no signs of life and stood like a lone sentinel in the semi-darkness. As he stood to strip down for a swim, Melanie followed suit. He raised his eyebrows then smiled to mask his thumping heart. She looked gorgeous in her one-piece swimsuit, her slender body and curves fully appreciated. His eyes stalled on her fore-arm. A faint curved scar with puckered edges marred otherwise flawless skin. Guilt rose for staring. He knew what it felt like. To give the impression he hadn't noticed he grabbed her other hand and tugged. 'Let's go,' was all he could think of to say as he led her to the water's edge. Why hadn't he ever noticed it before? He dived under and shuddered at the sudden cold. Because she always wore long sleeved tops, came to him as his head broke though the water.

Discovering Melanie was a strong swimmer, Guy kept pace with her until she tired and hinted it was time for her to return to the beach. 'Go back to the car and make sure you lock yourself in, I'll be only a few minutes.' He didn't go out any deeper but swam parallel to the shore, keeping an eye on Melanie as she breast stroked to the shallows then waded towards the sand. Once she was out of sight he swam hard.

As he turned and started swimming back, he searched the beach in the distance to see where Melanie was. At first his eyes settled on the ridge of dunes behind the strip of sand. Then he lowered his line of sight and spotted movement. A man was making his way down to the beach from the dunes. Guy couldn't make out any distinguishing features, the man being too far away but the lolloping gait was familiar. A sudden tensioning in his gut sent him a ghastly warning.

Stilling his arms and treading water, he searched for Melanie. Expecting her to be safely hidden in the car, his stomach muscles wrenched when he noticed her sitting on the sand. Her eyes were centred on him. She had no idea of the danger she was in but he was too far away to warn her. Oh, God no! 'Melanie!' he screamed but she didn't move.

A mantle of dread settled over him as he swung limbs back into action, increasing his pace to a speed he'd never swum before, aiming in a diagonal line for shore. His heart began pounding as he pushed his muscles beyond anything they'd ever experienced, fear gripping his insides, adrenaline forcing his body to act. He was a strong, fast swimmer but the distance he needed to cover was beyond what he or anyone could possibly achieve.

***

Observing Guy from a distance, Melanie sensed something was wrong. She'd never seen him swim so fast or make so many splashes when his arms hit the water. She stood to get a better view. His feet were churning the water like a massive washing machine, which was odd since he was such a smooth swimmer, hardly creating a ripple in his wake as his powerful arms cut through the water. It was something she had marvelled at, how such a large, muscular body could glide so smoothly and seemingly without any effort. Hugging her towel tight around her shoulders, she stood on Guy's towel, studying him, a little perplexed.

The sound of heavy breathing from behind startled her. Mystified, she twisted her head and shoulder around. Her heart lurched and breathing ceased when she recognised the man lumbering across the sand only a few metres away. For a brief moment she stood transfixed, utter shock rooting her feet to the spot like superglue.

A glint flashed as one arm lifted into the air. She screamed. The sound echoed in the stillness of the morning as her father lunged with a large knife. Twisting out of the way, she spun around on Guy's towel in a full circle then faced him again, ready for the next thrust.

*****

Guy hit the shallows. 'Melanie!' he yelled. His heart thudded as adrenaline surged. A second thrust of the knife. Melanie dodged, eluding the edge of the knife as it missed her by what seemed like mere centimetres from where he was.

Finally reaching shallower water he waded through the waves with his eyes glued to the ghastly scene.

The knife glinted in the sun as it was held high. It dropped in a rapid lunge. Melanie spun away, threw the towel at her father then tripped before plunging to the ground. She squealed as she raised her hands over her head in the automatic protective response he'd become so used to seeing.

'Melanie!' he yelled then choked on the salt burning his throat. 'Oh, God, no!' he screamed as he spied the abject terror on her face moments before she spun over on her back and covered her face with her hands. Casting his eyes upwards he saw her father grin in a sick delight as though he enjoyed seeing her suffer. It was as though Melanie's fear fed the man's maniacal frenzy.

At the same time Guy reached dry sand, his lungs screaming for air, the knife came crashing downwards.

'No!' he yelled as he watched Melanie twist on the sand to avoid the fast falling blade. But she wasn't able to move far enough. The blade penetrated then delved downwards. She screamed.

As Guy reached them he curled up his fist, tensed every muscle in his body and with all his might, lashed out. He didn't care where he hit the animal, or how hard, as long as he got him away from Melanie. The powerful punch hit

Jones on the cheekbone. A sharp crack broke the silence and an agonising pain shot up his arm. Instinct told him he had broken at least one bone in his hand as he watched the man drop to the ground.

Ignoring his pain, Guy sank to his knees at Melanie's side, gasping for air as he stared down through salt bleared eyes. She lay unmoving with her eyes closed. The blade was imbedded below her left clavicle with blood pouring from torn flesh. He had no idea whether she was alive or not. Tears sprang to his eyes while his turmoiled brain tried to figure out what to do.

Hearing the thudding of footsteps and a man yelling, Guy lifted his eyes. A man sped across the sand towards them. He held out a badge Guy recognised.

'I've called for the ambulance and police back up,' the officer yelled.

He dropped to the sand and handcuffed Jones then dragged him away several metres. Jones appeared to be unconscious. The officer approached Melanie. His shaking fingers found the beating pulse on her neck then he released an audible gasp of relief.

'Iain had us following you every time you left the house. I was too far back to stop him in time. We didn't expect him to be here. He just emerged from the sand dunes. I'm Sergeant John Matthews. I can't remove the knife because of where it is. If it has penetrated her heart or an artery, she could bleed to death much quicker if we pull it out.'

All Guy's brain registered was that Melanie was still alive. His unblinking eyes were still staring at her when her eyelids wavered then slid open.

'Don't move, Melanie!' he yelled as he reached out to hold her still. Knowing by her look of terror that they had frightened her again, Guy forced his voice to relax. But it was hard when she might not survive. 'The knife is still in your chest. If we pull it out it could do more damage. You need to lie very still and not move a muscle. An ambulance is on its way. Please, don't move!'

Her eyes widened. 'My father?' she croaked.

'Won't be going anywhere except to jail. Your boyfriend here knocked him out cold.' As he spoke, Sgt Matthews gripped the blade of the knife, his curled hand resting against her bloodied skin for support to prevent the blade from moving.

As Melanie swung her petrified eyes back towards Guy, he felt so helpless. He reached out and brushed loose curling tendrils of damp hair away from her face. Moving his hand down to hers, he grasped her fingers. He was so afraid he was going to lose her and there wasn't a damn thing he could do about it. He felt so powerless.

Hearing the sound of approaching sirens, Guy searched the road for the ambulance. It tore into a parking bay and juddered to a halt alongside his hired car. Please hurry, he willed as he watched the paramedics gathering essential items before racing across the sand. One took Melanie's vital readings while the other raced back to gather the extra equipment needed. Glancing down, he could do nothing but watch as the paramedic worked. Guy recoiled when he noticed the amount of blood that had flowed down Melanie's side onto the towel and through the thick fabric to the sand beneath. So much blood. How can she survive?

It felt like an eternity before he was sliding a board under Melanie. The two paramedics and Sgt Matthews went to great pains to keep the knife still while they eased Melanie onto the narrow length of moulded plastic. It was such a delicate manoeuvre with his heart in his mouth the entire time. The sergeant kept a firm hold of the knife while they lifted Melanie off the sand and carried her to the waiting ambulance.

Trundling alongside holding the moulded handle, Guy's hand hurt like crazy but he said nothing, trying his best to block out the pain. His injuries weren't life threatening. Melanie's life was the only thing concerning him and he felt very, very afraid.

Iain came running towards them, his unbuttoned coat flapping in the breeze and his laced shoes flicking up sand at every step. 'How is she?' he yelled as he closed the distance.

'Alive with a bloody great knife stuck in her chest,' yelled Guy. Releasing his hold of the board at the ambulance doors he felt Iain's hand grip his shoulder as they watched Melanie being slid into the back of the vehicle. The grip of brotherly love didn't ease his anguish one iota. One man climbed in beside her while the other slammed the doors and shot around to the driver's seat. Within seconds the siren was blaring as the ambulance sped off.

With his anger still seething, Guy turned and raced back to the comatose man lying on his back in the sand. He swept one leg backwards and let loose with a hefty kick to Jones's mid-section before he was grabbed around his shoulders and dragged away.

'No!' Iain yelled. 'The courts will deal with him. He won't be seeing freedom for a very long time. Come on, you follow the ambulance to the hospital and I'll be there as soon as I can.'

When he reached the hospital, Melanie was already in the operating theatre. Frantic, he raced down corridors grabbing people to ask directions then slumped into a seat in the waiting room when he was barred from going any further. Dropping his head in his hands, he felt tears spring to his eyes. Lord, please let her pull through? With his head low he tried to be surreptitious in brushing the moisture away.

'Guy?' Iain sank into the seat next to him.

'I promised her she would be safe with me and I let her down.' Embarrassed by his lack of control as tears swept across his eyes again, he kept his head low. He blenched when Iain ran two fingers along the already purple swelling of his hand.

'You need your hand attended to,' said Iain before rising from his seat and walking away, returning a few minutes later with a triage nurse. Guy bristled at their approach, sending his brother a savage scowl when Iain squatted in front of him.

'Here.' Iain handed him a clean handkerchief. 'You won't be able to see Melanie for a while. She's in good hands now and there is absolutely nothing you can do. Go and get your hand seen to while you wait.' Iain's voice was gentle. He made no comment about the remnants of moisture Guy was trying to swipe away.

He felt Iain grip his shoulder in a friendly squeeze. 'She means a lot to you, doesn't she, little brother? In fact, I'd hazard a guess that you've fallen in love with her.'

Only as a means of escaping his brother's too keen observations, Guy followed the nurse into a cubicle where his hand was examined and x-rayed. After a painful manipulation a second x-ray confirmed everything was in the correct places before they wrapped his lower arm and hand in strapping plaster.

While the plaster was being administered, Iain left him to find out how Melanie was faring, returning a few minutes later. 'The knife has been removed without further injury and with no major damage to any vital organs. Being the police officer in charge of the investigation, I'm going to insist on seeing her.' Guy felt an intense sense of relief at the news then willed the nurse to hurry so he could escape.

***

Hearing the squeaking of a shoe, Melanie forced her eyes open against the fuzziness of anaesthesia. 'Guy?' she called as she forced her leaden head around to see who was approaching.

'Sorry, it's only me. Guy cracked a few bones in his hand when he punched your father's lights out and is having it strapped. He's also feeling pretty bad about what happened. He feels responsible for letting you down and is blaming himself for you being hurt. He cares a lot about you, you know – more than he lets on. Your father is in custody and won't be causing any more problems. You take care, Melanie. You're going to be fine. I'll come to see you tomorrow when you're feeling a bit better. We're going to need a statement from you both.' Iain bent and brushed his mouth against her cheek then left.

Melanie's anaesthetically befuddled brain tried to recall all Iain had said while she continued to move in and out of consciousness. Somewhere in the fog, she became aware of her trolley rattling along the corridors while being moved to a ward from the recovery room but she was fully conscious when Guy approached. She was shocked to see he looked to be in worse condition than she was with his hand raised against his opposite shoulder in a sling. There was strapping plaster half way down his forearm to his fingertips.

He opened his mouth to say something but Melanie forestalled him. 'Don't you even think of attempting to apologise to me, Guy Harris'!

'And don't you be so damned cheeky after scaring me half to death. I've never been so frightened or felt so helpless in all my life. How are you?' He reached down and brushed the side of her face with the fingers of his good hand.

She shivered at his warm touch. 'Looking a lot better than you. All they gave me are a few stitches and a small plaster over the top. I hear you gave them a hard time demanding you have more to show than me.' Melanie managed a feeble grin.

'I take it Iain has shown his badge and been blabbing his big mouth off?' Guy perched on the edge of the bed, keeping her hand in a tight hold. 'Now tell me the truth, how are you really feeling?'

'Very sore but also relieved. There was no major damage. The knife missed all the important bits. And you?' Melanie forced a lot more bravado than she was feeling. She didn't want Guy to know how afraid she had been and still was. Her shoulder wasn't just very sore; it was giving her a great deal of pain despite medication.

'My hand hurts like hell, but it was worth it. Iain wouldn't let me have another go.'

'Pity, but let's not talk about that bastard. I'd rather talk about more pleasant things. Can you contact the girls to cancel our rehearsal tomorrow night? I'll be right for Thursday.'

'I don't think so, young lady! You're not doing anything until you are one hundred percent.'

'How long will your hand be out of action?' Melanie asked.

He groaned. 'Six weeks!'

'I'll be home in two days and back at work on Wednesday, as long as I don't lift anything.' She didn't dare reveal the true facts. She'd been ordered to have complete bed rest for a week but not being a relation, she figured the doctor wouldn't reveal anything about her condition to Guy. 'Now go home, Guy, wash all my blood off and let me have some sleep. I'm feeling really groggy from the anaesthetic. We didn't get much sleep last night and this morning I think I must have used up all my adrenaline supplies in one hit.'

'Are you sure?' She heard Guy ask as her eyes took on a will of their own and slid closed. She forced them open.

'Guy, in all honesty I'm feeling very sore and exhausted as I'm sure you are. Come back tonight. Please?'

'I'll see you tonight then. Take care.' His touch was gentle as he brushed his hand down the side of her face again then she heard him walk towards the door.

'I care about what happens to you too, Guy,' she whispered when she thought he had gone.

Chapter Seventeen

Having one hand strapped up was more than just a slight inconvenience. In the bathroom the jeans and bathers slid off with relative ease, one hand swapping from side-to-side to shove the clinging sandy fabric down his legs. The sweater was harder. Being able to only grip one side at the lower edge of the fine woven fabric, it was well nigh impossible to ease the garment up over a bandaged limb, especially when an agonising pain shot along nerves every time Guy so much as moved a muscle in the injured arm.

Shaving with a razor, using his left hand and with the right arm stuck in the air so it didn't get wet meant it took two seconds flat to decide he would be buying an electric shaver first thing in the morning. The next hurdle was using the towel, giving up on drying his back and leaving it to drip-dry with a growl of frustration.

He fell onto his bed naked, exhausted and with his hand throbbing in relentless waves. He swallowed two of the strongest painkillers he could find, not caring they were two years over the use by date. Who cared if they killed him?

When a shrill jangling woke him, he yelped when he used his hand to lever himself up as he reached over to lift the receiver.

'Harris!' he barked as he glanced at the clock.

'How are you feeling, little brother?' Iain sounded way too cheery.

'It wouldn't be polite for me to answer, and what exactly did you say to Melanie when you spoke to her and why didn't you tell me you were having us tailed?'

Iain had the temerity to chuckle. 'It was the only way we were going to be able to catch the bastard. We didn't expect Jones to know about or even get to the beach. Your tail was too far away to stop him on time. We suspect Jones was sleeping in the dunes waiting for the pair of you because he was covered in sand and we found a stolen car further down the beach. But then again it's possible he followed you since he had wheels.'

'And my first question?'

'I have no idea what you are talking about.'

Liar.

'What I rang for is to let you know Melanie will have to testify. She's the only living witness to the abuse of her mother. We don't have any evidence it was Jones who murdered his wife but with the attacks on Melanie we have enough to hold him in custody until the trial. Both you and she will have to testify. I'm not telling you it will be easy, it won't. Melanie is going to have to relive her past and I'm guessing it was pretty gruesome from the little she has imparted. I'm just preparing you. I'm on my way to see Melanie now.' Iain's voice softened. 'I'll be as gentle as I can. Will you be there?'

'Damn it, Iain! Is there no other way? I'm getting dressed now. I'll be there as soon as I can.' Slamming down the phone, Guy rolled from the bed then attempted to hurry but dressing was a struggle, taking way too long. He muttered a few colourful curses but at last was able to leave. It was good job the car was automatic, he thought, otherwise he probably wouldn't have been able to steer as well as change gears. Reaching the hospital, he ran up stairs and along corridors until he stood outside the door to the private room he'd insisted on. He paused to catch his breath. The moment he saw her face he knew Iain had been and left. Lying back against a mound of plumped up pillows Melanie was staring vacantly into space.

'Melanie?'

'They want me to testify. I don't think I can.'

Guy winced at the harsh whisper. Damn it. She looked so forlorn. He'd have to do something to wipe that desolation from her face. He slowed then reached out and ran one finger down her cheek. 'It will be months before they get this to court. Can we not think about it for a while? Right now we have more important things. Our first one is to get you home. Then we have a CD to produce.' Sinking onto the edge of the bed, he grasped one hand, rubbing his thumb around her palm. He now knew to let her see he was moving towards her. That way she didn't jerk in fear and shrink back into her skin when touched all of a sudden. She shrugged as though ridding herself of her negative thoughts.

'How was the shower?'

'Pardon?'

'The shower, how did you manage?' She pointed to his arm. 'And don't lie to me, I've been through it. I'm surprised you're wearing jeans. I could never get the zip up with my left hand and I notice you're wearing slip on shoes.'

Was that how she got the scar? What did he do to her? It was difficult fighting the need to ask but he figured she would clam up if he verbalised his thoughts. 'Yes, well let's just say that it was a very frustrating learning experience.'

'I want to be there when you try to cook a meal. Did you sleep?'

'I'll eat out and yes, I slept very well, how about you?'

'Guy, I want to go home - now. I don't think I can handle being in here alone during the night. Please?'

The fear in her eyes and desperate plea in her voice alarmed him. Then he realised she would more than likely suffer from her night terrors if left alone. Her self-confidence had taken a severe battering, knocking her fragile equilibrium skewiff. He left to see what he could do. It required a lot of talking and a lot of convincing but with a promise to return her for an examination first thing in the morning and a list of strict instructions, the medical staff finally relented.

Once home they sat at the kitchen bench sipping on the coffee Melanie made after watching Guy fumble in his vain attempt to unscrew the plastic top from the jar of ground coffee beans with his one good hand. They were chatting about inconsequential matters as a way of keeping her mind off less pleasant things.

'I was planning to find a place of my own as soon as my father was caught, but I guess I'd better stick around for a while to take care of you, as you have looked after me.'

Damn. He wasn't expecting this. The thought of her leaving sent his heart cold and he had no idea how to handle this new situation. Instead he changed the subject. 'I haven't rung your friends yet. I'll do it now. Are you sure you will be right for Thursday?'

Chapter Eighteen

'Where's Melanie?'

Guy spun around. 'Iain, what are you doing here?'

'Looking for Melanie. I went by the hospital and was told she checked out last night. So I went by your place and she wasn't there. This was my last option.'

'Not home? She should be in bed resting.' Guy crossed the room feeling a sense of foreboding when Iain swore under his breath.

'We need to find her, quick smart.' Iain brushed a hand across a brow that wore deep furrows. 'The judge released Jones on bail.'

'What? He's up on murder charges!'

'Actually, he's not. We have no evidence that he was responsible.'

'What about attempted murder on Melanie?'

'Jones claimed he only wanted to talk to his daughter and slipped on the towel. The judge gave him the benefit of the doubt as we had no proof.'

'He was armed with a bloody great knife! At the damned beach! I saw him attempt to stab her at least three times. That was no damned accident. Why in hell's name didn't you call me in?' He pounded his fist on the desk.

'It was only an initial hearing, not a trial. Regardless, we have to find Melanie. Where could she have gone?'

'Hell, I don't know. I took her to the hospital for a check-up and she was ordered to stay in bed for the day.' Guy began pacing, feeling like a caged lion, his unfettered hand running furrows through his thick hair. 'She could have been asleep.'

'I used your spare key to check the house. She's not there.'

Guy swore then tried to unscramble the cells in his brain. 'Look, she can only have walked. Maybe she went for a stroll to get some air. Let's start from home. I'll get Neil to help.' Striding past his brother, Guy yelled for Neil as he reached the passage.

Within seconds he was issuing orders over his shoulder about which areas each man would search as they raced to their cars. As he sped home, Guy wracked his brain for places to which Melanie could have walked. Turning into his street, he decided to check the house first in case she had returned. When frantic fingers fumbled at the lock, he dropped the keys. Cursing, he bent to retrieve them then sucked in a slow breath to ease his panic. Getting wound up wasn't going to help.

'Melanie,' he called as he raced inside. He tore through the house, checking the downstairs studio first. Finding no trace of her he slowed as he reached the kitchen, his mind whirling. He shot past the bench then came to a grinding halt when he noticed a half torn page on the note pad he used to jot down shopping requirements. Picking it up, he studied the indentations. There had been nothing written on it earlier and it had been moved from the wooden bowl of odds and ends. He scrabbled through the bits and pieces in the bowl searching for a pencil. Finding only a blunt stub, he grabbed a sharp knife and slewed off chips of wood into the sink until he had enough lead. He cursed the entire time, finding the task damned difficult with his left hand. Using the side edge, he shaded over the indentations then scrutinised the words until he could make out what Melanie had written. *Soap. Shampoo. Frozen stir-fries. Flip-flop juice.* What the hell was flip-flop juice?

He slammed the door as he tore outside and had his mobile open before he slid into his car. 'I think she's gone shopping,' he told Iain. 'The nearest shops are two blocks north. I'm on my way.' After repeating the message to Neil, Guy reversed from his drive, squealing the tyres as he swerved into the road and again when he planted his foot on the accelerator.

Supermarket, she has to be in the supermarket, he thought as he pulled into the main road running along the café strip. Forced to slow because of the volume of traffic and pedestrians he scanned the pathways as he crawled along. When a young woman pushing a stroller stepped onto the crosswalk he thumped the steering wheel in frustration. 'Come on, come on,' he muttered under his breath as a steady stream of people followed in the woman's wake. Finally free to continue he planted his foot, forcing the car to take off at too much speed. He swore as the car kangaroo-hopped then he eased back the pressure on the pedal. I'm going to kill someone at this rate, he thought then sucked in a deep breath to steady racing nerves.

His foot hit the brake pedal when he spied a mass of dark ringlets flowing down the back of a woman sitting with her back to him at an outside table of a cafe. 'Melanie,' he whispered as he scanned the area for any sign of her father and a place where he could park. He shot into a loading zone the moment a delivery van pulled out. Not bothering to lock the car, he slid out then jogged down the pavement, slowing as he neared Melanie. She must have either felt or heard him coming for she turned her head, her surprised glance bringing him to a standstill.

'Guy, what are you doing here?'

What could he say? 'I thought I'd come home to check on you.' Her raised eyebrows told him she didn't believe him.

'Then why is Iain behind you? And is that Neil as well?'

He twisted around.

'What's going on, Guy?' Melanie asked as she began to rise.

He spun back to face her then pulled out the wrought iron chair opposite. 'What are you doing out here when you are supposed to be in bed resting?'

'Relishing the freedom of being able to wander around without constant fear of being found. Enjoying the luxury of sitting out in the open under an umbrella while watching the world go by.' Pausing she lifted her cup and took a sip of cappuccino.

As Neil and Iain reached them, Guy took in the remnants of what looked like some sort of chocolate confection. Brown crumbs and a scraping of cream poked out from under a scrunched paper serviette. How long had it been since she had been able to indulge in such a treat?

How long since she had been able to sit out in the open like this? Nausea churned at the thought of having to tell her that her brief idyll was over. Glancing at her face, he noticed how her constant look of worry had disappeared. There was a happy serenity about her eyes. She looked so at ease, at peace.

'Melanie, how are you?' asked Iain as he pulled out another chair and Neil slid into the fourth seat.

'I was fine but seeing the three of you here gives me the distinct impression that things are quite the opposite. What's going on? And don't spin me the same line of lies Guy just spouted. None of you are here just to check up on me.' Her stiffening spine bounced against the backrest of her chair as she crossed her arms over her chest and sat back.

'Actually,' said Iain as he reached out and settled one hand on her arm, 'that's exactly why we are here. Checking to make sure you're okay. I don't know how to tell you this but your father was released on bail this morning.'

'No*ooooooo*!' The long loud wail rent the air, causing the people around to stop and stare in a sudden deathly silence.

As Guy sprang from his seat and crouched beside Melanie he heard Iain instructing the audience to disperse.

'Everything is fine. I'm a police officer.' A hand settled on Guy's shoulder. 'Let's find somewhere more private,' Iain added more quietly. 'There's a free table inside.'

Grasping Melanie's elbow, Guy eased her from her seat then assisted her inside. A tonne of concrete settled in his chest. Keeping his arm in place, he slid into a bench seat against the wall, dragging Melanie after him. Neil dropped a plastic bag of shopping on the other side of her.

'How did he get out?' Melanie's voice broke as she whispered against his shoulder.

'He's out on bail,' offered Iain. 'Without physical evidence we can't prove he murdered your mother. Fingerprints in your unit were dismissed since he was her husband.'

Melanie jerked from Guy's hold. 'But he's never been there with us. We were in hiding. It was a safe house given to us by the authorities! He had never been in that unit.' Her eyes flashed fire.

'I didn't know that. I'm sorry,' said Iain.

Neil leant forwards. 'He stabbed Melanie. Isn't that attempted murder?'

'He claimed it was an accident. Said he tripped on the towel while just talking to her. Said he was discussing her mother.' Iain slumped back, sucking in a breath.

'He had a knife!' Melanie cried out then glanced around at the sudden silence. She leant forwards. 'Why would you have a kitchen knife at the beach? And who paid his bail? He was broke. He's always broke.'

'Apparently he has a brother who put up the money.' Iain rested his elbows on the table, his hands spread fingertip to fingertip.

'Uncle Bill? But he's over east. I haven't seen him for years.' Melanie scrubbed at her eyes with a serviette.

'William Jones sent the money via the internet. We just didn't have enough evidence to prove intent or actual murder. The judge believed his story. Hell, I'm sorry, Melanie.'

'But what about all the other…?'

Guy spun his head to look at Melanie. Her eyes were shut tight and her lips clamped in a thin line. 'All the other what?' he asked.

Melanie dropped her head into her hands. 'Nothing,' she whispered. Then her head lifted. 'Iain, can I speak to you? Alone,' she added when all three men became alert and leant forwards.

Guy stared at her. Her eyes skittered around all three then settled on him. He read the pleading silent message. 'Okay, Neil and I will wait outside, but I don't want to be left in the dark.'

He hated standing outside watching the body language of Melanie and Iain. Whatever they were talking about was serious. He swore when tears began falling then felt a stab of jealousy when his brother put an arm around her as he handed her another paper serviette.

'She means a lot to you, doesn't she?'

Guy jerked around at Neil's words. 'What do you mean?'

'Come on, Guy, we've been best friends for years. I know you better than most. You've never looked at a woman the way you look at Melanie. In fact, if I'm not mistaken, I'd say you're in love with her.'

Guy didn't get a chance to answer. Iain joined them. 'I'm putting out an APB on Jones. Melanie has given me enough information to put him away.'

'What information?' Guy asked.

'Sorry, I promised I wouldn't relay what she told me in confidence. It was the only way I could get her to open up. Keep her with you until we find the bastard.' Iain turned away, leaving Guy gaping after him.

'Can you take me home?' Melanie's harsh whisper from his side sounded as though she had to force the words out. He turned back to find her standing behind him, her bag of shopping attempting to drag along the ground and looking as forlorn as Melanie.

The drive home was strained, the silence intense. All attempts to initiate a conversation were met with stony silence and a turned-away head. He followed her inside, handing her the plastic bag as they reached the kitchen. 'Your shopping.'

'It's for you,' Melanie said without stopping.

As she headed towards her bedroom, Guy peered into the bag then emptied the contents onto the bench. 'Melanie, wait,' he called.

She turned back with her hand on the doorknob.

'What is all this for?' he asked, pointing to the half dozen items.

'Soap sewn into a flannel to make it easier to wash with one hand. Pump action shampoo is also easier. You won't be able to manage screw tops. Same with the juice. Flip tops are easier than screw tops. Frozen stir fries are the easiest to cook.'

'I'm overwhelmed, thank you.'

'You're welcome. Lots of things are difficult to do with one hand.

Approaching her, Guy dared to ask, 'When did you break your arm?'

'I'd rather not talk about it.' mumbled Melanie as she turned away again.

'He broke it, didn't he?'

When Melanie stopped suddenly with her head bowed, Guy knew he was right.

'Please, Guy, can we not talk about things that are best left in the past.'

'It wasn't the only injury was it?'

Her backbone straightened then a single tremor wormed its way down her spine before it went rigid. He reached her in two steps and slung his good arm around her shoulders, giving her a gentle squeeze. 'I'm sorry. I'll not ask again. Go and lie down.'

She took only one step. 'Are you going back to work?' she whispered.

He thought for a moment. Did she want him to stay home? Would she be frightened alone? He moved so he could see her face to gauge her reaction better. Her eyes usually gave her away when she tried to hide the truth. 'Neil can look after things for what is left of the day.' He knew by the way she released her held breath and slid her eyes closed that it was what she really wanted to hear.

Chapter Nineteen

'Where do you think you are going?' Even though she had been expecting Guy to say something, Melanie spun around from preparing breakfast. Her heart began hammering from the scare he had given her.

'To work.' She hesitated, unsure how to plead her case. 'Guy, I need to keep busy, especially my brain so I don't have the opportunity to dwell on… you know… everything. I promise I won't do anything heavy and will take things easy.' After her non-stop ramble all she could do was stare at him in hope that he could read the plea in her eyes. 'I also need to have people around me to talk to. I don't want to be alone – please?'

She could almost see his brain churning during the ensuing silence. Please let him agree for she just couldn't stay here by herself with her father on the loose. If he found her at the beach then she had no doubt he knew where she was living and he only needed one opportunity with Guy gone to make his presence felt. Guy's security system wouldn't stop the bastard if he was determined. And after what happened he'd be more than tenacious in finding her. His only aim would be to get rid of her so she couldn't give evidence about his previous abuse. Nobody alive, apart from her, knew how he operated.

'Okay,' Guy finally said, 'but you can only carry our light work.'

'Yes, sir!' Melanie stood at attention, saluting him with a cheeky grin. Relief washed over her when he smiled, pulled out a barstool and began eating. That was much easier then she'd been expecting.

***

Hidden from Guy's eyes, Melanie worked harder than she should have. By lunchtime she'd caught up two day's mail and the pile of paperwork she'd found on her desk. Going out for lunch with her father free wasn't an option. Instead she ate a couple of pieces of fruit in the lunchroom before burying herself in any work she could find. Concentrating on tasks helped keep more sinister thoughts from invading although flashes of that knife kept stabbing through. She began shifting several reams of photocopier paper so she could dust the shelves.

'I promise I won't do anything heavy!'

Melanie jumped at the mocking sarcasm then squealed. Her head bumped on the underside of a shelf when she straightened all of a sudden. 'Don't sneak up on me like that!' she chided while rubbing her head.

One arm snaked around her waist and tugged her from the cupboard. Then she was steered towards the staff room where a chair was pulled out. Daring a peek she spied an arm indicating she needed to sit. She knew by his rigid stance that Guy was mad.

'I've just had a phone call from the hospital wanting to know why you didn't appear at your appointment this morning – the appointment you neglected to mention to me. I asked to speak to your doctor, who informed me you were supposed to take a week off doing nothing but rest your shoulder. He also mentioned your refusal of a medical certificate because I was your boss and I would understand. More likely it was so I wouldn't find out his instructions.' He moved closer and hovered over her like some threatening black cloud ready to let loose with a torrential downpour. 'That knife blade barely missed your heart!' He swept his hand down his face then through his hair as a long drawn in breath hissed through clenched teeth. 'Would you mind explaining why you didn't tell me and what the devil you are doing lifting piles of heavy paper? Tell me why you are not resting in your bed as instructed?' His glare said it all.

'Oh!' was all she could get out as guilt washed over her. Guy was mad: madder than she'd at first realized. If it was her father she would have had several backhanders across the side of her face by now. She cringed at the thought then wondered if Guy was mad enough to mete out the same treatment.

'Oh, is not an explanation.'

'Guy?'

'Nor is Guy.' He paused to suck in another deep breath then his face contorted as though he was biting his tongue, or maybe it was the inside of his cheek. 'Come with me,' he added more gently as he grasped her hand then led the way to his office. She had no choice but to follow and didn't dare say a thing. No way did she want him any madder. No way did she want him to turn out to be just like her father. That would destroy her. Too afraid to move an inch she watched as he swung one of the chairs from the front of his desk and placed it on an angle. 'Sit there for a minute and don't dare move,' he said as he strode from the room.

She sat, rigid and waiting, her face burning. By the sound of the mumbling she could hear through the wall she knew he was still irate. When he returned he plonked into the office chair at his desk without looking at her or saying a thing. She shifted uneasily, wondering what he was up to. It felt like forever in the more than ominous silence before two employees came in carrying the cane lounge from the medical room. Guy indicated where he wanted it then sent the men away with his gratitude before turning to Melanie.

'Do I need to explain what that is for?'

She dropped her eyes as she managed a single shake of her head.

'I'd like you to remain there for the rest of the day and do exactly what the doctor ordered: complete bed rest. You wanted company? You have mine. You wanted someone to talk to? Talk to me as much as you like.'

His stride as he moved towards her indicated his ire and she just held her breath and braced her body for the whack around her head. But much to her relief, he was incredibly gentle as he assisted her out of her chair and led her to the lounge. Pulling the mattress straight and plumping up the pillow he ensured she was comfortable before returning to his work. Her body might be comfortable but nothing else about her was. No way could she just lie there and do nothing – especially with Guy guarding her as though she was some la-di-dah queen. Sheesh!

***

She was so put out by his insistence that he didn't think it would happen but Melanie, who had turned her back to him in protest, was sound asleep within minutes. After unfolding the soft wool blanket from the foot of the lounge, he draped it over her. For a while he sat back in his chair studying her. He smiled when he realised he had finally figured out the only way to handle her strong independence was to meet it head on with the same steely determination. One up to me, he thought as he smiled in triumph.

Then an idea struck on how to keep the irrepressible, stubborn woman resting for the rest of the week. He dialled his brother's number as he leant back in his chair.

'Iain, you usually have a few days off after night shift, what are you doing tomorrow?'

'Not a lot, relaxing mostly, why?'

'How would you like to babysit for me?'

'You never told me, little brother. When did this happen? Was it a boy or a girl?'

'Very funny! I'm not in the mood for jokes right now.'

'Why, what happened?'

Guy explained the situation, what he wanted and together they hatched a plan.

He was struggling to work with his left hand on his computer when he felt Melanie's eyes on him. Without saying a word she stood and headed for the door, her head high with eyes staring straight ahead, ignoring his glance and making it obvious she was still chagrined.

Guessing where she was going, he called out, 'Five minutes or I come after you.' He then went to make them both a coffee, carrying them back in one hand moments before she returned. He indicated the lounge with a nod of his head when she attempted to sit on a chair. He handed her a mug. 'Are you ready to give me an explanation yet?'

Melanie shook her head with her eyes averted but he caught sight of grin shooting out from the corners of her mouth before she dropped her head.

'Drink your coffee. We're going home in a few minutes. I need to have a quick chat with Neil.' He picked up his own coffee and moved out to the passage where he leant up against the wall, fighting back laughter. Getting out of the room was the only way he could hide his amusement. Forcing his mirth under control, he continued on to the office next door to inform Neil that he and Melanie were leaving early.

Chapter Twenty

'Are you going to get dressed?' With her back to Guy, Melanie grinned. After assuming she wouldn't be going to work today she hadn't bothered putting on any more than a belted robe before wandering out for breakfast. Even though she had expected some kind of comment this one surprised her.

'Eventually,' she said as she turned from the toaster.

'I'm sorry but I was so upset yesterday that I forgot to mention that your doctor re-scheduled your hospital appointment for today. If you turn up like that they will probably re-admit you, which wouldn't be a bad thing. At least you would rest.'

Sending him a look that she hoped said she wasn't pleased with his high-handedness Melanie made a hasty retreat to change into jeans and long-sleeved cotton blouse.

When she returned to the lounge she was startled to see Iain chatting with Guy.

'Your chariot awaits,' Iain said with a grin as he swept his arm backwards and gave a slight bow from the waist.

'Excuse me? What's going on?'

'Oh, I guess I also forget to tell you that Iain is your babysitter for the day?' Guy's sarcasm was cutting. 'You didn't think I would be leaving you to your own devices, did you? Use your handcuffs if you have to, Iain. I'll see you both tonight.'

Without another word Guy left. Melanie stared after him feeling a spurt of anger rising. Upstart. She didn't need to be told she was blushing, she could feel the burning heat of her neck and cheeks. Too mortified to eat, she refused breakfast then scowled at the grinning Iain as he ushered her to his car.

'It seems you upset him,' Iain said as he held the passenger door open.

Not half as much as he upset me, she thought as she settled into the seat and crossed her arms.

'He was pretty irate yesterday when he rang me, more out of concern for your wellbeing than anything else.' Iain slammed the door then strode around to the other side. 'He cares a great deal about you and is worried,' he added as he turned the key and the engine rumbled to life.

Iain's words had Melanie thinking while they drove to the hospital. The funny, squishy feeling swirling around her insides was something new and something she didn't understand. Surreptitiously peeking at Iain's profile while he concentrated on the heavy traffic, she wondered why he didn't cause the same reaction to her innards. Iain was as caring and gentle as his brother and she liked him a great deal but she wasn't so cautious with him. Why? Her thoughts for the remainder of the journey centred on Guy, smiling when she recalled the feel of his arms around her and his exclusive masculine scent which sent her blood thrumming.

The examination of her wound was brief but thorough. The doctor was happy with how it looked and chatted to her as he ushered her to the door. 'You were very lucky, Miss Jones. The only thing saving you from more serious injury was the bluntness of the blade. Keep resting until the outer stitches come out on Monday. The inside ones will dissolve.'

Still facing the doctor, Melanie asked, 'Can I play my panpipes?' She didn't dare disclose that she had already done so. What they didn't know doesn't matter.

'Show me the action.' The doctor turned to watch as she demonstrated.

'I can't see any strain on the wound. Seems fine. But no sudden twisting and no heavy lifting.'

As an appointment for the following Monday morning was confirmed at the reception desk Melanie spied Iain sitting in a nearby chair and just knew by the sly look on his face that he had overheard the details. Feeling miffed, she stalked from the room, head high, chin jutted out, straight past and ignoring Iain. She knew damn well he would relay the message about the knife to his brother and it piqued her.

There was a plop, plop of Iain's shoes as he chased after her then his hand slid onto her elbow but he said nothing. Probably grinning like the damned proverbial Cheshire cat, she thought but didn't dare peek.

At his apartment, Iain showed Melanie around then settled her on the couch suggesting she stay put at which she sent him another withering glare.

He laughed as he turned on a large flat-screen television then placed a DVD in a slot. There was a pile of them with a well-known hire company sticker. He must have hired them for her. She was grateful in one sense but also miffed. They sat together on the long sofa, and after relaxing Melanie found herself laughing at a romantic comedy, after which they chatted. Wandering around while Iain prepared refreshments Melanie found a photo of both men when they were a bit younger, standing next to who were obviously, their parents. 'Tell me about your parents,' she said as she replaced the photograph.

'Dad was Scottish. He died in an industrial accident about three years ago. Guy was there when it happened. A sling rope lifting sheets of steel, gave way. Dad must have seen what was going to happen for he shoved two workmen out of the way but he was caught by the swinging load. The sheets slid on top of him. Guy heard the yelling and ran out to see what the ruckus was about. I was told that he was like a madman with super human strength lifting the steel sheets and tossing them aside and ignoring the blood pouring down his face.'

'How awful. Is that how he got that scar?'

'Yes. To him it's a reminder of how he failed.'

'Failed? What more could he have done?'

'Nothing. Dad was already dead, crushed by the weight. Guy took it hard.'

'Is that why he wants to keep in top condition? So he'll be ready if something like that happens again.'

'Maybe. I never thought of that. Maybe it's a subconscious thing. Maybe that's why he was so upset about not being there to protect you.'

'Now I feel guilty.'

'Don't. You did nothing wrong. There's only one person who needs to feel any guilt.'

But she did feel guilty. She turned away and sank back into the sofa. 'Tell me about your Mum.'

Iain settled on the sofa arm. 'Mum is Norwegian and is now living back there. She is also quite tall and you can see that Guy inherited her blonde hair and green eyes. He is much like her in nature as well. Guy took over the running of Dad's business. Dad was only fifty-five. He was much the same in build and height as me. We miss having Mum around but she lost heart after Dad died and wanted to go back home. We both see her whenever we can and she comes back here at least once a year, usually at Christmas.'

'I'm sorry about your Dad.'

'Yeah. It was pretty tough at the time. He was a good man. Mum and Dad were devoted to each other. Now, to change to subject, how about some lunch, care to help me?'

'Do I dare? Are you sure Guy will approve?'

Iain grinned. 'Oh, I'll give you the easy bits. What he doesn't know won't hurt him.'

'Trouble is he has a habit of finding out,' said Melanie. Iain gave out a shout of laughter.

After a delicious lunch Melanie watched a second film while Iain set about preparing a casserole for his evening meal. To fill in time, they went for an easy walk around the block then through a lush park dotted with large shady trees, passing only three people as they ambled along the winding paths. Even the playground was devoid of the happy noises of frolicking children. When they returned Iain looked serious as he sat her down. 'Melanie, I need to tell you something. We subpoenaed your mother's medical files from the doctors you mentioned. It didn't make pretty reading.'

A shiver coiled across her shoulders. She imagined the files would have been quite hefty since the injuries had been extensive over the years and she felt sure she didn't know about all of them. 'I don't suppose it did.' She couldn't face him.

'We also obtained your files,' Iain added quietly.

Melanie stilled. She hadn't expected this. She had no control over the tear that escaped and slid down her cheek. Then she lost the battle of willpower over her emotions and more tears leaked. Mortified, she swept her hands up to cover her face. She knew she shouldn't feel that way but a deep sense of shame enveloped her.

'Please don't tell Guy? I don't want him to know any of it,' she whispered.

'Hell, Melanie, he'll find out the details during the trial. Why don't you tell him first?'

'I can't ever talk about it. Please don't make me? It's too… oh, Iain… I can't.' Unable to stem the tears, she curled up against him. She felt him drape an arm around her shoulders and tug her closer. It felt good but in no way did it alleviate her humiliation.

'What I read disgusted me,' she heard him say. 'I've never seen anything like it before. You both went through hell and I now understand why you are so afraid of your father. I've handed copies to the courts to have your father's bail overturned. We were granted a Restraining Order. He can't come within a hundred metres of you.'

'A piece of paper!' As she shot up straight, Melanie heard her voice screeching but couldn't control it. 'You think a piece of paper is going to stop him? He wants me dead, Iain!'

There was a loud knock followed by Guy calling out. Melanie flew off the sofa and headed for the bathroom where she wasted as much time as she could trying to gather her shattered emotions together before returning to the lounge. Copious amounts of cold water over her eyes went only a small way to ease the red swelling from her bout of tears. Why did they come so easily now? It was as if she'd lost the ability to control her emotions when in the past she was stoic in hiding them. She'd had plenty of practice in blocking out painful memories but the sight of her distraught face in the mirror told her Guy would know something was up. She pinched her cheeks and pulled grotesque faces to loosen tight muscles before forcing smiles then sucked in an enormous breath before daring to leave the privacy of the bathroom. Please, Iain, keep your promise of not relating their private conversation to Guy.

She noticed Guy frown as she stepped into the room. She wanted to turn and run but her feet felt as though they had been nailed to the floor. Dropping her head, she heard Guy mutter something uncouth under his breath before moving towards her. She felt his arm slip around her shoulder before being gently tugged close without placing pressure on her shoulder. He kept her in an embrace for what felt like ages then he stood back with his hand on her elbow while he searched her face.

'Are you all right?' he asked.

She glared at Iain. Blabbermouth.

Iain held up his arms in submission. 'I just told him you were upset because I'd read your medical records. That's all, I promise.'

Feeling mortified and unable to control a bevy of emotions, Melanie pulled away then moved over to the DVD player to put on another movie. She had a desperate need to have something to do. She sat staring at the flickering screen in silence, but didn't absorb a single detail of the film. She had no idea what it was about especially since she had her ears attuned to the two brothers nattering. She could make out inconsequential chat but at the same time could feel their eyes pressing into her.

When she discovered they were staying for dinner she remained in a contemplative mood, hanging her head lower when Iain revealed what he'd heard the doctor say. She heard the hiss of Guy's sucked in breath but couldn't face him.

Iain broke the intense silence by standing up to collect their plates. 'Anyone for coffee?'

'Not for me.' Guy stood.

'Nor me,' Melanie whispered.

'Let's go home,' Guy said as he grasped Melanie by the hand.

'Fine by me.' She tugged her hand free then turned to Iain. 'Thank you for dinner and… well… everything.'

Heading for the door, Guy called over his shoulder. 'I appreciate today.'

Well, she didn't.

Chapter Twenty-One

'What have you got planned for me today?' Melanie asked as she began spooning cereal into her mouth.

'You make me sound like an ogre.' He smiled at her ire. 'Iain is taking you to the concert hall so you can make arrangements for the first concert. Then he's giving you a day out, mostly driving so you don't overtax your injury. We have your rehearsal tonight.' He leaned closer. 'I note you checked whether or not you could play,' he whispered.

'You have been busy. What else have you arranged without asking me?' Her voice dripped with sarcasm.

Guy laughed. 'I'll have more information tonight. Nothing else is finalised. I promise I'll go through all the details with the whole group.' Hearing a knock at the door he paused while he headed to open it. 'Here's Iain. Enjoy your day and take it easy.' As he passed she felt his fingers run in a gentle sweep down the side of her face. The barely there sensation remained with her all the way to the concert hall.

Melanie felt overwhelmed when she was met with an over-enthusiastic manager who greeted her with a hug then held out a folded sheet of paper. 'I kept this list of people who were disappointed at not being able to obtain tickets to your previous concert.'

'Truly?' She unfolded the paper. The list filled two columns of neatly typed names and contact details. 'This is unbelievable.'

'We had dozens of follow up calls after the event. With proper advertising I'm certain we'll have no trouble filling the hall each night. Are you sure you can't extend?'

Melanie felt her cheeks heat as she refolded the paper and handed it back. She'd had no idea their previous concert had been so well received. She hadn't really cared at the time for she knew she'd never dare to perform in a second. And she'd been right. Even the first had been a monumental error. It had gotten her mother killed. She fought off a wave of guilt.

'I'll just be happy if we can have reasonably full houses over the three performances. Maybe if the interstate tour is successful we'll think about more, but right now…' Words eluded her. 'Can we just go over the details now?'

A drive up the coast and lunch by the ocean after the lengthy meeting was a pleasant surprise, filling up most of the day before returning to Guy's home in time for Iain to put together the evening meal. The meal was almost ready when Guy arrived home, interrupting a session of light-hearted banter. Melanie couldn't understand why the mere presence of Guy seemed to completely alter the atmosphere and her tongue seemed to cleave to the roof of her mouth.

***

Even though he'd met them before, Guy formally introduced each girl to Iain as they entered with their instrument.

'Tell me more about that one,' Iain asked as one particular woman began descending the steps.

'Jenny. I'm not sure of her second name. Twenty-five, single and works as a music teacher in a private school, I think. I'm gradually learning about each but remembering which facts go with which lady is still a problem. Takes your fancy does she?' Guy teased while Iain's eyes followed the lady in question.

The first haunting bars drifting up the stairs had Iain setting down the sponge he had been using to wipe down the benches. 'Can we go down there?' he asked.

'Sure, they don't mind an audience.' Guy led the way downward. Violins raced to catch up to the panpipes. Violas were steadier, deeper and slower. The harp quivered up high.

'That's incredible,' Iain whispered. 'Melanie is brilliant and the other girls are also pretty darn good.' He sank to the ground, perching on a step with his legs outstretched and crossed at the ankles.

Knowing Iain wasn't one for classical music, Guy was surprised at his interest, which boded well for the concerts. If Iain could enjoy it then maybe they had a chance of being successful. Leaning back on his elbows his eyes kept flicking between the particular cellist and Iain who was studying Jenny in detail. She was tall but lean with mousy shoulder length hair caught back at the sides with hairgrips. Jenny was no stunning beauty but had a natural prettiness that appealed. She must have felt Iain's scrutiny for she glanced his way and smiled.

Guy leaned towards Iain. 'I think she likes you.'

Iain jumped then turned his head. 'I think I like her,' he replied as the piece came to an end. Iain rose, applauding loudly.

Guy tugged on his arm. 'Let's get supper prepared then we can come back.' While they worked, with the bulk of the work being carried out by Iain, Guy explained what they were planning. It wasn't too long before they were again perched on the bottom steps, immersed in the concert. Having now worked out all the changes, the girls were rehearsing the repertoire over and over again - for the CD first, then tagging on the other pieces they would be playing at the concert; a full two hours of pure entertainment.

Guy couldn't help but notice the spark between Jenny and his brother as they kept glancing at each other. Grinning to himself he wondered how long it would take for Iain to invite her out. Not long if he went by Iain's previous dating patterns. He scowled when he recalled how quick Iain had been in taking Melanie on a date. Too darn quick.

By the end of the rehearsal Melanie looked drained giving him cause for concern that she had overdone things, so when the girls clamoured up the stairs he held her back.

'Are you all right?'

'I'm fine, just a little tired.' He noticed the telltale shrug of her shoulders as she turned to leave. 'Let's go and eat, I'm hungry.' Some inner instinct told him she was hiding something as she spoke over her shoulder. The words, he felt sure, were a decoy to prevent him probing further. It disappointed him that she still kept things from him.

When Melanie swayed on the second step he knew his gut feeling was right. He closed the gap then wound his arm around her waist as they mounted the stairs. She leant against him until they reached the top when she straightened her spine and pulled away. So she didn't want to be seen having any weakness by her friends. His unease didn't lessen as he watched her struggle to maintain an aura of brightness during a supper she barely touched. Something was definitely wrong.

When he noticed a couple getting ready to leave, Guy handed out a schedule of dates and events he had almost finalised. 'This is only a draft so feel free to offer any suggestions. Taking into account the time needed to produce the CD and have it ready for sale, tentative bookings have been made in three other cities; also for the relative flights and accommodation. One more thing, can the next rehearsal be changed to Sunday? Melanie and I are flying interstate on Monday to check out the other venues.'

Keeping his eye on Melanie he noticed her jaw slacken as she studied the schedule. Since he hadn't given her some of the final details he was expecting some sort of reaction.

'What is this, Guy? Photo tomorrow,' she finally asked.

'Ah! Tomorrow you are scheduled to have the main promotional photos taken for the cover of the album. The doctor okayed it.'

'Did he now? I think we might need to discuss this later, Guy Harris.'

He pondered the adding of his surname then smiled when he figured there was something she was not so happy about but Melanie Jones was in for a bit of surprise tonight. He sighed. She would still probably have stern words with him for being so presumptuous. He was actually looking forward to it. Far better than the Melanie of last night. When she had fighting spark she wasn't in an emotional black hole.

'The photographer will be attending your Thursday rehearsal to take further shots of the girls and has asked if dress, hair and makeup could be as you would be on stage,' he added as the girls collected their belongings together.

After seeing off the visitors Guy shut the door, grinning when Melanie planted her body right in front of him, arms akimbo. He forestalled her. 'Before you say one word go and look at your bed.'

Her face screwing, she obeyed, prancing across the room to her bedroom. Guy followed then leant against the doorframe as he watched.

'Oh, Guy! How on earth did you… it's so beautiful… it's exactly the same. Oh, Guy!' She took hesitant steps over the carpet and then fingered the replica of her black gown. Picking it up from where he had laid it across her bed, she held it in front of her body as she stared at her reflection in the mirror.

'Try it on to make sure it fits.' Guy whispered, his heart doing strange things as he marvelled at the beautiful woman spinning around, her unabashed pleasure delighting him. He'd never seen her so happy. This is how she should always be. Such a simple gesture on his behalf and she forgot about her life. He felt choked up as she lifted her eyes and glanced at him in the mirror. She was fighting back tears but he knew they were not of the sad variety. His breath caught.

Sweeping her fingers to indicate he should leave her in privacy he pushed away from the jamb and reached in to grasp the door handle, pulling the door closed as he retreated. He waited at the end of the passage. His heart jammed somewhere in his throat when she walked out with her un-braided hair tumbling around her shoulders.

'It's perfect,' she whispered, her eyes glistening with unshed tears.

He took one step towards her then paused. 'You look so beautiful, just like the very first time I saw you.' Moving closer he stood staring into her eyes, his heart hammering against his ribs. He felt sure it was going to explode.

Reaching up on her toes she brushed her mouth against his, the simple gesture of impulsive appreciation causing Guy to crush her into his arms while he rested his chin on her head. Her display of affection was no more than a thank you kiss but it was the first time she'd freely kissed him, which was huge.

'I took your old dress to Neil's wife, Louise, and asked her if she could find someone who could replicate it for you. I think she found the right person. I would very much like you to wear the gown for the photos tomorrow, and we will need to take your instrument with us. Now, you said you wanted to discuss something.'

She pulled away. 'I think it can wait until tomorrow. Thank you so very much. You have no idea what this means to me.'

'The look on your face tells me plenty. It was my very great pleasure. Now go to bed and rest well, we have a busy day tomorrow. Goodnight.' His shower was long and freezing cold. He didn't know how much longer he could keep his intense feelings for Melanie hidden.

Chapter Twenty-Two

She looked stressed, her face ashen with dark half circles under her eyes. Now that she had cleaned off the makeup, Guy realised the photo shoot had been far too exhausting. Guilt stabbed. While he had been sitting at the back of the room determining which poses would be chosen for the album cover, programmes and advertisements, Melanie had been uncomplaining but was now so obviously stressed. Then he recalled how last night she had been below par. Damn but he should have probed further.

Instead of going for the quiet drive he had planned, Guy returned home so Melanie could rest. He grew more concerned when she asked for a couple of painkillers as she toyed with the late lunch he prepared. She ate no more than a couple of mouthfuls. After swallowing the two white pills, she sank into the sofa as though unable to take the few extra steps to her room.

His concern mounting, Guy put on some soothing background music then cleaned away the remnants of her uneaten lunch. Within minutes she was asleep. He lifted her legs onto the sofa, placed a pillow under her head then covered her with a blanket. He felt her brow to make sure she wasn't feverish then dared to brush a kiss across her lips.

Lowering into his favourite chair he studied her. It wasn't often he had the opportunity to examine her like this; she usually melted out of sight into her bedroom. He wondered if she still intended moving out. He hoped not.

Small frowns flittered across her face and she kept flexing the fingers of the right hand in her sleep. He wondered if she was reliving bad thoughts or was dreaming of playing, although her fingers didn't move like that whilst playing. He had planned on taking her out for dinner but now changed his mind. Instead, he searched the freezer for something he could manage to cook by himself with his one-handed helplessness. Removing a couple of frozen stir-fries, he studied the instructions before setting out the one pan, plates, forks and the other few items needed. Much as they both preferred freshly prepared food, desperate times called for frozen meals. For a few weeks they weren't going to kill him.

Hearing a rustle, Guy glanced up to see Melanie sitting upright in the lounge and studying him. 'Are you feeling better?' he asked. She didn't look much better.

'Yes, thank you. The throbbing has eased but I feel like some fresh air to clear my head, would you come for a walk with me?'

Throbbing? What throbbing? Must have been a headache. 'Sounds like a great idea since it will be the only type of exercise I will be able to undertake for a while.'

He was about to slide his feet into a pair of loafers when the phone rang. He paused as he considered whether or not to answer. 'Go on ahead, I'll just get that. It might be Iain.'

As Melanie stepped onto the pathway Guy headed for the phone, leaving the front door ajar. He lifted the receiver then heard Melanie scream. Dropping the phone, he ran full pelt towards the gate. Twisting his head both ways down the road, he spied Melanie backing towards him with her hands held over her head and whimpering his name over and over again. He sped towards her.

'Melanie, what happened?' He ignored her flinch when he reached for the hands scrunched over her head and drew them down.

'He's here. He was waiting for me. He ran when I screamed.' She pointed towards the corner.

'Get back inside and call Iain.' Waiting only long enough to ensure Melanie obeyed, Guy raced for the corner. 'Make sure you shut the door,' he yelled over his shoulder.

Bare feet slapped on concrete as he jogged down the footpath. Nearing the corner, he slowed then carefully peered around the bend. With no sign of any person walking or running, he rounded the corner and ran whilst twisting from side-to-side, peering down driveways and into backyards as he went. The man could be hiding anywhere, he thought as he made to cross the next street.

Hearing a squeal of rubber tyres spinning on bitumen, he glanced in the direction the sound was coming from then leapt out of the way as a battered red sedan bored down on him. 'Christ!' he muttered as he leapt backwards then tripped on the concrete kerb, falling on his backside.

There was a whoosh of wind as the car sped past. Lifting his head, he saw the tail of the car vanish around the corner heading back towards home.

'Oh! God, no!' Scrambling to his feet he raced back along the footpath, cutting the corner then swerving out of the way of an elderly gent who had just stepped out of his front gate.

'Sorry,' Guy panted as he sped past. The red car was nowhere in sight when he reached his gate but he searched the environs as he bent over and leant on the top of the gate trying to catch his breath.

'Has he gone?' Guy straightened and twisted around at Melanie's voice. The front door was open just a few centimetres but he could see her hovering in the gap.

'Yes. Does he own a red car?'

'If he was in a car then he stole it.' The front door opened wider and Melanie peered around nervously.

'Did you manage to get a hold of Iain?' Guy asked as he neared her.

'He's on his way.' Melanie hovered on the doorstep.

'He'll be peeved since its still time off for him.' Guy slid his arm around Melanie's waist and turned her before guiding her inside.

They were discussing the upcoming interstate trip when Iain arrived. It was a safe topic to keep her mind away from her father. Melanie prepared coffee while the three stood around the kitchen discussing details of the latest little adventure. Leaning against the refrigerator, Guy gave as much a description as he could recall about the car.

'I'll get my boys to see if we can get a match with recently stolen vehicles and have them search the area but I guess that now he's been spotted, he'll dump it and steal another. I don't need to suggest that it wouldn't be wise for

Melanie to step foot outside without you. There's not a lot more I can do except keep searching. Although with his frequent sightings he has to be holed up somewhere close by.' Dropping his empty mug on the sink, Iain headed for the door. 'Are you two still going east for a few days?'

'Yes, we head out Monday lunchtime and get back late Wednesday night.' Guy followed his brother to the door.

'It's probably a good thing to be out of harm's way for a while. I'll keep your place under surveillance,' said Iain as he reached his car.

***

It was early, too early when they'd both visited the hospital. While Melanie was having sutures yanked through barely healed skin, Guy had been having the plaster on his arm removed then replaced by a hard removable plastic cast, which was able to get wet, making showering a far more pleasant experience.

Then they'd landed at their first destination mid-afternoon. They caught a taxi to inspect the first concert venue before seeking out the hotel. Standing in the middle of the bare stage, Melanie played a short piece to test the hall for acoustics. To see if there were any dead spots she sent Guy walking around the entire upper and lower sections of the auditorium while she played.

'What in heaven's name is a dead spot?'

'You'll know when you experience one.' She shoved him towards the seating.

A sense of elation hit when Melanie showed no resistance to him draping his arm around her shoulder or holding her hand wherever they went until she became dissatisfied with the second venue the following day. He soon discovered what a flat spot was by finding quite a few places in the theatre where he could barely hear her playing. After only a few minutes of playing and Guy calling out his inability to hear clearly, she cancelled the booking then asked Guy if he had any other options on his list for this city.

Guy learnt a valuable lesson after having to eat humble pie for not considering they may need to inspect a second venue in each city. His chagrin worsened when after a few phone-calls on his mobile phone by Melanie, they were inspecting a second venue, which turned out to be perfect.

The third day was a repeat of the first. The venue was ideal leaving Guy pleased he had managed to get at least two out of three correct. Stunned by the efficiency and professionalism of Melanie he began to think his presence was superfluous. Miss Melanie Jones was far more experienced than she had let on and he was keen to find out a lot more about her professional playing history. There was only one way to find out.

'Exactly how many concerts have you done? It's quite obvious you know what you are doing.'

'Only the one night back home, the one you went to.' There was a telling sly grin on her face.

'And in Greece?'

'Only in Greece?' she queried with a certain air that made Guy even more wary.

'For a start and then tell me the rest.' Now he was certain there was a great deal Melanie hadn't divulged about her past.

'Greece - about twenty-five. Other European cities - about another twenty-five.'

'But you were only away for four years.'

'I only played the Panpipes in the concert arena for the last twelve months I was there. It took me three years to learn how to play. I toured with Stephan.'

'I can see you are a lot more experienced than I thought. You've been keeping things from me.'

'You never asked.' Melanie's smile was very cheeky but seeing her like this sent waves of pleasure galloping through him. This is how she should always be.

On their return home, Guy was most surprised to see his brother turn up at rehearsal, and was that Jenny with him? Surely not. But then he noticed the surreptitious brush of fingers as they parted. Then he recalled how Iain had spent entire suppertimes at the past few rehearsals chatting to Jenny Moore. Seems there was more to it than casual conversation.

Guy sidled beside Melanie. 'Iain and Jenny seem to be getting on well.'

'They went out for dinner last night,' Melanie whispered back.

'He is a fast worker. How do you know?'

'Jenny told me. They've been out three times.'

'Already!' Guy was stunned. 'Good luck to them. It's about time Iain settled down.' It was about time Guy settled down too and he knew exactly with whom he intended settling.

After taking time out for the photographer to snap various poses of the girls they only had time to rehearse for the CD. With the recording only two days away, it took precedence.

Chapter Twenty-Three

They were so exhausted after two very long days of recording the CD that Melanie suggested they cancel rehearsals for the next week. She grinned when there was not one voice of dissension. It gave her the opportunity to inspect a couple of advertised vacant units. After overhearing Guy whisper to Iain how her father had tried to run him down, she had spent many restless nights stewing. Guilt and shame about Guy becoming an object of her father's hatred had intensified. She had to leave. She cared too much for Guy to allow him to be a target. Even though she feared her father finding her, her own welfare meant little compared to that of Guy.

To leave without raising his suspicions, she ordered a taxi, telling Guy she was catching up with a couple of the girls to discuss individual details of their solo parts for the concert pieces. Lying to him didn't sit well. To her delight she found the ideal unit within walking distance of work and felt even more overjoyed that she could move in over the weekend. Not having a driver's licence meant the proximity to work was important. Her father would find it hard to attack, especially if she kept her movements within daylight hours when the streets would be full. All she had to do now was break the news to Guy, somehow.

During the week, she was surreptitious about packing her few belongings. She had never owned much but had bought a few clothes during her lunch hours since beginning work. At night she spring-cleaned her room and bathroom so that when she left they would be spotless. The day before she planned to leave she still hadn't found the courage to tell Guy. Fate ended up playing into her hands when he mentioned he was spending Saturday with Neil and a few other workers, setting up the new factory, premises he'd finally purchased.

Two trips in a taxi were all it took to have her belongings moved. She wrote a note with her new address. Guilt about being such a coward swamped her as she placed the note in a prominent position. But at least she had told him although her note merely explained she had found a place of her own and thanked him for all his care and hospitality when she had nowhere else to go. She managed to find the courage to ring Iain to tell him what she was doing, finding it odd how easily she could talk to him. He at least understood and promised he would call in to see Guy later.

***

Guy felt shattered when he arrived home and read Melanie's brief note. With an all-consuming emptiness tugging his innards into a taut clench, he sat slouched in a chair reading the short missive over and over again. When she'd not mentioned moving out again he had hoped she'd changed her mind. With her being more open and less skittish with just the two of them he was at a loss as to why she wanted to leave. Why now? With her father still on the loose and not afraid to tackle her in broad daylight, why leave? She was far more vulnerable on her own, so what made her decide to leave? He'd been certain he'd been making headway in breaking down barriers but now he wondered if he was seeing things that really weren't there.

He wandered into her room and shuddered. It looked as though she had never been there. The place felt desolate and empty. At the sound of his doorbell ringing he scooted to answer. Maybe Melanie had changed her mind. Quick strides of eager anticipation quickly changed to waves of bitter disappointment when he found his brother standing on the doorstep.

'Guy, how's things?'

'Melanie's gone.'

Iain winced. 'Yeah, she told me she was going.'

'She told you? Did she tell you why? I thought we were getting on so well.'

'Can I come in?'

'Oh, yes, of course.' Guy stood aside to let Iain pass but began pacing the floor as Iain plonked into a chair.

'Guy, she didn't tell me why but I think it's because you are getting on so well she felt the need to go.'

'I don't understand. That doesn't make sense.' Frustrated fingers were creating a bird's nest in his hair. The moment he realised what he was doing he brushed a hand over the tangle to straighten the short strands. 'She'll be such an easy target alone? Hell, I'm going to worry myself stupid wondering if she's safe.'

'Stop pacing.' A hand landed on Guy's shoulder to bring him to a standstill. 'Melanie has lost everyone she ever loved or trusted. Her mother died by her father's hand. He is a cruel, sadistic monster who taught her to not trust men or show her emotions. Her grandfather died while she was in Greece, after which she came home.'

'I never knew about the grandfather.'

Iain smiled. 'You don't ask the right questions. She's petrified of her father and has very good reason to be. I believe she left because she cares about you. I think she overheard you telling me how you were almost run down. She told me she didn't want anyone else to be a target because of her. In fact I would lay odds that she's in love with you. Deep down, I think she's afraid something's going to happen to you.'

'So where does that leave me? I just want her back here. With me. Permanently.'

Iain raised his head and grinned. 'Permanent, eh? That doesn't surprise me. It's obvious you're in love with her. Everyone can see it but you're going to have to do the old-fashioned thing and woo her. Ask her out, treat her like a girlfriend. There are a couple of things you may not know. Her outing with young Rod was the first time she had ever been on a date.'

'Ever? I find that hard to believe.'

'From what she told me I'm certain she's never had a boyfriend of any description. Her father would have killed her if she dated and her traditional grandparents chaperoned her everywhere while she was in Greece. Hell man, she's never even been kissed in the romantic sense.'

'You kissed her.'

Iain grinned. 'Ah, so you were jealous. I'd already figured she had strong feelings for you even back then. And it was only a chaste goodnight peck. The worst thing you can do is to not accept her reasons for moving out. Go and talk to her. Tell her you miss her but don't lay it on. I hope she misses you and comes to realise why. Keep the rehearsals here, pick her up and drive her home, but stick around; she's going to need you. The trial date has been scheduled for the week after the last concert.'

Guy snorted. 'Only if you can catch the bastard.'

'As far as he knows, Jones is out on bail and required to attend the trial on a certain date. He isn't aware that his bail has been revoked. But we hope we'll find him beforehand. We can't alter the trial date just because we haven't been able to serve new papers and arrest the man. Even so, the entire thing is going to be tough for Melanie and you may be needed to pick up the pieces. You are the only person she really trusts.'

'I'd like to know how you found out so much.' Finally ceasing his incessant pacing Guy perched on the arm of the sofa.

'She's not emotionally involved with me and I'm a cop. I guess I've learnt to ask the right questions.'

'What did she tell you at that café?'

'Come on, to get her to talk I promised not to disclose anything. We're both men of our word. You don't really want me to start breaking promises do you?' Iain clasped a firm grip on his brother's shoulder.

'No, but not knowing makes it damn hard to know what to do. I feel so helpless. I just want this bastard caught and then I want Melanie back here.' Guy stood and faced Iain. 'Look, you've given me plenty to think about but before I forget, I was going to ring you tonight anyway. We found signs of someone camping in the factory we bought, and it may have been Jones. In fact I'm sure it was because the jacket stolen from my car is there. I've left everything as found. There could be some evidence. Come around in the morning to have a look. I'll be there.'

Iain gave a brotherly hug. 'I'll have a team there early. Look, Guy, how about bringing Melanie out to dinner with Jenny and me next Saturday night? The two women are fairly close so she might feel more comfortable in a group. Ask her.'

'How is it with Jenny?'

'Pretty special. I've never felt this way about anyone before.' Iain had a dreamy smile on his face as he turned and headed for the door.

Guy grinned. 'I'm pleased for you. I'll be at the factory by seven.'

Sleep was non-existent. Thoughts of Melanie consumed him. He recalled the first time he saw her. Those images were forever imprinted on his brain. He replayed all the times she had been paralysed with fear. After receiving the comfort she needed, she seemed to be able to shake off her terror and turn back into the confident and efficient person she really was. Who was going to be there during the night to comfort her now? How would she cope during those long lonely nights of darkness and fear? Did she really leave because of a perceived fear of him being hurt? Then his thoughts turned to all the laughs they had enjoyed together, her work, her incredible music and mostly on what the heck he was going to do now to win her over.

Chapter Twenty-Four

The moment of reckoning had arrived. Melanie dropped the internal phone back into its cradle and huffed. Guy wanted her in his office. How was she going to handle this? Petrified, she approached slowly, pausing outside his closed door where she breathed in slow and deep to compose her racing heart. Expecting him to demand an explanation she stepped through the doorway with a hesitant frown.

'Good morning, Melanie, I have the proofs from the photo shoot. We need to select one for the CD cover and another for the advertisement and programmes.'

She shot him a glance then hesitated. He wasn't even looking at her as he spread photos on his cleared desk, sorting them into rough rows, keeping his eyes on what he was doing until he had them all the same way up. Then he separated those of her from those of her instrument. A third pile was of the entire ensemble.

'What do you think?' He finally glanced up, catching her staring at him, which further tightened already tense nerves.

Blushing at being caught out, she averted her eyes, glimpsing his smile as he dropped his eyes back to the photos. Why was he smiling? What was he up to? She peeked and listened as he selected a few he felt didn't work, explaining what he didn't like about them. With wildly palpitating heart, Melanie followed suit until they had discarded about half the shots, spreading out the rest for further scrutiny.

Never enjoying photos of her, Melanie pointed randomly to one of the panpipes. She didn't really care about the darn photos. She was more concerned about when Guy was going to slip in a comment about her leaving. 'I like this one best.'

Murmuring in agreement, Guy set the photo aside then removed all the remaining photos of the flutes. 'Now which one of you do we select? I like them all but my choice would be this one for the CD and programmes, and this one for the advertisement.' Pointing to one of her alone, and one of the group he glanced up. 'What do you think?'

As the dreaded heat rose in her cheeks she wished she could bolt from the room. Her innards felt as though they were about to explode like one of those party poppers. 'They're fine with me. You choose.' There was no way she could bring herself to look at him so she pretended she was still studying the photos but all she saw was an unfocussed blur.

She was vaguely aware of him sliding the two photos aside before he gathered up the rest. Thinking she could at last escape, she turned to flee.

'Melanie, something else came up over the weekend that you need to know about. Please sit down?'

She stilled, her feet incapable of moving as her heartbeat increased to a thundering pace. This was too hard. How was she going to explain things she didn't even understand? Drawing in a breath for courage, she turned and crept to the chair, plonking with a whoosh onto the fabric covered cushion, still unable to lift her eyes to look at him, still waiting for his questions.

'We found a camp in one of the buildings at the new factory. Iain brought a team over yesterday to investigate. We're certain it was your father's bolthole. Your jacket was there. They think they may have found the bloodied lump of wood he used to beat your mother. It's being tested for DNA now.'

Her eyes shot up of their own accord. Moisture from unbidden tears threatened to spill over but she fought them back. No more tears. Be strong Melanie Jones. Please, no more tears.

'Are you okay?' He sounded so concerned which weakened her resolve to not cry. She nodded even though nothing felt okay, then swiped at her eyes with the back of a clenched fist, determined to not embarrass herself again.

'Melanie, my house is bleak without you. I can't explain how much I miss you. I do understand your need to be independent but I'm so worried about you. What I don't understand is why you found it so hard to tell me. I would have helped you move. Please ring if you need anything - day or night, especially if you suspect your father is snooping around.'

'He doesn't know where I am.'

'Yet! How long before he realises you're not staying with me? How long before he finds you? With no one to protect you, how long before he has another go?' His voice rose with each question.

Melanie shot out of her seat. 'At least he won't hurt you now!' she yelled then winced when Guy sped around the desk towards her.

'Is that what this is all about? Me? You think I'm worried he'll harm me? I'm big enough to look after myself.' He grasped her shoulders so suddenly she jolted with fright. He'd moved so quickly.

'It's you I'm concerned about. God, Melanie, you are so vulnerable. How the hell do you think I'm going to be able to sleep knowing he could be breaking in and dishing out some despicable acts on you?' He wheeled away thrusting his hand through his hair in frustration. The silence was deafening before he turned back. 'I'm sorry. I can't tell you what to do. I just care what happens to you and I miss having you around.' As he wheezed out a long breath, he paused in front of her. 'May I pick you up tonight for rehearsal? Please?'

She felt stunned at this sudden turn-a-round. 'I'd like that but as for the rest, I've spent all my life eluding him. That's why I chose a place near here. It's not far for me to walk and there is a supermarket nearby. I'll be as careful as I've always been.'

'You think that will stop me from worrying?' He sounded almost hysterical and must have realised for he paused and appeared to fight for control. His shoulders rose and sank twice and his breath hissed through clenched teeth. 'I have a suggestion. The company is supplying you with a mobile phone as from today. At least promise to keep it charged and carry it with you at all times otherwise I'm going to be camping outside your front door every damn night.'

All Melanie could manage was a weak grin as she nodded a couple of times before making a hasty retreat back to her office, an image of the huge man sleeping curled up in a sleeping bag on her miniscule doorstep flittering through her mind. A sigh of relief whooshed as she set about concentrating on her day's work. When she carried his mail into him later in the morning Guy mentioned Iain's invitation to dinner.

'Would you like to go? It appears Iain and Jenny are getting on very well together. I'm pleased for them. I think it would be rather pleasant to join them, but it's up to you.'

Hesitating for a moment she thought, why not? 'Thank you, I would love to go.'

***

As she neared her desk a few days later Melanie was stunned when she spied a large flower arrangement sitting in the centre. Advancing at a snail's pace she removed the card from the front of the glorious blooms and opened it. *Happy birthday, Melanie. With all our love, Guy, Neil and all the staff.* Unable to hold back the flood of tears springing from her eyes, she flopped down in her chair, completely overwhelmed. Her head dropped into her hands as she allowed the tears free rein.

'Melanie, what is it?'

She jerked up at Guy's voice then scrubbed at her wet eyes, feeling stupid for being caught out at such a weak moment. She felt him lift her damp fingers before he eased her from her chair and tucked her close.

'What on earth is wrong, aren't you pleased? We didn't mean to upset you.'

She couldn't prevent the shudder winding down her body as she drew in a deep breath to gain control. This was all too much. How to explain why flowers brought on such a deluge? Would she ever learn how to control her emotions? Sucking in a second deep breath, she stood back a fraction. 'Thank you so much, I love the flowers.'

'Then why the forty-day flood?'

'I'm so overwhelmed. Nobody has ever bought me flowers before and the only person who ever wished me a happy birthday before was Mum and it was never very happy.' She paused as she brushed a clenched fist at her traitorous eyes, daring them to leak again.

'Never?'

Poor Guy looked so stunned. She managed a soppy wet grin. 'I seem to recall vague memories of birthday parties before I went to school but after that we certainly never celebrated. Mum never dared unless she was sure Dad wasn't around. This is the first time anyone apart from Mum… has cared it was my birthday.' Fighting back a fresh deluge, she pressed her face into Guy's shoulder with her fingers pinching the bridge of her nose. She felt such an idiot.

Still holding her close he shuffled them both to the door. She felt him close it before he shuffled her back to the desk. There was a whoop of tissues being dragged from the box on her desk then they were pressed against her face.

As she mopped her eyes, Guy reached for the intercom phone. 'Neil, can you please bring two cups of white coffee to Melanie's office?'

At the gentle knock a few minutes later, Guy stepped outside then returned with two steaming mugs. 'I've asked Neil to keep everyone away until you feel better. Drink up.'

The mundane action of sipping coffee while chatting about inconsequential matters helped her to gather her shattered wits. Reaching out, she fingered the velvety petals of pink roses. 'How did you know it was my birthday?'

'Your records. I took note of it when you put them on my desk. We always acknowledge our office staff's birthday in some small way. I had no idea something as simple as flowers would result in such a dramatic outcome. Tell me, even in Greece, no one acknowledged your birthday? I find it hard to believe.'

'I never told anyone the date of my birth so no one knew.'

'I guess I'd better warn you then, the staff have organised a morning tea for you. Melanie, I would really love to take you out somewhere special for dinner tonight to celebrate. Would you like to come?'

Completely overwhelmed, Melanie forced a smile through bleary eyes. 'I would love to go, thank you. Now I need to get the mail sorted. Thank you again, I really do appreciate the flowers, more than you will ever know.'

'I can't believe someone has actually bought me flowers,' she whispered as Guy left. She reddened when she realised Guy had heard when he paused in the doorway. To cover her chagrin she rushed past him, 'I need to wash my face so I look as though I am as happy as I feel.'

She was more than thankful Guy had warned her about the morning tea, especially when she saw the beautifully decorated cake with her name written on top in pink icing. She fought back tears of pleasure while cutting the jam and cream layered sponge into pieces, her face averted while she fought for composure but this time she managed to keep moisture at bay. What she couldn't understand was why the tears seemed to have a will of their own and fall so often and so easily when she'd never allowed them to fall prior to meeting Guy. Heavens but he must think her to be some kind of a wimp. By the end of the extended break, she was joining in the friendly banter she felt certain Guy had instigated and was back to the normal Melanie every one in the office knew.

At lunchtime she took the entire hour she was entitled to. On her return she had a couple of parcels under her arm, which she hid in a cupboard. When Guy arrived to pick her up that evening she was wearing the new dress and shoes she'd bought - her birthday present to herself. When she opened his gift, a gold locket on a chain, more tears threatened. Although delicate and exquisite, it looked expensive: the type of thing she could only drool over in a shop window. Never had she received such a personal gift of such quality and she knew she would treasure it for life.

Chapter Twenty-Five

As every morning, Melanie entered Guy's office to pick up the pile of unopened mail and obtain instructions for the day. With her thoughts centred on the previous night's rehearsal, which had been much longer than usual while the girls practised a new piece, she moved like a robot, taking little notice of her surroundings. Each girl had solo sections somewhere during the programme. Last night they had worked Jenny, with her cello, into their rendition of *Amazing Grace*. After a lengthy rehearsal the piece sounded really special but Melanie was still not happy with the ending. To her the last ten bars didn't draw it to a solid conclusion.

Stifling a yawn, she lifted and flexed aching fingers to cover her mouth. They were throbbing more than the usual unrelenting background ache and she wondered if her decision to not take a couple of painkillers with breakfast had been such a good idea. To add to her discomfort her lungs felt sore and raspy from the effort of playing for such an extended period. She knew her physical limits but had overstepped them last night.

Still concentrating on how she could alter the ending of the new piece, Melanie swept past Guy's desk, mumbling a good morning as she continued on to a side table to pick up the mail.

She stopped short when she noticed a photograph of herself on his desk. It was one taken at the photo shoot but not one she recognised from the proofs. But then she wasn't really concentrating on the proofs at the time. Aware of Guy watching, she picked the framed photo up to study it.

'There's another one in my lounge room, one by my bed and two in here.' His open wallet appeared in front of her dropped eyes. Two different photos were nestled in the front of it. 'This way, I can have you with me twenty-four hours a day.'

Mortified, she returned the frame to its place with hands that had begun imitating a wobbly jelly but she kept her eyes averted. She heard Guy move to the door and close it, barring the escape she was desperate to make. Was he a mind reader now?

'Melanie, I can't keep my feelings for you hidden away any longer. Iain reckons the whole world can see how much I love you.'

'L-l-l-l-love?' She knew her voice sounded squeaky but her tongue just wouldn't move properly.

'Yes, love. It's something new to me, being in love with a woman. I've never felt this intense passion about anyone before.' Footsteps neared. 'Looking back, I think you melted my heart the first time I saw you. All I knew was that I needed to see you again. I thought it was just your music that I wanted to hear again but now I know better.' His legs came into view as he settled one hip on the edge of the desk. 'It hit me for sure when you were stabbed. The feelings I had when I thought I was going to lose you are something I can't begin to describe and never want repeated.'

Too stunned to move, Melanie just stood there. The desk groaned as he moved. She could feel his presence right behind her. He stopped. After placing his hands on her shoulders he turned her around. Not having the gumption to look up she couldn't help but grin when he bent his knees to lower his frame so he could peer up into her eyes.

'I love you, Melanie Jones and I hope, one day, you can learn to love me the same way.'

As he straightened, her unblinking, stunned eyes followed his face upwards.

'I know you need time but I'm prepared to wait for as long as it takes. I would never pressure you but I think it would be dishonest of me if I didn't let you know exactly how I feel about you. You are a beautiful woman and one day I hope you will be a permanent part of my life. But that will be for you to decide. Now, love of my life, I feel very tempted to explore your very inviting lips but once I start, I might find it impossible to stop.'

Releasing her shoulders, he planted a soft kiss on her forehead then stepped backwards and had the nerve to just stand there. She just knew he was waiting for some kind of reaction but what was she supposed to say? Bemused, Melanie tried, but found it impossible to formulate any words in her brain. With escape the only option she spun around on one heel and fled, her haste causing her to fumble with the round door handle.

'I can't, I don't know how,' she mumbled to herself as she gripped the handle even harder. He must have heard for he grasped her shoulders again and drew her back against his body.

'Don't know how to love? You loved your mother.'

'But she was my Mum,' Melanie whispered. A really weird sensation clawed at her innards. It felt like some huge hand squeezing, then all her heated blood gushed along her veins leaving behind a tingling sensation of warmth.

'So you can love.' His warm breath brushed against one cheek as she felt herself being spun around. Then his fingers cupped her chin before gently forcing her face upwards. 'Look at me, Melanie.'

Slowly raising her eyelids, a different but at the same time familiar heat rose up her neck and face: an unwanted blush over which she had no control. Unable to drag her eyes from his, she could see the sincerity in his look.

'Don't be so hard on yourself and follow your heart. I know you find it difficult to trust men and you have every reason to have those fears. I'm also pretty sure you care about me. You care enough to put your life on the line in the mistaken belief you are keeping me safe. Only a woman who cares deeply about a person would do that. Search your heart to discover exactly what those feelings mean. '

Suddenly released and with Guy's words spinning around in her head, Melanie turned and fled, this time managing to turn the lock without fumbling.

For the first time in her working career, she sat at her desk doing a big fat nothing. Her mind was like a swirling maelstrom while she tried to sort out everything she'd just heard. The same strange, fuzzy warmth that had enveloped her body on previous occasions swept up from her toes and settled in the region of her heart. She placed her outstretched fingers on either side of her face, feeling the heat in her cheeks, which she felt sure, must be bright crimson.

When Guy strode into the room and grinned, her heart shot to her mouth. He handed her the pile of unopened mail. 'You forgot something.' He chuckled at her deepening blush then strode away.

She stared after his retreating back then forcing her brain to function, began slitting the flaps of the envelopes open with the end of a pen while three words kept repeating over and over. Guy loves me. Once the opened mail was piled in a heap in front of her and the envelopes scrunched up and tossed into the small plastic bin at her feet, she forced her concentration on the written words until she could comprehend them then worked liked a slave for the rest of the day, not daring to go anywhere near Guy's office.

Melanie was most surprised when Neil dropped by her desk before he left for the day to hand her a note. Opening it out, she read: *I'll pick you up at seven - tomorrow night. You look stunning in your new green dress. Will you wear it for me? Please? Guy.* At the very bottom of the page he had drawn a heart in pink highlight pen and placed his initials in the front of it and her initials after. Her mind and thoughts in utter confusion she refolded the paper and slid it into the pocket of her jacket then left for home. Her concentration level was shattered. There was a desperate urgent need for space - alone.

When Guy arrived the following evening he acted as though nothing had been said, treating Melanie with the same care and tenderness as he always did. But there was no holding hands, no kiss or looks of… she didn't know what but nothing was different. While enjoying a wonderful night with Iain and Jenny, Melanie wondered what was going on. Had it all been some kind of fantastic dream?

With the four of them, she didn't have to talk much, for which she was thankful. It was obvious Jenny and Iain were very much infatuated with each other and she wished she could be as open in showing and voicing her own feelings, even though those feelings were a complete muddle. She was at a loss to understand why she was so afraid of returning Guy's affection because she was certain she had strong feelings for him and didn't want to lose him, but she just didn't have the confidence to open up the same way he had. She wished her mother was still alive so they could talk. How she missed those rare times when just the two of them could chat about private girl things.

To add to her confusion, Guy didn't kiss her goodnight. After driving her home and giving her a hug, he bent and whispered in her ear, 'I love you, Melanie,' and then left her standing outside her door as he strode to his car then drove away.

'Why didn't he kiss me?' circled through her brain as she readied for bed then lay awake for ages. Maybe it's because you don't deserve to be kissed, kept coming back at her.

After a restless night with only short bouts of sleep between long sessions of trying to figure everything out, Melanie knew she needed to talk to someone. After a lot of soul searching, she figured Jenny was the only person she knew well enough to ask for a girl-to-girl chat.

The wait for the minute-hand to move around the dial to a reasonable hour to phone someone, felt interminable. Even though she and Jenny had become quite close over the months, Melanie wavered between being convinced it was the right way to go, to not be so ridiculous – solve your own problems. What finally had her dialling Jenny's number was the knowledge that Jenny had mentioned how she thought Guy was in love with Melanie and had teased her about him.

Approaching Jenny's front door an hour later, Melanie felt more nervous than on her first concert appearance. Was she doing the right thing? Frustrated and confused, she turned from the front door and strode back down the brick-paved footpath and bent to open the gate to flee.

'Mel? Are you coming in?'

Melanie paused then twisted around, forcing a smile at the puzzled frown on Jenny's face. 'I guess so. I'm just so confused and need some advice but... I don't know... maybe this isn't the right time.'

As though she knew Melanie was about to scarper, Jenny ran towards her and hugged her. 'Seems you have a bit of a problem. Come inside.'

Melanie didn't have any choice but to walk side-by-side with Jenny gripping her waist so tight. At the door Jenny stood behind, giving Melanie a gentle shove inside. With a firm grip on one hand, Jenny led her down the passage to the kitchen and pulled out a chintz-cushioned wooden chair from the table.

'Sit here and I'll put the kettle on.' She pulled the makings of coffee from white painted cupboards. 'Tell me what the problem is.'

'It's Guy.'

'Guy? What happened?' Jenny paused then turned to eye Melanie. 'He's in love with you.'

'That's the problem!' Melanie grimaced when her words squeaked out. She felt such an idiot.

'Why is that a problem? He's a terrific man.'

Feeling ridiculous, Melanie had an overwhelming urge to skedaddle but Jenny moved over and flung an arm around her shoulder then settled in the chair next to her.

'Don't you feel the same for him? Is that it?'

'I don't know how I feel about him, that's what's so confusing.' Melanie's head was so low she was speaking to the table.

Jenny reached out with one hand and drew Melanie's face around. 'I see the way you look at him when you think no one is watching. It's obvious you have feelings for him.'

'I do, I know that but I don't understand what my feelings are about. I've never felt like this before.'

'Felt like what?' Jenny asked as she grinned.

'Funny… confused. I miss him heaps when we're not together but am scared witless when we are.' Melanie paused. 'That doesn't make sense does it?'

'What are you afraid of? He would never harm you like your… well you know. Sorry,' Jenny added when Melanie shuddered. 'I shouldn't have mentioned him.'

'It's okay. I know Guy wouldn't hurt me; that's not what I'm afraid of. I want to touch him the same as he touches me. I want to be able to reach out and hug him… and kiss him… but I'm too scared. I've never… it's all new to me… and I… help me, Jenny.' Her plaintive wail sounded so stupid, even to Melanie.

'You've never had a boyfriend have you? I find that hard to believe. You are so gorgeous and sweet.'

Melanie cringed. 'Heavens, Jenny, don't you think I feel bad enough already. I just don't know how I should act, what I should do. I feel so embarrassed.' Melanie sank her head into her hands in despair.

'Oh, Mel, just act natural. You're in love with him aren't you?' Jenny brushed a finger against Melanie's cheek. It felt as though her entire face was a flaming inferno.

'Let nature tell you what to do. If he kisses you, don't pull back. Has he kissed you?'

'Yes. He took me out for dinner on my birthday and kissed me goodnight.'

'Did you enjoy it?' Jenny asked.

Melanie felt mortified at the intimacy of the question. 'Yes, very much but last night, after he took me home, he didn't and now I'm worried.'

'Has he told you that he's in love with you?'

'Yes.' The word was no more than a whisper. Melanie had to force it out through a throat that felt as though it was full of superglue.

'That's wonderful. So what are you worried about?' Jenny sprang from her seat and finished making the coffee, handing one to Melanie before she settled back into her chair.

After sitting in quiet contemplation for a few minutes, Melanie turned to face Jenny. 'Why didn't he kiss me last night?'

'I can't answer that but I guess it's because he's unsure of how you feel about him and he doesn't want to push you. If he's anything like his brother he'd always be a gentleman, make sure it was what you wanted before forcing the issue.'

'That's what he said when he told me how he felt. He didn't want to pressure me.'

'What else did he say?' Jenny had such a wide grin on her face Melanie just knew she was enjoying her discomfort.

'That he wanted me permanently.' Melanie felt so many things as she uttered the words she'd thought about over and over again since Guy had told her. Her heart felt as though it was exploding and a curious heat flooded low in her pelvis.

'That means marriage, Mel. He wants to marry you. This is so wonderful. I'm so happy for you.' Jenny jumped out of her seat and grabbed Melanie in a tight bear hug then stopped and whispered in her ear. 'I'm just hoping Iain feels the same way about me.'

Melanie stared at her friend. 'You want to marry him?'

'Oh, yes! I'm crazy in love with him. He's gorgeous, handsome, funny, sexy and so caring.'

After a long discussion over several cups of coffee Melanie received so much advice she felt even more confused than when she'd arrived. But all the while they chatted it became more and more obvious what her feelings for Guy meant. Especially when Jenny asked her how she would feel if she knew she would never see Guy again.

Melanie paused while attempting to visualise her life without Guy.

'Devastated.' A shiver shimmied down her spine. 'If I were to walk out of here right now, knowing he was gone… oh, Jenny, I think I'd want to die.' A sharp clamp squeezed at her heart followed by an all-encompassing knowledge. She loved Guy Harris.

As she lifted her eyes she felt radiant. 'I love him,' she whispered. Grinning, she leapt from her chair and began prancing wildly around the kitchen table. 'I love him!' she yelled. 'God, I love him.' She plonked back into the chair and grasped Jenny's hands. 'But how am I going to tell him?'

Jenny grinned a supercilious looking smile. 'I have an idea on how to not only knock Guy for six, but also Iain.'

Chapter Twenty-Six

Sitting back in the upholstered seat of the concert hall, Guy surveyed the packed auditorium. News had spread fast after the success of the first concert. He'd been amused at how eager eyes had scanned the early morning paper for reviews then whoops of delight audible down the phone when congratulatory phone calls between households followed.

Catching his brother's eye, Guy grinned as the lights brightened after the applause finally died for the final concert for the state. Each night there had been fewer empty seats. CD sales soared to the extent they would have to order another production run. Knowing the timing would be tight didn't concern him. They had enough for the next city. He was more delighted with the number sold: double what they had predicted.

Knowing it would be useless to try to reach the girls backstage until the noisy throng dispersed, they remained in their front row lounge seats for a few minutes.

'I can't believe how good they are,' murmured Iain as he stood and sidled his way past the empty seats.

'They seem better than the concert a few months ago.' Guy joined his brother in the aisle. 'Do you think they are good enough to go international?' He grinned as Iain stopped suddenly, almost tripping up a step in shock. Reaching out, Guy steadied Iain.

'Are you serious?' asked Iain.

'Yes, why not? Melanie has played overseas before so why can't we take the entire troupe? This tour is already in the black and we've got three states to go. We'll make enough profit to fund an overseas tour plus each woman will receive a substantial payment. I just wish all my business endeavours were as profitable in such a short time.'

Instead of taking the same route as the audience, they veered through the empty auditorium, leapt onto the stage then entered the labyrinth of passages behind to find the women chatting excitedly amongst themselves.

Guy glanced around. 'Where's Melanie?' he called over the ruckus.

'She's gone downstairs to find Jenny. Jenny wasn't feeling well,' someone called from the middle. Guy recognised the voice of Sophie, the harpist.

'Not well? She was fine earlier.' Iain sounded worried as he grasped Guy by the shoulder. 'Let's go down to find them.'

'You concerned, big brother?' teased Guy as they strode away.

'Too damn right I am.' Iain tugged harder as he lengthened his stride.

'You're really serious about Jenny aren't you?' asked Guy as he struggled to keep up with Iain's frantic pace.

'Serious enough to be considering marriage. I'm sure Jenny is the woman for me.'

Guy tugged his brother to a standstill as they reached the final door leading to the dressing rooms. 'I'm really pleased for you. I see the way you look at her. It's the same way Dad always looked at Mum. Have you asked the big question yet?'

'I was going to wait until the end of the tour. What the hell was that?'

They both twisted to face the direction from whence the sound of a scuffle and whimper emanated. Guy recognised the quiet voice coming from behind a partially open door as Melanie's. She sounded tense. Holding up one finger to his mouth to indicate silence, he crept closer, taking care to not make any noise with his leather soled shoes.

'Let her go, Dad.'

Guy shot upright as Iain swore under his breath. A tug at his sleeve and he turned to face his brother. They made their way back to the end of the passage, pulling the door shut as they exited.

'Jones has Jenny. I'm calling for backup,' Iain whispered.

Feeling a sense of panic swirl, Guy wondered how his brother could be so calm as he listened to Iain mumbling into the speaker of his mobile phone. Seeing the instrument sliding into a pocket, Guy took a few steps closer.

'You don't appear worried. You know what the man is capable of.'

'Not worried! My heart is pounding. He's got my woman in there and if he so much as lays a hand on her I'll beat his brains out. But we need to keep calm, think, and ensure neither of them is hurt. Scoot upstairs to make sure none of the others come down here, let them know to send the squad down. I'll wait here while I think of a way of getting them all out in one piece.'

Not wanting to alert Jones of their presence, Guy crept as rapidly as he dared and after pacifying panicking women, was soon back with Iain. 'What can we do?' he whispered as he neared.

'I snuck closer. Melanie is standing just inside the door, which is open about twenty centimetres and from what I heard, Jones has Jenny on the other side of the room. If I remember correctly, that room is about three metres square. I'm not sure if he has a weapon but I have to assume the worst. He has never used a gun, but prefers whatever bludgeon he can lay his hands on. Melanie is remarkably calm, trying to talk him into releasing Jenny. He wants money.'

'I recall Melanie hinting that he never used violence in front of an audience for fear of the authorities.' Guy reached for his wallet. 'How much cash do you have on you?' He rifled through the few notes he had. 'I've got about three hundred and fifty.'

'Two hundred, I don't carry much cash. But I doubt we could buy our way out of this.' Iain handed over four fifty-dollar bills then slid his wallet back into his jacket pocket.

'We could try. If he's desperate, it might be enough.'

'I need to think of Jenny's safety first. We both know what he's capable of and especially now that he has a witness. He must be desperate to have resorted to involving a third person – which really concerns me. Let's get closer. I'll move to the far side of the door, you stay this side. When I say *now*, we rush in. Me first, you follow. Head straight for Jones. You to his right. We grab his arms and wrists and drag them away from Jenny in case he has a knife.' Iain paused then sucked in a breath. 'Hell but I hate this sort of situation. Being Jenny makes it a hundred times worse.' As though searching for courage, he lifted his eyes to the ceiling, dragged in a few more breaths then squared his shoulders. 'Let's go but keep quiet.'

Guy felt for his brother but Melanie was in there as well and he'd experienced first hand the terror of seeing her stabbed. His own heart was doing a great job acting as though it was in a world drumming competition with the loudest and hardest drumbeat being the victor.

Step by slow quiet step, they crept along the gloomy passage. Iain paused at the door, slid back against the far wall, peered through the crack then shot to the other side before creeping close to the doorjamb. He indicated with hand-signals exactly where Jones was and outlined a knife held across Jenny's chest. Guy swore silently to himself, the visions of another knife plunging into Melanie obliterating any other thoughts for a few moments before he dragged his mind back to the present.

'You think any of us would bring money here?' Melanie's voice was clear but held a slight tremor.

'Then you go get some and bring it back here.' Jones was drunk, his words slurring. Guy shuddered. Jones would be at his most dangerous. Surely the man knew there would be plenty of people around here. He must be really desperate or so drunk he couldn't think. Guy slid the money from his shirt pocket and held it in the air, shrugging his shoulders in question. Iain shook his head.

'Let Jenny go. I'm not leaving this room until she has gone.' Melanie sounded determined.

'I won't harm her. She's my insurance.' The whimper from Jenny belied his verbal assurance. 'Stay still you bitch.' Jones growled.

Guy tensed at the ensuing scuffling, imagining Jenny struggling to get free.

'Dad!' Melanie yelled. 'Don't harm her. Let her go. Take me instead. Come with me.'

God, no! Guy tensed then listened for any sign Melanie was exchanging places with Jenny. Please, please don't.

'She'll call the cops. I can't let her go. You want her free then you go and empty your bank account. I want the lot.'

'I can't get more than five hundred dollars at a time. You know cards have a daily limit. It's the middle of the night for God's sake.'

'Then she stays here all night. I've got nothing better to do.'

Guy heard a suppressed scream, recognising Jenny as the source. He saw Iain tense his shoulders and screw his eyes tight and understood what he was going through. Gut instinct told him that unless they made a move soon neither woman was going to escape unharmed. A picture of the bloodied, pulpy remains of Maria Jones' face centred in his brain. He shuddered then forced the picture away as he caught Iain's eye then lifted one hand in the air, made the motion of running and pointed to the door. Iain shrugged his shoulders in a helpless motion then paused for a few seconds before nodding. There was no doubt it was a reluctant agreement but there was no other way. He caught a movement from Iain, who held up one hand while placing the other on the door.

'Now!' he whispered.

Iain shoved the door open and leapt inside. Guy followed on his tail. He flicked his eyes around the room, hoping he could grab Jones before the knife could be used. The door was thrust with such force it swung back and collected Guy on the shoulder as he surged inside. He couldn't avoid Melanie, knocking her to the ground as he powered across the carpeted floor. He heard Melanie yelp as she sank to the floor. At the same time Jenny screamed a long eardrum splitting wail.

Keeping his eyes planted firmly on Jenny and Jones, Guy felt as though he was in some slow motion third world as he saw Iain grab hold of the knife blade as it sliced upwards towards Jenny's throat. Red liquid spurted. Iain grunted and Jenny squealed making it impossible to figure out to whom the blood belonged. An adrenaline surge pushed him further forward. He reached out with both hands and closed his fingers over the hand holding the hilt of the large curved boning knife. It looked vicious, glinting like sparkling diamonds in the harsh dressing room light.

Using all the power he could muster he dragged the knife downwards and outwards. 'Let go, Iain!' he yelled.

Released suddenly, the knife slid from Jones's hand and went flying across the room.

'Oh, Christ!' Guy yelled as he scrambled after it and threw himself over Melanie to protect her from the falling blade. The air gushed from Melanie's lungs in an almighty whoosh as she was squashed into the floor beneath him.

Guy felt the nick of the knife point stabbing him through his trouser leg. A warm trickle told him he was cut but he didn't much care. Easing his huge torso up, he glanced down at Melanie. 'Are you okay?' he asked as he knelt back on his heels.

'Yes, just winded,' she managed to gasp out before dragging in a deep breath to refill her lungs.

Grinning, Guy dropped a quick kiss on her lips then straightened to ascertain the extent of the damage. 'Jenny?' He stepped towards her quivering body huddled on the floor.

'He missed me,' Jenny squeaked.

Now knowing it wasn't Jenny's blood, Guy stepped towards his brother who had Jones prostrate on the floor, face down, with one knee pressed into the man's back. Iain was holding Jones' arms behind his back in a bloodied grip. 'Damn it Iain, you're hurt. Show me.'

'Find something to tie him up with first. I'll live.'

With the amount of blood, Guy wasn't so sure Iain wasn't bleeding to death as he scanned the room for some type of binding. Spying a curtain held back with a twisted cord, he yanked the cord from its restraining hook and unwound it, using force to snap securing cotton threads as he stepped back to Iain. 'Here, hold him still while I wind this around.'

They bound the man's wrists together then left him lying on the ground. Then Guy examined the deep cut on his brother's left hand. 'You're going to need stitches. I need some kind of bandage.'

'Here,' piped in Melanie as she reached into the large bag she'd brought with her earlier. 'Use this, it's clean.' She handed Guy a T-shirt then reached into her handbag and withdrew a tiny pair of nail scissors.

Guy nicked the seam of the shirt then grasped the end and tore the fabric apart. He made another nick about ten centimetres up then tore a long strip from the fabric. 'Cut me another strip,' he said to Melanie as he wadded the first strip into Iain's palm pressed hard to stem the flow of blood. Using two more lengths he bound the wad into place, tying off the ends around Iain's wrist. 'That should do until we can get you to hospital.'

Iain was about to say something but was cut short as two men burst into the room, weapons drawn. Jenny squealed then sprang into Iain's arms.

'You're a bit late fellas,' said Iain with a wry grin. 'But read this bastard his rights and lock him up. I'll be in to charge him in a couple of hours.' He turned to Jones as he was hauled from the floor. 'You made one hell of a mistake tonight. That was my woman you held at knifepoint. Don't ever expect to see daylight again, you slimy bastard.' Iain turned and hustled Jenny out of the room with her ensconced firmly against his side. 'Guy, Melanie, we'll leave the statements until tomorrow,' he said over his shoulder.

Guy turned to Melanie. 'You look how I felt waiting outside - petrified.' He slid his arms around her and drew her shaking body close.

'You were petrified?' There was mocking scorn in her voice. 'Now you can call off your security guard who has been planted outside my front door every night.'

Guy couldn't help but laugh. 'You knew, did you?'

'Figured it out the very first night. Who do you think has been sitting in my lounge-room watching TV all night, every night?' Melanie giggled, the sound delighting Guy.

'Sounds like you've become very friendly. You didn't mind me being so presumptuous?' Guy asked as he tugged her close and led her outside.

'Oh, I was pretty mad at you, but at the same time quite relieved. He's a very nice man.'

Guy stopped mid-stride. 'How nice?'

Melanie giggled again then battered her eyelids at him. 'Not quite as nice as you,' she whispered then reached up and kissed him. 'By the way,' she added as she pulled away, 'you're bleeding.'

Reaching down with one arm, he felt the back of his thigh, her words making him aware of the injury he'd forgotten about. He felt sure the blood had ceased flowing.

'Compared to Iain, it's just a nick. I'll live.' He slung his arm around her waist. 'I'm all for getting home and tonight there will be no arguments, you're sleeping in my spare room.'

Chapter Twenty-Seven

Exhaustion was taking its toll. It was difficult keeping her eyes open let alone concentrate on music. Even with a few days rest between cities a heavy mantle of weariness hovered over Melanie's shoulders. To make it worse she missed Guy like something she'd never felt before. He and Iain managed to join them for the final night of each city but work commitments forced them to return home the following day. His two brief visits eased the relentless leaden hollowness but what hurt was how restrained his greeting had been each time. Where Iain and Jenny flew into each other's arms and kissed passionately, Guy always held back. His restraint hurt but she couldn't find the nerve to take that first step. Each time she felt him watching her she wondered if he could read how happy she was that he was there or whether he thought she didn't care. But why didn't he show her any physical affection? Because you don't deserve it kept coming back at her. He'd been sorry for his outburst about love and didn't really mean it. Heaven knew she was unworthy of his love; of anyone's love.

A weary sigh escaped. There was only an hour before the curtains opened for the final performance of the entire tour. Melanie hovered in the open dressing room doorway. Nerves prickled as she waited for Guy to arrive. Excitement bristled at the sound of his voice talking to Iain. No way did she want to be caught looking as though she was waiting so she scooted inside and grabbed her brush. She heard Jenny squeal followed by running feet. Blood thrummed through her veins in anticipation.

'Hi!'

The brush dropped and she spun around. Everything inside her clenched so tight she felt as though her body was going to ping apart. 'Hi.' It was a struggle to get it out with her mouth as dry as desert sands. Her feet were super-glued to the floor as he neared.

'So, the final night. Are you nervous?'

'Terrified.' But not about the performance. Please, please kiss me.

He reached out and gave her a loose hug. 'I've missed you.' Then his mouth settled on her brow. The kiss was no more than a friendly peck. He drew away. 'I'll leave you to get ready. I'm looking forward to this.'

A wave of sheer disappointment washed over her as she watched his back retreating down the narrow passageway between the rows of dressing rooms. Dear, God, is that all? She buried her face in her hands. She just knew that what she and Jenny had planned was going to be disastrous. She had to talk to Jenny but no way could she disturb what she knew would be a very passionate reunion.

She paced. Down the corridor and back - desperate for Iain to leave. The ten minute bell rang. Melanie spun around and watched the door. The moment Iain left she rushed inside to see Jenny re-arranging her mussed hair then re-applied her lipstick.

'I can't go through with this, Jenny. I'm going to make such a fool of myself. He doesn't love me,' Melanie muttered as her legs took on a will of their own and began pacing again.

Jenny's reflection peered at her in the mirror. 'He loves you, Mel. And more important – you love him.' Jenny recapped her lipstick and turned. 'We have to go ahead. It's too late to change the programme with the technicians. Come on. It's right. I'm dying to see how they react.' Gripping Melanie's shoulders, Jenny smiled with a quizzical uplift of one side of her face.

Melanie wavered, convinced it wasn't in the least bit right and she was going to make an utter idiot of herself. But she couldn't let Jenny down. If it all went pear-shaped then she'd just have to hide away and make her own way back to the hotel. Hiding. That was one thing she was expert at.

'Oh, all right then.' Before she could change her mind she grabbed Jenny's hand and dragged her down the passage, unable to suppress nervous giggles even though she was certain this was going to backfire.

The concert was received with tumultuous applause, which was only broken when a voice over the PA system announced, 'As a special treat for the final performance of the current tour, the group has added a debut piece dedicated to Iain and Guy Harris.'

The audience settled with an expectant hush. Melanie's stomach tightened so much she felt bilious. Daring a glance to the centre front seats, she spied both men hunch forward in anticipation. Dread settled in her innards.

The soft violins quivered their introduction, making it impossible for her to leave. Jenny stood, balanced her cello against her stool then moved to centre stage. Melanie swallowed down rising bile and lifted the panpipes to her mouth. Please let this be right, she thought as pink spotlights bathed the girls in a rosy glow while another, in blue, highlighted the men. Hearing the rest of the ensemble join in the lilting harmony brought her to her senses. She was a professional. She could do this. Even it was just for Jenny.

The music built up in intensity.

Jenny moved forward a step.

With her eyes planted on Jenny, Melanie drew in a lungful of air then blew the first note as Jenny began singing her own personal words to the first verse of *I Will Always Love You.*

As she played, Melanie kept glancing between the men and Jenny. Iain stared at Jenny as she moved to the front of the stage, her beautiful soprano voice echoing through the auditorium. A sudden rush of moisture spread across Melanie's eyes at the poignancy of the words. She fought the tears back as she dropped her instrument to her side and joined Jenny in harmony for the chorus. She ignored the rasping pain of her vocal cords, forcing a rich tremolo to her mezzo soprano voice. She would suffer for this moment of madness, in more ways than one, but she figured it would be worth it for Jenny. Melanie could handle her own humiliation – she'd had enough practice it was almost second nature.

⁎⁎⁎

Stunned, Guy sat unmoving. Melanie had such a brilliant voice: one she'd kept secret. Why? She glided to the edge of the stage and stilled for a moment, catching his gaze then looked away as though embarrassed. There was a flicker of something in her eyes. Was that sadness? Her poignant solo words brought an unfamiliar prickling glaze to his eyes and his heart swelled to what felt like gigantic proportions. Even as the two women sang the remainder of the song in harmony, he couldn't drag his eyes from Melanie as she told the entire world what was in her heart. He felt humbled by her courage, especially knowing how hard it was for her to express her inner emotions. He felt sure his heart was about to burst, but why did she look so… mortified?

Feeling like he was in a time warp, he perched on the edge of his seat watching this beautiful woman open up her heart in the presence of over two thousand people. When the song drew to a close he couldn't move so stood in awed silence. Iain stood beside him. Together they stepped towards the edge of the stage, accompanied by a sudden outpouring of thunderous applause, cheering and heckling.

The volume increased as Iain leapt onto the stage and dropped to his knees, sliding the final couple of metres to end up at Jenny's feet where he yelled his proposal. The cheers increased. Guy was desperate to follow suit but Melanie looked terrified. He slowed then stopped right in front of her.

'Are you sure, my precious love?' he croaked out.

Ever so slow her face changed from fear to the tiniest of smiles then she grinned, nodded then flew off the stage. He opened his arms, caught her then lowered his mouth and held nothing back. No longer was there any reticent restraint that had caused him so much agony. Much to his delight, Melanie returned his passion measure for measure.

Somewhere in the background he was aware of the continual cheering and wolf-whistles. He grinned with their mouths still melded together. Then he lifted Melanie into his arms and carried her through the side exit. He wanted her alone. With mouths still attached he strode along passages until they reached her dressing room. Using the fingers of one hand, he turned the handle then shoved the door open with his hip. Easing her through the door, he then dropped her feet to the floor, cradled her face and covered it in searing kisses and tender caresses; emotions, he noted with delight, that were matched with equal intensity. When he finally came to his senses he was at a complete loss for words. Nothing he ever said would equal what Melanie had done for him tonight. Sinking down into the only chair in the room he eased Melanie into his lap.

She laid her head on his shoulder as her arms slid around his neck. Before either had a chance to say a word, there was a tentative knock at the door, followed immediately by heavy pounding.

Sighing, Melanie called out, 'Come in.'

'I need privacy,' Guy growled in her ear as the girls crowded in, with Jenny and Iain bringing up the rear, still wrapped up tight together. There was non-stop chatter and congratulations. Guy sighed. He didn't have a hope in hell of having a quiet few hours with Melanie.

'Limousines are waiting to take us to a celebration supper,' he called over the hubbub. 'Come as you are and leave your belongings in Melanie's dressing room. We'll pick them up on the way to the airport in the morning.'

The supper and celebrations continued into the early hours. Returning to the hotel, Guy crawled into bed, tired and happy except that he still hadn't had a chance for a single moments' privacy with Melanie.

A wake-up call dragged his tired eyelids apart. After a quick shower to wash away cobwebs, he flung clothes into a bag then joined the group assembled in the foyer waiting for the small bus hired every time the group needed to get from one place to the other. A call in at the concert hall to retrieve belongings from the previous night and they were on the homeward journey.

It wasn't until they were soaring through the sky that Guy had a chance to voice private thoughts. With Melanie's curled up hand in his he turned to her. 'I'm positive my heart stopped beating the entire time you sang your song last night, and it has been pounding ever since. That was very precious to me. I'll treasure the memory forever.' He leaned over. 'You never told me you were a singer as well. What other surprises do you have in store for me?'

'I don't often sing any more, it hurts too much.'

Startled by her words, he stared as Melanie clamped her mouth shut then slid her eyes closed. He edged closer and grasped her chin. 'What do you mean by hurts too much?'

Pausing, she opened her eyes but wouldn't look at him. 'I damaged my voice box. If I sing too much, it puts a strain on my vocal chords and it hurts. Last night was fine, but I couldn't have done much more.'

'I appreciate it even more. Thank you. And just when did you plan your little surprise?'

'Before the first concert. Jenny helped me sort out what my feelings for you were. I guess I was a bit screwed up in the emotions department. I had no idea what the turmoil inside me, about you, was all about.'

'Are you telling me you have known about this for three whole weeks and I've been in agony, aching for you the whole time? I've been so desperate to be with you, but kept away because I promised I wouldn't pressure you. The number of times I've picked up the phone to ring you and put it down again for the same reason. I've missed you so much.' Leaning back in his seat he sighed as he brushed the back of his hand against his forehead. 'All that suffering wasn't necessary?' He leant forwards again and hooked one finger under her chin to force her to look at him. 'You have been in my thoughts constantly, day and night. I love you so much, Melanie.'

'Was the surprise worth it?' She grinned as he swept his arm around her to keep her as close as the seats would allow.

'Oh, yes!' Melanie received and gave back, a very ardent kiss after which, she sank back in her seat. Then something she said finally registered.

'What happened to your voice box?' Leaning against the window, he studied her face. It paled. Her eyelids slid shut then she tugged her hand from his grip. Turning her head away she unlatched her seat belt then raced to the toilet cubicle. He followed, reaching out as she shoved on the door. His fingers slid from her arm as she jerked her way inside. Gut instinct gnawed at his innards while he waited.

As she stepped into the aisle after a lengthy visit, Guy snaked out his arm and grasped Melanie around the waist. 'You didn't damage your voice box, did you?' She shuddered. 'What did he do to you?' His grip tightened when she attempted to pull away. He drew her closer until they were standing chest to chest in the confined space. 'The only thing I can think of where a person's voice box might be damaged is through strangulation.'

When a mewling sound escaped Melanie's lips, Guy hooked his fingers under her chin to lift her face so he could see those eyes that were always hidden away when she was forced to face unpleasant things. 'He strangled you?' He felt positively ill as he slid one hand behind her head then eased her against his heaving chest. 'Sweet mercy, Melanie,' he murmured as he held her close, having a desperate need to protect her from all harm, past and future. So many emotions swept through him: anger, disgust, regret, sorrow and an enormous dose of helplessness.

'Please, Guy, I don't want to talk about bad things. Especially today.' The heartfelt plea rumbled against his chest.

Releasing her, Guy stood back with a hand on each of her shoulders as he searched her face, tortured at the bleak look of sadness. 'I'd give anything to take away your pain, sweetheart. But you are right. Today is for happy thoughts. Please forgive me for bringing up things you'd rather forget.' Ignoring the curious onlookers queuing for the toilet, his mouth swept down in a possessive kiss.

Lifting his head, he forced a smile. 'Let's not give the passengers any more floorshow. Come back to our seats.' Easing her in front of him, he trailed her down the aisle. Once settled back into their seats, he wondered how he could change the subject, which was almost impossible since ghastly scenes of possibilities were forcing their way into his grey matter.

'How would you like to take the tour back to Greece?' he asked quietly, fighting to suppress his grin when Melanie twisted around and stared at him with her mouth agape.

'Are you serious?'

'Never more serious. You could launch your CD onto the European market and you know Greece well.' Pleasure engulfed him in seeing the changing expressions flit across her face while she thought of the idea.

'I would love to go back.' The smile faded. 'I could take Mum's ashes back as I promised.' Then she brightened again. 'If we did, could we include Stephan? He is a much better player than me and could help us organise the tour. Being so well known and admired in Greece, he would be a huge draw-card. You'll like him. He is a wonderful, wonderful person.'

'First, I doubt anyone could play much better then you. Second, I think I'm jealous of your Stephan and third, I can't see why not if you say he is as good as that. I've learned to trust your judgement.' He paused at Melanie's giggles. 'What's so funny?'

'You being jealous of Stephan. I'm so looking forward to the day you meet him.'

'Please explain.'

'Not on your life. I can't wait to see your face.'

He sent her another questioning glance when she let out another delicious giggle, a sound so rare but he was overjoyed with its increasing regularity. She said nothing in reply to his look, just sent him a serene smile as she settled back into her seat and closed her eyes.

It was late afternoon by the time he returned Melanie to her unit. While she turned her percolator on for a much-needed coffee, he unloaded her bags and carried them inside. Coffee made, she settled close to him as he draped his arm around her with a loud sigh of contentment. Things had changed for the better but he couldn't rid his mind of the day's revelation about her past. What other ghastly torture had she been through? What caused that scar?

He was reluctant to break the wonderful sense of peace but had no choice. The weight of dread settled in his innards.

'Melanie, you know the trial starts in a week.'

There was an immediate tensioning of her body. Damn but he hated doing this to her.

'Your lawyer needs to spend time with you so she can plan her strategy. The appointment is for Tuesday and will take most of the day. I'm sorry but it can't be put off any longer. Meg Nelson has done as much as she can with the other witnesses but needs you to give details about what happened in both your past and your mother's. Iain will pick you up and stay with you.'

'Can't you take me?' Her voice was stilted, telling him how much she hated the thought. She wasn't the only one.

'I can't be there because I have to testify about the attacks I witnessed. I'll pick you up afterwards and will only be a phone call away if you need me. Without your statements your father could be set free or serve only a minimum time and I certainly don't want him roaming around again and I don't think you do either.' He kept his fingers caressing the soft skin on the inside of her arm while he raced through his spiel, not daring to pause. From the little Iain had been able to tell him and what he now suspected, Melanie was going to find the whole ordeal beyond arduous.

'I want to come into work tomorrow,' she whispered.

Of all the things she could have said, this was the one he expected least. 'You've been working hard for the past three weeks, you need a rest.'

'I need to keep busy,' she growled. 'Please, Guy? I don't want to be by myself all day. If I'm not busy, all those bad memories will be running through my head and I don't think I can handle it.'

'What about tonight? Are you going to be all right by yourself?' He very much doubted it and would prefer take her back to his house.

'I'll be fine. I'm so tired I should sleep like a bear in hibernation. I'll think of you,' she added with a cheeky grin that looked forced, pulling herself up to plant a kiss on his cheek.

Thrilled at the way she was far less inhibited, he moved his mouth to capture hers, deepening the kiss. Coming up for air, he paused for a moment, wondering if the time was right. Yes, she needed something very positive in her life.

'Well, my love, I'll give you something you can really think about if you do happen to wake. Think about whether or not you are going to put me out of my misery and marry me.' He was stunned when Melanie broke out into laughter.

'Oh, I don't have to think about that, I already know, I was just waiting for you to ask me.'

'And the answer?'

'Of course, I thought you would have known from my song. I couldn't have done a very good job if you didn't get the message but the rest of the audience certainly did.'

'Melanie!' He hoisted her out of the seat, plonked her onto his lap and kissed her. It was a while before he re-surfaced, trying to grasp the shreds of sanity together and gain some coherent thought. There was one thing he was certain of - he couldn't risk destroying the fragile trust Melanie was developing towards men and him in particular. To take things further would be a mistake. With a great deal of regret and mental effort, he lifted Melanie from his lap, slid her onto the cushion beside him then dragged his body up, away from temptation.

He stumbled on legs that felt unsteady as he crossed the room. 'I'm leaving now so you can get the sleep you need. Ring me if you need me, even if it is only to talk. I'll see you in the morning.' He almost ran out of the unit.

Chapter Twenty-Eight

He was pacing again. Damn but this waiting was getting to him. Why hadn't Iain rung? Guy paused at the coffee machine and poured black liquid into a mug. Then to ensure he ceased pacing he yanked out his office chair and plonked down, settling the mug next to two other half-full mugs. He frowned then snorted. He might as well have gone with Melanie and Iain to the lawyer's office for all the work he'd accomplished. He scanned the desk. The mail was still unopened and the computer screen blinked back the same screen saver it had been blinking since he'd arrived seven hours ago.

He made a grab for the phone at the first ring, sending one cup of coffee tumbling in his haste. 'Damn it,' he mumbled then barked, 'Harris,' into the receiver as he righted the mug and lifted dripping envelopes away from the spreading black puddle.

'It might be a good idea if you were here before this ghastly interview is over.' Guy searched for somewhere to put the letters then dropped them onto the floor.

'How's it going?' he asked.

'Rough – very rough. Melanie's doing it tough. God, that man is an animal!'

A hiss escaped as he sucked in a breath. 'I want to know it all! Hell, Iain, how am I going to help Melanie get through this if I don't have a clue what I'm up against?'

'Give her all your love and you know I can't reveal details until they are heard in court. You are a witness. Can you be here in half an hour?'

'Hell, man, I'm leaving now. God, I hate this.'

'You and me both, little brother,' Iain muttered before the line went dead.

Guy stared at the receiver. Was that all? How could Iain leave it at that? Was Melanie all right? What wasn't Iain telling him? He slammed the receiver down as he shot from the chair then padded his trouser pockets to ensure the car keys were there as he bolted from the room.

Fearing he would find Melanie curled up in a ball tucked away in some dark corner, Guy arrived at the lawyer's office to find his brother hitting his fist against the outside wall. His heart began hammering when he noticed traces of moisture in Iain's eyes. 'What the devil is wrong?' asked Guy, his rising unease leaving him with a sensation of doom that began gnawing at his innards like rats chewing on something disgusting.

'Hell, Guy, I'm a hardened cop who has seen almost everything, but what that poor woman and her mother have been through beggar's belief. She's going to be in a really bad space when she comes out. Melanie is going to need you more tonight than ever before.'

'Tell me one thing. Was she strangled by her father?'

Iain stilled then slowly turned. 'How did you know?'

'Something Melanie let slip. How did she escape in time?'

'She almost didn't. She says she was unconscious when her mother intervened.'

With one hand covering his eyes to hide his pain, Guy paced the reception area, up then down before pausing in front of Iain. 'Why would any man do something like that to his wife and daughter? What sort of animal is he?'

'He's an entrenched alcoholic who can't hold his liquor or his temper, not that that excuses his disgusting behaviour.' Iain dragged his body upright, puffed out his chest and released a long sigh. Then he sucked in a slow, deep breath with his eyes closed before taking a step towards the door. 'Wait here. I have to go back in. I don't think we'll be much longer.' He caught Guy's eye. 'I can tell you one thing. I'm almost certain Melanie was never sexually abused.' Iain paused then forced his face into a trace of a composed smile before re-entering the office, leaving Guy standing there with his stomach churning. Thirty minutes of torment later the lawyer came out with a messy pile of papers grasped against her chest and obvious signs of distress on her white, drawn face. She indicated for Guy to go in and stay as long as he wanted. He'd never felt so terrified as he stepped into the office.

Melanie was slumped across the arm of her chair leaning against Iain's shoulder. Iain had both arms stretched around her upper body in a tight embrace. It was quiet, way too quiet.

With his heart feeling as though it was being ripped apart Guy called softly, 'Melanie!'

She lifted her tear streaked face then scrambled from Iain's hold, leaping across the short distance then plastered her body against his chest as though she wanted to melt into his skin. Her hands gripped tight behind his neck, her feet not touching the ground. A torrent of tears escaped.

Iain left to give them privacy, closing the door behind him.

Guy held Melanie tight before reaching behind her knees and lifting her legs then sinking into the nearest chair. They sat unmoving for what seemed like an eternity, while Melanie released a lifetime of agony through her tears. When he felt her relax and her sobs ease he drew out a clean handkerchief and wiped the moisture from her face with utmost gentleness. 'Let's get out of here, sweetheart. I'm taking you home.'

Assisting her to walk by latching her to his side, Guy couldn't think of what he could possibly say or do to lessen her distress. Iain was sitting in a chair in the reception area with his head in his hands. The moment he saw them, Iain stood and led the way, opening doors as he went.

After settling Melanie into the passenger seat, Guy moved around to the driver's side. 'I'm taking Melanie to my place. I'll ring you.'

With Melanie staring hollow-eyed into space, Guy's tension didn't ease one iota as he drove. Once home, she didn't resist as he led her to the guest bedroom and laid her on the bed and removed her shoes. It was as though she were in a catatonic state. With no idea how to handle such emotional trauma, he removed his jacket and shoes, sank to the floor beside her and caressed her back while murmuring quiet, comforting words as one would to a young, frightened child. It seemed to take forever before he felt her relax. Hoping she was asleep he lifted his hand and held it just a few centimetres from her back while he leant closer to see if her eyes opened or her breathing changed. At last. She was asleep but he figured it was through sheer emotional exhaustion.

Unsure whether or not to leave her alone, he had a quick shower and change of clothes, his mind in turmoil. One thing he was sure about – Melanie shouldn't be alone during the night. He rang his brother. 'I'm going to keep Melanie here overnight. Can you sit with her while I collect clothes and toiletries from her unit? She's asleep at the moment but I'd hate her to be alone if she wakes.'

'Sure, I'll be there in fifteen. Has she said anything?'

'Not a word and that worries me. It's as though I'm not even here. How can I explain this?' He rubbed a hand through his hair as he thought. 'It's like she's spaced out. What happened, Iain, and don't beat around the bush?'

'I can't give you any details but her life has been as bad as you could ever imagine – probably worse if I were being honest. Melanie and her mother have been through sheer hell. From what I understand about this type of trauma, the mind's natural defense is to retreat into an emotional fog that numbs the senses. That's probably the space she's in right now. Let her sleep. I'll be there shortly.' Then Iain hung up.

Lord, he hated the way Iain wouldn't give more details. To give him something to do Guy searched the fridge to see what he could make for dinner, taking out bits and pieces and placing them in groups on the bench to see what would go with what. Then he began peeling and chopping vegetables and had just dropped them into a pan of cold water when Iain arrived.

He wasted no time at Melanie's unit where he packed as many items as he thought she would need. Once home, he checked Melanie to find she was still asleep. Back in the lounge he was determined to force more information from Iain.

'What happened today?'

Iain smiled and held his arms up in submission. 'Meg managed to get Melanie to disclose things I feel she's kept locked up inside all her life. It was tough but maybe it will start the healing process now that she's managed to admit horrific things. That girl has a lot of fighting spirit. Many people wouldn't have come through the way Melanie has, indicating she has a very strong mental constitution. You know I can't give you details but take real good care of her. Be gentle when you touch her as she still has a fair bit of ongoing physical pain. I'm going home to have a stiff drink – no, make that at least two. Today was one of the most harrowing days I've ever experienced.' Iain farewelled his brother then left, leaving Guy none the wiser but just as afraid.

After ensuring Melanie was still asleep he set on some quiet background music then continued preparing a casserole. He had it simmering in the oven when he felt he wasn't alone. Lifting his eyes, he spotted Melanie standing in the doorway watching him. She looked too pale, too damn fragile, causing him to hesitate, not knowing how she was going to react or what in hell's name he was supposed to do.

'Melanie?' he questioned quietly as he took a couple of tentative steps towards her then paused.

'I'm fine, Guy. I just need you to hold me,' she whispered.

Swinging his arm around her shoulders, he led her to the sofa where he settled at one end while she stretched out with her head in his lap peering up at him.

'Do you want to talk, sweetheart?' He paused, giving her a chance to start but then changed the topic. 'How about getting married in Greece while we're on tour?'

A weak smile escaped. 'I'd love to, especially since I have no family here and my only friends are the girls. I have my grandmother and a few other relatives in Greece plus Mr Panegyres and Stephan. I would like them to be at our wedding. Since the girls will be in Greece in any case there will only be a couple of people needing to fly to join us. I just have to convince the man I love to agree.' She eyed him with a beseeching stare but her colour had improved and the vacant expression gone. Thank goodness.

'I don't think he will take much convincing but how do you propose we plan a wedding in another country, from here?'

'I have a few people I could ask to help. What about your Mum? Will she come to Greece?'

He grinned. 'It wouldn't matter where we married, she'd be there. I rang her to let her know. She's despaired of either of her boys ever finding the right woman so she was shocked when she heard that we both have. You'll get on well with her.'

'Iain told me you are very much like her and I think I get on pretty well with you. Will you come to my wedding?'

'That's a certainty.' Guy grinned at his bride-to-be, bent and pecked her on the mouth. 'Do you want a traditional Greek wedding?'

'No. I'd prefer something smaller and more intimate. I'm sure we can organise it from here, I know of a few places that would be rather special.'

Guy smiled at her ramblings, sending a silent thanks to the heavens for the change in her demeanour but he wondered if her rapid chatter was a deliberate attempt to shove away unpleasant thoughts. 'Come here, my beautiful fiancée. I think my lips have forgotten what yours taste like and they need a gentle reminder.'

Melanie wriggled around then knelt on the lounge, snaking her arms around his neck. He sighed, delighted at her actions then he explored and found out again exactly how soft and warm her lips were. Lifting his head he suggested she stay the night.

'I can't. I don't have any clothes.'

Without saying a word, Guy pointed to the bag he'd taken the liberty to collect. He could tell she was going to argue so he forestalled her. 'I'm keeping an eye on you tonight, whether it is here or at your place. You choose.'

'And if I choose my place?'

'That's fine by me but since you have only one bed there, I would see it as you inviting me to share it.' He tugged her close as he lowered his head, planting soft kisses down the side of her neck, lingering while he gently nibbled on her ear lobe. Her barely audible moan told him exactly where to pause and explore with the tip of his tongue. Feeling her quiver he moved his mouth to hers while his fingers caressed her back. He smiled against her mouth when he heard her gasp, his thoughts centred on how he was going to thoroughly enjoy awakening his chaste little musician when the time was right. Deliberately releasing her he leant back, watching her face while she tried to regain her composure.

'And if I stay here?' came out soft and husky.

'Then I regard you as a guest in my home, as you were before. I promised you then that I would never betray your trust or take advantage of you. My promise still holds. The choice is yours.'

He left her to think while he checked the casserole and willed his libido to settle. He knew damn well she would be staying since he hadn't really given her any option. Instinct told him she wasn't yet ready for a more intimate side to their relationship especially if, as he strongly suspected, she was still untouched. He heard her bedroom door close then the shower start.

After a tensely quiet meal, Melanie offered to wash the dishes while Guy undertook a gentle workout. Only seconds after he heard the silence from the region of the kitchen, he noticed Melanie settle on the top step of the gym. Appearing to be deep in thought she sat with her arms around her drawn up knees, her hair fanning around her hunched body like a glistening cloak. She was so caught up in her thoughts that she didn't notice him moving closer then standing in front of her.

'A penny for your thoughts.' He smiled when she jerked her head up and blushed hotly. Wondering what brought on her embarrassed pinkness he said, 'I'm going for a swim before work. Would you like to join me?'

Melanie shivered, her face changing abruptly to one of fear. Guy moved closer, drew her to her feet then mounted the steps with her tucked close. 'Sweetheart, I haven't been back to that beach and have no desire to ever go there again. It has too many bad memories for me as well, so I've taken to swimming in the river. It's a beautiful spot and you could stay in the car if you felt safer. There's a little café, which is open early. You could even sit in there. I'd enjoy your company.'

Melanie was dressed, ready and waiting when Guy exited his room next morning. He smiled as he draped his arm around her shoulder, more than happy with the way she was now far less inhibited with him and best of all - she didn't jerk at his touch. Progress.

Chapter Twenty-Nine

Guessing it was to keep her mind away from unpleasant thoughts, Guy wasn't surprised at the way Melanie kept busy at work, continually asking for more tasks. In the end he set her a special task. 'Make contact with Greece and put some hours into making sure the concert tour is organised, then see what you can come up with regarding a wedding venue and setting a date.'

For the rest of the day he didn't see much of her. Glancing in every time he happened to pass her office, she was either working on her computer or chatting on the phone, mostly in Greek, so he had no idea what she was saying or to whom, but he sure enjoyed seeing the sappy smile on her face.

Melanie spent only one night at his place and with no rehearsals for a couple of weeks, he saw very little of her after work hours until Saturday when they were going on a date. This time he drove up into the hills to a restaurant where they had a magnificent view through floor to ceiling windows over the glittering lights of the city while they enjoyed the wonderful ambience of the restaurant set in a wild-life park.

'Are you going to let me know how your planning went?' Guy asked as he grasped one hand.

'The concerts are booked. Stephan has made the arrangements. I emailed him a copy of the programme and advert we used here and details of each girl. He's going to work out harmonies from the CD I sent him. I also sent him a recording of our last show, so he will also work on those other pieces.

'He sends you his congratulations and is looking forward to meeting you. He wants to make sure he approves of you as suitable husband material for me.' Her glance was coy but cheeky. 'Virtually all we have to do is turn up. I have accommodation and transport booked. We're touring for three weeks but they will be full weeks with only two days rest each week and quite a bit of inter-island travel. Flights are booked and I will confirm them as soon as I have a meeting with the girls and run everything by them. Is there anything I've forgotten?'

Guy sat in awe. 'I thought there was to be a wedding somewhere in all that,' he said. 'Or is that to be on one of the few days rest?'

Melanie smiled a very sweet smile. She'd been up to something.

'I've found the perfect venue for our wedding but it is going to be a surprise for you.'

Her pointed jab into his ribs told him not to ask questions.

'I can promise you the day will be magical. The date is the day after our final concert. Nobody, but me, and of course, the owner of the place will know the venue. Our guests, including you, are going to be picked up from their hotels and driven to the venue where I will be waiting for my golden Adonis.' Melanie glanced at Guy. 'The reception will be catered for and I have someone special organising it for me.'

'You have been busy. Is there any room for any kind of a honeymoon in your plans, Miss Super Efficiency?'

As Melanie lowered her eyes, he didn't miss the rising redness of her cheeks. 'I think that might be your department,' she whispered.

He couldn't help smiling at her innocent blush. 'Do I get any idea where we are getting married so I can have a starting point?' He placed his long fingers under her chin, lifting her face. Embarrassed didn't begin to describe how she looked.

'I'll give you the city, but not the exact location. Start in Athens, well more like the coast outside the city.'

He noted her quietness but wasn't about to let her off the hook. 'Oh, my beautiful darling, I can recall a few romantic spots where I might like to finish off what I started the other night. But make sure you don't tire yourself out too much on the tour, because you certainly won't be getting much sleep in the days,' he leant forwards, 'or nights, after. I can promise you that and as you know, I am a man of my word.'

Chapter Thirty

After a day and a half of giving his own testimony and listening to various witnesses, Guy leant against the rear wall of the empty courtroom with his eyes closed, trying to make sense of grisly details. He sucked in a breath and swallowed but it didn't dispel swirling nausea. He had about fifteen minutes to pull himself into some semblance of a supporting fiancé and not a wretched mess of a human being. What he'd learnt so far sickened him. This morning's session had been the worst. A Senior Medical Registrar detailed Melanie's injuries. There were so many of them - far too many. And they hadn't outlined the cause of those injuries.

Kneading long fingers against the taut muscles at the back of his neck to ease the pounding tension, his memory lingered on two things. Melanie is in constant pain and she had been a professional opera singer in Greece. But why had she never said anything?

Glancing at his watch he straightened and went in search of the men's room. After the recess, it was Melanie's turn and he needed to bring it together for her. He sent up a silent prayer of thanks to his brother who had offered to keep Melanie company in the witness lounge so that Guy could sit in on the hearing.

Peeking in the mirror above the washbasin he realised he needed to do something drastic to rid his face of the devastation he was feeling. Melanie would be able to read him like a book. He dunked his entire head under a stream of cold water then dabbed his face dry with paper towels before finger-combing his hair back. Staring into the mirror, he pulled various faces until he felt the stiff smile he'd forced his lips into was somewhat passable.

***

Terrified was the only word she could think of as to how she was feeling about having to testify. If the bastard wasn't sentenced to a long term of jail, he would find her and his reign of terror would begin again.

He would kill her. But it wouldn't be a quick bullet to the head. Oh, no. He would make sure she suffered as much pain and torture as he could manage. She just wished she understood why he hated her so much. Why was he so cruel? It had been the alcohol to start with all those years ago but now? It had to be something else that drove him. He'd already carried out one threat. He'd killed her mother because she dared to leave. Melanie had always believed it was an idle threat. Now she knew better. And she was next.

Would she be strong enough? She snorted in doubt. How she wished the length of prison term didn't depend on her testimony and the way she presented it. And when she had answered all the questions and revealed all the details of her sad, sorry life. What then? Guy was going to hightail it out of her life. There was nothing in her past she was proud of and certainly nothing any man she was with could be proud of. With these thoughts niggling she made her way towards the closed door with Iain's arm slung around her shoulders, gently nudging her along. The nudges were needed for if he wasn't there she'd turn the other way and head straight outside and keep on walking.

'Melanie.' At the quiet word she paused and glanced up. Guy stood a few metres away with his arms open.

'Guy!' Desperate to feel the security of his arms one last time she ran the few steps and flung herself at his chest.

'My beautiful love, I needed to tell you how very much I love you but I don't think they have invented the word to explain how I feel.' His mouth swept down in a searing, long kiss as he held her tight. All she wanted to say was - please don't let me go. Just take me away so I don't have to endure this. Every cell in her body felt as though it were made of lead at the thought of entering that room she could see was just a metre away as she peeked over his shoulder.

'Ahem, you two, we need to go.' A nudge on her shoulder as Iain spoke and Guy pulled away.

He smiled down at her. 'Keep remembering how much I love you and look at me if you need support. Feel my energy because it will be pouring across the room to you.'

'I don't want to do this.'

Guy framed her face with his hands. 'You want your father to pay for what he did to your mother? You want him locked away?'

'Yes,' she whispered.

Another quick kiss brushed across her tense mouth. 'This is the only way that's going to happen. Don't think about anything else except, *you are going to jail you bastard and I'm going to put you there.*'

Iain grabbed his shoulder and dragged Guy away, leaving Melanie with the court usher and feeling suddenly bereft. A rumble of voices drifted out for the few seconds the door was ajar. Then there was silence when a deep gruff voice from inside said, 'Will you all stand?' Her heart squeezed tight along with every muscle in the region of her stomach. Then her pulse began to thunder when her name was called and the usher pushed the door open.

For a moment her feet wouldn't move. Meg Edwards had shown her how to walk in, pointing out where the bastard would be seated so she could keep her eyes averted from him. She also knew where Iain and Guy would be. If at any time she felt she couldn't continue, she was to let Meg know so they could call for a recess. Well they hadn't even started and she was itching to tell Meg she couldn't continue.

'Miss Jones!' The usher's voice sounded impatient.

Melanie straightened her spine and willed her right foot to move.

One step.

The left foot followed suit. She had to force her muscles to keep going.

Right foot, left foot, keep going.

The few scant metres felt interminable and now she knew what it felt like to walk to the gallows. Wriggling back in her seat, she sucked in a long slow breath then lifted her eyes towards Guy. She noticed the slight turning up at the corners of his mouth as he nodded his head ever so slightly then mouthed the words *I love you.* For the very briefest of moments she felt as if there were only the two of them present as she felt a definite surge of energy reach her, just as he'd promised. But after all this, he was going to be disgusted with her and walk away. Of that she was sure.

She swung her eyes towards the jury who were seated across the other side of the room. After sweeping the length of the jury box, she dragged her eyes away from the end before they reached the small enclosure where she knew the bastard would be. She didn't have to look at him to know he was staring at her with hatred: she could feel that hatred boring into her. A shiver ran from her toes to the top of her head. Her old terror enveloped her and she shuddered again.

Meg Edwards' clear voice broke the electric atmosphere. Melanie swung her eyes to the petite middle-aged woman who began leading through what she knew was going to be several hours of re-lived torture. The first question was about her mother's abuse. This she could handle.

Unable to recall how a lot of the earliest incidents had come about, Melanie pointed out she had been too young, but as they worked their way through the years, her memories became more vivid, her answers more explicit and more chillingly graphic. Even she shuddered at some of the words that seemed to pour from her mouth. Considering the awfulness of the abuse, Melanie felt she handled the testimony well. On several occasions she had to hide her face in her hands to seek composure when she felt overwhelmed. Each time Meg gave her time to calm. Good use was made of the large box of tissues on the narrow wooden bench in front of her whenever she lost control of dreaded tears. A plastic lined refuse bin sat hidden from view to one side of her feet and it was filling rapidly.

On top of the shelf and to one side, a plastic lidded jug stood next to a glass tumbler. She took regular sips of water, mostly for something to do when she found it too difficult to voice an answer. Sipping and swallowing gave her a few precious seconds to grasp composure. Not once did she look in the bastard's direction. Seeing his face would have snapped her tenuous control.

On the odd occasion she sought out Guy, and every single time he gave her a brief nod and direct glance.

'Tell me about your Mother's abuse after you returned from Greece.'

At Meg's quiet question, ghastly memories tore through Melanie's mind causing the dreaded tears to surge in a deluge. She fought for control but the tears just kept flooding and falling. Grabbing a handful of tissues she held them against her eyes, pressing hard in an effort to dam the torrent. It didn't work.

'I can't,' she managed to stammer out then heard Meg asking for a break.

Somewhere in the background she heard the judge dismissing court for the day but she had to be nudged by Meg to stand while the judge left. She turned towards Guy and saw through a bleary haze that he almost tripped in his haste to reach her. His comedic actions in regaining his balance caused a smile to creep along her face as she stepped from the box into his arms.

'Sweetheart,' he murmured in her ear as he slid one arm around her waist and assisted her to the privacy of a separate anteroom across the passage from the courtroom. He sank into a chair then drew her down and she settled into his lap. One hand cradled her head against his shoulder. She snuggled into the warmth of his body, breathing in the familiar, safe scent of him. A sense of security swept through her and she just let go, soaking his shirt while he whispered soothing words she didn't absorb but the quiet rumble of his voice eased her raging turmoil. Using a handkerchief from his pocket, Guy mopped up her sodden face then gave her a sweet kiss. Not one word was said about the day's proceedings for which she was more than thankful.

When she heard a knock at the door, Melanie raised her head. She could only just make out Iain through watery eyes and gave him a weak smile.

'You were great today, Melanie. Meg sends her thanks. She'll catch up with you for a chat before court tomorrow.' Iain almost galloped over to give her a brotherly hug as she eased her cramped body from Guy's lap. Deep down she knew both men were forcing the niceties but it sure helped.

They left the premises, a brother each side of her. Without them physically holding her up, she felt sure her legs wouldn't have the strength to support her body, she felt so drained and weak. Feeling disconnected from reality she wasn't aware of passing scenery until the car stopped. They were at Iain's apartment where Jenny stood waiting at the open door. Jenny gave Melanie a hug as she walked with her into the bathroom to freshen up. Apparently they were staying for dinner.

'Mel, I'm here if you want to talk, but if you don't want to that's fine,' Jenny whispered as she put her arm around Melanie and gave her a second friendly squeeze. 'You look worn out, are you all right?'

A sigh slid from her lips. 'Yes, but it was pretty hard going over all the things that happened to Mum. I'd much rather forget them. I'm glad the men were there; I don't think I would have coped without them but it's going to be harder tomorrow. I don't have a lot of choice. I hope I can be strong enough but I doubt it since I fell apart today.'

'You're a tough cookie, Mel. You'll make it. Come on, come and help me in the kitchen. It'll give you something to do. You can tell me all about Greece and what I've got to look forward to.' Jenny's arm was latched around Melanie's waist as they walked out together.

She could feel the two men watching as they entered the kitchen. 'I'm okay,' she muttered. As okay as I'll ever be, she added in her thoughts. A crystal bowl, a pile of salad vegetables, chopping board and knife appeared on the bench before her face. Grateful she had something to do she set about putting a salad together. She listened intently as Iain led the stilted conversation by outlining the plans he and Jenny had made for their own upcoming nuptials on the Saturday before Christmas, the first day of the school holidays for Jenny.

She heard Guy tossing in some teasing comments to the pair in an effort to keep the conversation light and by the end of the meal Melanie felt more human and joined in the laughter. She was delighted when Jenny asked her to play the panpipes while signing the register and this led to planning special rehearsals without the men. There was quite a bit of overactive protest from the two men about this, but both women insisted some parts of the wedding had to be a surprise for the men. Melanie didn't miss the look from Guy who seemed to be questioning, *only some parts?*

After the meal, Guy drove Melanie to her unit and followed her inside. 'Go pack enough clothes to last until the end of the trial. You're staying with me.' When she opened her mouth to argue, he placed one finger on her lips before leading her to her bedroom, opened the door and pointed to her bed. 'You stay here, then so do I.'

She understood implicitly. Either he stayed and shared her bed, or she stayed with him. Boy, did she want to stay. Instead she shooed him into the sitting room while she packed. Deep down, she was relieved he had insisted because she knew she wasn't going to sleep well over the next few nights. At the same time she wished he hadn't made her that promise. She felt so ready to turn their relationship into a physical one. Even though she was inexperienced, she didn't feel afraid of taking that step with Guy. She wondered if she dared suggest they share a bed. Maybe not yet. Maybe it would be better to wait until the trial was over. Then he would leave her for sure. It would break her heart but then not having slept with him, she wouldn't miss him so much for she wouldn't really know what she was missing. She glanced around the room to see if there was anything she'd forgotten.

Before zipping her bag, she packed her instrument. She hadn't played since the tour, but tonight she had a deep urge to lose herself in music. It was when she played that she was able to leave the harsh world of reality and be transported to a world of beauty and harmony. Tonight she needed it more than ever.

Once at Guy's home, they sat over a hot drink chatting. 'I was wondering how come my brother knows all the details of his wedding except for the music soiree you girls are planning and I get the whole shebang kept secret from me. Would you mind explaining the difference, sweetheart?'

'I'm not marrying your brother, I'm marrying you,' she replied trying to keep her voice light but inside her thoughts were different. Because there won't be a wedding, her subconscious was telling her. But she needed to keep up the pretence for now.

'I'm mighty pleased about that,' Guy murmured before leaning over and planting a warm peck on the mouth. 'But I still think it's unfair.'

'You give me the details of the honeymoon and I'll swap you fact for fact,' she said, trying to keep a serious face.

'Ah, well, we're having a honeymoon.'

'We're having a wedding.'

'We'll be gone for two weeks.'

She laughed. 'I'm only asking for one day of your time. That gives me about thirteen facts I can keep from you.'

'You're cheating, Melanie.' Guy's protest was in mock seriousness, a grin accompanying his stern words.

'I promise you will enjoy every minute of our special day but there is one thing we need to discuss, and that is the words we want in the actual ceremony and I guess I have to tell you one more thing, the ceremony is not in a church.'

'So I do get to have some say, thank you. As to the church thing, that suits me fine but we have to keep in the bit where I get to kiss the bride. That's mandatory. And just so I get that bit right,' his face hovered close, 'I need some practice.' He kissed her. 'Lots of practice.' Body to body he practised some more until he drew back and sucked in a long breath. 'I need to get out of here. I don't suppose you have any idea what you do to me?' he mumbled as he walked away.

'About the same as you do to me,' Melanie called after him as he made a hasty retreat downstairs to the gym. She grinned as he paused in the doorway. 'You're a minx, sweetheart. I need to work off my frustration. Go to bed.'

Melanie rushed to the shower to cool off, grinning as she went and wishing once again that he hadn't made his promise. She wanted him to make love to her. How she wished he wasn't so bent on keeping his promise. Her wedding day if there was even going to be one, couldn't arrive soon enough.

After a long shower, Melanie lay on her bed thinking about the wedding but thoughts of the earlier court proceedings kept interfering until all she could think of was what was going to happen the following day. Sleep wasn't going to happen so when she felt certain Guy was asleep she unzipped her panpipes, crept through the house then downstairs, pushing the door closed with her foot.

***

The music drifting from the gym was sad and mournful, creeping through his soul. Knowing Melanie would have trouble sleeping he'd left his door ajar so she could come to him if needed. But she hadn't. Instead she was creating the heebie-jeebies in his soul with such haunting tunes. He figured it was going to be a lot worse after Melanie related her own trauma. He still hadn't figured out what he could do the next night to try to keep her mind off the trial. He would have to play it by ear. Iain and Jenny would be available if needed. He only had to make a phone call.

Guy heard and was disturbed by the sudden lengthy silence and went looking for Melanie. She sat huddled on the ground with her arms wrapped around her folded legs, her chin on her knees. He settled next to her and tugged her close. Arms crept around his waist and clung like a limpet. They sat in silence until Melanie sighed then stood. She smiled.

'Thank you.'

'For what?'

'For being there.'

'Are you okay?'

'I am now. You gave me what I needed. Goodnight.' She picked up the panpipes and mounted the stairs.

Chapter Thirty-One

After a lengthy consultation with Meg, the day in court began where they had left off the previous afternoon. As she entered the room, Melanie sucked in a deep breath and huffed at the stray wisps of hair tickling her brow. You can do this, she thought. Keep strong. Make sure he rots in prison. And let it be a rat-infested hell-hole.

She sank into the leather chair full of determination. As she related the most harrowing parts of her mother's abuse there were a few lapses in her willpower when she sat in silence trying to gather her thoughts, along with a few quiet tears. She was glad the judge didn't have to call a recess during the session before lunch. The sooner she got it over then the sooner she could escape.

The moment they were outside the courthouse, Guy guided her to an eatery where she picked at her food in silence. She wasn't hungry and Guy's idle chatter washed over her head. He soon fell silent and grasped her hand. It was warm and welcome, especially when his thumb rubbed gentle circles around the inside of her palm. The soothing warmth felt good but inside it felt as though a huge vacuum had sucked out all her innards. Words defied her.

When they arrived back at the courts, Iain was waiting. He gave Melanie a brotherly hug before leading them into the courtroom where they left her with the clerk of the court while they resumed their seats. She appreciated the concern but words still eluded her. She felt as though she was in some mystical world where people communicated by thought processes.

Meg Edwards began in a quiet sombre voice. 'Melanie, the court has heard the medical details of your own injuries and we now need you to tell us how they happened.'

Shocked, Melanie glanced up from the spot on the table she was staring at and turned to peek at Guy. Nobody had told her he'd already heard details of her abuse. Not sure whether she was glad he already knew, she dragged her eyes back to her lawyer.

'Could you start by giving us the details of any injuries you received as a child?' asked Meg. 'We heard there were several healed fractures in your arms. Can you tell us about them?'

Unable to move, Melanie sat still, a tight muscle in her jaw flexed as it begged for release. She made several attempts to speak but her throat felt so thick it struggled to move. It took a monumental effort before any sound came out.

'I don't recall everything. I was too young. I don't think there were any before the age of five. I'm not sure. If there were, Mum never spoke to me about them. There were always hard back-handers to the side of my head, constant hard shoves and yanks. They were just a way of life. I only remember four really bad times.'

'Speak up please,' the judge called.

Breathing deeply, Melanie closed her eyes, paused then forced the words past what felt like a block concrete in her throat as she began reliving the horror of her life.

'The first I remember was when I was about six. I was late home because we had a practice for our Christmas concert after school. Yes it was at the end of the school year when I was six. When I arrived home, the bastard…' She'd forgotten Meg's advice to not call him that. 'Umm… my father was really drunk and very angry because I was late. Mum was still at work so she couldn't vouch for me. He wouldn't listen to my reasons for being late or that Mum knew where I was. She'd signed a permission slip but he didn't believe me. He kept screaming at me, calling me a liar… then laid into me with a piece of firewood… he often used a piece of wood.'

'Speak up please,' Meg urged.

'It hurt,' Melanie yelled so loud she jolted before lowering her voice. 'A lot. When he had finished belting me he locked me in the broom cupboard. I couldn't sit down. There wasn't enough room. I didn't dare cry aloud… but I can remember using my uniform to brush my tears away because my arm hurt so much. Mum wasn't allowed to let me out until the next morning. I heard her coming up to the cupboard, whispering and she attempted to open the door but he hit her and dragged her away. The teacher at school took me to the office because I kept complaining about the pain in my arm. The school nurse said she thought my arm was broken and they took me to the hospital.'

'You'll have to speak up so the jury can hear,' called the judge again.

Melanie hadn't realised her voice had dropped. 'Sorry,' she called louder as she stared into space. Seeing nothing but a haze in front of her, she shook her head and tried to focus her eyes, suddenly becoming aware of a hushed silence around her. Daring to peek around the room, she saw that all eyes were fixed firmly on her. Searing heat rose up her cheeks, increasing her mortification.

'And the second time you can recall?' Meg asked, bringing Melanie back to awareness.

'Was about a year later.' Melanie paused then sighed. Lifting her eyes she sent a quick glance over at Guy then dropped her eyes to the ground, staring at a dark spot on the carpet. She wondered what had caused the mark, knowing she was being ridiculous but thoughts about the mark were far better than answering the question. Keeping her eyes on the spot, she began describing the day. 'I dropped a glass on the floor and it broke.' The pause was long while she wondered what Guy was thinking. Was he recalling the incident at home? Will he think her an idiot for reacting so stupidly? Would he want anything to do with her after this was all over? After all who would want a crazy person that went ballistic over a broken glass?

'The p... my father had been drinking and he went absolutely berserk. He grabbed me by the arm and just hit me... and hit me... and hit me... he wouldn't stop. I don't remember him ever stopping. All I remember was his continual hitting with his clenched fist.'

Vivid images crowded into her brain. Remembered agonising pain coiled along her nervous system as she paused. She shuddered then continued relating her gruesome past. 'Mum found me unconscious on my bed when she arrived home from work. The... he wasn't around. She took me to the hospital. My arm was broken again but I had so many bruises it felt like every bone in my body was broken.'

She fought to control the silent tears that began coursing down her cheeks and plopping onto the wooden bench but made no effort to wipe them away. Seeing a handful of tissues from the box on the bench thrust in front of her face, she grabbed them and swiped at her face. After blowing her nose she peered at the clerk through bleary eyes before scrunching the tissues up into a tight ball and dropping them into the bin. 'Thank you,' she murmured before seeking out the dark spot on the carpet.

As though in a dream, she heard the disconnected voice of Meg ask the next question.

'Didn't the authorities do anything?'

'The police came. He lied. They believed him. They always believed him.'

When a sense of deep bitterness rose she glanced up at Meg. 'I was seven years old. Do you honestly think I would tell the truth so I could get beaten again the moment the police walked out the door? Because that is what would have happened.'

An eerie silence fell over the room causing Melanie to wonder if these people really believed her. Who could blame them if they didn't, but it was true. The authorities always took the bastard's word as gospel.

'Can you remember the third time?' Meg's voice was firm but quiet, breaking Melanie from her inner thoughts.

Melanie dropped her eyes back down to examine the spot in intimate detail. *I wonder if it is blood.* 'Yes. I'll never forget it. I still have nightmares about it.' She inwardly grinned, wondering if it were possible to be two people at once. Here she was answering questions about one thing whilst thinking of something entirely different. Did she have a split personality?

'Please tell us about that day.' The question was louder; the tone pleading. Meg must know she wasn't concentrating.

'I think I was about ten. Mum and I were singing together and dancing around the room. She had a beautiful voice, much better than mine. I loved listening to her.' She felt herself smile at the memory. Then another picture surged. What had happened next? Her smile vanished as a shimmy of unease slithered across her shoulders.

'My father came home drunk... he was so, so drunk... he yelled at us to shut up then he just laid into the both of us... he was so angry... just because we were singing. He grabbed me by the arm... dragged me to the back door... threw me down the concrete steps and left me there. I fell headfirst and landed with my arm caught on the edge of a step, under my body. It was my other arm this time. I wasn't allowed back inside all night. He bolted the doors from the inside and then bashed Mum up some more. I could hear her screaming and I think she must have fallen unconscious because it went suddenly quiet.' Out of breath she hissed in a long breath. Then she dragged in another but it didn't stop her feeling nauseous as ghastly pictures flickered in her mind like an old black and white movie. 'It went so quiet I thought she was...' Melanie glanced at Meg. 'Dead. All night I was locked outside and all night I thought she was dead. She didn't find me until the next morning.'

'Where did you sleep that night, Melanie?'

'I don't remember.' A tremor snaked down her spine. She'd been shivering. 'I recall being very cold. My arm ached so much that night and I knew it was broken.' Searching for guidance from the ceiling she squeezed two fingers against the bridge of her nose to prevent a severe leakage. 'I relive that night over and over again in my dreams… it is so vivid… the pain wakes me it is so real.'

Feeling suddenly cold and clinical she stilled, staring ahead at the same spot on the floor without even blinking. She didn't respond when asked if she was all right but after a long pause she heard from somewhere, far off, the next question but since she was only ten years old, standing at the bottom of those wooden steps, the voice wasn't talking to her.

'Melanie,' Meg called, 'were the police called?'

A hand touched her and she jolted, shook her head then focussed on Meg. 'Yes. The hospital called them, but they didn't come until about a week after I returned home.'

'What happened?'

'The… my father told them I fell down the stairs. When they asked me if that was true… I said yes.' The bitterness returned with a vengeance. She lifted her eyes and stared at Meg. 'I didn't have any choice. It was the truth and he was standing behind them glaring at me. If I'd said anything else he would have beaten me again after they had gone. And besides …'

There was a palpable pause which was only broken when Meg moved in front of Melanie to gain her attention by tapping her on the shoulder.

'Besides what, Melanie?'

Twisting her head, she stared at Guy then replied to a hushed audience who appeared to be straining their ears in order to not miss one word of this horror. Her horror. Why did they want to know?

'I was young and knew no better. At the time I honestly thought all men treated their wives and children the same. I believed all the girls at school and their mothers were bashed the same as I was. If I said anything to the police, they would just laugh at me because they were men. I never had any really close friends who I felt I could trust to tell them about my bruises. It wasn't until High School when I learned any different.'

A loud collective indrawn breath was followed by profound silence. Melanie figured it was because all those present didn't believe her. She felt like a fool for being so naïve.

'Tell us about the fourth time, Melanie.'

Startled at the tremor in Meg's voice, Melanie shot her gaze towards her lawyer and noticed Meg fighting for control. She looked angry and upset. Stunned and confused by Meg's obvious distress, Melanie forgot the question. 'Can you repeat the question please?'

'We want to hear about the fourth time,' Meg repeated.

It took every ounce of Melanie's mind to formulate an answer. How could they want her to recall all this horror? Her mind felt as though it was in a concrete mixer and she was in a surreal world. Concentrate, she told herself. Get it over with. Focus. She searched for the spot on the floor then whispered hoarsely. 'He hit me with an axe.'

The gasp was much louder as Melanie squeezed her eyes shut to prevent that ever threatening dam-burst. She gripped the edge of her chair until she felt the pain in her fingertips, forcing herself to concentrate on the pain instead of tears, determined to not make a further fool of herself.

'He said he was going to chop my arm off because I took an apple off the table without asking him. I didn't even know he was in the room when I took that apple. Mum said I could have one, but he wouldn't listen... said I had to ask him before I did anything.'

Even though tears began flowing she raced on without hesitation, desperate to get this ordeal over with.

'It was only an apple. He dragged me outside. My feet bounced down the back steps. Then he dragged me through the dirt to the woodpile.'

Sniffing then gulping in an attempt to regain a modicum of control, she paused as she saw vivid pictures of what had happened next. She felt Meg nudge her.

'Tell the court what happened.'

She tensed then gripped her fingers together. 'I don't think I can,' she croaked.

'Just try, Melanie,' Meg patted her on the hand.

Screwing her eyes shut, Melanie sucked in a breath then blurted, 'The axe was too blunt to cut my arm off but it snapped my bone and cut my flesh… a big flap of it here' Releasing the tight grip she had on her fingers she brushed her hand against her left arm just below her elbow. It was why she always wore long sleeves: to hide the ugly scar. 'It hurt… so much. Mum hit him over the head with a rock to stop him. She kept on hitting him until he dropped the axe and let me go. God, it was so awful and it hurt so much.'

Melanie felt utterly drained as she paused. 'Please stop? I can't…' she begged. With the painful memory causing the tears to well again, she dropped her head into her hands and sobbed great wracking sobs that echoed around the silent room. She didn't bother to try to gain control. She'd had enough and didn't have the strength to fight back a deluge.

The next thing she was aware of was Guy kneeling by her side, murmuring tender words into her ear. He was incredibly gentle as he eased her out of her chair and held her tight. 'My darling sweet Melanie, how could any person be so cruel to a child?' he whispered.

***

It took ages before Melanie ceased sobbing. By the vacant look on her face there would be no laughter or chats about weddings tonight. He would be lucky to get her to eat anything. Iain was waiting by the door, opening it as Guy assisted an unresponsive Melanie to his car. She leant against his body like a limp rag doll.

'What can I do?' Iain asked.

'Apart from giving that bastard some of his own medicine - I wish I knew. I'll take Melanie home and put her to bed. Can we call a halt to tomorrow if needed?'

'I'll have a chat with Meg to see what we can do. I'll call you later but I have to go in to work tonight. Jenny says to call if you need her, don't worry about the time.

Sending his brother a brief wave Guy drove Melanie home. She walked straight into her room, slamming the door behind her. Feeling such utter helplessness, Guy paced around outside until he heard the shower going. He forced himself to the kitchen to find some nourishing food although he doubted any of it would be eaten – he certainly had no appetite. The thought of swallowing anything made him feel bilious. He felt sickened by what Melanie had revealed.

When Melanie didn't come out, he began to worry. It was too quiet. He tapped against her door but heard no response. He hated invading her privacy but was concerned for her wellbeing so tentatively opened her door. Melanie sat cross-legged in the middle of the bed with a towel wrapped around her torso, her hair dripping onto the doona, hands clasped in her lap and vacant eyes staring into space. Her skin was pink as though she had scrubbed and scrubbed to rid it of the filth of the day. Dear God, why did she have to re-live such horror?

'Melanie?' When there wasn't even a movement in response, he strode across the carpet and perched on the edge of the bed. 'Melanie,' he repeated, 'Please talk to me?' Still she didn't move so he eased her up and carried her into the lounge, grabbing the spare blanket from the bottom of her bed as he went. Standing her up, he wrapped the blanket around her then settled her on the sofa. Returning to her room, he found another dry towel and her hairbrush then set about rubbing the water from her hair and then brushing it. Finding it too awkward on the sofa, he carried her to the kitchen bench, sat her on the stool and placed her meal in front of her while he stood behind, rubbing each strand of her sodden hair dry. It was the continuous, gentle brushing that seemed to pull her back to reality.

'Guy,' she whispered, 'I love you so much, please hold me?'

'Dear heaven, Melanie,' he cried out, crushing her against him, planting small kisses on top of her head, then moving down to her lips where his kiss was searching and deep. When he tasted the saltiness of silent tears flowing freely he knew she was back. He grabbed a tissue and dabbed at her tears, still raining kisses on her in between.

'Sweetheart, my heart is just about bursting for you right now. I love you more than life itself. You are so precious to me.'

Leading her back to the sofa he settled her in his lap with her cradled in his arms, sucking in his breath when she began running her hands down his arms then across his chest. He said nothing. The last thing he wanted was for Melanie to retreat back into a vacuum. If she needed to touch him to ease her tension, she could touch all she liked. It might kill him in the process when his hormones fired up but compared to what Melanie had been through, it was the least he could do.

'I never wanted you to know about my past, but I'm glad you are there for me. I couldn't do it without you. I feel your energy from across the room, pushing me to keep going. Guy, can we go out somewhere tonight? I need lots of people around me, normal people, talking and laughing about normal things. Somewhere noisy, where I can't think. I don't want to be able to think... or remember.'

Stunned by this about face, Guy understood her need. Who would want to dwell on such inhumanity? But for the life of him, he couldn't think where he could take her. The cinema would be too quiet, so would a meal out or a pleasant drive – as if it would be pleasant! Suggesting she dress in jeans and jumper while he showered, he set her on her feet. While showering, he racked his brain as to where they could go with lots of people talking and laughing. It was while he was rubbing his skin dry that an idea came to him, Wednesday night was pacing night at the trotting track just outside the city centre. He hadn't been there for years but there would be lots of noise, crowds of people and they could have fun. It could be exactly what Melanie needed. He prayed it would be as he emerged from his room carrying a couple of jackets.

'Have you ever been to the trots before?'

'No, never, is that where we're going?'

'Yes, but you'll need a warm jacket. You can borrow one of these. It'll be a bit on the large side, but will keep you warm.' He handed one over as he eyed her hair. She had tied it back in a ponytail, which fanned out in damp ringlets at the bottom, another hairstyle he'd never seen before but it looked cute. 'You're hair suits the outing. You must have been reading my mind. A pony tail.' He laughed out loud at his own inane joke hoping to drag a smile from Melanie but she just rolled her eyes. At least it was a reaction.

They had a lot of fun and were able to put the unpleasantness of the day aside whilst mingling amongst the crowd arm-in-arm to inspect the horses. They put on crazy small bets based on nothing more than horse names or what the horse looked like, and snacked on hamburgers and chips. They yelled as their horses rounded the track and were surprised but ecstatic each time one of them had a small win. Their winnings totalled a little more than their outlay, which maintained their high spirits until they almost danced back in the door late that evening.

'Guy, that was the best fun. Thank you so much.' Reaching up Melanie gave him a kiss, which deepened as he wrapped his arms around her and drew her close until the ringing of the phone broke the silence.

'Where the devil have you been?' asked a perplexed sounding Iain, 'I've been worried about you two. I've been trying to ring you all night.'

'Sorry. Melanie wanted to be amongst happy people tonight, so we went to the trots. I forgot about your call. Sorry if we kept you up but it was worth it. It was a great night. We had fun and most important, Melanie is still smiling.'

'I'm at work and will be up most of the night in any case. So you won't require the day off tomorrow? That's wonderful. I'm glad things are okay but remember tomorrow is going to be tougher still. Take care. I'll get there if I can.'

Chapter Thirty-Two

The way Meg Edwards broke into the day's questioning was unexpected. Melanie squirmed as she listened to Meg outlining the medical report on the first incident of abuse after Melanie had returned from Greece. Pain descended into her gut and stabbed. She didn't need to hear this, she'd lived it – and barely survived. So why should her dark secrets be made public? It was nobody else's business.

'Please explain to the court the exact details of what happened on this occasion.'

Wishing she had magical powers to transport her to some far off planet, Melanie glanced at Guy to see if he looked as disgusted as she felt. He was looking right at her, his face a mask. He caught her eye, nodded then held his hand to his heart before pointing her way. Her innards turned to warm mush at his silent message but it gave her the impetus she needed.

'I learnt to play the panpipes in Greece. Soon after my grandfather died I returned home with the intention of taking Mum back on a return flight. I had tickets for both of us. My father wasn't around the first day I was home. Probably passed out drunk somewhere.'

'Objection!' The opposing counsellor yelled. 'Supposition!'

'What does that mean?' she whispered to Meg.

'It means you are only guessing. Since you weren't with him, you don't know the fact.'

'Since he was nearly always drunk it's a pretty good guess.'

'But you can't state guesses as fact. Stick to what you know to be true. Now go on. Your father wasn't around that day.' Meg straightened and moved away from the private discussion.

When her voice cracked on her first attempt to answer, Melanie coughed to clear her throat. 'Early the next morning I pressured Mum into packing a bag so we could escape. I called a taxi to take us to the airport. But we weren't quick enough. As we came out the door he was standing between the taxi and us. The moment he saw us he sent the taxi away then went off his face. He stormed down the path yelling obscenities and threats. I managed to elude him and locked myself in my bedroom. Mum wasn't quick enough. He laid into her for daring to attempt to run away and for letting me come back.'

'Objection! Supposition!'

Melanie glared at the other lawyer. Was he ever going to let her finish? 'I'm not guessing,' she yelled back. 'I could hear every darn word he said. The entire neighbourhood could hear.'

'Calm down,' Meg urged with such a wry smile Melanie wondered if she really meant it.

'Fact,' Melanie emphasised, 'Mum didn't know I was returning and I wish now that I hadn't for Mum would still be alive. I feel so guilty. I heard every word he yelled and knew then how much he hated me, but I still don't know why.' She closed her eyes as she tried to come to some reason for the hatred.

'Go on,' urged Meg, breaking Melanie from her reverie.

Concentrate, she told herself, or this is going to take forever. 'He belted Mum unconscious then came for me. I had seen him angry, but never that angry. He broke down my door and dragged me to his bedroom and held my hand against the doorframe. Then... he... slammed the door on the fingers of my left hand using all the force he could muster. It wasn't just the slam. He pushed hard against the door with his body. My fingers were jammed in the crack. The pain was beyond imagination. Because I yelled out... he did it again... this time across my hand.' She drew in a shuddering breath then whimpered, 'He said it was to teach me a lesson.'

'Why didn't you fight him off? You were an adult. You're as tall as him?' Meg asked.

The unexpectedness of this question brought Melanie up short. Unbidden tears welled then began rolling from the corners of her eyes as she looked to Guy for help. He stared back, giving her a brief nod of his head. She didn't pull her eyes away, not wanting to answer. She felt his energy as he silently urged her on with a couple more discreet nods. Feeling stupid for allowing her tears to fall so readily, she swiped at her face, willed no more to fall then sniffed back any more moisture as she straightened her back, filled with a new determination.

'I tried to, but when he dragged me through the lounge… Oh, Lord… I could see… he had strung Mum up with a noose around her neck. One end of the rope was in his hand. She was unconscious… he jerked the rope a bit and the noose tightened. He said he would pull the rope tight if I fought him. That's when he slammed the door on my hand. He scarpered as soon as he hurt me the second time. He always did. He never waited around to see the results of his abuse. He never gave any assistance.'

'What happened then, Melanie?' Melanie dragged her eyes from Guy to Meg.

'It was difficult because of the injuries but I undid the rope and put Mum to bed. Then I bathed her cuts, put cold compresses on her bruises and tidied up the mess.'

'What about your hand, didn't it hurt?'

'It hurt like hell!' Melanie yelled then noticed a few people across the room jump in their seats at her sudden outburst. It was the first time she'd really vented her rage but it felt good. Then she had an incredible urge to laugh and had to bite the inside of her cheek to quell the ridiculous notion. Stupid question – did it hurt? 'What do you think? You try slamming your hand in the door and see how it feels.'

The heat of her anger began to cool while Meg perused her notes. The pause was so long Melanie began to wonder if there were going to be any more questions.

Meg glanced up. 'The medical report said that you went to hospital. How did you get there?'

'I walked. I had no choice. I had little money and no transport.'

'You say you had little money, but you had earned a considerable sum with your concerts in Europe, what happened to that?'

'What has this got to do with anything?' Melanie whispered behind her hand.

'Just answer the question, please?' Meg said loud enough for all to hear.

'Okay.' It wasn't okay. Her finances were private. 'I left most of it with my grandmother. After my grandfather died she had no one to support her. They live the traditional life so their house reverted back to his family and she had no security so I bought a house for her and left her enough to live on. She lives on the interest of a term deposit I set up. It's not a lot but she manages. I couldn't bring any money home. My father stole every cent I ever managed to save. I left a small amount in another bank account in Greece, which is still there and I still own the house. It was my nest egg to set Mum and me up in Greece. I came home to take Mum back to Greece but it never happened. One of us was always in hospital, too injured to fly.'

Daring to peek at Guy, she saw that he couldn't mask his surprise at her revelation. Iain leaned over and whispered something in Guy's ear. Guy nodded then smiled. What were they discussing? Were they laughing at her? At how naïve she was?

'Melanie, why did your mother stay with your father?' The question was a shock bringing her attention back.

'I remember her taking me away to hide several times. But we never had enough money to go far. He always found us and the beatings were far, far worse when he did. It was better to stay. We lived under constant threat. If Mum left, he would kill me and vice versa. We stayed to protect each other. We stayed because we were too afraid to go.'

'Tell me about your right hand Melanie.'

The moment her other hand was mentioned Melanie flung her hands up to her face and leant against the front of the witness box. She could still feel the agony of that day. It never left her. She knew she should answer, could feel the expectant hush but it was too hard. Words eluded her.

'Miss Jones, do you need a break?'

The compassionate question from the judge surprised her. She straightened and dropped her hands onto the bench, staring at the hand in question as it took on a mind of its own and flexed. 'No. I want to get this over and done with.'

'Melanie, how did you sustain those injuries to your right hand and when did it happen?' Meg repeated.

With her eyes closed and forcing her brain to concentrate, she drew in a couple of deep breaths, releasing the held air in a gush, seeking strength to continue. 'My left hand was in plaster for three months. After that incident, I moved my things into the spare bedroom because we couldn't afford to get the door fixed. I always locked the door to my room the moment I heard my father coming home. As well as turning the key, I put a chair under the doorknob so he couldn't get in. He was always drunk. Since returning from Greece I noticed that he drank more than ever and he never, ever came home sober. Once he passed out I could come out, and every morning I would leave home before he woke. You have no idea what it is like to be too scared to come out of your bedroom during the night to even go to the toilet.' A snort of derision escaped from her nostrils and she smiled. 'I even resorted to climbing out of my window during the night to pee under the bushes in the garden - anything to avoid being caught. It wasn't easy getting back in with my hand bandaged but I rolled a large rock into place to make it easier.'

Hearing a couple of sniggers, she twisted her head around to see who dared to find the situation funny. The grin on one of the jury members altered instantly at her glare.

'Go on,' urged Meg.

Still staring at the man, Melanie answered. 'Two days after my hand was finally free from the strapping, I was talking with Mum and we were laughing. He came home early but I didn't hear him over the noise we were making. God, how I wish I had heard him. Mum still had her leg in plaster and couldn't walk. She tried to warn me he was there but he caught me before I could escape into my room. He knocked me unconscious. I don't know why but I guess it was just because we were laughing.'

From the corner of her eye, Melanie saw a movement. Focussing on the lawyer who was half-way from his seat, she added loudly, 'I know - supposition.' A titter from the other side of the room preceded utter silence. In the ensuing hush during which the man reddened then plonked back into his seat, Melanie felt the blood drain from her face as remembered images flickered through her mind. She felt positively ill. 'When I came to, I was on the floor and he was sitting on my stomach with… with… with a pair of pliers in his hand.'

She shut her eyes as her innards constricted into a tight knot. It felt as though her lungs had forgotten how to move. The silence was downright eerie. Then she realised that it wasn't only her that couldn't move. Nobody moved. Everyone seemed to be holding his or her breath. The tension felt unbearable as she fought to forget the pain that still lived with her every day.

'Go on Melanie, what happened?'

She couldn't help it but all control disappeared and she started sobbing.

'He used the pliers on each of my fingers,' she stammered then gulped. 'He squeezed and twisted until they cracked. I passed out in agony after the first finger. Was he happy with that? Oh, no! He waited until I came around. Then he did the next one. It took what felt like forever to finish the job because I kept passing out. He kept waiting. Every time I came to… he started again.' She raced to get it out. There was a desperate urge to flee.

Feeling the agony of that day surge, Melanie dissolved. She had no control. The more she struggled for control, the louder her gasps. Through the blur of moisture she made out Meg turning from where she had been referring to her notes.

'Do you want a break or to go one?'

Swiping the moisture from her face with the sleeve of her plain white blouse, Melanie fought to pull herself together. Deep down, she knew she had to finish. She had to make sure the bastard went to prison for ever.

'I want to finish this now, because if I leave here, I'm not coming back.' Her voice rose, along with her anger. 'Mum tried to help me. She limped across the room on her plaster but Dad knocked her to the ground. There was a loud sharp crack as her head hit the floor. Then, when he had finished with me, he left. He always left. He is such a brutal bully when he does these things but such a coward afterwards. The very thought of us going to hospital where the authorities might become involved, he would vanish from our lives for a while, sometimes weeks at a time.'

Meg broke the intense ensuing silence. 'Go on, Melanie.'

Melanie shook her head trying to remind herself what her last words were. 'When I came around, Mum was still out cold. I had some coins hidden under a brick in the front garden. I had to crawl down to the phone box to call the emergency number. I don't remember anything else until I came around in the hospital. I was told that they found me unconscious in the gutter outside the phone box. I was given strong painkillers to deaden the pain. The doctor wanted to amputate some of my fingers but I wouldn't let him. It was six months before I could use my fingers again.'

'Melanie, do you still have pain?' Meg asked.

Not daring to look at Guy, knowing he would add things up, Melanie stared at the floor, seeking out the dark stain. A deep sense of shame smothered her. 'Twenty-four hours a day, seven days a week. It never goes away.'

'Can you describe the pain and how you handle it?' asked Meg.

'It's like having permanent toothache. I try to put it to the back of my mind and keep busy so I have other things to keep my mind occupied. I can cope most of the time. Sometimes it gets really bad and I have to resort to painkillers but I try to avoid them as I don't want to become dependent on drugs.'

Shame kept her head down. Guy would be thinking about the time she had asked for some pain relief. When the judge called a recess a deep sigh escaped. Now used to rising for the judge to leave, she pushed her seat back and stood before daring a glance at Guy. Disappointment washed over her. He was leaving. Dear God, he was leaving her so soon! He couldn't even wait until the end of the trial! Devastated, she dropped back into the seat, her innards feeling as they were going to implode.

An arm slid around her shoulders and squeezed. 'Guy will be back soon, nature calls. You're doing well, very well. How are you coping?'

Her chest heaved when her lungs remembered how to suck in air. Toilet. He was only going to the toilet. In an effort to hide the effect Guy's vanishing had had on her, Melanie frantically scratched around in her brain to recall what Iain had just said. Coping, how was she coping? She wasn't. She was slowly dying.

'Better than I thought I would, but I need to get it out and over and done with. I didn't ever want Guy to know. I'm so ashamed. How could he ever want to be with me now?' She couldn't look Iain in the eye.

'Are you serious? Melanie, none of this is your fault. You've done nothing wrong. You are one of the bravest people I have ever met. Most men couldn't have endured what you have. You don't honestly think Guy is going to think any less of you, do you? Get that out of your mind this instant. He loves you for the wonderful person you are.'

She prayed that was true but didn't believe it. At that moment Guy returned. He didn't look so good, his face pale and a decided shade of green.

'What's this, big brother? Holding my fiancée in your arms behind my back? You wait until I see Jenny.' He sounded as if he were deliberately trying to lighten the atmosphere. She didn't mind but was mighty curious as to what he had been thinking all morning. And why did he look so ill? She dared to snuggle close as his arms wove around her because in his arms was the only place she felt safe, but for how long would it continue?

'How are you, sweetheart? Do you want to keep going, or call it quits?'

She would like nothing better that to call it quits. 'I have to get this finished today. I can make it. Iain was right, it helps if you let yourself feel angry and I'm pretty angry at that bastard right now. I just hope I can last out the day. I need the ladies' room.'

***

As Melanie left, the two men resumed their seats. 'Is that Melanie there or is she going to fall in a heap any minute?' Guy asked.

'I think she has dug deep and found some inner strength. You need to know she's ashamed about what happened and feels you might think less of her, not want her.'

'What? How can she think that? Hell, is she still so insecure about the way I feel? Thanks for the warning. I'll have to think of some way to convince her otherwise. I can't believe she doesn't trust my love for her.'

'It's not that she doesn't trust your feelings for her. It's more of a syndrome of self-loathing that's instilled in battered people. They don't believe they are worthy of being loved. I can find some literature about it that you might find worthwhile reading. Help you to understand. The fact that she had such a strong loving relationship with her mother is probably the reason she's as normal as she is.' Iain nudged him in the ribs. 'Here comes your beloved,' he hissed from the side of his mouth.

Melanie perched her backside on Guy's knee with her head on his shoulder. Tension radiated from stiff muscles. Helplessness filled him. What could he say or do to ease her trauma? The clerk returned to indicate the next session. Before releasing her, Guy gave her a brief kiss. It was all he could think of. It wasn't enough.

'Keep strong, sweetheart and remember how much I love you.' As she moved to the witness box his mind felt tormented by Melanie having to endure this whole ordeal. What was more unsettling was what Iain had said about how Melanie may not feel worthy of being loved. How in hell's name was he supposed to prove to Melanie that she was more than worthy?

At the very first question Guy wondered if it was a precursor to how traumatic this next session was going to be. Melanie was asked to explain how the hospital she had been sent to called in the police to investigate the brutality of her father.

'How did things change from then on, Melanie?'

'From then on, because the police became involved in investigating my father, he tried to kill me. I knew it without his continual bragging and threats about how he was going to get rid of me forever.'

'Why would he do that?'

'Apart from mum, who was too darn scared to say anything against him, I was the only living witness to his brutality. Every time he attacked me it was with the intent to kill.'

Guy's spine stiffened the moment he heard the cold, callous tone of Melanie's voice. Something was wrong. He frowned as she continued. There were no hesitant pauses. Her eyes hardened and her lips jutted. He sensed a new determination in her demeanour but it still worried him.

'I kept out of his way as much as I could. I wanted to leave but knew things would be much worse for Mum if I did. How could I live with myself if he killed her in retribution for me leaving? I couldn't. At the same time I needed regular examination of my healing injuries and Mum still had her leg in plaster so we were in no position to be fleeing in any case. I kept my door jammed closed and would never come out if he was around. I must point out he wasn't home all the time. He came in when he was desperate for food, or money, or drink. I think he was afraid we would call the police again. I hope he was afraid. I hope he was terrified. I hope he is still terrified. I'm glad there is no capital punishment in this country because dying would be too quick. He needs to know what it is like to be imprisoned in hell for the rest of his life.'

The opposing lawyer springing out of his seat yelling out several objections caused a stir. There was a bit of uproar while he yelled and the judge attempted to call order. Guy couldn't help but smile at Melanie's affronted glare. It took Meg several attempts to shake Melanie's arm before Guy detected a slight grin on Melanie's face. Iain must have noticed as well because he elbowed his brother in the ribs.

'Atta girl – keep it up,' Iain muttered.

With silence reigning again Meg asked Melanie to continue.

'Keeping my door locked worked for a while. I found a job to feed Mum and me and pay the rent. I hid my money and that was probably a mistake because he always tried to find it. He usually came in during the day while I was at work and tore my room apart until he found my stash of money. In the end I found a spot outside the house to hide my cash. One night I went out to go to the toilet, I didn't put the chair back because it was almost morning. I didn't know he was in the house. He hadn't been home when I went to bed. I didn't hear the usual ruckus when he returned. He was waiting for me when I came back into my room. He wanted my money. He knew I had some because I was still working and he hadn't been able to find it. He slammed the door shut and came at me with a hammer.'

At the sound of Melanie choking, Guy tensed, ready to spring from his seat. He watched the muscles of her throat trying to swallow. She coughed then dragged a tissue from the box and wiped her mouth.

'He demanded I tell him where my money was. He said he was going to kill me to get me out of his life. I refused to disclose my hiding spot. Said I didn't have any money. After knocking me to the ground with his elbow he lifted the hammer over his head. I knew… I knew… I knew I was going to die.'

Guy felt his pulse rate hammering at the same rapid pace Melanie was talking. It seemed she was hell bent on getting the words out so she could get away from this re-lived torture and his heart was hell bent on thumping right out of his chest.

'He was holding me down with his stinking, smelly body but… I… I… managed to twist onto my left side at the last minute. The hammer came down with such incredible force on my right rib cage. The pain was excruciating. I was instantly short of breath and began gasping but I just couldn't drag in enough air. At the hospital later, I was told my lung had collapsed. I think my father thought I was dying because of the way I was fighting for air. He fled. Mum called the ambulance because I couldn't move… couldn't breathe. They had to take out one rib and part of my lung, which was crushed and bleeding internally and there were so many splinters of bone embedded in the lower lobe. I guess I was lucky it was only one blow and no more damage was done. I was in hospital for a couple of weeks after which the authorities found a room for us in a women's refuge. I wanted to fly to Greece but the doctor said I wasn't fit to fly until my lung healed. Something about the pressurised atmosphere.'

'What happened after you were released from hospital?' asked Meg.

'We could only stay in the refuge for a limited time. The people there found us a flat to rent. We lived on welfare payments. Before I was well enough to leave the country he found us again. He beat Mum. Her left leg was fractured in three places. Then he laid in wait for me. He gagged Mum so she wouldn't call out to me as I stepped in the front door after work.'

Guy caught her quick peek in his direction and noticed her face screw in pain. His own breath stuttered. He knew what this was about.

'This time he tried to strangle me. Almost succeeded.' She looked hesitant and nervous as her voice trembled and faded. Her entire body shivered then a hand went to her throat. He'd noticed the habit, knew why she did it but hadn't had the gumption to mention it to Melanie. Now he would find out all the facts: facts he shouldn't have to find out about.

'I had passed out when Mum dragged herself over and hit Dad over the head and knocked him out.' Turning to the opposing lawyer, she added, 'I know, I didn't see it but Mum told me later. She was there, so she should know the facts.'

Guy felt a nudge to his ribs when Melanie emphasised the last word. He turned to Iain.

'Smart girl has his mettle,' Iain whispered behind his raised hand.

Grinning, Guy turned back as Melanie continued.

'Mum said she dragged me out the door and called for help. We were both in hospital at the same time. Mum had to have her leg reset and they operated on my throat to repair the damage to my voice box. The police were called in to investigate but they couldn't find him. When I left hospital we were sent to a new address where I hid Mum away. We were safe for almost two months but he found her again and that's when he killed her.'

'Objection! Pure speculation!'

Guy twisted around to see Jones' lawyer prancing about.

'Then he tried to kill me again when he stabbed me at the beach.' Melanie interceded in a loud voice. 'There were witnesses to that,' she yelled even louder. 'They found his fingerprints and DNA in our flat,' she added. 'There was Mum's blood on the wood they found at his hideout! Evidence!' Melanie shouted. 'Not speculation!'

'Go for it,' Guy murmured as he watched Melanie's heaving chest. She was standing, leaning over the bench, resting on straightened arms. It delighted him that she was so angry and determined. Standing in front of her, Meg was frantically trying to get her client to settle down but it appeared Melanie was just as determined to keep going.

'We were in hiding. He had never been in that particular unit in all the time we lived there. So there is no other explanation for his DNA to be there!' she emphasised as she finally dropped back in her seat, her face hot with anger.

After getting her non-stop story out, Melanie slumped back in her chair staring at the floor. When her vacant look returned Guy knew she had used up everything she had. He felt inordinately pleased when Meg Nelson stated that she had no more questions.

He couldn't help but grin when the defence counsel could get nothing from Melanie despite barraging her with questions and statements, none to which he received a response.

'Miss Jones,' he yelled to gain the entire room's attention, 'you keep mentioning your father, but Mr Jones is not your biological father is he?'

Guy jerked upright and swung his gaze towards Melanie who snapped alert out of her trance.

'What did you say?' she gasped as she straightened and swung her eyes to stare at the man as though he was completely out of his mind.

'Mr Jones is not your father.'

She paled so suddenly. 'Oh, I wish that were true. It would be wonderful to know I don't have his disgusting genes or blood in my body,' Melanie spat.

'Well I've studied all the medical records and your blood type is B positive, whereas both your mother and father are A positive and I believe that is impossible. Mr Jones claims he is not your biological father.'

Meg shot from her seat to ask what the relevance of this was to the case but was cut short when Melanie folded like a concertina and slid downwards until she was nothing more than a heap on the floor behind the wall of the witness stand.

Guy didn't wait. He heard the judge call for the court medical orderly then lunch recess as he flew from his chair and leapt across the room. Crouching on his haunches in the confines of the witness box was difficult but he wriggled his body then felt for a pulse in Melanie's neck before lifting her from the floor. He was about to carry her outside when he was joined by a lady who claimed she was a nurse. Frantic with worry, he could do nothing but watch as the woman spent a few moments, but what felt like hours, checking Melanie.

'I'm sure she's just fainted. Settle her on the floor with her lower legs up on the chair,' the woman finally said.

With relief washing over him, Guy followed instructions then knelt beside the two women until he heard Melanie groan. He reached out to support her wobbly body as she regained consciousness then sat behind her on the floor, holding her limp body against his torso while the nurse continued her ministrations.

'Guy? What…?' Melanie began to struggle.

'Sweetheart, stay still for a moment. You fainted.'

'I've never fainted before in my life.'

'You've probably never had such a shock before. Do you remember what happened?'

She brushed a hand against her brow. 'Could it be true? Is that why he hated me so much?'

'I can't answer either of those questions but Iain will find out. How do you feel? Do you think you're up to walking? I'm taking you home. I won't allow any more of this badgering.' Standing, Guy eased Melanie up but tightened his hold as she staggered on unsteady legs to the door.

Iain was waiting outside. The moment he spied them Iain swung to the other side of Melanie and together they assisted her through the building, out onto the street and kept going until they reached Guy's car parked in a council car park.

With Melanie settled into the passenger seat, Guy pulled his brother aside before moving to the driver's seat. 'Can you ask Meg to tell the judge that Melanie is in no fit state to give any more evidence? I won't allow her to step foot in the courtroom again even if it means I spend time in jail for contempt of court.'

There was a stunned look on Iain's face. Guy wasn't surprised. He had sounded rather vehement, but damn it, Melanie had been through torture, twice now.

'I'll send around the doctor we use for the station and explain to him what she's been through. He might issue a certificate. I'd like her to agree to a DNA test so we can be certain about her paternity. We have both parents' DNA on file to compare them with. I can't believe we didn't pick up the discrepancy in the blood types.'

'Did you have Melanie's on file?'

'Not sure, no, probably not. It wasn't thought to be crucial evidence. But it would have been on the subpoenaed medical records. See if you can talk her into it. I'm going to bed after I've made that call. I have to work tonight. I'll call you in the morning.'

For the entire deathly silent drive home, Melanie stared into space. There was no argument when Guy suggested she lie down to rest. When he checked on her a few minutes later, she was asleep but he could tell from the restless, jerky movements that it was not peaceful. When the doctor came Guy hated rousing her. Before leaving the room he discussed the DNA test and felt relieved when Melanie agreed.

Guy paced up and down the passage until the doctor emerged.

'Mr Harris, your brother outlined the ordeal Melanie has been through. She is mentally and emotionally exhausted. I've suggested counselling but she refused. If she wants to talk about things, it would be a good thing, but if she doesn't, leave it at that. Let her rest as much as you can. If you get worried about her, give me a call. Here's my card, and Iain always knows where to find me.'

'Melanie is going to insist she returns to work. What do I tell her?' Guy asked as he studied the card before slipping it into his wallet.

'Physically, she is fine. If she finds work helps her keep focused on normality, let her go. I believe she works as a PA for you. Gear her workload to what you think she can cope with. She will probably find it easier to keep busy.'

Guy snorted. There were no doubts about that. She never stopped. 'Thank you, Doctor, I'll be in touch if I need you.'

After showing the doctor to the door Guy checked on Melanie. She was curled on her side, asleep. He drew a blanket over her then left the door ajar so he could hear if she roused. Then he rang Neil to see what was happening at work before spending the afternoon making various phone calls from the list Neil had dictated. His work completed, he lay down on the sofa listening to quiet music while mulling over all he had learned over the past few days.

***

When she woke, Melanie found Guy asleep on the sofa. She stood looking at him for a moment, then knelt beside him and explored his arms and chest with her fingertips before planting a gentle kiss on his lips. All of a sudden Guy's arm whipped out, wound around her waist and tugged her close. As he deepened the kiss a myriad of sensations coursed through her body, heating it with primitive hunger. She couldn't move, didn't want to move, so relaxed and wallowed in the exquisite pleasure.

'You can do that any time you like, sweetheart,' Guy whispered against her mouth as he slowly released her and straightened. 'What would you like to do tonight, stay in, or go out? How about the cinema and supper afterwards?'

With a weird sensation of disappointment at the kiss ending, Melanie fought for sanity through the fug of what she realised was pure sexual pleasure. 'Sounds good to me, I need to keep my mind busy. I'm not going back into that courtroom tomorrow. I'm going back to work,' she added, expecting an argument and secretly amazed she had been able to get such a well-strung sentence out. Pins and needles were still stringing their way along her nerve endings.

'That's great. Neil said he misses you and is making a mess of sorting the mail and everyone is complaining because they can't find anything.' Guy smiled. 'But don't make plans for Saturday morning because I'm taking you shopping and Saturday night we are going somewhere special for dinner.'

'I don't get a say?' Melanie teased, suspecting Guy was doing his best to keep her mind from the courtroom. Well so was she.

'No.' He grinned. 'Do you want to freshen up, or do we go as we are?'

'Give me five minutes.'

Chapter Thirty-Three

Concentrating was hard but Melanie felt at peace with the normalcy of everyday work. But pictures of her return to the courtroom kept interfering. Her cross-examination hadn't been anywhere near as gruelling as she'd thought it would be. What had angered her were the belligerent denials by her father. Even after all the evidence he still professed innocence. His outlandish lies explaining every injury were beyond belief to her but she'd been so afraid the jury would believe him. The entire ordeal had drained her to a physical and emotional low to such an extent that it hadn't registered when she heard the verdict of 'guilty of all charges.' What had sent her heart soaring was a phone call saying that it was highly unlikely the animal was her biological father. They still had to wait a couple of weeks for the final results but ninety percent surety was enough for her.

But this left her with another dilemma. Who was her father? And why hadn't her mother ever said anything? The thought kept surfacing as she worked catching up. It was amazing how much paperwork had been piled on her desk over the past week. But thank goodness there was so much to do. The only dark moment was when she'd told Guy she was moving back into her unit after work. His smile hadn't fooled her. She had become adept at reading his body language.

When Guy left work early, saying he had business to attend to and wouldn't be back for the rest of the day her good spirits seemed to have gone with him. He would pick her up in the morning, he'd reminded her, but refused to say where he was taking her, despite her pleas.

Melanie was waiting outside her front door when Guy arrived. A sense of exuberance had kept her innards twanging since she had woken in the early hours. She couldn't explain what it meant. She had actually giggled when she realised she was skipping down the paved pathway like some young schoolgirl. Freedom, she thought as she laughed at Guy's weak jokes while they drove into the city. I feel free!

She caught Guy's frequent glances and wondered what he was thinking about her over-bright demeanour. After parking the car he wrapped his arm around her waist and guided her down the main street. 'Are you going to tell me where we're going?' she asked after they'd walked almost the entire length of the mall.

'Yes, my love, we have an appointment upstairs in this building.' He turned a sharp right into an arcade, using pressure from his arm to steer her in the right direction and laughing when she almost continued on straight ahead. He then led her to the elevator where they rode up two storeys. Once out of the enclosed space he guided her along the walkway, stopping in front of an exclusive jewellery store. 'I thought it was about time I made it official that you were mine.' In an instant his grin changed to a frown when she backed away with her hands held against her mouth.

'No, Guy… you… I… you can't want… Oh, no, you deserve someone who isn't… tainted.

'Tainted!' Scowling and looking stunned, Guy stepped closer and grabbed her hands, drawing them down and holding them firmly when she tried to tug them free. 'You can't believe that. Sweetheart, there is nothing tainted about you. You are perfection with a pure gentle heart, an incredible will and talent in buckets. Just because you had such an appalling father doesn't mean you are the same - especially since you aren't even related to the animal.'

She shivered as his hands slid up her arms and his fingers bit into her shoulders. But the sting of his powerful grip didn't hurt, in fact it felt as though he was surging his strength into her. She felt – protected was the only word that came to mind.

'If what his lawyer said is true,' Guy continued, 'then you don't share the same blood or DNA.' Releasing his hold for only a brief second, he slid one arm around her shoulders and drew her against him. 'Sweetheart, I am thirty-three years old.' His voice sounded muffled. 'I've spent the past thirteen years searching for the right woman; the one who rocks my foundation and turns me to mush on the inside. Someone I can share the same kind of love my parents had. You hooked me the very first time I saw you on stage. Then I spent a very frustrating four weeks searching for you. At the time I had no idea why but there was this deep gnawing need to find you.'

Grasping her shoulders again, he held her just far enough away that he could search her eyes. She liked what she saw in his.

'Once you were staying with me it didn't take long to figure out that this,' he grabbed her right hand and placed it over his heart, holding it in place with his flattened hand, 'belongs to you. You stole my heart. You turn my innards into goo every time I even think about you. Sweetheart, don't you realise how much I love you, how desperate I am to spend the rest of my life with you?'

An incredible sensation of tingling joy swept through her, sending everything in her gut into a squishy concoction of something she couldn't describe. But it felt so darn wonderful. 'I love you just the same but I thought that once you knew all my ghastly secrets you wouldn't…'

She got no further. Guy's mouth latched onto hers in a searing kiss. He drew back. 'Don't ever even think that. Yes, your past was ghastly, incredibly so, but not because of anything you ever said or did. The only person who should feel shame is that poor excuse for a human being, who had no idea how to care for a wife and child. Now, my precious love, are you going to allow me to put a ring on your finger to show the world how incredibly proud and delighted I am that you have agreed to marry me?' His raised brows emphasised the question.

Dear Lord, she'd never felt anything like this before and couldn't put words to the sensations rippling through her. Warmth, relief, disbelief, love and most of all safe. For the first time in her life she felt safe. 'If you're sure, yes, I will be honoured to wear your ring.'

He blew out his breath then smiled. 'Thank you, my love. I've never been surer of anything in my life.' Grasping her by the elbow he gave a gentle tug as he stepped into the shop. 'Let me get you inside before you have a chance to change your mind.'

She couldn't help but laugh at his expression – the giggle just slipped out, the same way so many had unconsciously escaped over the past couple of days. It felt and sounded strange and she couldn't recall ever having giggled before.

It became obvious, by the way Guy was greeted, that this was his business the previous day. Melanie felt self-conscious at the thought of selecting an engagement ring but she was soon put at ease by the very experienced saleslady who displayed a range of gorgeous sparkling rings Guy had already pre-selected. One immediately took her eye but she said nothing, feeling mortified by the entire process. They spent an hour trying on each ring until finally Melanie settled on the one she had preferred from the beginning.

'Yes!' Guy yelled at her decision.

The saleslady grinned. 'Mr Harris bet me you would select that particular ring.'

Still feeling embarrassed she hovered near the door while the sales lady completed the transaction. What was she supposed to do in this type of situation?

With a wicked grin Guy slung his arm around her shoulder. 'We are celebrating tonight, so my lovely, I'm keeping it until tonight.' He guided her along the street, the small box hidden in the depths of his trousers' pocket. 'I'm really looking forward to tonight,' he added as they stopped at a small open-air café for coffee and a light snack.

Presuming the meal was a celebration dinner Melanie spent the rest of the day in preparation. After washing her hair she brushed it dry until her curls sparkled in smooth waves down her back. Apart from on stage, she rarely wore make-up but this time took care in applying a small dash of green eye shadow to highlight the dark brown of her eyes. Around her neck she clipped her most treasured possession: the locket Guy had given her for her birthday. As a finishing touch she draped the front strands of her hair back and pinned it up with a fake jewelled hairgrip that matched her dress. Her preparations complete, Melanie spun around in front of her mirror to make sure everything was perfect, feeling on top of the world and still in utter disbelief that Guy hadn't dumped her.

She felt particularly delighted at Guy's stunned look when she opened the door at his knock. His mouth gaped then closed a couple of times before he managed to formulate words. 'You look absolutely stunning,' he whispered as he turned her around to admire her. 'I'd better get you out of here, sweetheart for you are doing strange things to my sanity.'

Another unbidden giggle slipped out as she slid her fingers into his hand. She felt so alive, so wonderful. With her father, no, not her father. With that animal locked away for a very long time, she had no cause to ever feel afraid again, giving her an extra reason to be feeling so incredibly alive.

While they drove, Guy informed her they were not dining alone. Surprised, Melanie guessed Iain and Jenny were joining them. She was even more surprised when she spotted Neil and Louise also sitting at their table. As she settled into the seat Guy held out for her, Melanie felt apprehensive. Being the centre of attention had always caused her discomfort and the presence of the other four was a little disconcerting. Her tension eased as the meal progressed with a lot of the talk about Iain and Jenny and their looming nuptials. This, she could handle.

After the main course, Guy called everyone's attention. He turned to Melanie, reaching out to grasp her hands. What was he up to? Nerves tightened and pinged.

'Melanie, the reason I asked these four to join us tonight is because they are my dearest friends and I'm proud to declare my deep love for you, in front of them and for them to be a part of our official engagement.' He drew the ring from his pocket and slid it on her finger, which was shaking like a good panne-cotta and over which she had no hope of controlling.

'Sweetheart, I love you so much and I must be the proudest and happiest man on this earth right now.'

She reached up to whisper in his ear. 'You don't do things by half measure do you? I'm speechless.'

Guy chuckled then bent his head to kiss her again.

'Hey, you two, I'll have to arrest you for indecent behaviour in a public place if you keep that up much longer.' Iain's laughing words broke them apart.

Both Louise and Jenny took her hand to admire the ring with a central oblong emerald flanked by two diamonds on each end while Guy kept a hold of her right hand, gently rubbing her palm with his thumb, which created tingling warmth that spiralled up her arm. From the corner of her eye she spied a phone being studied by a grinning Iain. Wondering what was going on she sat as Iain showed the digital images to everyone at the table. As Guy was handed the phone he leant towards Melanie. They peered at the tiny screen together. Iain had captured all the relevant moments very well including several of their rather tempestuous kiss. Despite her heating cheeks, even Melanie was pleased with the results.

'Take photos of everyone,' she said to Guy, 'so we will always have the memories of our special night.'

After leaving the restaurant and farewelling the other two couples, Melanie was mystified as to why Guy just sat in the driver's seat before turning the engine on. Concern turned to worry when he faced her looking really serious. Oh, God, not now. Please don't let him say this was a mistake.

'Melanie, tonight was the second most special night of my life and I don't want it to end. Please come back to my house tonight? You still have some clothes there. I need you near me. I won't break my promise to you, but I want to hold you in my arms.'

She melted at the incredible tender plea in his eyes. 'I don't want it to end either. I'll stay. But tell me why tonight only rated second, to me it was the very first.'

He grinned. 'My favourite night was the night you sang that amazing song, declaring your love for me in front of all those people. I can't tell you how much that meant to me.' Leaning over he angled his mouth over hers, his kiss tender. 'Let's go for a walk along the beach before we go home.'

Chapter Thirty-Four

Miffed that the girls were on Christmas holidays during the Greek tour and didn't have to arrange time off, Melanie created a comedic form to apply for special leave. She left it in Guy's mail tray tucked amongst the pile of work letters. She was even more put out when he sent back a note refusing her leave because she was under contract with him for the tour and he would only grant her two week's annual leave for her honeymoon, on condition he chaperone her so she didn't get up to any mischief.

Her return note informed him how piously she would behave, exactly like a nun.

Guy arrived at her office door with her note in his hand. 'That's not quite what I meant,' he whispered, shoving the door closed with his foot. Her heart thundered at the way he stared as he stalked like a panther across the room, swept his arms around her and lowered his head. Fire raged in her veins during a long, slow, and very hot kiss. Intimate caresses with his fingertips delved under the neckline of her top leaving her breathless and her skin tingling. Then as suddenly as he arrived he released her and moved back to the door. 'We'll see how pious you are after I have finished with you,' he murmured before leaving the room again.

Her legs shaking, Melanie stumbled to her chair and plonked down. It took ages to recover her equilibrium enough so she could get back to her work – and then she had to really concentrate on the tasks.

For the next week the only time she saw Guy was at work and despite filling all after-hours time with wedding dress fittings and sorting the myriad things she needed to organise for the big day, she began to wonder if her lack of response to his more ardent than usual encounter had put him off. But how was she supposed to react when he took her by surprise like that.

With only a week before Iain and Jenny's wedding her agitation grew, especially since Mrs Harris was flying in from Norway and was to stay with Guy, which meant they'd have yet more time apart. Even when she agreed to go to the airport to meet Guy's mother, they had Iain with them so there was no opportunity for private conversation or any type of intimacy. She even felt a stab of jealousy when the two men hugged and kissed their mother with so much fervour. When Guy straightened he reached for her.

'Mum, this is my beautiful Melanie. Sweetheart, my gorgeous mother, Ingrid Harris.'

'You are much prettier than your photo shows, I'm so glad to meet you at last. Guy never stops singing your praises so you must be a very special lady.' While receiving a warm embrace Melanie was intrigued to know just what Guy had been telling his mother and what photo?

'The boys never stop talking about you either so I feel I know you already. I've been looking forward to meeting you.' Melanie murmured against her future mother-in-law's ear while she was in the process of being hugged to death. Having never been greeted before with such zeal by a stranger she felt shaken by the depth of the greeting.

While they waited for the luggage at the carousel Melanie stood back, listening while the other three caught up with snippets of news and gossip. She was intrigued by Ingrid's strong husky voice that had a Norwegian accent mixed with a strong Australian twang.

***

Contentment settled deep as Guy studied his mother preparing Norwegian treats for the girls. Having her here was beyond fantastic. He missed her, wished she would stay but knew she wouldn't. Her heart had been ripped to shreds when his father died. Grief had consumed her to the extent that Guy had worried for her welfare. She'd found some consolation amongst her family in Norway. Now she looked better, happier, her ready smile returning. Both he and Iain understood but hell, he missed having her around.

Scuffling and chatter rose from downstairs as the girls readied for rehearsal. There was sudden silence. Then a long note from the panpipes followed by screeches of too tight or too loose strings until pegs were twisted, drawing each into tune with the pipes. Another note, more strings until silence reigned again.

High harp notes twinkled an introduction. His mother lifted her head. Melanie played and the knife clattered as it dropped to the bench.

'That's amazing. Can we go down there?' Ingrid dried her hands on a tea-towel.

'Of course.'

As they reached the bottom step all Guy could see of Melanie was her back. She must have noticed the other girls peering over her shoulder for she turned suddenly, paused briefly then continued playing. He hated the way she blushed as though embarrassed.

As the piece drew to an end his mother clapped. 'Please don't stop, that was exquisite.' Ingrid paused. 'Melanie Jones.' She looked thoughtful then glanced up. 'You don't sing as well do you, Melanie? Are you the same Melanie Jones I saw performing the lead female role in The Pearl Fishers in Oslo?'

Stunned, Guy stared at Melanie then concern hit as she dropped her eyes to the ground, looking as though she wanted to crawl under the carpet she was staring at. The girls eyed her with curiosity. So they knew nothing about her past either. Seeing how distressed Melanie looked he strode over and gently grasped her hand.

'Melanie doesn't sing opera any more, but tell me, Mum, was she any good?'

'Oh, yes, very good. She sang the lead role so well I figured she must have been a lot older. Her voice was very mature for her age. She had us all sitting on the edge of our seats.'

With the sudden tension in the air, he figured Melanie was struggling with what to do or say so he suggested the girls continue. For a couple of pieces, Melanie's playing was a bit shaky. Guy heard the difference while he explained to his mother about Melanie's voice.

'That's so awful and now I've brought back terrible memories. I'm sorry.'

'I doubt Melanie will stress over it. She's remarkably strong, especially now the bastard is in prison.'

'Back home I have a couple of recordings of Melanie's singing. I listen to them often.'

'Excuse me?'

'Didn't you know?'

'No, she has a habit of keeping her past locked away. Maybe the fact that she can't sing anymore is still too raw. It wasn't all that long ago when this happened.' He kicked himself for only searching for recordings of her playing the panpipes but heck, how was he supposed to know these things when Melanie was so good at keeping her lips sealed about anything personal. But why? And here he was thinking she was beginning to drop her barriers.

When Melanie approached his mother during supper, Guy edged closer. 'I'm sure Guy has explained why I don't sing any more.'

His mother nodded and mumbled something he couldn't make out.

'You don't need to apologise. You just took me by surprise. I didn't think I would ever meet anyone who had heard me sing because I only performed in Europe. I'm sorry I reacted the way I did. I don't mind talking about my singing career but I feel uncomfortable talking about my injuries.'

His mother smiled as she patted Melanie on the forearm. 'Thank you, I fully understand. I have two of your recordings at home. Would you mind if I sent them over for Guy? You really were rather good.'

'I have a copy of all my recordings. I did four operas and one album featuring various arias. I guess I could leave them lying around and he can listen to them if he wants.' She turned to Guy. 'I didn't think you were into opera.'

Ingrid smiled. 'Oh, he's been to a few in his time. He appreciates a good voice and is particularly fond of the duets and chorus sections. You'd be surprised. I'll make sure I get to Greece in time to hear one of your concerts. You are very talented.'

When Guy drove Melanie home she asked him to wait. She returned only minutes later with something clutched against her chest. She looked so scared with her eyes downcast and seemingly not breathing. Releasing the held breath her body shivered as though releasing a dark spectre from her life. She planted a smile on her face before daring to peek up. Damn it all but what was she so afraid of?

'Your mother would like to listen to these.' Melanie dropped her eyes while he read the various labels, his eyebrows rising in surprise.

'And is it only my mother who is allowed to listen or can other people hear them as well? You are continually full of surprises, sweetheart.'

Much to his relief Melanie laughed. 'If I'm not there I won't know who's listening will I?' A contemplative frown appeared. 'I'm not ashamed of the recordings - I just never thought you would appreciate opera.'

Something twigged. 'Tell me, how many of those fifty or so concerts you did were with the panpipes?'

'Oh.' She paused. 'About a third,' she whispered.

'And the rest, I take it, were you singing. I think I'm looking forward to finding out more and more about you. I also think I might be asking a few questions when we get to Greece. Goodnight, my love. I'll see you at work in the morning.'

Eager to leave, Guy gave Melanie a brief kiss and hug then set the first CD playing while he drove. Her voice was very, very good with her arias sending tingles down his spine the same as her playing did. What a loss to the opera world, he thought as he slowed in order to hear as much of the CD as possible on the journey across town. He set a second CD in his sound system the minute he arrived home. His mother appeared from her room at the sound of the voice she obviously recognised.

'She was a very talented singer, Guy. Such a pity. I've not heard this one before. Leave it on please. Melanie can sing us to sleep.'

Chapter Thirty-Five

After a traditional wedding then seeing Iain and Jenny off for their honeymoon, Guy was delighted that his mother was staying to celebrate Christmas. To make the day easy for everyone, he arranged to dine out for the evening Christmas dinner. As per normal he closed the company down over the Christmas break so that all his employees could spend quality time with their families.

He woke Christmas morning to greet an early morning grey edging through the window. After lying awake for a few minutes he reached over and lifted the receiver from its cradle, expecting to rouse Melanie from sleep. Surprise hit when she answered after the first ring. 'Happy Christmas, sweetheart. How about coming for a swim? I can't sleep and am anxious to see you. We could come back here to have breakfast with Mum.'

'I'm awake in any case. Why not?'

'Pack all you need and spend the day with us. I'll be there shortly. Bet you're not ready when I get there.' After hanging up he left a hurriedly scrawled note for his Mum, changed into bathers then raced to his car.

Melanie was waiting with a zippered bag and a dress over her arm. 'What took you so long?' she asked with a grin. 'I've been waiting for ages.'

'And like Pinocchio, your cute little nose is beginning to grow. Happy Christmas.' He pecked on said nose and grinned.

The sky had turned smoky grey as they neared the river whilst listening to Christmas carols on the radio. When Melanie sang softly in accompaniment, Guy rejoiced in the sound. She certainly hadn't lost any quality to the tone, which made him wonder why she didn't sing any longer. One way to find out.

'When did you begin singing?'

'Oh, err, at high school.'

'Opera? At school?'

'Yes. My music teacher was an opera singer. She taught me.'

At the definite quiver in her voice, he glanced at her. Tension tightened her facial muscles. 'Just you or the whole class?'

'Umm, just me.' A tear slid down her cheek.

Guy indicated and pulled onto the verge. She'd turned her face towards the side window. 'Melanie?' He grasped her chin and drew it around. 'Talk to me.'

A long sigh accompanied raised shoulders, which then slumped. 'I learnt how to play the violin in primary school. When I went to secondary school I switched to the cello. When I played music I was transported to a different world: one of beauty and harmony. A world where I could forget about… well, you know… bad things. I didn't have many friends so spent all my recesses in the music room, practising. The teacher took me under her wing, gave me harder pieces, extra tuition. When she heard me sing in the school choir, she asked if I'd like to learn opera. I agreed so she coached me.' Her eyes dropped then she yanked her head free and turned away.

Turmoil swirled around his brain. She looked and sounded so humble as though she was embarrassed. Yet she should feel proud of her talent and achievements. So many times he just didn't know what to say or do so stuck to the simple. 'Thank you.'

Melanie turned back. 'For what?'

'For opening up. I know how hard it is for you. Your teacher must be incredibly proud of you. I know I am.'

'Proud? Of me?'

'Yes, my love, very proud.' He didn't have a clue what else he could say so he checked for traffic then pulled back onto the road. It took only another five minutes before he turned into a shady parking bay near the water.

Hand-in-hand they waded in the shallows for a few minutes. Then they sat on the sand with Melanie nestled between his bent legs, her back leant against his chest while they watched the sunrise with the first rays of salmon and orange sparkling like prisms on the tops of the gentle waves. They sat like that until the sky lightened and then Melanie stood, stripped off her clothes and waded into the water.

For a few moments, Guy sat and watched, her very presence causing a strong physical need that wasn't about to be eased. He waded out to waist depth, brushing his lips against Melanie's mouth as he passed then swam hard into deeper water to give himself time to bring his raging libido under control. It was either that or roll Melanie under him in the sand. Only when his physical ache had eased did he swim back to her then dove under the water to catch her legs and pull her under. They both came up spluttering and laughing then spent time teasing each other while having fun frolicking in the waves.

'I've had enough,' said Melanie all of a sudden. 'You stay in and have a good hard swim.'

'Are you okay?' She didn't look okay. Now that it was lighter he could see dark rings nestled under her eyes as though she hadn't slept.

She smiled but he could tell it was forced. 'I'm fine, just a little tired from all this activity.' She bent suddenly and whacked her hand in the water, splashing him.

Taking her at her word he swam for a couple of kilometres before returning to shore to find Melanie sitting with her legs drawn up and his towel around her shoulders for warmth. She eyed him as he rose out of the water. She stood, handed him his towel, turned and walked along the narrow belt of sand at the river's edge.

Alarmed by the look on her face Guy chased after her. 'Melanie, are you all right?'

'I'm fine.' She smiled. 'You had the sun shining on your body and it turned you to gold. You looked so awesome and I'm just trying to catch my breath.'

Stunned by her words Guy had to turn away to hide his instant reaction. Damn but this was getting too hard. He dragged his towel around his hips and tucked in the end, ensuring the fold was hiding the evidence.

'Let's go and drag Mum out of bed and have breakfast.' Even though physical contact was sweet torture, he eased his fingers around her hand for the walk back to his car. To keep his mind off her nearness he joined her in the

Christmas carols while they drove home. By the time they entered the house they were laughing, easing his tension. He banged on his mother's door, 'Time to get up. Melanie's here waiting for breakfast.'

He carried Melanie's belongings into his room then sent her to have first shower while he started breakfast.

'And just what are you so happy about, Guy? Do you realise how early it is?'

He hadn't realised he was grinning until his mother spoke right next to him. He'd been miles away. 'It's not that early. I picked Melanie up before dawn. We've been and had a swim.' He eyed his Mum seriously. 'How did you feel just before you married Dad?'

'Wonderful. You love her that much, do you? That makes me very happy.' She embraced him, something he'd never been embarrassed about, even as a teenager. 'I'm glad you waited for the right person. I'll get dressed then give you a hand.'

As his mother went in one door, Melanie emerged from another. She wore white cotton cut-offs and a green Christmas emblazoned T-shirt on which white, red and silver Christmas tree motifs featured across the front. Her hair had been left flowing with the front strands tied back with a long matching green Christmas ribbon. Guy's heart started drumming at the sight of her, his body warning him to move away fast. How he was going to keep his hands off her for the next four weeks, he had no idea. This continual burning desire to make love to her was becoming harder and harder to deny. He bent to kiss her briefly then made a rapid retreat to drown under a cold shower.

Guy discovered the gift the moment he entered the bathroom. After unwrapping the silver paper, he set the CD into a portable player he had by his bedside, listening to the music as he showered. It began with his favourite, *The Swan*. He paused when he recognised the song Melanie had sung at the final concert, but this time she sang alone. Then a new song began, one he didn't recognise. He turned the water off, wrapped a towel around his waist and sat perched on the end of his bed listening in awe to the personal words from Melanie to him. He lifted the card that had been included and opened it out. It told him that she had written the song especially for him. When the recording ended he remained seated while attempting to drag his emotions under control. He finished dressing slowly, the effects of the freezing cold shower he'd just endured, having completely dissipated. With a loud groan of frustration, he opened his bedroom door to find the two special women in his life watching him. His Mum discreetly left, leaving the source of his painful discomfort within arm's reach.

He strode over to Melanie and whispered in her ear as he wrapped her in his arms. 'I'm beyond words, my precious girl. My heart is bursting with love for you. You keep coming up with the most incredible surprises. I can never thank you enough for my gift.'

He held her in his arms and showered her with passionate kisses leaving Melanie gasping. Despite the deep desire to continue holding her, he knew he had to take control. Dropping his arms, he moved away and yelled that his mother could come out now. It was only his mother's presence preventing him from dragging Melanie back into his bedroom and firmly closing the door. He didn't have to be told how Melanie was feeling; he saw the raw emotions in her face. The thought swelled his heart so much he felt it surely must burst as he busied himself serving bowls of diced fruit with hands that were shaking.

He felt ecstatic in the knowledge Melanie wanted him as much as he desired her.

Over breakfast, Melanie sat in silence toying with her food and eating little. Guy reached out and placed a hand on her arm. 'I keep getting the feeling you're not as fine as you claim.'

'I'm just a little tired. I woke very early and couldn't get back to sleep.' She smiled but again it was forced, which sent a gut-wrenching wave of concern to his innards.

After the kitchen had been cleaned up, Melanie retrieved another gift from her bag and handed it to his mother. 'I had these flown out for you. Mr Panegyres managed to find a copy of each and put them on a plane. I was worried they wouldn't arrive in time but they were delivered yesterday.'

His mother un-wrapped the paper to reveal a copy of the compact discs of Melanie's that she didn't have. 'Thank you so much. I listen to the other two quite often. I never knew you had recorded so many or I would have already purchased them. I have something for you as well.' Ingrid brought out a gift wrapped in blue embossed paper. 'It's a bit of a tradition in our family that a mother makes something special for their daughters for their wedding. I was only blessed with two sons so I made this for you, since you will soon be my daughter. I also made one for Jenny.'

Melanie tore the paper off and held up an exquisite small tablecloth crocheted in fine white cotton with both hers and Guy's names worked into the delicate pattern. Their dates of birth were under each name and the date of their wedding at the bottom of the heart shaped central design. Tears welled as she wrapped her arms around Ingrid and cried on her shoulder.

'It's so beautiful, thank you so much,' she sobbed.

Realising Melanie had probably never received such a gift before Guy wondered what her past Christmases had been like while he rescued his mother. 'The tears mean Melanie is very happy. You should have seen the flood when we bought her flowers for her birthday.' He drew Melanie to him as he attempted to lighten the moment. 'We almost ran out of tissues in the office,' he continued as he grabbed a pile of tissues and began mopping up her face.

Guy's weak joke managed to elicit a feeble smile from Melanie. 'I'm sorry,' she mumbled. 'I love my gift, it's beautiful. Excuse me a moment while I go and wash my face.' She fled.

Guy followed. 'Sweetheart, are you all right?' he asked as he knocked on the door.

Melanie stepped through the doorway, a wry embarrassed smile on her face. 'Yes, just embarrassed. I'm not used to such kindness and when she said the bit about being her daughter; it was too much. How I miss Mum, I wish she was here.'

Guy couldn't help tugging Melanie close, firing up his libido yet again. He sighed then led her back to the kitchen where he suggested they go for a walk in the park before the day became too hot. Any excuse to gain some relief.

They strolled arm-in-arm through the park, continuing around the block whilst avoiding young children as they rode their new bikes, scooters and skateboards, gazing into front yards and admiring the various Christmas decorations on the houses. When they returned, Melanie put the percolator on for coffee while Guy produced two gifts from a cupboard, giving one to his mother and then handing the other to Melanie. 'You can only open it if you promise there will be no more floods otherwise my next work project will be to build an ark.'

Melanie laughed as she un-wrapped the paper then opened the box to reveal a fine gold bracelet set with an emerald and diamonds similar to her engagement ring. 'Oh, Guy, it's gorgeous.'

'I had it made to match your ring,' he said, smiling at the image of the necklace to complete the set, which was already wrapped in silver paper and secreted away as her wedding gift.

As she reached up to kiss him, he saw Melanie fighting to hold her tears back and put his finger up to scoop up the one escapee bead of moisture then bent his head to return her kiss. 'No tears, sweetheart. Here, let me put it on you.' Removing it from the box he wrapped it around Melanie's wrist, holding up her hand to admire it.

'It's beautiful, Guy, thank you so much.' She reached her arms around his waist, standing against him while trying to maintain her composure but it sure didn't help his.

Guy presented his mother with a silver frame containing a composite group of photographs of their engagement dinner. 'Melanie managed to keep the restaurant dry, but our engagement dinner was a very special night and I'm only sorry you couldn't have been there with us.'

'So am I, but I'll be at your wedding. I won't be missing that occasion. And for you, Guy, I have this. Not the right time of the year over here for it but I hope you will wear it.' The parcel contained a close fitting sweater, hand knitted in very fine wool, the stitches so tiny it appeared as though it had been machine knitted.

They were sitting watching a Christmas programme on T.V. when Melanie reached up and whispered, 'Guy?'

'Yes, sweetheart?'

'Do you have any painkillers?'

He sprang upright in alarm. Searching Melanie's face, he saw the pain etched across her eyes. Without comment he retrieved a packet of strong painkillers from an overhead cupboard, removed two tablets from the foil and brought them back to her with a glass of water. He knelt on the floor in front of Melanie. 'I knew something was wrong. How long have you been in pain?'

'It woke me during the night.'

'Why didn't you tell me earlier? Hell, sweetheart, let me know in future. Would you like to lie down for a while?'

Melanie nodded shyly, looking as though she was embarrassed at her weakness. While she slept, he lay on the sofa dozing, ignoring the sappy Christmas film his mother was engrossed in. He felt startled when his mother asked him why he didn't join Melanie.

'I know Iain and Jenny lived together before they were married.'

How was he supposed to answer? 'Melanie has never slept with a man before. I'm not sure whether it is by choice or circumstances but she is twenty-five years old and kept herself intact all those years. I'm not sure how important it is to her, we've never really discussed it but for some reason I feel it important for her first time to be on her wedding night.' He then outlined how they had met and how he promised he would never take advantage of her so she would learn to trust him. 'I can't betray the fragile trust with men she has built up.'

'I'm very, very proud of you, Guy. A mother could never wish for a better son.' She stooped down to give him a motherly kiss on his brow. He didn't feel heroic – he felt downright physically frustrated.

Chapter Thirty-Six

Soon after settling into the hotel in central Athens, Melanie insisted her first stop was to be her old workplace. After negotiating hectic traffic in a taxi, the drive to the area around the Port of Mirolimano was less frantic. Her hands were wrestling each other in her lap when they pulled up outside the offices where she had worked. Guy grinned at her anxious pacing as he paid the fare. Then she almost dragged him inside, eager to see her old boss.

She didn't bother knocking on his door but shoved it open, causing a loud bang as it was flung against the wall. She stood motionless in the doorway. George Panegyres, with a grumpy frown forming, looked as though he was about to give the interloper a severe talking to when he glanced up. Instantly, a broad smile sprang across his creased features as he leapt out of his chair and opened his arms.

Guy stood back watching the pair greet each other with such warmth. He smiled as he recalled how jealous he had been of this tall sun-weathered man. After introductions George winked as he asked Guy if he was letting Melanie stay to work for him again.

'Not likely. My staff would strike if she wasn't there to solve all their problems.' He smiled. 'When you gave your referral I didn't think anyone could be so good, but she is. You can't have her back.' His long arm slid possessively around Melanie's waist.

He was fascinated as he was given the grand tour around the offices and factories while George Panegyres spouted a comprehensive outline of the machinations of the company. Guy was amused when they had to stop every few metres while staff members rushed up to Melanie to give her copious hugs and kisses. It soon became obvious that Melanie had been very popular. After the tour, they were taken out to a nearby Estiatorio for lunch. It was mid-afternoon before they were allowed to make their escape.

Another taxi took them in the direction of Plaka, nestled on the north eastern slopes of the Acropolis, to meet Melanie's grandmother. Guy was on tenterhooks after being warned that her grandmother didn't speak a word of English and wouldn't approve of Melanie being with him un-chaperoned. After a slow drive fighting chaotic traffic, they ambled along narrow labyrinthine laneways of the delightful old quarter to the south of Athens central then up a steep, but short set of stairs where Melanie knocked on a bright blue painted door. Most doors, window frames and ceramic pot-plants wore the same colour. There was a lengthy wait before the door opened by an elderly woman whose wrinkled face broke out in a smile when she saw her granddaughter standing on the tiny porch. Melanie spoke in Greek then introduced Guy, who didn't receive such a warm smile but was nevertheless welcomed inside.

He felt claustrophobic in the tiny rooms and had to stoop to get through doorways. They were offered refreshments neither of them wanted but Melanie whispered to Guy that they didn't have a choice. It wasn't polite to refuse the proffered refreshments. They forced down traditional strong black coffee alongside homemade Kadaifi, shredded wheat cakes sweetened with honey, the combination of tastes complimenting each other.

Understanding only a few single words, Guy felt like an interloper as Melanie and her grandmother spoke rapidly. The only hint he had of what was being said was through body language. The older woman looked angry, her arms flinging in all directions as she spoke vociferously. On the other hand, Melanie's face paled and then became rather strained. He was startled when the argument ceased suddenly and Melanie gave her grandmother a warm embrace before grasping his hand and tugging it as she headed for the front door.

'What's going on?' he asked while they virtually sped back down the street.

'I asked her about Mum. She didn't want to tell me, but I kept urging for information. My grandfather disowned Mum and sent her to Australia to stay with relatives when he discovered she was pregnant. He didn't approve of the man she was in love with and wouldn't let her marry him. It wasn't the man he had picked for her. Mum had shamed the family. He thought the man was too old and was furious she had been out with him unchaperoned and had become pregnant. Grandma told me off as well for being with you alone. Being engaged didn't make any difference. She eased her stance when I told her you were a very honourable man and we had never slept together. Like a good Greek man, you were waiting for our wedding night.' Melanie grinned at the astounded look he knew was on his face.

'I asked her if she knew who my father was. She knows but wouldn't tell me.' With a worried frown marring her features, Melanie went silent and Guy saw her withdrawing into herself. He slid his arm around her shoulders as they hailed a taxi.

'I'll go back to see her another day,' said Melanie as though to herself. 'Maybe I can use some excuse about hereditary conditions for any of our children.'

Noticing a flush rise up her cheeks at the mention of their possible offspring, Guy chuckled. 'Now there's something I'm looking forward to.' He nudged her. 'Especially all the practice in creating such delightful little beings.' A cab pulled alongside and he opened the door for Melanie.

'And whose fault is it we haven't had any practice to date,' he heard Melanie mutter as she slid into the seat.

Her comment floored him. He slid in beside her with his brain in a maelstrom of conflicting thoughts. 'We never really discussed this, did we?' Her head down, she stilled. 'Look at me, sweetheart.' When she didn't move he chucked two fingers under her chin to draw her head up.

'Where too?' Guy glanced up towards the intruding voice. For a moment he had forgotten where they were. He met the eyes of the grinning young man with typical Greek features, which had been a surprise since the voice had a strong British accent.

'The Divani Hotel. You sounded English.'

'Spent my school years in England,' the driver said as he sped off, jolting Melanie's chin from Guy's fingers.

Knowing the driver had heard and understood every word of the brief conversation Guy kept silent until they were standing on the footpath outside their hotel. Melanie attempted to rush off, but he grasped her upper arm and drew her back. 'I want to finish our discussion,' he said as he swung her around to face him. The way she was chewing the corner of her lower lip with her eyes firmly studying the ground told him she was feeling uncomfortable so he drew her into his arms and spoke with her head cradled against his chest.

'Sweetheart, when we met, I promised I would never take advantage of you. You were in no emotional space to be threatened by any man wanting more from you than you were prepared to give. You were frightened and very vulnerable. I try never to break my promises to people and with you I felt it important to keep my word if you were to learn to trust me as a man and more importantly as the man who wanted you in his life.'

'I always trusted you!' she mumbled against his shirt.

'You have no idea how that makes me feel, sweetheart. But if I'd pressured you to turn our relationship into a more physical one, would you have maintained that trust?'

'Maybe, maybe not, but so many times, I wanted you to.'

'Now, she tells me.' Guy couldn't suppress his chuckle as he cupped her face and drew it up to look at him. 'Your trust was fragile and there was no way I was going to chance losing you - especially through me losing self-control. Over the past couple of months my reasons changed slightly. So many times I've wanted to drag you to bed but somehow I got the feeling it was important for your first time to be on your wedding night; your first time to be with your husband and not some lover.'

'Even if that lover was you?' As though the words just slipped out, she bit her lip then reddened.

Guy grinned. 'It's probably a good job I'm flying home so I'm not tempted to break my word. You have no idea how much I want you in my bed.' He bent his knees until they were eye-to-eye. 'But it's not going to happen. It's me who now wants to introduce his virgin bride to the delights of marriage. Call me old-fashioned if you like, but oh, I'm so looking forward to our wedding night.' He swept his arms back around her and held her tight before leading her inside, content he'd finally broached the subject.

The following day they were on the way towards Lykavittos Hill to meet Stephan who lived on the edge of the National Park. For the last few hundred metres after alighting from the metro train, they ambled up into pine-covered hills. When they reached a certain spot, Melanie stopped, removed her instrument from its special bag she wore like a backpack, and played a short tune. 'Melanie,' echoed from a distance, followed by a replying tune on another set of panpipes. Melanie slipped her instrument back in the bag then ran the last fifty metres.

Guy followed at a more sedate pace; watching intently while the woman he was about to marry was gathered up in the arms of a young olive-skinned and way too handsome man and was thoroughly kissed. Jealousy surged. The man holding his fiancée so close and so avidly was no older than he was and it wasn't until Guy got much closer that a grin spread across his face. Wearing a perfectly tailored but wild coloured outfit of flowing trousers and shirt, Stephan was the most effeminate man Guy had ever seen.

A cheeky grin was plastered across Melanie's face when Guy reached them. She turned to Stephan. 'Guy has been jealous of you. He thinks we might have had a thing going.'

'But she is a woman, a lovely woman, but a woman. But you I could go for, where did you find such a hunk,

Melanie?' When Stephan edged closer with a somewhat predatory gleam in his eye, Guy stepped back wondering how far this man would go.

'Stop teasing him, Stephan, and keep your hands off my man or you'll have me to deal with. You've got your own.'

Relief surged. Guy smiled at the friendly shove she gave to Stephan's shoulder.

'Now I am afraid - Melanie getting cross with me.' Stephan laughed then turned to Guy. 'I'm sorry, I was only teasing. But you are very good looking and you don't often see your colour hair around these parts.'

After Guy's initial trepidation, he felt more at ease as he enjoyed a wonderful few hours with Stephan. He soon understood why Melanie liked the man so much. They discussed in detail the concerts then the pair treated Guy to a sample of the duets they would be playing together proving that Stephan was as good a player as Melanie had indicated. They made final arrangements about the one dress rehearsal they would have before Stephan walked them down to the main road.

'You might have warned me.' Guy remarked while they made their way back down the hill.

'Then I wouldn't have enjoyed the look on your face so much. Stephan is a wonderful, caring man and is harmless. He has a steady partner, Costas. They have been together for years. Costas is a singer in the same Opera Company I was in. In fact it was he who took me along.' Melanie grinned up at Guy. 'So, are you still jealous of the two other special men in my life?'

'You are a bit of a devil, but I understand your affinity to both men. Now what would you like to do tonight? It's New Year's Eve and we need to do something special.'

'Let's walk around the city. It will be alive with people and lots of fun. We can enjoy the atmosphere then find a seat in a little taverna somewhere.'

They crawled into bed in the early hours of the morning after sharing a plate of appetizers called mezedes in one open-air eatery and then souvlaki later in the evening. Guy refused the many offers of retsina, not ever having acquired a taste for the distinct pine resin flavoured wine. He felt as though they had kissed half the population of Athens at midnight then joined in the vibrant celebrations before returning to their hotel.

Weariness still dogged him when he and Melanie arrived at the airport late the next afternoon to meet the girls. After helping cart luggage back to the hotel and settling the girls into their rooms he retired for a much-needed nap.

The girls had the following day to wander around and catch up with jetlag while Melanie and Guy returned to the airport late in the evening to meet Jenny and Iain. Iain was remaining for the first concert before, much to his chagrin, having to fly home with Guy for work.

The following day a mini-bus arrived to carry the girls and their instruments to their first venue for a long day of rehearsal. The two brothers settled them in then went sightseeing for the day.

When he saw Stephan before the concert began, Guy was impressed. Wearing black trousers and a really smart cream satin shirt, he was the perfect contrast to Melanie's black gown. Alongside his brother, Guy moved up to the box where George Panegyres stood to greet them. The anticipation was intense until the opening notes.

The Swan opened the evening; this time the blue lights were to the right half of the stage. After the opening bars, gold lights lit up left stage as Stephan joined in giving the impression he was standing on the side of the lake entranced with the gliding black swan. The effects and the haunting sounds of the two sets of panpipes playing to each other in an unaccompanied duet were hypnotic. Guy sat totally entranced. The other ten girls were placed in strategic positions around the stage and each time one was featured with a solo performance, the spotlights highlighted them.

The performance was a magical wonderland and well worth the continuous, thunderous applause at the end. There were two encores planned. The first, their new version of *Ave Maria* to which Stephan had worked out intricate harmonies. They ended on the traditional *Swan* with Stephan ceasing to play as his gold lights were doused a few bars before Melanie moved back off the stage, completing the last few notes solo from the wings as the lights faded, leaving the hall in darkness. The auditorium lights came on slowly to indicate the performance was over.

'My word, they were good,' Iain muttered as the three men stood to make their way back stage.

Iain and Guy were booked on the same flight the following day. With not enough time for the women to return from the airport in time for preparations for their performance, farewells were said at the hotel. There were tears from Jenny as she found it difficult to let her new husband go, while Melanie was more subdued, which concerned Guy.

He found a relatively private little nook in the hotel foyer where he eased her close. 'I'm going to miss you, sweetheart. I'll ring as often as I can, but please phone if you need me - any time. I'll be back for your second last concert. The plane is scheduled to land in time for me to make the start of it. Always remember how very much

I love you and how very much I am looking forward to the time when I can kiss my bride.'

His farewell kiss was long and passionate. It was with deep reluctance he released Melanie. With a last brush of his fingers down the side of her face, he turned, picked up his bag and was gone, not daring to glance back.

***

Without Guy, Melanie had a constant hollow ache inside but forced a bright chirpy persona to hide her emptiness. How many years practise did she have for pretence?

She returned to visit her grandmother, coming away emotionally exhausted after a lengthy session of cajoling and threats; all to no avail. Frustrated, she caught a cab to call on her old boss, his name being the only one her grandmother would reveal. Stops and starts, along with traffic that seemed more chaotic than ever, notched her frustration levels so high during the journey that she felt as though she was about to explode. She had a more than generous bundle of notes waving near the driver's chin before the taxi even came to a standstill.

'Keep the change,' she muttered in Greek as she dropped the notes at the same time as she shoved the door open. Tense with anxiety, Melanie jogged through the car park, briefly nodded to the receptionist as she shot past and only ceased her brisk strides as she halted in front of George Panagyres's door. She paused with her eyes closed trying to calm her racing heart. Three deep breaths in, with slow exhalations gave her a modicum of calm. Lifting her hand she clenched her fist and knocked three times – something she'd never done before. The door had never been a barrier, with her always being free to enter at any time.

'Enter.'

The one word sounded stern and she wondered if now was the right time. She glanced at her watch. She only had an hour before the bus left – not enough time to pursue this. Deciding to come back later, Melanie turned and began walking back down the short passage, glancing through the narrow but long panels of glass into each small office. The orderliness of the office layout, contrasted strongly to the way her mind felt.

'Melanie?'

At the shouted question she paused mid-stride and twisted her head around. Her heart began pounding again but she turned and made her way towards the man standing in the passage with his arms akimbo and a worried frown deepening the wrinkles on his brow.

'You can't knock on my door and then walk away. What is it child? What's wrong?'

'What makes you think something is wrong?' Melanie stepped past him and kept going until she reached the nearest chair, which she pulled out then sank down.

'For you to even knock tells me something is wrong. For you to not enter makes me think it is very serious.' George paused in front of her then dragged a second chair away from the wall and settled it close. After sitting, he reached out and took her hands in his. 'Now tell me what is bothering you.'

Sucking in a breath of courage, Melanie hesitated. 'This is so hard but I was told that you know who my real father is.' She glanced up at the long hiss. 'You know?'

'I do, but I didn't always, much to my regret. A letter arrived from your mother the day before you first came to Greece.'

'You've known that long! But why?' A surge of anger swept through her. 'I don't understand. I always believed that… pi… bastard was my father. I could never understand why he hated me so much, especially after I returned home.' She paused, mystified. 'But why did Mum tell you? I didn't even know you knew Mum.'

'Oh, I knew her but she disappeared one day – just vanished. I spent weeks searching for her. Your grandparents would tell me nothing, except that she had run away from home. But she revealed the truth in her letter. Would you like to read what she wrote?'

Stunned, Melanie stared at the man in front of her. 'You still have it, but why?'

'Maybe you should read it and then you will understand.' George released her hands and pushed his seat back. He moved to the other side of the large, scarred wooden desk and removed a small key from the top drawer. Melanie watched as he lifted a picture from the far wall and couldn't disguise her gasp of surprise when a wall safe was revealed. She felt intrigued as he rummaged around inside then really afraid when he handed her an envelope that looked as though it had been handled many times.

'Read it carefully,' George said as he settled in his normal office chair on the other side of the desk.

Melanie found it difficult to control the slight tremor of her fingers as she eased folded papers from the envelope. After slipping the envelope on the desk, she unfolded the papers and began scanning the words. Her quick perusal altered to a slow study of each word as the truth of her background unfurled before her eyes. She didn't even know she was crying until a tear plopped onto the page. It felt like forever before she read the last words: *All my eternal love, Maria.*

Leaving the papers resting in her lap, Melanie dropped her head into her hands and wept tears of joy, of frustration, shame and anger. Why had she never been told the truth? When a large handkerchief appeared before her eyes, she grabbed it and scrubbed at her wet face then blew her nose before feeling strong enough to look at the man opposite her.

'You are my father?' she managed to force out of a blocked throat.

'It appears so. The moment I saw you, I knew it was true as you have my own dear mother's hair.'

'But why was I never told?'

'As you just read, your mother begged me not to tell you. Believe me sweet daughter, I wanted to. I felt desperate to acknowledge you as my child – my only child. I never married because there was never anyone to replace your mother in my heart. I wanted to marry my beloved Maria but your grandfather wouldn't give permission. I was too old in his eyes and not the person he had lined up for her. Your grandparents are of the old school. When Maria disappeared I had no idea she was pregnant. I didn't know until you arrived eighteen years later. It was an enormous shock.' George shuffled forwards then knelt on the floor in front of her. 'But such a wonderful shock,' he added as he wrapped his arms around her and hugged her in a tight embrace. Melanie felt the energy of his love pour from him.

'You should have told me. Mum should have told me.' Her words sounded muffled as she pressed her face into her father's shoulder and the tears began again.

'I felt honoured to abide by your mother's wishes. We will never know her reasoning but my guess is that she felt deep shame and didn't know how to confront what must have been a lifetime of lies. How about coming out for refreshment so we can talk at length?'

Suddenly remembering her time constraints, Melanie pulled away and glanced at her watch. 'Oh, heavens, I can't. The bus leaves the hotel in twenty minutes.' She scrambled to her feet. 'I'm never going to make it.'

George's rise from the floor was a little more ungainly, his age making it difficult. Melanie gave him a hand up and couldn't help but smile as she swept away the last vestiges of moisture from her face. The swell of happiness was almost overwhelming. That this man was her real father was almost beyond comprehension.

'Ring the hotel and I'll drive you. We'll meet the bus at the ferry terminal. Can someone collect your things?' George brushed down his trouser legs and straightened his clothes.

It was a frantic drive with little said but Melanie's mind was tumultuous, her dominant thought on why her mother had never told her the truth but now she understood why her mother had asked so many questions about Greece and in particular about her boss. It all made sense now. As they pulled into the busy ferry terminus, she glanced around but they had beaten the bus. When her eyes rested on her father, she discovered that he was watching her intently. 'Now I know why you let me get away with so much when I worked for you.'

He laughed. 'I could never be angry with you. You twisted my heart with wondrous joy every time I saw or thought about you. It saddened me a great deal when you decided to return home. Why did you leave?'

'I was going to bring Mum back here, but... oh, heavens, it was so awful. He was so awful.' She turned away so he couldn't see the pain in her eyes. 'We never got the chance.'

A hand rested on her shoulder. 'What happened, Melanie? Tell me how your mother died.'

Spying the bus drawing up in the queue for the ferry, Melanie flung the door open. 'She was murdered by that bastard,' Melanie spat as she shot from the car. She turned back and leant into the car. 'Ring Guy and tell him I said it was all right for him to give you the details but I can't talk about it.' She turned and began walking away then paused and ran around the other side of the car. George lowered the window. 'I'm glad it's you. I love you, Dad and please don't tell Guy that you're my father. I want to surprise him'

'I love you too,' she heard yelled back as she ran towards the bus, fighting back a new wave of tears.

Later that night when Guy called, she felt so excited. 'I've found my real father. I'm so happy.'

'That's wonderful news. Are you going to tell me who it is?'

'Yes, I'm thrilled. I can't explain it but I feel this strange completeness and sense of belonging. But I haven't had a chance to really talk everything out yet. I'm going to ask him to walk me down the aisle. Do you think he will?'

'I hope so, for your sake, sweetheart.'

'You have no idea how wonderful this feels – to be having my real father walk me down the aisle. What I found out is that he never knew Mum was having me. I now know they loved each other very much and it makes me so happy to know I was created from such love and not from the hatred I grew up with.'

'They couldn't possibly have loved each other as much as I love you, sweetheart. I miss you so very much. My heart aches for you all the time and I'm not sleeping so well with you so far away. You take care, my love.'

'I'm not sleeping so well either. I feel empty without you,' she whispered as she hung up.

Chapter Thirty-Seven

While preparing for the second last performance Melanie was far more nervous than usual. It was mind-boggling how the CD sales had soared after an incredible, successful tour playing to almost full houses. As they went, each theatre had fewer empty seats. Unbelievable reviews ensured tickets sold as the troupe travelled mainland Greece as well as several major islands – usually a single show at each. On the free days, Melanie had ferried back to Athens to spend time with her new-found father, and to complete the finer wedding details.

The constant to-ing and fro-ing sapped her energy and she felt physically exhausted but emotionally alive. Being kept so busy had helped lessen her anguish in missing Guy so much. It was a happy tiredness. She relished the constant feeling of joy instead of fear. Now they were back in Athens. Tonight Guy would be sitting in the box seat when the concert began. He would be there, he assured Melanie on his last phone call before boarding his plane. Iain had arrived the night before. He and Jenny had been inseparable ever since.

Her preparations complete, Melanie began pacing around her dressing room. Normally she would sit in quiet solitude to gather her thoughts but she felt so anxious to see Guy, feel his arms around her, smell his wonderful scent. The five-minute call bell sounded. Picking up her instrument, she scampered to the wings then pulled up near the stage door. She had to gain control. Deep, slow breaths – in and out. Stay calm. He'll be up in the box – he'll be there.

The moment the auditorium lights faded, the girls stepped into their places on the dark stage. Settling onto their stools, instruments ready, they waited in silence. Stephan stood beside Melanie, whispering encouraging words that floated somewhere in the vague background of her mind while her thoughts contained only one vision – her tall, golden Adonis.

The stagehand counted them in. She stepped onto the dark stage with Stephan leaving her side and moving to his position. Melanie lifted the pipes into place, breathed in then played the first note. Stage lights flashed on, and for the first time ever, she faltered when she looked up to the box seat at the empty space next to Iain. Even in the darkness of the auditorium, there was no reflection of the shimmering lights from Guy's blond hair. He wasn't there. If she could make out Iain's shadow then she should be able to see Guy. Devastation hit. Maybe he wasn't coming. The air left her lungs in a whoosh.

Still in a vacuum, she heard Stephan picking up her part as she stared at that vacant seat. Why wasn't he here? Years of being a professional performer finally kicked in. She was a performer so she had to perform. She sucked in to refill her lungs and picked up from Stephan. Very few people in the audience would have noticed anything was amiss but Iain, the girls and Stephan would have noticed. She forced her concentration back to the programme.

Feeling as though all life had been sucked from her body, Melanie stood apart from the others during intermission. She was sipping on a bottle of cold water when Iain approached.

'I rang Guy and his plane was delayed, he'll be here as soon as he collects his luggage. He said to tell you how much he loves you in between cursing the airline. And I'm to give you this.' Iain neared then planted a big sloppy kiss on her cheek then moved away.

Even though Iain's words didn't ease her concern, Melanie played better in the second half but continually peeked at the box, waiting and hoping. Bitter disappointment swamped her when the concert finished and he still wasn't there. While they were driven back to their hotel in the bus, she sat alone, huddled against the window, staring into the darkness, ignoring futile attempts at conversation by her friends. Her only hope was that Guy was at the hotel. He should be by now if he was collecting his luggage during interval.

The moment the bus drew up in front of the hotel Melanie rushed down the aisle and stepped off, her eyes searching for Guy's blond head. He'd be here, waiting.

He wasn't. She raced inside and scanned the reception area but at this late hour it was almost empty. She felt tears well but fought them back as she sped to the reception desk.

'Has Guy Harris checked in yet?' Her pulse throbbed as she waited for the young lady to scan the register.

'I'm sorry, no.'

He wasn't coming.

'Melanie!' A hand grabbed her shoulder.

She spun around. 'He's not coming is he? You lied to me!' she screeched at Iain. 'If he'd been at the airport at interval, then he'd be here now!'

'Melanie, no, he's on his way.'

'No he's not. He doesn't want me!' Ashamed of the tears running down her face, Melanie turned and shot towards the elevators. She hit the button, fidgeting until the door opened, ignoring the sick platitudes of Iain and Jenny. Despite fighting to quell the tears, they just kept coming as she rose. Running down the passage to her room, she dragged her concert gown off the minute she slammed the door shut and flung herself onto her bed. He wasn't coming. Her past was too bad. She wasn't worthy of his love.

***

It was early morning before Guy was able to walk up to the reception counter of the hotel. He was surprised to see Iain pacing around. 'Iain, why are you still up?'

'Where the hell have you been?'

'The plane was delayed. I'm sorry but there wasn't a lot I could do about it. How's Melanie? I feel really bad about letting her down.'

'Melanie had a meltdown thinking you weren't coming. She let fly saying you didn't want her.' He ran a hand down his face. 'Hell, what could I do when I had no idea where you were?'

'Where is she?'

'In her room. We wheedled another key from the manager.' He slipped it from his pocket and held it out. 'Jenny went to her but received an earful for her troubles.

Melanie was distraught. We checked on her about half an hour ago. She cried herself to sleep.'

'Hell, I must go and see her. I didn't think she was still this insecure.'

'Guy, she's had twenty-five years of insecurity and abuse to develop this sense of unworthiness. You read the reports I gave you.'

'Yes, of course. I just thought that maybe…'

'It takes more than a few months for victims to learn a new set of values. You go, I'll check you in and put your bags in your room. I'll slip your key under Melanie's door. Room 317. Third floor. You're next door in 319.'

'Thanks. I'll see you in the morning.' Guy turned and raced to the elevators with his heart hammering. He felt exhausted after being in transit for over thirty hours and wondered if he'd get any sleep or if it was going to take him what was left of the night to convince Melanie he hadn't deserted her. The ride up felt interminable. At last the doors slid open. He raced along the corridor scanning door numbers until he reached 317. He knocked. Hearing no sound, he slid the key-card in the slot and shoved the door open. Approaching the bed he noticed her tear-ravaged face in the light of the bedside lamp she'd left burning. His heart melted at the sight. She hadn't even removed her stage make-up, the dark mascara having left black streaks down her face.

Kneeling, he ran one finger through the mass of black curls fanning around her head. She hadn't even bothered to braid her hair before retiring. Even asleep her face wore deep sadness. He settled his lips to hers, savouring in the yearned for sweet taste and warm softness. At first it was gentle but as his blood surged the kiss deepened and his arms slid around her shoulders drawing her up. She felt so, so good.

'Guy?' mumbled under his mouth.

'Who else would be kissing you like this, my beautiful love?'

Suddenly her arms flung around his neck, dragging him down and gripping tight. Startled, he returned the passionate kisses from his previously meek, chaste nun. She paused. 'I thought you weren't coming,' she whispered.

'My darling, darling girl, nothing would have kept me away even if I had to swim all the way – which probably would have been a lot quicker. I'm really sorry for letting you down, but when you are thirty thousand feet up in the air, circling around and around an airport and they can't find a spot for you to land, there's not a lot you can do. My first flight was delayed, which meant I missed the second. They got me on a different airline but when we reached Athens late they didn't have room for us to land. I willed the flaming plane to land, but it was still far too late for me to get to your concert. I'm so sorry, sweetheart. I've missed you so much.'

Dropping his head to her brow, he paused as he wallowed in the feel and smell of her. 'Please don't throw me out. I need you near me but I'm dead tired. I've been flying or waiting interminable times in airports for over thirty hours and all I want to do right now is sleep with you in my arms.'

Melanie wriggled over to the other side of the enormous bed, holding her arm out in open invitation. Marvelling at her unrestrained actions he slipped his shoes, belt and black leather jacket off then lay down next to her, tugging her close while wallowing in the blissful sensation then heaved out a huge sigh of contentment.

He delighted in the warm sensation of Melanie running her fingers around his face. Then she leant over and settled her mouth over his in a long tender kiss. 'I love you so much, Guy,' she whispered as she snuggled into his body.

'Just as well, my love, since we are being married in thirty-six hours.'

***

Within seconds he was asleep. Melanie watched him for a while then reached up and rejoiced in the sensation of his skin against her fingers as she ran them around his face. Even the rougher than normal bristle on his chin delighted her. Her fingers ran down the arm holding her close, exploring all the bumps and hollows under the fine cotton of his shirt, the hairs on the back of his hands turning her nerve endings into fire. Wriggling her fingers under the unbuttoned cuff, she kept her hand there while she drifted off.

It was late when she woke again. Guy was still dead to the world, still holding her in a firm grasp around her waist. Unable to believe he had really come, she watched him for a while, feeling content and at peace. Then she reached up and swept her mouth against his in a brief kiss before taking care in wriggling free to go to the bathroom, collecting a fresh change of clothes as she crept past her suitcase. After a quick, refreshing shower she tiptoed back into the room to spy green eyes watching her.

'Do you have any idea just how beautiful you are, sweetheart?' As Guy sat up he glanced at the bedside clock. 'I think we may have missed breakfast. Give me ten minutes to freshen up and get out of these clothes which I feel like I've been wearing for a week, and we'll go find some lunch.' Standing, he stalked towards her like a predatory panther, pulled her into his arms then slanted his mouth over hers in a seductive kiss. 'I have three weeks of kisses to make up for. Heavens, how I've missed you. Wait here, I'll be back shortly.' But only after another lingering kiss did he leave.

Feeling so alive, Melanie grew restless waiting. Guy was longer than the time he stated but she filled the minutes by packing. After the concert she was spending the night at her father's house. As far as she was concerned it was bad luck for a groom to see his bride on the wedding day and she wasn't taking any chances with lady luck. She'd waited a long time for the right man and never believed it would actually happen, but now that it had, she was going to do everything in her power to ensure there were no hiccoughs before they were pronounced man and wife.

An incredible sensation of pure bliss hovered around her as they wandered outside to find a small taverna for lunch, spending the rest of the day arm-in-arm, roaming the city until it was time to prepare for the final concert. Guy's mother had arrived while they were out so they spent a short time with her before Melanie went upstairs. In her room, she removed everything she needed then called her father to collect her honeymoon case. What she no longer needed went to Iain's room as planned before she knocked on Guy's door.

He opened it with nothing more than a towel wrapped around his waist. A gasp of pleasure escaped. 'I'm not quite ready, but come in.' He left her sitting in a chair while he returned to the bathroom to dress, coming out wearing a suit befitting the importance of the final night. 'How was last night?' he asked.

'Tonight will be much better. Tonight I will be playing for you.' No way was she going to reveal the effect his absence had had on her.

'And tomorrow? Are there any instructions on what I am supposed to be doing?'

'Iain has them and what you are supposed to be doing is saying good-bye to your single life.' Melanie's happiness bubbled over, giving her the confidence to be bold and cheeky.

'Well my single life these past three weeks has been pretty bleak and incredibly lonely, so I'm very much looking forward to the change. How about you? Are you ready to say goodbye to your single life?'

The question had a double meaning but she no longer felt the same intense shyness with him. 'I think I might be willing to try it,' she whispered back.

Guy stared at her, but said nothing. Instead he moved close, bent his head on an angle and brushed his mouth against hers. 'What happened to the Melanie who was going to be a pious little nun?'

She grinned. 'Oh, that Melanie found herself a wonderful, caring and gentle man who stole her heart. She ends up marrying him because she decided it would be fun lying naked in his arms and making glorious love with him.'

Guy lifted his head and stared, looking stunned. Melanie giggled, knowing she had shocked him.

'Let's go,' he said. 'I've heard some rave reviews about your concerts so I'm looking forward to this one. Then my beguiling, adorable witch, watch out tomorrow night for I'll be acting on your words and not just once. That's a promise and I think you know by now, I always keep my promises.'

Feeling hot moisture puddling between her legs, Melanie laughed while he guided her downstairs to the waiting bus. She hadn't yet told him he would be coming back to the hotel without her.

As promised, Melanie gave it her all in her playing. Copious flowers were presented on the stage after the final encore and it was nearing midnight when she sought out Guy.

'Guy, I love you so much but I'm staying somewhere else tonight. I'll be waiting with great eagerness for you tomorrow afternoon. You have no idea how much I am looking forward to us being joined together.' Reaching up, she swept her arms around his neck and hugged tight with her mouth pressed to his in a brief but sensuous kiss then released him, turned and ran from the room.

***

Startled, Guy watched after her wondering what the heck had just happened. Iain and Jenny neared. Iain placed a restraining hand on his arm when Guy made to follow.

'This is where we take over, little brother. It's bad luck to see your bride on your wedding day before the ceremony. So you're stuck with us until then and I've been ordered to tell you, no phone calls.'

When Guy swore under his breath Iain laughed. 'This time tomorrow you'll have her by your side for the rest of your life. Believe me, a few hours of misery and it will be worth it.'

'I've just had three weeks of sheer misery.'

'Join the club, little brother. By the way, apart from becoming a husband, you're also going to be an uncle. We are pregnant.'

Guy spun around. 'That was quick work, congratulations.'

'Yeah, well, we jumped the gun a little bit there. Jenny's almost three months gone.'

'Is Mum pleased?'

'Your mother is delighted. I might even be tempted to spend more time in Australia with grandchildren coming along,' said the husky Norwegian voice beside him. 'Melanie was brilliant tonight. She plays as well as she sings.'

'She didn't play so well last night,' said Iain. 'Even I could tell. She kept looking up to that empty seat beside me and you could see and feel the life flow out of her. Stephan had to take over in her first piece. She actually stopped playing for a second or two. She was devastated.'

'I feel bad enough already,' Guy groaned. 'You don't have to rub it in, but there was not a lot I could do apart from jump out of the plane. Tell me, Melanie said she found her real father. Has she told any of you who it is?'

'We didn't even know that much. She's said nothing but I bet I can tell you what day it happened. Just before we moved to Napflion, she seemed a lot happier all of a sudden,' Jenny replied.

'By the way, Melanie asked me to tell you there is a letter under your pillow. Sleep well, because I doubt you will get much tomorrow night.' With a teasing and meaningful jab to his brother's ribs, Iain bade him good night.

Guy headed straight for his bed where he lifted the pillow. He found an embossed envelope with the words, *My Golden Adonis,* on the front. He left it there while he undressed and hung up his suit, after which he picked the letter up, nestled against the pillows on his bed and opened the envelope.

Guy

I know it has been a difficult road for us, more on my side than yours. You always knew exactly what you wanted but I seemed to be constantly confused. You asked me to trust you on more than one occasion. I always trusted you: right from the first time you saved my life. My instinct on that first night when you held me safe was to trust you. There was never any doubt. I don't normally believe in fate, but something had you following me at that place, at that time and I trusted you when I had no reason to ever trust any man. I needed to learn how to trust myself - and my own inner feelings to understand what they were.

The first time I saw you rise out of the water with the sun shining on you, I was left breathless and awed at the sight of you but I had no idea why I felt that way. My immediate thought was that you were a Golden Adonis. I wanted to run my fingers all the way down your arms and body and it scared me to feel that kind of yearning. I have never wanted to touch any other person the same way, before or since.

The number of times I have watched you and my heart has started galloping around in my chest or my body has started trembling or a tight clamp of something I could never make sense of, clenched my insides. I didn't understand what was happening to me. I watched you sleeping on your bed one morning and all I wanted to do was reach out with my fingers and allow them to run through your hair, to feel you, touch you, experience the sensations - but I was too afraid because of what you might think of me.

Jenny helped me understand what all these strange feelings were about. I have been miserable these past three weeks without you. The hollowness in my heart hurt me as much as my injuries do but there are no painkillers for this type of pain I experience when we are apart. When you weren't there on Friday night, I was terrified you weren't going to come, that you didn't want me because of what happened to me in my past. What I do know for sure is that I love you so much. I want to be with you, to touch you, to make love with you. The number of times I have wanted you to break your promise to me would surprise you but I know you respected me too much to do that. I believe you would have rather cut off your right arm before you broke a promise to me and I am so fortunate to have found a man with such honour. For that I am grateful in one sense because I can give my husband, and only my husband, my heart, my soul and my body on my wedding night. But at the same time I am regretful because I would have liked nothing better than to experience the delights of making love with you, on so many occasions up until now.

I know there will still be times when I am too afraid to say what I really want to because all my life I have had to hide my emotions except for those rare times Mum and I had with just the two of us, but I hope I can learn to overcome my fear of expressing my inner emotions.

Yes, I am going to be afraid tomorrow, but only because of my inexperience – I love you so much I don't want to let you down. I know you think me as completely naïve, but I am well aware of the intimacies I am so looking forward to sharing with you and I trust you enough to help me through it.

Adonis was a God in Greek mythology who was the beloved of Aphrodite, the Goddess of love. Tomorrow and for the rest of my life, I will be your Aphrodite and you will always be my Golden Adonis. This clue may help you understand what you will experience tomorrow when we are joined together. I love you, Guy, as I have done for a long time now. I'm so much looking forward to the time when you can kiss your bride and

even more, I am looking forward to the time when my Adonis accepts his Aphrodite into his bed.
Melanie

Guy read the words over and over again, his thoughts about how much he hated wedding traditions. All he wanted was Melanie in his arms, in his bed, and he had no idea where she was. He punched Iain's number into his mobile.

'Go to sleep, Guy.' Iain sounded too damned amused.

'Where is she?' Guy knew he sounded desperate.

'Let me look at my piece of paper with instructions on. Let me see. If Guy asks where I am, tell him I am at my father's place.'

'I don't suppose she has given you a phone number or a clue as to where that might be? I'm hurting here, big brother.'

'No clues, although I suspect Jenny may know because she's doubled up with laughter right now. So much for my romantic advances! Now, be a good boy and go to sleep and let me get back to what you so rudely interrupted. The sooner you go to sleep the sooner the wait is over. Good night, Guy.'

Guy tried, but it was in the early hours of the morning before exhaustion dragged him into unconsciousness. The incessant ringing of a phone dragged him awake.

'Harris,' he barked after fumbling around for the receiver.

'Guy, if you are one second late for your wedding Melanie will string me up and I don't relish the thought. Open your door and let me in.'

Guy flew from the bed then stumbled to the door wearing nothing more than the robe he managed to drag on and hastily wrap around his nakedness. 'What the devil is the time?' he asked when he noted Iain already dressed in suit trousers, shirt, waistcoat and tie.

'A lot later than you think. You've missed breakfast and lunch. Go and get in the shower and make yourself at least half presentable for your bride.'

'Why didn't you wake me?' Guy yelled as he vanished into the bathroom.

'I just did. I've ordered lunch, which should be here in a few minutes. Are you packed and is there anything you want me to take home with me? Some of us poor blighters have to work.'

After a lengthy wallow under the hot stinging shower to wash away the cobwebs of exhaustion and jetlag, Guy opened the bathroom door to see lunch spread out on a table. He ate the food with only a towel wrapped around his waist and accompanied by plenty of brotherly jesting until, after a glance at his watch, Iain insisted Guy dress.

Guy's luggage was to be sent downstairs. He had made arrangements for it to be picked up and transported to his honeymoon destination. Iain packed everything up for him while Guy dressed in the white suit Melanie had requested. He was reminded about the rings and this was double-checked. Iain read through his checklist, ensuring they had everything then grasped Guy by the arm, led him to his own room to collect his suit jacket and then went downstairs to wait for the limousine.

The luxury vehicle swept through the crowded city then out up into the hills overlooking the small harbour of Mirolimano near Piraeus. Guy rarely felt nervous but right then he was very much on edge. Iain did his best to keep his brother distracted, until they pulled into the driveway of what looked to be a private residence where they were met at the door by a valet.

'Welcome gentlemen, if you could wait here for one moment. I'll let them know you have arrived.' After delivering his message in heavily accented English, the man disappeared but was soon back. 'Follow me. Your guests are on the veranda but you are to move to the rotunda in the middle of the garden.'

When they stepped onto the veranda they stopped short. The garden was vast, containing a large number of mature shady trees that canopied the area, keeping the blazing sun out during the hot summer months. Now winter was upon them the area was a murky grey except around each tree, which was swathed in fairy lights. Each was a different colour, the lights reflecting off the number of white marble Greek statues placed at various spots around the garden. Guy's thoughts went immediately to Greek mythology and he wondered which were Aphrodite and Adonis. His eyes settled on the two placed either side of the entry to the rotunda and he smiled. The guests were seated in a semi-circle under cover on the veranda. There was a path leading down the centre of the garden to the rotunda in the middle and an equal distance beyond, with the ocean below in the background.

The two cellos were set up next to chairs on either side of the rotunda and the harp a little closer, edging one side of the pathway, but none of the musicians could be seen. As Iain and Guy stepped onto the marble pavement, Jenny and Mary, the two cellists moved out from behind trees, picked up their bows and began playing *Pachebel's Canon in D* as coloured spotlights shone on them, changing the white of each gown to a different hue. One at a time, the other musicians joined in and as each did, the player emerged from behind a tree with their dresses taking on the colour of the surrounding lights. The total effect was like a rainbow-coloured Greek mythological fairyland. What had stunned Guy was what the girls were wearing. They were all dressed in long white chitons to look like ancient Greek goddesses.

The celebrant beckoned the men forwards then led them to the rotunda. Under the roofed area stood a small round table with a Grecian urn in the middle. A flickering candle was burning in front. Peering close, Guy read Melanie's mother's name engraved on a metal plate. Her ashes. A lot of people would have thought it macabre but he felt pleased. Considering the circumstance, the presence was fitting. He straightened as the two men were asked to stand one side of the celebrant and to turn and watch the far end of the path.

All of a sudden a vision in white silk emerged, as though rising out of the water in the background, on the arm of George Panegyres. His mouth gaped when he realised who Melanie's father was. But then again, he now realised that the lengthy call the two had had when Guy related all the details of Melanie and her mother's life had a deeper meaning. No wonder George had wanted every single detail.

Melanie's dress was a simple white silk chiton that hung from her shoulders and was caught in under the bust and around the waist with a fine gold twisted cord tied at the back and left hanging down the full length of the gown to the ground. Her hair had a few curls bundled on top but the rest was in long ringlets down one side, also bound with the same gold cord. His Aphrodite came towards him. As she approached, the rotunda was bathed in gold lights reflecting off the white suit Melanie had insisted he wear, turning him into her Golden Adonis. Knowing the significance of the colour, he smiled at his bride.

George placed Melanie's hand into Guy's outstretched fingers. 'I give you my only child, my precious daughter,' he said, his voice cracking. Then he stepped back to join the guests, noticeable moisture swimming across in his eyes.

'You look so beautiful, my Aphrodite. I love you,' Guy whispered as he drew her closer, his heart feeling as though it needed to burst to relieve the incredible sensation settled in the region of his chest.

When the music ended, the celebrant began the short service, the main feature of which, were the vows the two gave each other. There was no shy, scared little Melanie while she recited what was in her heart with confidence. The rings were exchanged and placed on each other's fingers then Guy was finally granted his wish. He was asked to kiss his bride. He made sure it was long and ardent, and that his bride was left breathless. He smiled down at the smouldering look in her eyes when he lifted his head.

'Your Adonis awaits his Aphrodite with great yearning.' He whispered the words so only her ears heard then rejoiced at the tremor he felt coming from her.

While they signed the necessary legal documents, Stephan played his Panpipes while the girls accompanied him with a beautiful piece of music Stephan had created for the occasion. Guy felt overwhelmed as he walked his wife to greet the guests. He was most surprised to see Neil and Louise and was informed Melanie had flown them over, since it was because of them the two had met. He also learned they were in the audience the previous night. He didn't dare ask who was running his company. It was better he didn't know.

The bridal couple wandered around the gardens and the house, meeting and chatting to guests while partaking of the huge meal that had been prepared in traditional Greek style. There were a few speeches; Melanie hadn't wanted any but her father was so proud to show off his daughter and let the world know all about her that he insisted. Both Iain and Guy gave short speeches that left Melanie blushing and then Stephan and the girls played romantic music for the bridal waltz.

Melanie was passed from one man to another as the evening wore on, until finally her husband retrieved her and slid his arm around her waist and wouldn't let her go again. It was quite some time before he was able to drag his wife inside to find a private spot where he could talk and continue ravishing her lips.

He started with the lips and once satisfied he lifted his head and drew her close. 'Don't ever stop surprising me, sweetheart. You look incredible and right now all I want to do is whisk you off. I feel like I'm floating up in the clouds. So, George Panegyres is your father. Are you sure?'

'Come with me, I want to show you something.' Melanie curled her hand in his and led him into the vast lounge room of what now seemed more like a mansion than a house. She pointed to a couple of photographs on the wall. 'Do you recognise this lady?'

'She looks exactly like you, but a bit older. The same hair, the same face and build.' Guy stood back in amazement as he stared at the photographs.

'This is my grandmother.'

'My mother,' interrupted George as he neared. 'I don't think there is much doubt, do you? Plus Melanie insisted on a DNA test. It only confirmed what I knew to be true.'

He smiled lovingly as he swept an arm around Melanie's shoulder.

'We've had some lengthy discussions. Melanie has told me about the appalling life she and her mother experienced. It makes me feel ashamed that I didn't look harder for Maria but I had no idea where she went. It wasn't until I received a letter from Maria before Melanie first came here, that I even knew I had fathered a child. I knew the very moment I saw her that Melanie was mine. She is so much like my mother. But Maria begged me not to say anything, only to take care of Melanie.'

'Why would she do that?' asked Guy.

'I have no idea and it hurt me to abide by Maria's wishes but at least I could enjoy my daughter.' George bestowed a loving smile on Melanie.

'Half the people here today are relations I never knew I had,' said Melanie as she ran a loving finger over the photo. 'From someone who had only a grandmother and a couple of cousins, it seems I now have dozens of close relatives. Dad is thinking of selling up his business so he can spend half of each year with us.'

'Everything I own will pass on to Melanie. Before I sell, I want to offer you both the opportunity of taking over my business.'

Stunned, Guy jerked his head towards the man as the offer swirled around his head. 'If we lived in the same country I would probably consider your offer but from my point of view, no. It takes all my time to run my own business and it earns me a considerable income. More than I need.'

'I understand. Melanie intimated that was the way you'd react when I first mooted the idea. So I'll sell. I'm a very wealthy man who has more money than I could ever use. Now that I have a family of my own, I intend to spend as much time as I can close to Melanie and hope to enjoy a couple of grandchildren in the not too distant future.' He looked meaningfully at Guy.

'Oh, I think we could accommodate you.' Guy grinned at Melanie's red cheeks. 'My mother intimated she would consider coming back to Australia with grandchildren on the scene so I guess we're going to have to do something about it as soon as possible.' Drawing Melanie into a tight embrace he glanced at George. 'Right now sounds a pretty good time to get started,' he added, noticing Melanie's cheeks redden even more.

'Your car is here, and I've put Melanie's case in the boot. I suggest you slip away without any announcements?' George chuckled as he reached out to shake Guy's hand. 'Take care of my girl and enjoy your honeymoon. The crew have their instructions.'

He bent to give Melanie a warm embrace. 'You have chosen well for your husband. Take care. We'll get together on your return. I'm very proud of you.' Drawing back, George ushered them to the front door where the same limousine stood waiting.

'How did you know where to have the car waiting,' Melanie asked as they drove off.

'I didn't, but your father did. You're not the only one who has been making sneaky little phone calls and plans. I rang your father ages ago, although I didn't know he was your father then, to help me plan our honeymoon. I told him the places I would like to take you. He suggested a couple of others and arranged the transport, which I am told you will recognise. I'm also told you don't get sea-sick, which is just as well.'

'We're using Dad's boat?'

'We are, and we have it all to ourselves for two weeks, apart from a few necessary staff who I am told are very discreet and will hardly ever be seen by us. We have a few island destinations where we can stay as long as we want.'

The journey to the boat was not long since it was moored in the harbour below the cliffs from the house, the cliff edge now containing a bevy of onlookers. Their escape had been noted. The skipper and the few staff who would care for them, welcomed them aboard amidst loud cheering from above. After waving to their guests, they stepped aboard the luxury cruiser. Melanie's bag was carried on board and they were shown around the boat and then to their quarters, where Guy's bags had already been stowed. Their guide turned the main lights down in the huge main cabin then left. Guy swept his bride into his arms and started what he had been yearning to do since he first saw her on the stage.

Much to his surprise, Melanie grabbed his tie and tugged. As he leant forwards she kissed him then slid her hands under the coat lapels. Shoving her hands upwards, his coat slid from his shoulders then down his arms. He wriggled them free. The coat puddled at his feet at the same time Melanie yanked the tie tail from the knot. A wicked look seared him as the tie joined the coat. Shaking fingers slid shirt buttons free from their keepers then hot fingers sent a path of fire across his chest as they explored then lowered. His mind was mush.

'You forgot something,' Melanie whispered as she peeked from lowered lashes then yanked his belt apart. Her fingers went straight to the zipper tab.

With his brain about to implode he had no idea what she was talking about.

The zipper slid down. He groaned.

'The door.' She grinned wickedly as her hand slid lower.

'Who cares?' he managed to stutter as he hoisted her in his arms, stepped back and shoved the door with his shoulder.

www.ingramcontent.com/pod-product-compliance
Lightning Source LLC
Chambersburg PA
CBHW072200130726
47910CB00011B/1760